Praise for Counterpunch

'*Counterpunch: The Story of a World Champion Boxer* is a work of fiction in the sporting, interpersonal drama, and action sub-genres. Written for mature reading audiences due to the presence of some scenes of violence, inside and outside of the boxing ring, this is an engaging and inspirational tale of keeping up the fight through a long period of history. We follow Sam Smith as he starts out his boxing career in England in the 1960s, through to his rise to world championship status and the incredible life experiences and assistance which he gets from all sorts of unusual sources.

Author Chris Shaw has crafted a tale that sports fans of all ages are highly likely to enjoy and get a lot of satisfaction from. Boxers and fighters will especially enjoy the technical aspects of the work and the vibrant atmosphere of the piece, which really gets into protagonist Sam's head as he goes through the many different stages which make him an ultimate champion. The plot progression has a few little surprises, but overall it builds in a very logical structure and gets more inspirational with every chapter. I really loved the supporting cast of characters who each contribute something to Sam's journey, and I felt they were diversely penned with plenty of variation and character quirks.' *5-star review by K.C. Finn for Readers' Favorite*

'At the mention of each bell, my heartbeat rises in anticipation of what might happen next. Will our hero win the next boxing match? We soon discover that there's a lot more on the line than just winning. The author has the amazing ability to put us in the boxing ring right alongside the main character Sam, taking us on a journey through the boxing fraternity, particularly it's more sinister side. Binding this all together are characters we all wish we had in our corner. Beware when you read this novel - it will have you rolling with the punches.'

Armando Lepore, former Southpaw, South Australian lightweight title fighter

Also by Chris Shaw

The Imposter: A Norfolk Romance

It's All Relative:
Stories to Shorten Your Travel Time

HMS Warspite:
My Memories of World War II
(pp Wally Shaw)

My New Country:
Loving, Laughing and Learning to Live in Australia

Hey Guys! Here's How You Get More 'Nooky'!
How to Build the Happiest Relationship in Your World

Never Let the Truth:
Stories From My Imagination

A Trillionaire's Pathway:
My Fantasy Hotel

COUNTER PUNCH

THE STORY OF A
WORLD CHAMPION BOXER

Cover designed by Christian Hildenbrand
Cover image by istock
Typeset in Algreya 9/11.5pt, Courier 11.5 pt and Estrangelo Edessa 26pt
Printed and bound in Australia by IngramSpark
Prepared for publication by The Erudite Pen (theeruditepen.com)

 A catalogue record for this book is available from the National Library of Australia

Counterpunch: The Story of a World Champion Boxer/ Chris Shaw. -- 1st ed.
ISBN 9780980588262

I have woven my father's name, and his lessons, into this story as a 'thank you' to him for all his love and support in so many ways throughout my life, and also my sister Vicky's life, too. He was a lovely man, and we couldn't have asked for a better father.

This little story, from whichever universe it came, is for you, Dad.

Author's Note

I awoke one morning trying to spell a word that described the sound of a boxer's glove hitting an opponent's chin at speed. Thoughts that are half dream and half reality do not bear close analysis, especially first thing in the morning, so I didn't come up with anything initially.

After coffee and some routine pharmaceutical defence against the rigours of old age, I wrote down my best attempt, and the rest of the story just seemed to follow. I keep trying to explain the writing 'Zone' to people. The nearest I can get to an explanation of the 'Zone' is a meditative state, from which creative people, like writers, can draw their inspiration.

Three things have influenced my boxing knowledge:

1.   My father tried to teach me to box at the early age of eight or nine. In doing so he directed my fist to his midriff where it hit a button on his uniform, which hurt, and I cried. My father had considerable patience, but I think he realised that he had little to nothing to work with. A son who plays violin – I ask you!

2.   I had three compulsory boxing matches at boarding school. I lost two and won one. The two victors I forget, but the vanquished I do remember, and wish him well from all those years ago.

3.   My father told me he used to do some boxing in his youth. One story he told remains with me. At nearly five feet three inches tall, he was to fight a six-footer. He walked across the ring to tell his opponent that he didn't want to hurt him! Then, during the fight, he dropped his gaze to his opponent's solar plexus but hit him on the 'button' (a spot

on either side of the jaw about one inch back from the chin)
to finish the fight.

Chapter One

'Shug!' was the sound of my boxing-gloved fist as it hit a jaw. My opponent's jaw. Hah! I saw his left coming around the houses at me as a swinging high hook. Easy! My left fist crossed to his left bicep, crushing muscle to bone before his fist could reach my head. I saw his right trying to do the same. This action got the same reaction from me, and my opponent, Clark I believe his name was, dropped his guard from the pain. I knew punching muscle on to bone hurt. It was done to me once. Never again. Marciano used to do that, I'd been told.

I saw Clark's guard go down, hit his 'button', about an inch either side of the point of the chin, and watched his eyes. There was a glazing, a headshake, and he retreated. The rope was behind him. I waited for him to bounce off it and timed my uppercut nicely. His face was to the ceiling, and he bounced off the rope again. I clobbered him with a quick left, then a right as he came forward. His brain must have been Scots porridge by now.

I backed off to see his actual state. This one was tough, but his legs weren't good. There was a slight stagger, and his hands were up in defence but lower than when we started this dance. I crashed a left jab through his guard near the chin to check his reflex speed. No. He didn't cover up. It got through his defence, and he was basically gone. He just didn't know it yet.

My plan to finish him was to wait for his attack, then counterpunch. To make it go the way I wanted, I circled slowly and dropped my guard. Like a bee to honey, he spotted it and came for me. His right fist aimed at my chin.

Nah! Mate, that was far too bleedin' obvious, and much, much too slow. There was lots of time for me to dodge sideways, and now he was extended with no defence. I gave him a brisk left cross to the chin, and he joined all the others I'd fought in the tent tonight. He became predictably horizontal. I thought this one, Clark, may have given me more of a fight of it.

You see, beginners do a bit of skipping, a bit of running, a bit of work with the bags and think they can box. This one was better than most, but he wouldn't earn his fifty quid.

I can't count the number of fights I've had in the tents, where anyone can try their luck against me if their weight is about right. Must have been hundreds. Let's say an average of five fights every Saturday night for a couple of years, give or take, but the figures beat me. I haven't been put down yet so I feel almost ready for some real competition.

I'd done all this stuff for a long time now, and it's a bit like bricklaying: simple, as long as you know what you're doing. And trust me, I really do know boxers and boxing. I watch and 'read' everything about every boxer who climbs into the ring with me: body shape, movement, coordination, aggression and so on. Put it all together, and it means

I know pretty well what to expect. There's the occasional surprise, of course, but I've got a few of my own too.

The crowd was making some noise now. They wanted me to lose, just to let me know I wasn't Cassius Clay or Muhammed Ali as he later became known. Now there was a man, a boxer and a gentleman. I'd have given him a Nobel Prize if it had been up to me. Fighting whitey politically, fighting conscription, and still beating the best in the world at the Noble Art! What a man.

Hello. The next contender had stepped up. I checked the board and saw his name was Smith, the same as mine. So, let's find out who is the best Smith, shall we? I was watching him closely and saw his movements and his body shape. His eyes were saying, 'Cocky.' He thought he was good. He was not pasty white so he must have done some outdoor work. He had good muscles, but not on top of his shoulders, where it counted. The cocky ones were easy. The standard plan was to get in the first hurting shot, and they mostly gave in right there. *Try it.*

Bell!

I walked straight across the ring, touched gloves and hit him right between the eyes. That's it. He dropped like a stone. They carted him away, so I sat down in my corner and took a swig from the bottle.

'Alright, Sam?'

'Good as gold,' I told Mr Goldstein, my manager. 'You'd be too if no one 'ad laid a finger on you all night. Was 'e the best you could do?'

'Got one coming up you might enjoy, my boy.'

'Who's 'e, then?'

'African. Been told he's OK. And Sam, *do not* hurt your hands on this one. You know the heads on these guys are like blocks of solid teak, and you can't put them down by hitting them in the head. You'll have to find another way with him.'

'Thanks, I'll think of somethin'.'

The announcer gave his spiel, and the new guy, Smith, climbed into the ring. He looked across at me as he swung his leg over the rope. Now that was very rare. Usually, their focus was all over the place, what with the crowd, the noise, and the lights. His eyes told me he was focused. Good muscles. Good coordination. Looked fast. But there were ways to slow a boxer down. I'd take this one slowly to see what he had.

Someone once asked me about fear. How fearful was I about fighting? They had to explain what fear was, and I still didn't really get it. So, here we go. Another dance.

We touched gloves, which was usually a formality, but he tried to hit mine hard. See? You learn by doing. I remembered a bloke in the ring with me once before, who was all aggression, but he had no finesse. He'd kept coming at me, so I dodged and counterpunched him all through the fight. He couldn't believe that he'd lost to me. I could have told him why, but he didn't ask.

This one was circling and bobbing up and down. I thought I'd try a little rush to see what he did. A quick left-right-left, then I jumped back. He was startled! That surprised me. Why would he be surprised? Okay, so what was he going to do next? Nothing. *Try this then.* A slow horizontal hook from my right, which got all his attention, and he went through all his defence strategy. He just didn't see the left uppercut coming, and it stunned him. He made a quick recovery though and was still bouncing. I wanted to see how he took to a little crowding in the corner. I came with the left-right-left combination again, left a gap of a heartbeat, then did it again, and we were back in the corner with him covering up. He landed a good right from the floor, but he seemed like a rabbit in headlights when there was no room to move.

The Ref moved us. I used my tactic again in another corner and got the same reaction, except that he missed with the uppercut because that was his ploy. Okay once, but never twice with me.

Bell!

I sat and watched the other Smith. He looked a little tired, and this was only his first round. If I could slow him a bit more, he'd be mine. How strange, this corner thing of his. Usually, boxers fought like hell not to go into a corner. They used all their ringcraft to keep out. He seemed to want to go there or didn't fight hard enough not to get caught there. Maybe he was putting all his eggs in one uppercut basket. Maybe I should find out.

Bell!

I jabbed at his forehead – once, twice, three times. His guard came way up, but he didn't work out what I was doing. Bam! A big right jab to his heart. I gave it lots of toe! That's when you punch, starting from your toes and using the muscles in your ankles, knees, thighs, and then put your whole twisting back into it before the punch even got to the strength in the shoulder and arm. Got him. Distinct wobble. His knees gave him away.

Now, I followed up with a left-right-left to the chin, and then backed off. I wasn't hitting him in the head, but I was jerking his brain around inside his head by beating it from side to side. Big difference. Not hurting my hands either.

Hurt my hands, I'm out of the game, and my family goes hungry.

Now I needed to get him into one more corner and see how he worked it this time. Left-right-left-right, hold, part, then left-right-left-right, quick as a snake, or a 'Golden Gloves' contender. Maybe one day. There was confusion on his face. He came back to do the same to me, but of course, I wasn't there. I'm not silly; hanging myself out to dry. He located me beside him just as I hit his 'button' from the side. His head spun and sweat beads soared into the lights; his eyes went dull, and he went down. He got a leg under him to get up, but there was no strength there. That was what my heart shot did to him. It killed his legs.

I leaned on the ropes in a neutral corner and watched him. He did his best, but his strength just wasn't there anymore. The Ref counted 'the other Smith' out.

I sat down, and that was my night over. I had a nice wedge of bread to take home for my Donna. She would be pleased, and we'd planned to go to Epsom Downs tomorrow. I'd bought a kite each for our girls, so we'd have a great time if there was enough breeze.

'I fought he might have given you more of a problem, vat one, Sam.'

'Nah! 'e knows nothin' about ringcraft. What's with that corner thin'? 'e seemed to want to be there.'

'I think he wanted to use his uppercut as a finisher.'

'Maybe once, but 'e'd never get me a second time. You saw that?'

'I did, and if he'd got enough power in it, he could have dropped the average Joe.'

'Yeah, a simple plan, but 'e 'ad nothing else. Same time next Saturday?' I asked.

'You betcha, Sam. And, there's a tournament coming up in Camden next Wednesday. They want an 'oppo' for a geezer from Wapping. He's got good wraps, is about your weight, and there's a couple of hundred in it for you if you win. What do you say, my boy?'

'Suits me. You'll pick me up?'

'Sure thing. About six?'

'I'll be ready,' I said.

'Yes, I think you are ready, my boy; ready to start workin' your way up the ranks without getting hurt. That's what these two years of practising against all-comers has given you, and now it's about time you started in the real world of boxing. Your apprenticeship is over, Sam. Unless you get hurt, Saturday's on too. That's bread and butter for both of us. See you Wednesday at six.'

'G'night Mr Goldstein.'

'Do call me Reuben, Sam. We've known each other long enough to dispense with all that mister rubbish.'

I just grinned.

Chapter Two

It was a cracking weekend in the middle of summer, 1964. On that Sunday we had a great day with the family at Epsom. We loved this little market town in Surrey, famously known for its racecourse as well as its Epsom salts. The weather was beautiful, with lots of wind, so the kites I'd bought worked a treat. Our girls, Anna aged six and Ella aged four, had a great time. They had ice creams too.

Donna, my wonderful wife of seven years, still had a gorgeous figure, even after having two children, and a bang up-to-date hairstyle. When I first met her, she had a full-on beehive, but she reckoned it was too much like hard work. Now, her lovely honey-coloured hair fell from her head like a waterfall and turned up at the ends. It looked so cute as she snuggled up to me on the bus, which was always nice.

We got fish and chips from the shop, still wrapped in newspaper, then it was home to our little terraced house in Whitechapel. The rent was very reasonable, but in the back of my mind I knew I wanted something better for my girls.

Since I was a pre-War baby, born in 1938, I had done my schooling and left in 1954, having learned not very much at all. I enjoyed the physical side of things, so I worked at construction sites around and about the area. After being all at sea for the first six months, I started seeing the pattern of the work needed and became quite productive and much more relaxed.

Donna and I had been in love since school and got married when her eighteenth birthday came along. We rented a little place in Whitechapel, and there we would have grown old together, but for a silly bugger on one work site.

We were loading bricks; he was throwing them, and I was catching and packing them. He started to throw too many at a time and then to throw them awkwardly. I told him to cut it out. He had this really annoying laugh that was more like the noise of a donkey. He gave me the laugh and threw one right at me. I dodged it, but something cold came over me, and I walked over and bloodied his nose.

The foreman came over and I explained what had happened. He sacked the 'donkey' and said to me, 'If you can't keep your temper, you'd better learn some discipline. Here's the name and address of a bloke who may be able to help you. And don't ever assault anyone ever again. See me first, right? RIGHT?'

'Yes, Boss,' I told him, and I contacted a Mr Reuben Goldstein, who managed boxers in the tents. These were places that held boxing matches between established boxers and anyone who fancied their chances – for money. I watched and learned. Then Reuben loaned me a pair of gloves, and I remember the feeling of winning my first fight. That was in 1962, and I'd been doing this on Saturday nights ever since. It brought in a nice little wedge for Donna, enough for an outing on Sundays, like Epsom Downs.

Come Monday, I'd have to find out about the boy I'd be facing on Wednesday. I'd ask Reg Benson. He'd know. Reg was a fixture at the Waterloo pub, who knew everything about the boxing game, so I'd get a heads up from him for the cost of a pint or two.

Monday came around quicker than I'd wanted. I ran down to the gym to get the kinks out from Saturday and worked on some speed. I sparred with Rollo Tarantino, another welterweight boxer. Rollo had been around the gym for some time but never seemed to want to work up the ranks to professional status; just to spar. He was good and could adjust to different styles, but he had nothing I couldn't handle. My moves were fluid and adaptable; I knew what to look for, how to tackle it and how to shut it down. He was always trying something different in striving for the upper hand, so I had to keep sharp; otherwise, he could slip in a crafty punch and that would upset me.

I went to see Reg, who was predictably sitting in 'his' seat in the Waterloo pub.

'Reg. How're you goin'?'

'Good, Sammy boy, good. I hear you're on the Camden ticket with that bloke from Wapping.'

'You always do know the drum, Reg. Let me get you a pint, and you can tell me all about 'im.'

'Yeah. Thanks, Sammy. He's actually quite good, and I've seen him take down some decent fighters. He's a hustler; busy, you know. Always on the move, like, bobbing and weaving then leading with his long left jab. I reckon if your timing's good, you can make all that dodging work in your favour. Know what I mean?'

'Reg, mate, you're worth another pint. I can deal with 'is jab; just 'it his elbow the wrong way; and 'is dodgin' will be into my oncomin' fist so, with luck, 'e'll knock 'imself out. That's definitely worth another pint. Thanks, Reg.'

'Just watch that jab, Sam, because sometimes he follows up with a dynamite right that seems to come out of nowhere. I've seen him put down half a dozen good fighters with that.'

'You aimin' for another pint, Reg?'

'Nah, Sam! Just want you to have the best info, mate.'

Come Wednesday, Reuben arrived at six precisely. I kissed Donna and the girls goodbye, grabbed my holdall, and we were off.

'Know what you've got to do, my boy?'

'Yeah, and thanks to Reg, I know how.'

'Oh, yeah. I remember Reg. Short bloke, balding, thick horn-rimmed glasses. Drinks at the Waterloo?'

'That's 'im. This one's a bouncin' ball with a jab and an occasional right. Busy with it, too. So, I'll let 'im do all the runnin', and see how good my timin' is. Be interestin'.'

Kitted and gloved, I sat in this Camden Hall to wait. Cleared my mind by thinking of next Sunday with the girls. I thought they were about ready for a trip to the zoo. Anna had mentioned an interest in animals, which for a Londoner was odd, because, apart from the pigeons in Trafalgar Square, there's not a hell of a lot of animal life – well, apart from the East End, that is. Little joke there. That was good. Meant my mind was not fixed on the fight.

I got the call, walked to the ring and climbed in. My oppo, Wallingford by name, climbed in after me, so I got a good look at him. He kept his eyes away from me, so I knew

I had him beaten already. He just didn't know it yet. Good muscles, but the definition was from the gym, not the ring. Long muscles, not short, which meant speed, but probably not endurance. Not a lot of toughness there. I'll cook him slowly. Wallingford was a bit of a mouthful, so I'd try to fill his with my fist. Another little joke, well, well.

Bell!

Reg was right; this guy was a bouncing ball. I waited in the middle of the ring, letting him circle me. Dropped my guard an inch. Nothing. Another inch, and in came the jab. I slipped it, waiting for the right, but he was saving that. Keeping my guard down, here came the jab again. I slipped it so his wrist was against my neck and punched his elbow from the outside with my right. I heard his sudden intake of breath. I'd hurt him, so he wouldn't be so keen on the jab from now on. So, how was he going to bring in this famous right of his? He feinted with his jab and in came that right. Slipped that too, and that meant his arms were crossed, so I gave him a taste of uppercut and watched his eyes go out as he dropped. He hit the canvas just as the bell rang.

Nice round. I must buy Reg another pint. That was good info. What would have happened if I hadn't spoken to Reg? I'd have had to work it out for myself. Could I have done that? Yes, but not so fast maybe. I'd test my timing with his bouncing this round and try to drop him.

Bell!

He was slower out of the corner. Bounce, bounce, bounce. When his feet were on the canvas, he could dodge sideways, but when his feet were in the air, he was mine. So, up jab, up jab, up leave. Now he was very confused as to when I would jab and when I wouldn't. He gave me his left jab, and the right; both slipped with a side-to-side motion of my head, but I got in a left uppercut again and followed with a downward right. Not only did I get the timing right, but got the punch very close to his 'button'. He was gone. The Ref counted him out. The roar of the crowd was huge as I put my fists in the air. I didn't go in for this self-congratulation thing much, but the crowd seemed to want it, or maybe they needed it. There were smiles all around as I went off to get changed.

'Nice one, Sam. That was sweet to see. How much do you owe to Reg?' asked my manager.

'I really hope you're not talkin' money, Reuben!' I snarled, getting my face close to his and looking him in the eye.

'No, Sam, not at all. Remember me? I know you, and I know you're as straight as a die. What I meant to say was: how much did the info Reg gave you help you in the fight?'

'Yeah, quite a bit really,' I said, relaxing. 'I definitely owe Reg another pint. If I'm goin' to be doin' this sort of thin' regular-like, maybe you could toss 'im a fiver now and again – for 'is 'elp, you understand. You're the moneyman, Reuben, not me; but 'e could be 'andy.'

'Quite right, on all counts, my boy. There's another competition in Ilford next Wednesday. What do you think?'

'Yeah, well, 'e didn't 'urt me one bit, so why not. I'll do the Saturday tents too. Donna will be extra pleased with all the money.'

'Sure, she will, Sam, my boy. And Sam, I'll always see you're alright – all right?'

I nodded. My gut said I could trust him with my life. But only time would tell.

Chapter Three

Ilford, Fulham, Balham and Clapham fight cards all came and went. The cards were regional fights, so called because of the black and white posters put up about a week before, which were brushed onto lampposts and bridge columns with a bucket of water-paste and a big, wide brush. It was very cheap advertising.

All my oppos had their own strengths, but my job was to find out their weaknesses, and I did. One had class, but a glass jaw. Another based all his skill on his right hand and kept it cocked for when he needed it, while I 'kicked' him six times to Christmas everywhere else. He never did get to used it. I just didn't understand it. Their job was to beat me, but how could they do that unless they found a weakness to exploit. We could box, yes, and go around and around, hurting each other in the process. But if I could find their weakness, I could drop them and be safely home with my missus for an early evening with my girls.

Reuben interrupted my reverie. 'Sam, that last one. I thought he had you after his blistering final round. He hit you that many times. You okay?' Reuben seemed to have developed two little worry lines over his nose.

'Yeah, not a worry in the world, but I don't think you were really watchin'. What you thought you saw was a barrage of punches hittin' me. What really 'appened was that 'e tried to break my forearms with his fists. Not one of those punches landed. Must have looked good to the punters, but you did understand the finish, didn't you?'

'I saw you put him down, but I don't know how that happened.'

'He miscalculated and thought I was done for. But I was playin' dumb. I dropped my 'ead as though I'd 'ad it. He lost concentration just for a moment, wonderin' if I was goin' to fall, but 'e left his 'button' free and clear. One punch, just a little to the left of 'is chin and it was lights out, Bob's your uncle. Nice one that, if I do say so meself.'

'Just for a moment, I thought we'd lost the momentum I've been working on, Sam, my boy.'

'Nah! Leave it out! You ought to know me better than that!'

'Listen, Sam, you're all right, aren't you?'

'Yeah. Good as gold. Not even tired. What 'ave you got on your mind?' We were alone in the locker room, and there was a change in my manager's attitude that I hadn't seen before.

'I need to talk to you serious-like, Sam, so listen hard. You're young, just twenty-six. You're a very experienced boxer now, and you're a thinker. You're good by any boxing standards. You've got all the moves, you're very fit, and everything is looking rosy. So, I'm thinking of putting you on to some fights that're with professionals. They'll start you on a journey that could take you to the top. Up to now, it's been penny-ante in the tents, but it has developed your experience and your skill levels.'

'Some of those fighters have been quite good,' I mused.

'No, Sam, they haven't. They were quite good at your level then, but you now need to change gear as you go up the rankings. But listen to me; this is, "Only if you want to." Are you game to make this journey – just a quick yes or no?'

'Well, yes, of course, Reuben.'

'Okay then. Listen hard to this next part. You'll talk to your missus and make sure that she is behind you. The reason I say this is that I've seen fighters who were fighting two oppos in the ring at once. There's their boxing opponent, and there's their wife, who didn't approve of what they were doing. But the wife seemed to be in the ring too, upsetting his concentration. If your missus says "No," then it's "No," and we'll settle for the tents and the occasional cards around and about. I think you're better than that, Sam, but you've got to want it, and so has Donna. Do you understand that?'

'Yeah! I do, and you're right. Not to 'ave the missus in my corner would really upset me. You got that so right, mate. So, I'll ask 'er, and then what?'

'I'll take you to every professional fight around and show you every film of boxing that's ever been made, to let you see how the big boys do it. At the end of that, I'll ask you again if you want to travel that route. If you and Donna both agree, then we start in earnest.'

'That sounds excitin', Reuben.'

'We'll have Reg on our side because he knows the game like no one else I know. I've also got an old manager picked out, who is almost as wily as you are. I've got a ring man and trainer called Charlie Browne, and I'm here to back you, financially.

'I'll make this solemn pledge to you, right now, Sam Smith. I'll deal fairly with you and your family all the way. If it turns out that we all make a lot of money out of this, it'll be by your effort, your skill and your body that the rest of us will rely on. Let me ask you, Sam, what do you want to get out of all this – and think first?'

I sat apart and did think, trying to see my future life. If some smart and very fast bastard managed to beat me, then I guess it would be all over. But I couldn't live the rest on my life playing the tents and the occasional card around London. That would be a real dead-end for me. I also wanted something better for Donna, and for our girls too. I wanted them to have nice things, not make-do and hand-me-downs. I didn't want 'posh'. Wouldn't know what to do with 'posh'. I just wanted 'nice'.

There was something else buzzin' in my head that I couldn't quite get hold of. It was shadow boxing me. Then I had it. Respect! I wanted all my boxing skills and my boxing knowledge to be respected. I wanted boxing people around the world to say, 'He was a great boxer – clever too. How did he do the things he did? How did he beat fighters who we know were better than he was, but he always managed to beat them somehow? How did he do that?'

'Well, Reuben, here's the thing. I want to earn some good money for Donna and the girls so we can live nicely, not big, and not loud. Just be able to get some nice things for 'em. Maybe even get our own house, somewhere nice.' I paused.

'But what I want most of all is to be respected for what I can do. I 'ave a lot of experience, earned in the tents plus some from the cards. If I use that, and keep really fit then I can beat anybody, and I want people to know that. I'm not "King of England," know that, but "Douglas Bader," know that; "Captain Cook," know that; "Muhammed Ali," know that. I want to be the best, but quietly. I expect it gets pretty loud at the top, but that doesn't mean that I've got to behave like an American, does it?'

'No, Sam, you can do it the way you want to, and I'll go right along with you. Now, go and talk to your missus. When you have her decision, phone me. Incidentally, if I had had to write your little speech just now, I would have said almost exactly what you said, so we're on the same wavelength. See you, my son, and I wish you luck.'

Well, that was an eye-opener. It felt as though I'd just gone ten rounds, but that's what thinking can do. And people think that boxing is all fists and gloves.

Chapter Four

I had my tea and waited for our girls to go to bed, then turned off the new songs from the Beatles. Great music. Our girls were so lovely and lively. I'd promised them a stroll down King's Road in Chelsea next weekend, to see all the new stuff on sale in the shops. Mary Quant was a name on everyone's lips. When I told them, their eyes sparkled. They were a lot brighter than me at their young ages. I had to do the best I could for them, but not spoil them – well, maybe just a little, now and again. I had to give them the best start in life that I could. I may have had a way to do that now.

'Donna, my sweetheart, come and sit beside me, I want to talk to you.'

'Good, because I want to talk to you too, but you go first,' she said, plonking herself down beside me and placing a smacker of a kiss on my lips.

'I've 'ad a long talk with Reuben. 'e has plans for me to move forward – big plans. 'e says that with my experience and my knowledge of boxin', I should be movin' on from the tents and the cards around town, and startin' to move up to the professional boxin' circuit.

'My love, this is one of those times when I can look back and see what I 'ave been doin', and where I am right now. I will go nowhere doin' the same thing, but I can challenge myself by movin' up the scale. To do that with any 'ope of success, I need to 'ave your support and your blessin' first. Without that, I can do nothin'. What do you think?'

'Sam, darling, I love you. I've been watching you over our years together, with the money you're bringing in, and wondering where we'll be going as a family. So, tell me about the plans.'

'Reuben asked me what I wanted out of boxin', which is quite a clever question when you think about it. I told 'im I wanted you and the girls looked after, perhaps our own house and even a car maybe? I'll need some money to buy a few really nice things for all my girls. And I also told 'im I want respect for my boxin' skills and ability. Love, I 'ave been pitched against all-comers in the tents. I 'aven't been put down, and I've won every fight I've been in.

'Now, this is going to get a lot bigger if I go through with it, but I don't want to stay put. I want to get better. This is a bit of a gamble, but I've got my family to support. Now I need the support of my family if I'm to move forward.' She nodded, so I continued.

'Reuben wants me to see lots of professional fights, and films of fights, so I can judge whether I can be a part of that or not. 'e 'as a small team in mind that can 'elp me be prepared. All this will be put into place once we've made up our minds that this is what 'we' want to do – together, as a family. What do you think, love?'

She held up her hand, and I waited. I recognised that this was one of those special moments; like when you see an opening that your oppo hadn't planned, and you know you've got a winning punch coming up. It was that sort of special moment, and I savoured the tension.

'Sam. You're not cut out to be a banker or a doctor. I knew that even when we were in school. We were so young when we married, but I knew you were true and you've proved that over the years. You're also a really good father to our girls.' I looked at her expectantly.

'So where are we going?' she asked. 'The girls are going to need stuff like clothes, education and lots of other things that we can't afford at the moment. But here you are presenting me with exactly the plan that I wanted from you! Tell Reuben, "a great big yes" from me. Let's see you get some respect for all the work you've done in the tents, and let's start getting among some real money. You've done most of the work, my love. Let's see how far you can go, shall we?'

'Oh yes! Oh yes! Oh yes!' I shouted, jumping up in the air. 'I'll go down to the corner and ring Reuben right now.' I plumped a great big smackeroo on her lips.

Needless to say, Reuben was delighted, and invited me and the missus to dinner in the West End. He picked us up in his car the following evening and dropped us home afterwards. The restaurant was a posh place, decked out in the current Spanish-themed fad, with posters advertising bullfights, guitars, fans and castanets on the walls, and wine in bottles encased in straw. Reuben seemed genuinely excited, and we thoroughly enjoyed the evening.

'Donna,' he said, just before we got out of the car, 'you've made a very wise decision, my girl. Sam has been doing very well, but I could see him starting to get into a rut, good as he is.'

'Is he really any good, Reuben? Only, I've never seen him fight and apart from being knocked out, I wouldn't know what to look for.'

'Listen to me, m'dear. I've been in the fight game for most of my life. A long, long time ago I started looking for a boxer who I thought could go all the way to the top of his weight; one that I would want to manage. I've seen hundreds of fighters, literally, and some excellent ones, too. But I've never come across one like Sam, who can read his opponents so quickly and so accurately. He's young, quick, fit and fast, but he's clever too, and that's very rare. I did wonder whether he was just going to stay in the tents, which is why I have challenged him to do better, but not without your help. He couldn't do any of it without you at his back. So, it's all agreed then? We'll start to get him a new perspective by seeing how the big boys behave in the ring. It'll also allow him to gain that experience without getting beaten – sorry, that was a bit clumsy of me. He'll be fine, you'll see.'

'Just make sure he is, please mister. I wouldn't want him and me to be taken for some sort of ride. I could get very, very upset if I see any unfairness; do you understand me, Mr Goldstein? Nice meal, by the way. Thanks.'

'Just now, I'm thinking of getting an amazing pair of boxing gloves made just for you, Donna, for when *you* climb into the ring. You've got the makings of a good fighter too,' Reuben said, smiling broadly.

'Sorry. Didn't mean to come on that strong, but so many things could go wrong, and I don't want you to be one of them.'

'I understand perfectly, and you have my word that I'll do my very best for Sam and his family.'

'Let the games begin then,' she said with a wry grin.

Chapter Five

Over the next two months, Reuben put his team together.

Art Dutton was brought in as my international manager. Art was in his sixties and had managed many good fighters, three of whom had gone on to be world champions. He had recently suffered a much-publicised heart problem with a heart that 'gave me a jazz rhythm rather than a waltz,' he liked to say. It finished him in the public eye. However, with a proper drug regimen of a beta-blocker, he told us, together with a fitness and nutrition programme, he was now much healthier than before and raring to go.

His demeanour was one of a lazy, scruffy, undisciplined geezer who wore rumpled mismatched clothes, much like Hoss Cartwright in Bonanza, played by Dan Blocker. However, if you watched his beady little blue eyes, you'd see intelligence, humour and focused attention on everything around him. He looked as though he had once been a big sloppy man living on a bad diet and inadequate sleep, which, if true, may well have contributed to his heart problem. However, his international contacts and his organisational skills were legendary.

Reg Benson was brought into the team for his encyclopaedic knowledge of the boxing game, its individual fighters and their styles, as well as his contacts, both local and international. He was an interesting man in an English eccentric sort of way. In his late forties, his father had been a successful doctor with a practice in Wimpole Street, but had died before his time. His mother had been killed in a motor vehicle accident two years later, leaving Reg to inherit quite a bit of money to indulge his one passion: boxing.

His waking hours were focused entirely on boxing; nothing else. Everything he'd heard or read or had seen on TV or in documentaries had been filed away for possible future use. He seemed to always be in the same olive-green suit, brown shirt with a yellow paisley tie, and unpolished brown brogues. He could sit on half a pint for most of the day in his local pub, the Waterloo, or enthusiastically join in with drinking buddies who had boxing stories to tell. He was a confirmed bachelor, but one who was very happy in his own skin.

The last member of the team was an old 'pug', as they used to be called, referring to an ageing fighter who hung around gyms and pubs re-living their glory days. His name was Charlie Browne, and he had slipped getting into the ring for his World Championship Heavyweight fight as a contender. His lumbosacral spine had been damaged, but he had fought on with no feeling in his legs. In his own words, 'I ended up mincemeat, man!'

He was a great big chocolate-coloured man with a smile that brought joy to the world – a gold tooth putting a highlight to that smile. His family, he told us, had originated in Jamaica, where his father had managed a paint wholesale/retail outlet. They had lived well in a big high-set house on Halfway Tree Road in Kingston, the capital. In the early 1950s, Charlie's father had been offered a position in New York, and the family had moved there. Charlie had grown up as a large athletic boy who had taken a fancy to boxing in his teenage years, working his way up to be a world heavyweight contender.

After his disastrous championship fight, he'd gone to college. However, boxing had called him back, which is why he was in Reuben's lounge room, eating sweet biscuits and drinking tea with the rest of us.

Apart from Charlie's warm and gentle approach to life and having come up through the boxing ranks, he knew all there was to know about ringcraft, stamina, strength, speed and accuracy, as well as all the tricks used in the boxing game, whether inside or outside the ring.

Charlie was of indeterminate age; let's say mid-forties. He still had a solid frame and good reflexes but preferred to live in the shadows. He was arguably the best man in the world at 'running a corner'. He could staunch blood flow and reduce pain almost instantly, but most importantly, gave the best advice to his boxer, *succinctly*. Most ring men chatter on to their boxers, leaving them with a head stuffed full of words and no target. Boxers are not known for their learning, in the main, so 'keep hitting his head' is about all they can cope with.

With his long history in the game, ascending to world championship status combined with an in-depth knowledge of the human body and its workings, he was my ideal trainer too. Reuben thought that with Art, Reg and Charlie, he had all the bases covered, and that they would make a focused, professional team.

We gathered at Reuben's house for our first meeting, and introductions were made. He had an 8mm Kodak movie projector and a real screen, not a sheet on a wall.

I was in seventh heaven with these guys, since they were on my wavelength as no one else had ever been before. Half the day was spent on films and documentaries of boxing matches that had been fought and recorded, films of fictitious fights or what Hollywood thought were boxing matches, together with in-depth discussions. Reg, too, was like a child with a bag of lollies with all this material. Charlie proved worth his weight in gold in his attention to detail of movement, direction, accuracy and tactics. Art didn't need to be there as he'd seen it all before.

The other half of the day was spent in training – in the gym with the weights and the bags, and then sparring with some selected characters that Reuben brought in. I also went on long runs, which were monitored to show my improved times and distances.

While I proved to be no slouch when it came to ringcraft and reading a fighter, there were many subtle nuances that Charlie was able to show me. Combination punching started as the more obvious, followed by analysis of attacks and defences – some that worked and some that didn't and, most importantly, why they didn't. Charlie went into anatomy and physiology of the human body that he'd learnt during his training so I could see the effect certain punches had on the body. That was a really beneficial part of my training. Also, my punching had to be harder and more precise, especially if the oppo was dodging and weaving, and Charlie started to work on this too.

Charlie commented, 'I've seen professional fighters miss a hundred or more good punches in one fight in exactly the same way. The oppo ducks to one side so the fighter's right goes over his head, time and time again. Now, that's just slack and bloody unforgivable, and it's all because their timing and pattern recognition are rubbish. Now, if the oppo dodges and ducks, remember, they always have to come up, and the way that they do that will probably be repetitive. So watch it, learn it, and when the moment comes, they'll come up into a big right-hander, if you time it right. Also, I've seen massive men with huge bellies, which some boxers make the mistake of thinking are vulnerable. If they're professionals, those bellies hide abs of steel. Not that it will ever concern you as a tiny little welterweight, of course.' I took it all in.

'Sam, the last thing I want to do is to fill your head with so much "stuff" that you're still thinking about it in the ring as words, instead of watching what you're doing. So, we talk, then we put it into practice in the ring, slowly at first, then work up the speed, adding the new skill to your muscle memory. When you've done it enough times, you can forget it. Right?'

'Good, Charlie,' I said, 'because I'm beginnin' to fill up with "stuff," to be 'onest.'

We went on to break down the films and documentaries, with alternative ways of dealing with precise situations, which was best, and again, more importantly, why. Best of all, the Saturday tents were there to put some of this stuff into practice, and the cards midweek to further the experiment, putting into play some of those learned lessons.

'All I can say is, "they'd better look out!"' I grinned.

Chapter Six

After two months, Reuben said I was ready to start my professional career, having had Donna's blessing, again. He had already booked a fight with Tom Johns, rated #3 at my weight in the United Kingdom. My usual weight was about 150lbs, and like every boxer and jockey, I could play around with a pound or two either way when it was needed. At 147 pounds, it made me a welterweight at the top end of the scale. Reuben said he would take the team to Arena Birmingham in his car, where the fight was being held.

I felt as though I hadn't learned anything – that it had all been just a chat, even though we had been through many new moves in the ring. Time to find out.

Charlie said, 'Sam, this is a situation you haven't been in before. My best advice to you right now is to keep your head down while all the razzamatazz is going on and start paying attention when you get into the ring. My old trainer had a saying, "When all the razzamatazz is over, there remains just two boxers in one ring." And you are quite at home in there, Sam; it's where you live. That you can beat this man, I have no doubt, as long as you don't do something silly, like an amateur. Both Reuben and I want a verbal report from you after the match so we can see what needs to be corrected. You're fit, handy and ready. Go get him, Champ!'

Well, I changed in a very classy room that had carpet on the floor! Charlie fussed over me a bit with the bandages and gloves, laced the boots just so, and gave me his summary. He then sat back to give me some quiet time.

There was a need to focus on something. I realised that there wasn't an image in my head to support why I was doing this. Donna and the girls were my primary focus. This was for them. So, I created from memory a picture in my head of my girls enjoying themselves on Epsom Downs with their kites. *Plug it in, remember it, then tuck it away.*

Me. What did I need from now on? I had said 'Respect', and meant it too. But what did that mean, and how to get it, or more realistically, earn it?

First, I had to win. There was no respect for losers. Second, I had to show my skills to boxers and enthusiasts, not just the crowd. They would just be happy with the win. Third, I would have to keep it tight, keep it hard and keep it smart. Then respect would come naturally.

I was ready. Head down, hood up, with Charlie leading the way. I had to keep inside myself and ignore the roar of the crowd baying for blood. *It won't be mine, people.* I put the mental picture of my family up there on the inside of my forehead. *I'll be okay. Give me your blessings, and I'll get it done.*

I stepped into the ring and looked for the oppo, but I'd got here first. Shrugging my hood off, I moved about to smooth out any muscle kinks, then closed my ears to the noise but opened my eyes wide to everything about my oppo's corner. It was well organised, with a smooth operating team, which had obviously done this before. In came the oppo, Tom Johns. *Nice threads.* He was moving about already. He had a lean, well-muscled form, but not much reach, maybe. I'd be checking that out.

I moved to the Ref in the middle of the ring, and saw John's eyes were steady, but he was not seeing the things I was seeing. Instructions from the Ref, touched gloves, then we danced.

Bell!

His left was up high as a guard, but he'd dropped his right. He wanted me to worry about his right, so I expected the left jab. It arrived quickly, and the right followed as an uppercut. Predictable, but I was not there. I took a step back, so his uppercut nearly knocked the lights out over the ring. It left his right side wide open, which I punished with my left. I heard his sharp breath intake. *Gotcha! Try that again, and you'll get the same result.*

We circled, we circled and we circled some more. It was like when there's silence in a conversation, which someone has to fill. It would be up to him because, as top dog, he wouldn't want to give the impression of fear or laziness. Sure enough, double jab and another uppercut. I'd warned him with my first punch and punished his right side once more. Then he sent me his right hook, but it was a bit of a haymaker, going 'around the houses'. It left him vulnerable again, so I hit him with my left, but I just knew that he was going to protect that right side immediately, and, as his left opened up, I gave him a right to the heart. There was the wobble in his legs, and I could hear his heavy breathing. I could see him gathering his thoughts, so gave him a left-right-left combination to the head, and, while he was thinking about that one, I gave him another, and the wobble was back.

Bell!

'Nice,' commented Charlie. 'What's he going to do next round?'

'Go to the canvas,' I smiled, rinsing my mouth. 'But 'e'll try to 'ustle, so I'll let 'im. 'e'll have to chase me around, and that will give me the opportunity. Watch, Charlie.'

Bell!

My mouthguard was in, and I got up feeling really good. Johns came forward, jabbing, and missing, I have to say. I was bobbing and weaving but kept my eyes on him, waiting for the moment. He brought a right from the floor. I was backing away, but it caught me in my groin. The pain hit me like a freight train, and I dropped. I could hear the Ref going crazy with him, and the crowd was hysterical. I did some very heavy breathing, and the pain subsided. The Ref was above me and starting to count. I was up at 'seven' and felt like I'd just had a fortnight's holiday. I was fine.

We touched gloves again to show there was no hard feeling, backed away, then I took a quick skip forward and dropped him with a sweet right to the 'button'. He'd had no idea it was coming. I moved to a neutral corner, leaned back and waited, but he was not getting up. I knew how hard I'd hit him. He was out. The Ref held my left arm up. I held my right fist next to my face – and winked. I'd got them! I'd got the crowd. They were with me one hundred percent because of the low blow, and the wink just topped it off.

The crowd was shouting, 'Sam-my! Sam-my! Sam-my!' as I left the huge arena. Charlie loomed over me for protection, but only from the mass of people, the noise and the questions. What I was thinking as I left the arena was: Respect! You can't win respect by behaving like my oppo.

I got back to the changing rooms where I showered and dressed. The bruising would come out later, no doubt, but for now I was relatively comfortable. He had put me down with a low blow. I had redeemed myself, and the crowd loved it.

Did that mean more money? Well, more people would know me. A bigger audience would mean more money. I was second on the programme so the money would not be that great, but it was a start. I thought about the picture from Epsom and smiled as though I was in touch with my wife. But for now, it was home and sleep. I'd meet the gang tomorrow to report on the fight, and the wink!

Chapter Seven

All our team sat around a table in Reuben's house in Hampstead talking about Saturday's fight. Everyone said I had done well. Of course, they did. I'd won, hadn't I? Charlie said that the low blow was just one of those anom... strange things that sometimes turn up in a fight, and there was nothing that I could have done to avoid it. I was backpedalling at the time, so it wasn't my fault, and the crowd was well on my side because of it.

'There was a sudden burst of applause at the end,' said Reuben. 'What was that about? I didn't see.'

'I winked at the crowd,' I said.

'Why?'

'I wanted 'em to know I was okay, that I wasn't 'armed or in pain, and that I bloody well nailed 'im,' I said.

'I think you did yourself a bit of good there,' he encouraged. 'People will remember that gesture, and remember you, and you'll be more popular and get bigger audiences because of it. Well done, Sam, my boy. You got a good fee for this one, and I'm throwing in an extra "fifty" for you to treat Donna and the girls.' He actually said, 'A couple of po-nies.'

'Thanks, Reuben. That's fab, but you'll earn that back in no time, trust me,' I assured him.

'Back to work tomorrow,' interrupted Charlie, 'after you've seen our doc. Light training to start, mind you, then we've got you another match in three weeks if the doc gives you the go-ahead. Will you be ready for that?'

'Yeah, Charlie. No trouble. Reg, who's the oppo?

'A Liverpool bloke by the name of Jimmy Verance. The Scouser's about your weight. They say he's tough and hard to put down. Been fighting a while. I'll get the gen on him, and we'll have a little talk, eh?'

'Thanks, Reg. It'll be useful to know what I'm up against; it saves time in the long run, and usually a punch or two findin' out.'

The doc gave me the 'all clear', and we were off again, with some new sparring partners that Charlie had brought in. Needless to say, I wore some heavy-duty protection so as not to get knackered again!

In the meantime, I got smart and asked Donna what she'd like to spend Reuben's 'ponies' on. Did she want a meal with the girls? Did she want a bunch of flowers, or a box of chocolates, or something else?

'No,' she said, 'the girls need some new threads, and I'd like to take them shopping for some little girl things. Thanks, my love.'

I seemed to be getting the hang of this husband and wife thing, but I never relax. It's a bit like being in the ring, or the Boy Scouts: 'Be prepared,' I always say.

The time flashed by towards the next fight. Reg booked a time with Charlie and me, and again we met at Reuben's house.

'The thing about nearly all fighters is that they know what they can do, but they don't seem to care what other fighters can do,' commented Reg. 'That's where you're so different, Sam. You look for what other fighters can do, and then work out what they can't do, and that tells you how to beat them. It's a part of pattern recognition. Left jab, left jab, straight right. If you pay attention, and if your oppo keeps doing that, you work out that if you jab him before his second one, you put him right off his stroke, and you can get a nice right cross in there while he's working out what's going on. You see what's going on and mess up his rhythm. Tell us how, Sam?'

'Well, there's backward and forwards. You backpedal so 'e can't reach you, so 'e starts coming at you faster, then you change direction, and 'e's on top of you and just beggin' for a sweet right cross or an uppercut. Or, 'e jabs, you go left; 'e jabs, you go right; 'e jabs, and you 'ave faked right, and 'e misses over your left shoulder, leavin' 'is left side open to a nice 'eart punch. Or you attack 'im as 'e would attack you; left jab, left jab, straight right. 'e probably knows only how it works for 'im but 'as no idea 'ow to deal with it in return,' I explained with a grin.

'Look, gang, I'd like to say this, especially after all Charlie's 'elp. I need all the technical boxin' tools I can get, but they're just backup. Ninety percent of my boxin' is done in my 'ead. I play chess with their boxin' skills; and yes, I do actually know how to play chess.

'Sometimes, I ask a question by lettin' my guard down. Does 'e see it, and if so, what does 'e do about it? This gives me a 'uge amount of info. Crowd 'im, smother 'im, and see what that brings. A simple jab will bring a response, which'll tell me a lot about his defence. Action/reaction. So, from now on, I'll be startin' my fights at what will be seen as a slow pace, while I build up a profile of their skill sets. Strengths, weaknesses, attack, defence, 'is preferences for dealin' with his opposition, but mainly 'is weaknesses, which I then exploit. I'll put 'im on the floor, and we all go 'ome for an early night with a nice wedge in the back pocket. I see this slow start as being the way to go for the professionals. With amateurs, it didn't matter so much, because most of 'em were all over the place anyway.'

Charlie nodded his approval. 'If you can do that, man, with your full skillset, I can't see you losing a fight. We have to work on your punching weight and speed, get your legs even stronger, and then see what happens.'

Reuben interrupted. 'You've got just three days until your fight with the Scouser. Feel ready, Sam?'

Yes, mate, as right as rain.'

'If you win this next one, we're going to get really serious, but we'll leave that until after the match.'

Chapter Eight

The training went well, and I felt on top of the world. Reg had told me the Scouser, Jimmy Verance, was tough, hard to put down – and a bit of a brawler. This meant that he would be coming forward all the time, trying to smother me with punches, and messing up any timing I might have. If he was a brawler, I'd have to give him a boxing lesson, so I spent a lot of time on counterpunching practice with both my sparring partners and the floor-to-ceiling ball. Charlie, my ring man, said I was coming along nicely – rare praise from him.

The fight night came, and we went in Reuben's car again. It wasn't far to Bethnal Green from where I lived in Whitechapel. The Scouser may have some travel disorientation away from his beloved Liverpool, but I wouldn't bet on it. So, we'd see what he had. I was feeling terrific, but I'd take it slowly and punish him for brawling. That was the plan.

My hood was up. It was dance time again. I hated all the audience noise and the falseness of it all. Only the dance mattered, and whether I could get the best result in the ring.

He was up first, and I watched him as I got nearer the ring. He was keen and showing me his aggression. He was showing me a preview of his tactics. Not very clever, mate!

Bell!

The dance began. He was straight across the ring and tried a quick right, which I slipped. Then I clipped the side of his head. He tried again, but I wasn't there; I moved the other way and left-hooked his body. He tried to counter counterpunch, but I'd been doing some of that too, so was nowhere near where he punched, but gave him a nice body shot again on the return.

He insisted on coming forward, thinking this gained him some points, I suppose. I reversed it to see how he liked a taste of his own medicine. I advanced, and we met sooner than he had expected, and a right cross to his jaw brought him up a bit sharp. I saw his eyes open in surprise. I didn't see his uppercut coming, and I was momentarily out of the action; backpedalling quickly. When I got my control back, I crowded him into a corner. I gave him some really nice body shots and finished with a sweet right to the side of his head and then retreated. This puzzled him because if you have your oppo in a corner, surely you'd want to keep him there for as long as possible? So, why did I let him off the hook? He was still trying to work that out.

Bell!

'Nice bit of work that, Sam,' said Charlie. 'Why'd you let him out of the corner?'

'For starters, because this fight 'as to go for more than one round, or it'll look rigged. Also, I need to know more about 'im. I 'aven't explored 'is arsenal yet. 'e's a brawler and a bully but can't handle the same tactics used against 'im. 'e's got a reasonable punch, but 'is timin's way off. 'ere we go.'

Bell!

Again, he came out like a whirlwind, throwing punches all over the place. I circled right to see which way he came at me, then I circled left to see his alternative strategy. This was a ten-round fight, so I mustn't end it in two. It would do my reputation no harm, of course, but it wouldn't be good for the sport. So, I kept him going – circled, counter-punched with the old left-right-left at speed. Mainly, it was practice for me in combating this sort of brawling fighter at this level, and finding out, again, how good I was – or was not. In fact, I felt quite comfortable.

The third round went about the same as the second because I'd learned nearly all of his technique in the first round. Now, there was the question of how to drop him. His defence was a bit better than I'd thought it would be. Gloves were held high beside his head, but it left his body open. Next round, I'd see if I could drop his hands then drop him with a right on the 'button', or maybe my left hook. We'd see how it turned out.

Bell!

'Okay,' said Charlie, giving me a drink, 'what happens next?'

'Next, I drop him. 'is guard is good but it's 'igh. If I get 'im to lower it, I'll drop 'im. You reckon that'd work, Charlie.'

'Just what I was thinking, Sammy. From a boxing point of view, you've done well tonight.'

Bell!

He came bustling towards me with his guard up but not throwing a punch. I circled to the right and used my right to punch the side of his head. He came on again, and I circled to the left and still used my right, but into his guard this time, which still rocked his head back. His guard was still high, so I gave him a quick left and right, with a follow-up left just north of his belly button. He countered with a right to my head, but it wasn't there. I dodged right, and my left hook to his chin came into play. It dropped him, so I went to the neutral corner thinking that my punch was nicely timed with a fair amount of power behind it. Let's see how tough he was. Yes, he was tough. He made it on eight, but he was wobbly. *Did I let him off, or would I finish him?* I'd learned all I could from him, so I might as well go home.

He hung back now and that was his main tactic gone. I had about a minute left. I used a series of combination punches to put him in a corner, went downstairs and upstairs until he didn't know who he was. I jumped back, and he just dropped. He was gone. The Ref held up my left hand, and when I had the camera just right, I winked and smiled. I had a mouthguard that looked like teeth and gums, so my smile looked natural; from a distance, anyway. The small but select crowd roared their approval.

Chapter Nine

After the fight I had to have a meeting with Art Dutton, my international manager from America, and it was a bit daunting, to be honest, although Reuben was there too.

I started by calling him Mr Dutton, but he squashed that, saying, 'You goddamn Limeys are so polite. For crying out loud, Sam, call me Art and we'll all get along just fine.'

He told me that even though he hadn't been in the picture much, he'd been keeping his eye on me.

'Charlie does bloody good work at your level, Sam, and that is exactly the point. If you hadn't got through these preliminaries with the change of status from amateur to professional, I wouldn't need to be here, and you would fade into insignificance. The fact that you made that transition successfully means that you now have something for me to work with.'

'I thought I'd done pretty well, Art,' I said, more in hope of a return compliment.

'Yes, so far you have, and I do admire your thinking processes. But to be successful at the top, some things have got to change, even though you're truly a boxer's boxer. Now, Sam, what does it take to be at the top?'

'Well, I guess, 'ard work, good thinkin' and a suitable prep for each fight,' I speculated, more in the hope that that was what he wanted.

'True enough, but the answer that every top coach in every sport in the world would tell you is: "You have to beat the best". Sam, the top ten boxers in the world, at your weight, are some really tough nuts. Most of them are scared out of their wits about the possibility of losing because they have nothing else in their lives. Now, I truly believe that with this team behind you, plus a massive amount of commitment and hard work from you, we can put you up there in contention with a pretty good chance at a world title.'

'Really?' was all I could think of to say. I could feel my eyes were huge. This was goin' so fast. Could I keep up?

'I've spoken to Reuben and the others, and they're all on side. What you need to do now is to explain this to your missus, and make sure she's still with you. Among other things, it will mean you spending up to two months away in training; some here in Britain, and some overseas. The money will be there, somehow, but I don't want you to think about that aspect – ever. I hope Charlie has told you that he doesn't want to fill your head up with words that you don't need to use in the ring. This is like that. There are some things that you should not need to concern yourself about. Money is one, and your wife's support must be another.'

'Thanks, Mr Dutton, ah, Art. I'll talk to 'er tonight, but I'm sure it'll be okay. She just wants what's best for our girls and me.'

'I gathered that. Now, you are a welterweight, so speed, stamina and strong-punch boxing are what you need. If you're clever with it, that's a real bonus. You're not a heavyweight who can get away with being a "one-punch wonder". You need to have all the skills. You're fine at this level, but among the top fighters, you'll need a great deal more stamina. You've spent all your training in the gym, so while you're good, you're not hard. I want you to be hard – as hard as nails before you meet any of those guys – hard and fast and lethal. If we can give you this as a platform, and you use your lessons learned through experience, you can most definitely go all the way. If you're short in any department, you'll be history. Do you read me?'

'Yeah, I do, and I'm prepared to work 'ard.'

'Mercifully, you have no idea of hard work – yet. Tell me, Sam, why are you doing this?'

'I want to provide for my missus and the girls, and I want respect for my boxin', meanin' my skills, my knowledge and my behaviour. I 'ope to raise the public's idea of boxin' as an entertainment as well as a sport. With my wink, I seem to 'ave got a whole new set of fans, and if one wink can do that, what else can I do to communicate directly to the public about good sportsmanship?'

'Who's your idol, Sam?'

'It 'as to be Mohammed Ali. 'e is the greatest boxer ever. 'e uses politics, and then gets politics to use 'im. e's clever, and 'e's funny. I've also said before that if I were in charge of things, I would give 'im a Nobel Prize.'

'Sam, my friend, I hope you never have the enormous pressures put on you that that man has had put on him. At any other time in the history of the human race, he would have been fine, but these are bad and brutal times, especially for black people in America. Amen.'

'Are you religious?' I blurted out.

'Not really, but "Amen" means, "Let it be so" in Hebrew, and I use it quite often. We'll have a meeting at the gym at 9 o'clock on Monday morning, and I'll have a plan for you. Go and talk to your wife, and we'll start from the very beginning.'

I turned to Reuben. 'If I'm goin' to be away, what will Donna do for money?'

'Don't you worry about that, my boy,' reassured Reuben. 'I'll give your missus quite enough to live on while you're gone. She'll be all right, and if there's a sudden problem, she only has to phone me.'

'Let's get started then!'

Chapter Ten

At the next training session, Reuben had this to say. 'Sam, you must experience the world, and some of the places in it so that you know more than just Whitechapel.

'Soon, you'll be going on a trip with a man I know and trust called Kit Sayer. Kit's an old mate of mine who's been everywhere and done everything. He'll take you to places and show you things that few know about. It'll have to be a bit of a whirlwind because it'll cost a lot of 'ready'. Have you got a passport?'

'Sure 'ave.'

'What about Donna and the girls?'

'No. We've 'ad no reason to get any organised.'

'Tell your wife to sort that out, and I'll pay for it. She'll need to get the forms from the post office, but there's no urgency. What's the essence of travel, Sam?'

'Take everythin' you're likely to need, I'd say.'

'And that tells me you need to get out more. The answer is quite the opposite: "Half the luggage and twice the money" is a much better plan. Pack what you think, and I'll meet you at your house tomorrow at nine in the morning. Oh, and you won't need a suit, trust me.'

'Where are we goin'?'

'That's part of the learning curve. You'll find out when you get there.'

* * *

'Sam, Donna, this idea came from the whole team,' stated Reuben, 'and it's with my financial blessing. I've told you never to consider the money, and I repeat that to you now. Sam, you'll be away for about two months in all, and I envy you this trip more than I can tell you, but it'll be a growing-up trip for you. When you get back, I want to see a worldly man who has had his eyes opened way beyond Whitechapel. I want to see a hard man, with confidence and even a slight swagger, maybe. You won't understand that yet, but you'll be a changed person – for the better.' I just stared at him.

'Donna, I'd like you and the girls to join Sam in New York at a later date. I don't want to change your husband only for you to remain "Donna and the girls, just of White-chapel". You too, need to grow by experiencing different things, and a trip to New York will start that. You can relax. I'll come with you to make sure you don't get lost. Now Sam, are you packed?'

'Sure am.'

'Show me.'

I reached behind the sofa for my suitcase, which was quite heavy.

'Do you have passports, money and tickets?'

'Not tickets! No! I thought you 'ad them,' I said, with panic echoing in my voice.

'That's good, my boy. I wanted you to feel a little fear brought on by being disorganised and ignorant, not only of travel procedure but lots of other things too. You'll have my good friend, Kit Sayer, to look after you. He'll be your guide and mentor and will have everything you need. I'll take you to the Underground, and you'll get a Tube to Cromwell Road then a coach to London Airport. Can you do that?'

'I reckon I can,' I said, but with some lingering doubt.

'I'll see you in the car. Give me your case.'

He took the case as I said a teary farewell to my wife. As soon we were on the Tube to Cromwell Road coach station, he said, 'Kit will show you some stuff that few get to see. You'll go places and see things beyond your understanding. However, I give you my word that you'll be safe. What you're feeling now is the very edge of what I call, "The Foggy Curtain", where the present is scary and the future is unknown. I want you to explore all this so that when you come back to us, you'll never again fear that feeling. You will always embrace it, be excited by it – and in control.'

'Cheers, Reuben, and thanks. I won't let you down.'

'Go and be educated, my boy,' he said, with a wave of his hand.

I bought a ticket to London Airport, sorted out where the coach went from, and sat with my thoughts for about an hour. I was already missing Donna and the girls, but there was no value in doing that. I had to look forward, and since no one could do that, I thought through some fights and some moves I could make to counter any oppos' attacks in the ring.

Eventually, the coach dropped me at the appropriate terminal. Waiting at the coach stop was Kit. He was a smiling man in his mid to late forties, with the beginning of greying hair at the temples, slightly ageing his brown mop. He was a bit taller than me, and very relaxed.

'You're Sam?'

I nodded and held out my hand, which he squeezed unnecessarily hard. His eyes said 'Dominance' and in the ring I would have hurt him quickly, but this was different. He was in control, and I had to like it.

'Sam, I've been tasked to look after you on a short holiday, and to show you some things outside London, which shouldn't be hard. I will have no drunkenness, no playing with the ladies, and you will do what I ask of you at all times. Understood?'

I nodded again. This man should have been on a Regimental parade ground, with a waxed moustache and a swagger stick. Still, if those were the rules, then those were the rules. The last thing I needed from him was to abandon me with no money and no resources in some far-flung corner of the Empire! *So, suck it up Sam, and do exactly what you are told.* 'Yes, Sir!' my mind replied, silently.

'I will train you, and educate you, and then return you to London in one piece, is that clear?'

'Yes, Sir!' I answered, which strangely relieved a lot of stress because he didn't understand my sarcasm. *It is what it is, Sam. Get used to it. It's not for long.*

'We'll go to the check-in now, so pay attention, because I want you to look after the arrangements from now on. You'll need your ticket and passport, weigh your luggage and be polite to the staff. Got that?'

'Oh yes,' I told him. *I think I'm going to have fun with him because he doesn't understand me and my humour, so we will have two conversations; one that I say to him, and the other words that speak to me. Let's see.*

'Follow me, then.'

We checked in and I watched exactly how this was done to the two passengers ahead of me so I understood the pattern.

'Thank you, Sir,' said the smart young lady.

'You're welcome,' I replied.

'Don't get all gushy,' grimaced Kit.

I smiled at him. I was right, he didn't read people well; he just knew what he wanted.

'Where are we goin'?' I asked.

'You'll see when we get there,' he said abruptly, but I'd seen Jamaica on the ticket and also Antigua. Where was Antigua?

'Look,' pointed Kit at some big wall-tables, 'these are the destinations and gate numbers, so marry those with the right airline and flight number, and make sure you don't get on the wrong plane and end up in China!'

Yes, Sir! almost came to my lips again, but he may detect some sarcasm and I wanted to keep that to myself.

We climbed on the aeroplane, got our seat number from the boarding pass, did up the seat belt and waited.

My assessment was that I would have to remain quiet during this holiday since Kit's whole personality was dominant and controlling. I would learn, but I would have to appear submissive. Right! *Sam, you're organised. Now, take it all in, and enjoy, even if the company is ex-Gestapo.*

The take-off in the very sleek Boeing 707 was very exciting, but I soon fell asleep, waking as we were on approach to Coolidge International Airport in Antigua, a small island, which was an intermediate stop. We were directed to the 'In-Transit' lounge in the airport, disembarking into heat, the like of which I had never experienced. The sun beat down rather than shone, the sky was blue and cloudless, and nearly everyone was black except Kit and me. Closely watching the whole scene, I soaked up the style of dress, the movements of people, their smiles and the generally relaxed feeling.

Where were the steely-eyed officials, the high-visibility vests, the barriers and all those signs saying, 'Do this!' or 'Go there!' and especially 'Don't... or, NO...!'? There was such a mass of people, dressed in bright colours, all milling about, seemingly with no order or direction. It looked like a chaotic village market in Africa, which I had seen as some pictures in a National Geographic magazine in a doctor's waiting room once. We went back through the iron-furnace heat to the plane again, experiencing that exciting feeling on take-off, flying up above the sea.

Kit told me about the West Indies, showed me a map of all the islands, and where Jamaica was in relation to Antigua, Cuba and the United States. We landed at Palisadoes Airport near Kingston, the capital of Jamaica. Apparently, the airport was built almost on top of Port Royal, the old pirate capital of the West Indies. However, it sank in an earthquake in 1692, leaving no trace above the waves now, according to Kit.

While Kit saw to all the official stuff on immigration and customs, I picked up my case and, sweating profusely, made my way to the taxi rank. I was so used to the black London Taxis that I was pleasantly surprised when our taxi turned out to be an American Plymouth. I'd never ridden in an American car before, with its tail fins and lavish chrome. The driver talked to us, but I couldn't understand much of what he was saying.

I did hear him say, '...and what are you nice white folks from London doing in Jamaica?'

Kit told him, 'We've come to spend lots of lovely money so that you can get paid, man!'

The driver threw his head back and laughed. 'Got me!' he conceded.

Kit and the driver spoke in a sort of dialect as we glided and floated our way to Kingston along the airport road on the Plymouth's ultra-soft suspension.

We stopped at a very modern hotel. The foyer was decorated with light coloured woods and tinted glass. Outside, the gardens were as pretty as Kew and the Chelsea Flower Show.

Having checked into our rooms, we met at a thatch-roofed bar near an unspoiled swimming pool in this tropical garden. A local guitarist quietly played island music. This was a very long way from Whitechapel.

Kit approached with two cold drinks with condensation on the outside of the glasses.

'Cheers,' he saluted, 'and non-alcoholic. It's called, 'Lemon, lime and bitters', and is a nice-tasting refreshing drink that avoids the alcohol but allows you to sit comfortably in any bar. Now, Sam, we have some talking to do. How are you liking Jamaica?'

'Hot! No, very hot! Everythin' is so bright and colourful. I love it.'

'Good,' said Kit. 'You're going to need some clothes for this temperature if you are not going to boil, as we say, or 'broil' as the Americans say, meaning 'grilled'. So, we'll get a cab to a shopping centre, which will be air-conditioned. T-shirts, shorts, thongs and a hat make up the uniform worn by tourists and Jamaicans alike. We'll also pick up some sunglasses and heavy-duty sunscreen to stop you burning, peeling, and probably getting skin problems in later life.

'We'll be here about a week. Tomorrow, we'll drive to Montego Bay on the north coast.'

Chapter Eleven

We were about a hundred yards out from Montego Bay's golden sand beach on the north coast of Jamaica. The sea, ruffled by a slight breeze, was as blue as an advert, as warm as a bath and as clear as glass. It had been my home for a week under Kit Sayer's careful watch.

'Change to your regulator and go through the hole below us. You'll be in a cave. Swim to the end, and I'll meet you there. Okay?'

'Right,' I said, givin' him the sign of thumb and first finger in a circle. I exchanged the snorkel for my scuba regulator mouthpiece, blew through it to clear it and followed Kit down to the bottom at around twenty feet, clearing my ears as I descended.

There was a hole in the coral, through which I squeezed both myself and my scuba tank. The cave was dark, but I saw light coming from one direction and swam towards it. In no more than twenty yards I was in brilliant sunlight among a forest of spectacular sponges. Kit was standing on the sandy bottom, holding his hands and arms in a position which said, 'Ta–DA!'

It was a heavenly scene for any diver: from the multicoloured sponges up to six feet tall and lots of coral and small, brilliantly coloured fish. I cast my mind back to London, for comparison, and wondered how I hadn't known about places like this.

'Do as I do,' wrote Kit on his underwater slate. I gave him the 'OK' sign and followed him closely, wondering what was next. Very slowly he searched the sides of a small canyon covered in corals. Every so often he pointed at something he'd seen. I nodded to show him I'd seen it too, whatever it was, but knowing we would identify and discuss it later.

At one point he held up his hand signifying me to stop. Then he made the sign for me to slowly sink to the sandy bottom of this small canyon, only five feet or so below us at around forty feet. He held his finger up to his mouth for silence. We waited, lying side by side on the sandy bottom. I spotted a small hole in the sand, about half an inch in diameter, the size of the old sixpence. We were about three feet away from it. We waited, and we waited.

The tip of a pink antenna came slowly into view, waving around. Then another. After about twenty seconds, a small pink shrimp, much of which was transparent, climbed out of the hole in the sand, taking time to observe its environment. It spotted us, but we were some distance away, unaggressive and immobile. It ducked back into the hole only to re-appear, shepherding half a dozen baby shrimp. 'It,' the parent presumably, was no more than an inch long, although its antennae were three times that length. The babies were smaller than a baby's fingernail clipping and almost see-through, but they started playing, moving around and tumbling about on the sand under the very watchful eyes of their parent.

I couldn't believe what I was seeing. Here was a tiny shrimp family with a parent making a chance for the 'kids' to play safely outside their burrow. Their whole play area would have been within a circle no larger than 3 inches, or 75mm in diameter.

For whatever reason, the adult suddenly seemed to sense danger and ushered the youngsters back into the hole with one sweep of a tiny claw. It retreated with, I swear, a very accusing and angry glare at us. How could I see that, or even understand that look? I really don't know, but that was what I felt: guilty about interrupting their playtime. What an honour to see that little scene. It was probably unique in the experience of just about everyone else on earth, except for the two of us.

We smiled and nodded at each other through our masks. Kit checked the time and depth, and then pointed upwards. I acknowledged and we began a very slow ascent. After about ten feet Kit pointed to something he'd seen in the open water. I looked. In the deep-blue distance was a shark - coming towards us! It seemed about ten feet long and was swimming at us with a flowing stroke of its very long tail.

I could feel my blood pressure rising. Kit came in front of me and gave me his 'Don't Panic' signal, very forcefully. I watched that shark like an unexploded bomb. It seemed to see that we were slowly rising and, with a flick of its tail, changed direction. Kit winked at me, and we continued our ascent.

I still had about a third of a tank of air left, but we had been between fifty and sixty feet for some time, so a slow, controlled ascent would be needed to avoid the 'bends' – a very nasty and painful consequence for not obeying scuba diving's basics.

We surfaced under the hot Jamaican sun, replaced our snorkels and made for the beach. A five-minute lazy swim, watching the bottom change in depth and character as we approached the beach, took us into the shallows. We dragged our equipment up the furnace-hot sand into the shade of the palm trees bordering the beach that were clattering in the breeze.

Kit asked, 'How was that?'

'That, Kit, was the best thing I 'ave ever seen in my life. There were amazin' colours and movement, and nothin' I've ever seen before.'

'There was too much going on for me to give you a lecture on all the things we saw, but do you remember a thing that looked like a dinner plate made of red lace, standing on its side?'

'Yes, I remember that.'

'Was it an animal or a plant?'

'Well, it 'ad to be a plant, lookin' like that.'

'Wrong! It was an animal. Let's call it a Sea Fan because that's what it looked like. I thought the little shrimp family was quite charming.'

'Kit, that taught me more about divin' and beauty than I ever expected.'

Sam Smith should be in a boxing gym in Whitechapel in London, under grey skies and cold, soaking rain at this very moment. How did I get here, and, more to the point, why was I here, swimming with what turned out to be a Thresher shark, which swam as easily as Roger Bannister can run?

Sadly, at the end of the week we left 'Mo Bay' behind, together with the happy, smiling Jamaicans with their Reggae music and their apparent need to dance all the time. The flight we caught from Montego Bay International Airport, where Kit watched me negotiate emigration and customs, proved we were going to Canada! Whoa! How good was that? Of course, I'd given no thought to weather conditions or appropriate dress, but that was part of my training; learning to think forward and anticipate needs. I was getting there.

We had a farewell Red Stripe beer in the lounge before take-off, but Kit offered no more information about our stay in Canada. I fell asleep soon after take-off and awoke with Kit instructing me to, 'lift your window blind'.

For a whole minute I could not work out what I was looking at. There was the deep blue sky above, the sun shining down very brightly on to a flat, white, porcelain dinner plate with what looked like heaps of ice cream standing up on it. What?

My mind was scrambling to make sense of what I was seeing. Then I got it. We were high in the air with white cloud cover below us, flat and unruffled in the still air.

'Outta sight, man,' I told Kit.

'You would say that, of course,' he criticised.

A little later we dropped down through the cloud, which was as grey as an average English day. When our plane finally broke through, there was a modern city spread out around a bay.

'That's Vancouver,' said Kit. 'We won't be staying there as we have another flight to Kamloops in the Rocky Mountains soon after we land. But Vancouver is a very modern and innovative city. I lived here as a child. A building company put up an office complex on a complete city block on Robson Street. The safety fence around the outside was made of plywood panels, and the mayor offered a reward for the best artwork, in whatever medium any sponsored artist cared to work with. So, for however long it took for that building to be erected and the fence to come down, was the length of time the general public had to appreciate the work of local artists. I think that was a good idea.'

'I agree. That would 'ave been good to see. Of course, we 'ave pavement artists in London, but they do it for coppers from the public passin' by. Sponsored artists?'

'Yes, the artists would be sponsored by a company, which could attach their company logo to the artwork. They would pay the artist's joining fee and donate a set amount to the Mayor's Charity Appeal. They call that a 'Win/Win/Win' situation.'

I got us through immigration and customs, but as we went to pick up the luggage, the cold suddenly hit me. I realised I was still in my shorts, T-shirt and thongs, lookin' like a complete idiot among the ski outfits and warm woolly hats of the native Canadians.

'Here,' said Kit, handing me a holdall. 'Go and change into something warmer. And next time, start to think about what you are going to need at the other end.'

This was quite a learning curve, based on embarrassment. Then I realised that there was as much embarrassment as I put on myself. No one else cared. Two more lessons learned.

We climbed aboard a tiny little plane with only one propeller, and a pilot who was an Elvis Presley look-alike.

'Greetings!' he said. 'Welcome to our little flight to Kamloops. The weather is good today so get out your cameras because there's some brilliant scenery between here and Kamloops.'

He was right. Every five minutes it seemed, as the aircraft struggled for height up the side of the Rocky Mountain range, there was a new and beautiful calendar-picture scene. Soon, snow started to come into the picture, literally, and it began to get very cold, even though there was a heater in the plane. We landed on an airstrip that had no snow on it, so I think there must have been some underground heating. A taxi took us over snowy roads to a men's clothing shop to get me some very welcome warmer clothes.

'In this environment, "Comfort is all,"' advised Kit, 'and comfort basically means warm and dry. If that means wearing seven or eight layers of clothing, then so be it. If your feet are dry, comfortable and warm, and your head is warm, then the rest will cope. If you're warm all over, you are one happy little Canadian.'

I phoned Donna, as I did every night at 7 pm, her time. This was another learning curve to work out time zones to make that call on time. The girls were always excited about where I was, and what I was doing. Donna and I missed each other, but I usually had her laughing by the end of the call.

A good night's sleep was followed by a huge sweet breakfast of bacon and eggs, pancakes and maple syrup, then we were ready to rent skis and all the rest of the stuff. Being fitted for skis was not something I'd thought about. I imagined you just picked out a pair from a bin or something; maybe choosing the ones with the brightest colours, like you would a snorkel. But no! A careful measuring took place, and it was part of the 'Comfort is all' advice.

I went on the 'Nursery Slope' with the 3- and 4-year-old Canadian children! Now that's really starting at the bottom. For an hour, I was hauled up a short towline, skiing down a gentle snow slope doing little curves by putting pressure on the outside ski, which was counter-intuitive, then stopping at the bottom by bringing the front of the skis together. The practice confirmed that the theory worked, then Kit turned up.

'It's time to get you on a slope. Follow me.'

He used his poles and some sideways skiing, like roller-skating, to progress, leaving me in his wake. I tried like hell to follow him, but the skis didn't want to cooperate. Then suddenly I was moving forward and caught up with him in a queue.

'Right, finally you're getting there. When it's our turn on the lift, get into position beside me and just stand still. The lift bar will collect you. Just sit back, and it will take you to the top. I'll be on the other side of you since they're double seats, so just relax and let it all happen.'

I had my doubts that this was going to happen as Kit predicted. I imagined my body in a mangled heap caused by the machinery being unable to stop, or embarrassing the hell out of myself in front of most of the population of Canada, together with a crowd of sophisticated international tourists!

Front page news: 'Idiot Brit injured by lacking the simplest of ski-slope skills! Read all about it!'

In the actual event, however, it all went smoothly. The assistants noted that I was a first timer, so took extra time and patience to get me settled. The thick green bar touched me behind the legs. I sat down and was whisked, 'up, up, and away', into the sky!

'This is a gas!' I said to Kit.

'Told you.'

'How do I get off of this thing?'

'It's the same process in reverse. You just stand up. Your momentum will propel you forward on your skis, and the bar will go off to the right. You keep going forward out of the way but remain upright. Okay?'

'If you say so.'

I counted twenty-six main pylons on the way up, and then we went over a lip in the mountain and continued for another couple of miles. *I've got to get down from 'ere*, I thought, *by skiin'!* That was really being thrown in at the deep end!

'Here we go,' said Kit. I stood up and was propelled forward. The bar went off to the right, just as Kit told me. However, I found myself on top of a short, snow-covered hill, about twenty feet high, and before I knew what was happening, I was careening down it at a high rate of knots. I fell over in the middle of a circle of people having, what looked like, a cocktail party. They were standing around with glasses of champagne in their hands and smiles on their faces. And there was I, like an immobilised turtle on its back, in their midst.

'Who let the "hoi polloi" up here?' one asked.

'Some people will do anything for attention,' said another.

'Should give him a good clip round the ear!' said another. Strangely, they were all English accents. I finally got to my feet and looked at 'clipped ear'.

I muttered to 'im, 'You should be very careful who you're talkin' to, saying somethin' like that, my friend. Remember the name Sam Smith of Whitechapel, and please – anywhere – anytime. Bye!'

I made off as quickly as I could. The Aussies call them 'Pommie Bastards', and right at this moment I savoured the idea of gloves and a ring. I think, in truth, I was missing the ring! Never mind, now I had to get down off this bloody great mountain before I froze to death, or got lost, which would amount to the same thing.

Kit skied up behind me like an Olympian, of course. He did everything like that.

'Follow me,' he said, swanning off. I did the best I could to keep up. We stopped at the top of a slope, at the bottom of which was a toy-town inhabited by what looked like tiny, tiny ants.

'This is called the "Five Mile," so take your time getting down, and I'll meet you at the bottom.' He skied off, curving at speed down this enormous slope.

In my mind, it was an enormous white–tiled frictionless roof that reached the ground from the top of this mountain at a near-vertical angle, and here was me, standing on the peak of said roof, on shiny, smooth skis with no brakes! This could be interesting, let's see what happens.

I started off, tried to curve, moved slightly from the middle to the side, at which time I was confronted by an incredible drop, covered, at my level, with the tops of a thick forest of massive pine trees. I tried reversing the curve by putting pressure on the outside ski but kept going towards the edge at an incredible speed. Only one thing for it: 'bail out!' I did, by throwing myself sideways, landing in the soft snow just a few feet from the edge. My skis were stuck in the snow behind me. I couldn't reach them as they were crossed and well buried in the snow from the speed I'd achieved.

Well, that's the end of my career, I thought.

More headlines: 'Promising boxer, Sam Smith of Whitechapel, was found dead at the top of the Five Mile slope outside Kamloops in the Canadian Rockies. It appears that he became immobilised when his skis stuck in the snow and, being unable to save himself, froze to death.'

'Do you still fancy a spot of ring work with me, Sam?' asked a voice. I recognised 'Clipped ear' and inwardly cringed.

'Can you 'elp me up? This is my first attempt at skiin'.'

'I would have guessed that. Let me give you a hand.' Between us, I managed to rise unsteadily to my feet.

'If it's any consolation to you, I would never get into a ring with you again. You're far too good. I fought you in the tents about a year ago. You found my weakness and dropped me in the second round. I've never been hit by anything quite that hard before. Keep up the good work, and I can see you as a proper champion not that long from now. Who did you fight last?'

'A Scouser called Jimmy Verance,' I said. 'I dropped 'im in the third.'

'I believe you. Now, put much more pressure on your front ski. You can't break it, but you will cut across the slope harder, and not get up to Olympic Slalom speed. Did you hear your skis screaming? I did, and it was quite terrifying because you had to be going well over 50 miles an hour to get that sound, sport! Also, I really thought you were going over the edge, and that would surely have been the end of you. Nobody gets to stay alive at that speed in dense forest. I'll follow you for a little way to make sure you've got the hang of it.'

'Thanks,' I said. 'I thought you were just another English prat, but you're actually kind.'

'Sam, win your next fight and we'll call it quits. Now, off you go with lots of pressure on those skis.'

I found he was right. Using nursery-slope pressure was not enough. He waved cheerily and disappeared down the slope as if in a puff of blue smoke. Maybe he was a genie.

I finally got to the bottom, and there was Kit's teacher's face.

'There, that wasn't so bad was it?'

'I don't know whether to curse you, punch you or thank you. I need coffee.'

We took off our skis and walked to a crowded coffee shop.

'So, tell me your story, blow by blow.' I did and had him belly laughing for a full ten minutes. My! That was a new experience. Maybe that was a chink in his armour. *Keep it in reserve, Sam.*

'They're the funniest set of circumstances I've ever heard about skiing. You'll entertain a lot of people with that story over the years, trust me.'

'What 'appened to, "keepin' you safe, Sam"?'

'Are you harmed? No! Of course not. There's nothing out there you can't handle. Now, finish up your coffee, and we'll go again. Then I'll introduce you to some steeper slopes. I predict that by the end of the week you'll be skiing like a professional. You started out by being very fit, having great reflexes, and your legs are getting a workout that will stand you in good stead for the rest of your career.'

Again, he was right. By the end of the week, I had conquered almost vertical cliffs of snow, seeming to spend more time in the air than with my skis on the snow. It was exhilarating. The lumps, bumps and bruises were far outweighed by the adrenaline rush. The coordination of using my eyes to work out a safe route through the snow, avoiding the rocky outcrops, then choosing a course I could negotiate safely was a real challenge. Then, I had to navigate that safe route a few milliseconds later as I checked further ahead. However, when I got it right, it was like being on the best roller coaster in the world. 'Exhilarating' is the best word I can find to describe it as it included risk, adrenaline, dizzying speed and sheer joy.

At the end of that 'exhilarating' week, we regretfully took the small feeder flight with 'Elvis' back to Vancouver and caught a plane to Toronto. It was an afternoon flight, and Kit advised me to watch the scenery of the Rocky Mountains. What could I say except that the whole journey across the Rockies, until we landed in Calgary, was absolutely amazin'! I had so many pictures on my camera to take home to Donna and the girls. I'd have to get those negatives developed really quickly so I could show them my adventures.

We glimpsed Banff Township with its famous hotel and cable cars, and the appealing aquamarine colour of Lake Louise as we flew over. It looked a great spot to bring Donna and the girls as part of a skiing holiday sometime in the future, maybe. The afternoon became evening became night much quicker than usual because we were flying east against the sun. Kit explained all this to me and told me to watch out for thunderstorms.

'Thunderstorms? You sure we're safe in a plane in a thunderstorm?' I asked Kit.

'Relax! These will be the safest and prettiest storms you'll ever see.'

The captain told us we were flying at 40,000 feet to avoid the dry electrical storms, but that we might enjoy the effects of the lightning below us.

Soon, individual clouds lit up in pink, like Christmas tree lights.

'Pink?' I asked Kit.

'Probably the effect of lightning on water droplets within the cloud, I would think, but I don't really know. Does it matter?'

'Not at all. We're at 40,000 feet, watchin' natural Christmas tree lightin', lit by lightnin', and it's all included in the price of the ticket. I'd call that a bargain! Blimey, you couldn't do better'n that down the Portobello Road.'

Kit told me that we'd be landing in Toronto, but then travelling on to New York to meet up with Reuben, Donna and the girls. That was really exciting; my stomach was giving me that tickly, anticipatory feeling that a kid gets on Christmas Eve.

I managed all the immigration, customs and visa requirements for the United States, which was rewarded by a nod from Kit. From here on, life got much busier with a larger population hurrying about, as in London. I thought I was used to this, but when compared to the Canadians, it was much more aggressive.

We took a Yellow Cab from the airport to the hotel, which was an education in itself. The girls were in the foyer as we went in, and I got smothered in 'girl' for a long time. It was brilliant to see them again. Donna was in a new dress, looking a million quid, and I told her so. I shook Reuben's hand and told him, 'I don't know 'ow to thank you and Kit for such a wonderful trip. I've 'ad the time of me life, and Kit has taken care of me every step of the way. Thank you again, Reuben.'

'You're welcome, Sam. How are you feeling?'

'Exactly like the fighter you described that you wanted to see. I'm on top of the world. The skiin' has given me legs like steel girders, and the divin' means that my wind is great. All I need is some ring time to sharpen me up again, and I'm good to go.'

'Not yet, my boy. I have some tough work for you before you fight again, but we'll talk about that later. Tomorrow, you, Kit and your family will go shopping. In the evening I'll take us all out to dinner. The following day we'll all go to Madison Square Garden. It's an indoor arena where some of the top fights in the history of boxing have taken place. If you're familiar with the layout, then you'll have a big advantage over someone who isn't – providing you get to fight there, that is.' I just grinned at him.

'Now, go and enjoy a lovely evening with your family. Eat in the hotel restaurant tonight and put the bill on your room tab. Enjoy the shopping tomorrow, and I'll see you in the evening. Kit will make sure you don't get lost.'

Kit added, 'I'll leave you to your family, Sam. I'll be here tomorrow morning, and we'll have a look at New York City. I'll see you all in the foyer at ten, sharp.'

We went up to our rooms. They were huge. Great big bathroom, beautifully decorated bedroom, and a massive bed. What a treat! The girls were in love with their bedroom too but had to toss a coin for who slept in which bed. I had a shower to smarten up since Kit and I had both been travelling for an 'extended period of time'. Kamloops to Vancouver to Calgary to Toronto to New York, and we'd gained three hours in the process, although I hadn't quite got a handle on that yet.

We all went to dinner and caught up on the gossip back home. I told the family some stories of the things I'd seen, but I couldn't properly describe the skiing because of the scale and the speed, so I told them about my first slope, and the scenery. It was just wonderful to see them again, laughing and happy – all my girls with their eyes a-sparkle.

Chapter Twelve

The next day we walked, we shopped and we bought. We have tall buildings in London, but here they were the rule, not the exception. The buildings were crowded, the streets and sidewalks were crowded and the shops were crowded. I was glad my upbringing was in London – a country boy would never have coped with this lot. But the energy was fantastic, and the shop assistants were so helpful.

I had to curb the spending since it wasn't our money but promised my girls that if I ever won enough money, we'd come back and do it properly. I gave the girls the same amount of money each and let them spend it on what they liked. As a father with two daughters, aged six and four, many lessons were built into that exercise.

Our lunch had huge servings, then we shopped some more before heading back to the hotel. Kit was true to his word, and got us safely around this town, and back. We went up to our rooms, and the girls opened what they'd bought, sorting out the things amid squeals of delight. Donna had picked up a couple of things for herself, some presents for Anna and Ella, and a ring for me. She told me she had wanted to get me one for a long time.

We'd gone into a jeweller's where a smart, beautiful and very focused young lady approached us. Donna explained what she wanted, and since she hadn't discussed it with me, I had no idea where she was coming from. We had the sort of relationship that allowed me to refer to a ring potentially going through my nose, and she didn't get upset. Having looked at my hand, the young lady returned with a tray of men's rings. Donna chose one, which was chunky and gold with an embedded small sapphire and an equally small diamond.

'Try that one,' Donna urged. I did, and it didn't look at all sissy or overly flashy.

'Why this one?' I asked.

'Silly! The blue sapphire is to remind you of the colour of the sea in Montego Bay, and the diamond is to remind you of the snow in the Rockies. I thought that this ring would remind you of your adventures, and also of time spent away from us, which I hope is not going to happen too often.'

'You are my love, my 'eart, my dearest and totally cherished wife, and I am constantly underestimatin' you. 'elp me not to do that, will you?'

About twenty people went, 'Awww,' and I realised we had an audience, so I grabbed her, planted a nice kiss, and said, 'Thank you, my love.' The audience gave us a round of applause as we left, which put huge grins on our faces.

We got out of there with the girls giggling and rolling their eyes. Me? I was wearing my handsome ring as a highly prized trophy.

Reuben met us at 5.30 pm in the foyer, where we were sitting on the ultra-comfortable furniture.

'Well, Sam, how are you feeling?' Reuben asked. He kept doing that!

'Absolutely on top of the world, physically and mentally. Just a bit stale as far as the ring is concerned. It's this city and all the travellin', I think. I'll be as right as rain when I climb in the ring with an oppo who keeps me sharp.'

'That's exactly how I expected you to be. And you and the girls, Donna?'

'This is all wonderful, and we do thank you. I don't know what you have in mind for my Sam, but he'll give you a hundred percent, always, to make up for this treat, won't you, Sam?'

'Always 'ave – always will.'

Reuben nodded. 'I know, and I'm pleased it all worked out nicely for everyone. Now, while we're all together, here's what's going to happen. Tomorrow, we'll all go to see Madison Square Garden, which is an indoor arena, holding 20,000 plus screaming fans. They usually have ice hockey or basketball games there, but some of the most important fights in boxing history have also taken place at "The Garden". Sam needs to familiarise himself with the layout, so that when he fights there, he'll have the advantage over any boxer who hasn't. Sam, you'll need to say, "Hi!" to some of the staff so you can call them by name when you fight here, and you'll be familiar to them as part of their family. OK?'

'Yes, I understand. Donna and the girls can go on one of those guided tours. Then they'll know more about the place than I do.'

'Exactly! Now, we'll all have dinner tonight, my treat, and then Donna, the girls and I will fly back to London tomorrow evening after their trip to The Garden. Kit will fly with you to Birmingham. Charlie will meet you there, pick up a rental vehicle and drive you to Yorkshire. You'll walk, then run as far in Yorkshire and its surrounds as you can in ten days. One week will not be enough, and two weeks will become dull, repetitive and mundane. After that, you'll drive to Hereford, where you'll spend ten days with some SAS boys. At the end of your time in their company you'll come back to London and do some ring work. By then, you'll be ready for anything that comes your way. Questions?'

'Who will I be fightin', and where?'

'You don't need to concern yourself with any of that right now. Let's just say, it's being taken care of, as we speak.'

The restaurant and the meal were both fab. Reuben let down what was left of his hair, telling us stories of past boxing events – some serious, some really funny. It was a great evening. He saw us back to the hotel, saying he'd meet us at ten the following morning. I wondered why so late, but I think it was for family time: some relaxing time for Donna and me, and to generally take pressure off the whole group.

There was more to Ruben Goldstein than met the eye. He was forty-five to fifty and had been on the outskirts of boxing all his working life, until he met me. I believe he thought I could be his salvation for money and prestige in London. He would probably buy a black Homburg hat and start to smoke cigars, generally coming over as a bit of a Toff, if we became successful. Well, he'd seen me and my family right, so he could do what he liked. We'd see what happened with my money. I hoped his worship of 'Shekels' didn't get the better of him. He'd also seen what my right fist could do. However, ultimately, he also understood 'Respect'.

The following morning, we all took a cab to Madison Square Garden, and, while Kit looked after my family on their tour of the place, Reuben took me 'backstage'.

'Hey, Rube, ya old son-of-a-gun! I'd recognise that stoop anywhere! It's all that money weighin' down ya pockets!'

'Hi, Lou! Still doin' a bottle-a-day?'

They embraced. I was stunned as Reuben mostly had on his serious face. Lou looked like a younger and more benign version of Ernest Borgnine: big, loud and ugly, yet focused and strangely attractive.

'Lou, meet the next world champion. Sam, this is Lou. He doesn't have a fancy moniker, and don't let him tell you he doesn't get paid much, but as far as The Garden is concerned, he is Mr Boxing.'

'Pleased t' meet you, Lou,' I said, shaking his huge mitt.

'Ya look real good, Sam. One forty-five? Welter?'

'That's me,' I said. 'You're good!'

'Thanks, my boy, but trust me when I tell ya, I've seen 'em all: Joe Louis, Rocky Marciano, Cassius Clay, now Muhammed Ali, and I'm even old enough to remember Jack Dempsey, and they're only the big boys. In your league, there's Sugar Ray Robinson, Kid Gavilan, Johnny Saxton and Emile Griffiths. That's a list o' the best boxers in the last half-century. Ya reckon ya can beat 'em?'

'If you put me in a ring with any of those at my weight, I'd find out their weaknesses in the first two rounds, spend two rounds sorting out 'ow I'd beat 'em, then drop 'em in the fifth. That's 'ow I work.'

'He serious?' Lou asked Reuben, his eyebrows up near where his hairline would have been, with a voice to match.

'Yes, and don't ever bet against him, Lou. You'd lose for sure.'

'When ya fighting here, Sam?'

'When it's all arranged by Reuben and Art Dutton.'

Lou looked hard at Reuben. 'Ya got Art on side?'

'I sure have, and he rates Sam.'

'Well, Rube, if that don' beat all? I've known Art for a t'ousand years, an' he's never been wrong about a boxer – nor a fighter, if it comes to that. Sam, you're a lucky man ta have Rube an' Art in your corner. Look me up when ya come over, and we'll share some coffee and some talk. What d'ya say? An' I'm buyin'!'

'I'd like that, Lou. Can I get a look at the ring?'

'Sure ya can! Follow me downstairs. We've got a big Basketball League series on just now, so the ring is stored in the basement.'

After seemingly endless corridors and stairs, we were presented with a ring in a large room. Lou put the lights on.

'This gets up to the arena on hydraulic jacks, an' can be ready for work in twen'y minutes, tuned ropes an' all.'

I jumped up and went through the ropes. I leaned against one, and it was a little saggy. 'Needs some work,' I told Lou.

'Yeah, I know that, but how do you know that?'

'Because I like my oppos to come off them rather faster than this so I can get in a three-punch combo before they get too far. If the ropes are too slack, the oppo has a chance to see what's comin', and, if he's good enough, maybe he gets in a punch of his own, but only one,' I said.

Lou looked again at Reuben. 'He for real?'

'Oh yes! But he's in training just at the moment; and no, Lou, I'm not letting you in on that. Only that he's working hard. I have no doubt we'll see you for a fight sometime soon.'

'What ya doin', Sam?' asked Lou.

'I'm leavin' a parcel of energy in the corner that I can pick up if I need it, when I fight 'ere,' I told him.

'OK. How d'ya know which corner you'll be in?'

'I left a parcel in each, but no oppo will know it's there, nor how to get at it, see.'

'Yep,' said Lou to Reuben, 'he's a thinker all right. Rube, I look forward t'ya comin' here. Allow some time for us t'get together, huh? It'll be my treat.'

'If he comes and he wins, it'll be my treat. If he loses, you pay!'

'Fair enough!' There were more bear hugs and smiles all around. Lou shook my hand, and it was like a baby's hand in a big adult's.

'I look forward ta seein' ya fight here, Sam. Stay safe.'

'Thanks, Lou. See you.'

All of us went topside, and I saw the size of the indoor arena. It was huge, but warm, free from smoke, bright and clean. I spent about ten minutes soaking in the sound, the echoes, which were few, the architecture, the seating and the playing area. I imagined the brightly lit ring in the middle of a vast crowd in the dark, all baying for my blood. That was fine. I didn't feel the least bit depressed about that because I'd be super fit, had fought hundreds of oppos and had a huge experience of boxing behind me. If I was put down, so be it, but I'd fight like hell for Reuben, Donna and the girls.

'Any time you're ready,' I said, and Lou shook hands with me again. 'Hasta la vista, Sam!' said Lou with his outdoor voice and huge, booming belly laugh.

We all met upstairs in the foyer, with Anna and Ella taking it in turns to give me information on The Garden.

'Now you'll know where I'll be, and what it's like when I fight here,' I told them.

'Wow!' they said in unison.

My girls are so cute. Yes, I know, I'm besotted. I was just so lucky, but now it was nearly time for me to go to work again, so I could put myself against the best the boxing world could throw at me.

Chapter Thirteen

From Madison Square Garden we travelled back to the hotel for another teary farewell to my family as they were flying out to London soon. Kit and I went to a different airport because we were landing at Birmingham – that's in the UK, not Alabama. See, I was learnin'.

I was lucky enough to sleep over the Atlantic but awoke just in time to descend through grey cloud into a grey world of rain and wind. I looked after the airport routine then went with Kit to pick up a rental car from Avis.

Charlie was there, and I said to him, 'Owmanw'appen!' A huge and happy grin split his face.

'Yea, man,' I told him, and he shook my hand.

'That was just like my father used to greet me,' he said

He took over driving duties from Kit, who was going home. I shook Kit's hand, and thanked him profusely for his time, his instruction and his care for me.

'I predict you'll be a great boxer. I won't lose touch with either you or Reuben. Good luck, Sam.'

Charlie drove north then exited on the A64, where we stopped at a small village pub on a hill overlooking a long green valley.

'Have a look at that while I get this sorted,' he said. I strolled over to a five-bar gate that had moss and lichen growing on it. I doubted the wind ever stopped blowing here, and probably only intermittently stopped raining. So growing conditions were great, as long as you were a plant that didn't need a whole lot of sunshine. The valley was green and lush, had curved sides and ran for as far as I could see. *Very, very different from 'Mo Bay,'* I thought with a smile.

Inside, the pub had a warming fire, sturdy chairs and tables, and lots of dark wood. Classic! I'd missed this. Charlie had bought me a beer and returned with it to our table.

He got straight to the point. 'I need to talk to you about your next ten days, which will be walking, running and climbing. I know you've just done a lot of skiing, but you're going to need all the help you can get in the ring at the level you're approaching.

'Starting tomorrow, you'll leave here and walk/run as far as you can. When you're tired or have had enough, ring me from a phone box, and I'll come to collect you.

'For you to get the full benefit from all this exercise I thought you'd need ten days. One week would be too little, and two weeks would be wasting the extra time. Your progress, as in speed and distance covered, will be monitored on the map, so we need to see improved stats every day. Don't kill yourself on Day One, so walk more than you run. Soon, you'll be running all the time. Your results will be of great interest to all concerned.' I nodded.

'At the end of ten days, we'll go to Hereford, to the SAS Regiment HQ. Reuben has made some arrangements there, so you'll come out of there a very tough man indeed.'

After a good sleep in the pub, I was dressed in a tracksuit and a groovy pair of running boots – yes, boots! They were like a basketball player's boots that were designed to support my ankles. I'd be walking and running on rough tracks, and if I turned an ankle or fell and fractured a leg bone, that was my career out of the window, meaning that all this would be wasted. My skiing had given me powerful legs and ankles, but there was no point in taking chances. I was also given a backpack, specially designed by Charlie. It had only a small volume, which, when it was full of two litres of water, a couple of Mars bars and a tiny first-aid kit, was tight and didn't jiggle around. The straps were elastic that would give with my movements but didn't hinder them in any way.

The following morning, I said cheerio to Charlie and set off down one such track, walking until I got into a rhythm, then jogging. I spent a fair amount of the day watching the track, which stopped me looking at the lovely scenery. However, the aerial skiing technique soon re-asserted itself, allowing me to run without apparently checking the ground. While it didn't compare in grandeur to the Rockies, Yorkshire did have a beauty all its own.

Over the next few days, I started running from dawn to dusk, with no great huffing and puffing; just a smooth gliding action that became nearly effortless. There were fells over 2000 feet that had mountain status, and vales with streams of icy, crystal-clear water. Day after day I pounded through these beautiful areas. I'd phone in just before dark, and Charlie would pick me up. He'd give me a massage after a hot shower, and we'd discuss the results of my running. During the first few days I was exhausted, but as time went on, the ease of running was far out, and the hillsides and the warmth of the people I met were outta sight.

'Ey up lad, what's thy 'urry?'

'Ow do, where's the fire?'

'Like as not, you're already late, lad.'

'Th's nowt s'queer as folk!'

These were some of the comments I'd had from well-wishers, who were travelling the same tracks, but at a somewhat slower pace. I had a great time and met some really cool people.

'Did you know you're famous in these parts?' asked Charlie, one evening.

'What's that about?'

'The local paper, called "The Press," had an article about some mythical runner who was seen in two different places at the same time,' he smiled.

'Someone's clock's wrong then,' I said.

'Maybe, but your route today says that you did close to seventy miles in the eight hours since you left me this morning. Now that's bloody good, considering that it's not an Olympic track but rough sheep tracks through some very rugged and hilly country,' argued Charlie. In truth, my runs were more like a steeplechase than long-distance running.

'Time for some dancing lessons,' Charlie told me.

We moved to a pub outside York and drove to a dance studio, with which Reuben had made an arrangement. The lady in charge, Jean Smith (another Smith!), was beautiful, and very cooperative and supportive of what I was trying to do. I showed her the sort of movements I had to make in the ring, and she converted that into a dance with music, which was very clever.

We didn't dance as a partnership, but individually. Jean put on some jazz music, and I started to improvise steps. After an hour, I was still utterly confused. After four hours, I had begun to be able to get into the rhythm, with my feet at least talking to each other. Also, by then, I'd stopped watching them.

The following day, I started to get a backward and forwards movement, which would keep me out of trouble from a jabbing oppo, and then incorporated a sideways movement of my upper body too. By combining the two, I could do a 'Cobra'. This was my description of sinuously weaving about – first from the waist up, and then, by incorporating my feet, I could cover at least twice as much ground as before. This would stop my head from being hit, many times more than just bobbing and weaving, which is what all other boxers did. Major breakthrough!

On our last day, Jean showed me some ballet moves – yes, stretching, but mostly balancing exercises. She explained the importance of stretching, and I vowed to incorporate that in my pre-fight routine. I was rubbish at standing on one leg and had to include my fists being out in front of me. However, by mid-morning Jean said that I had integrated all she needed to teach me. With those lessons, I had learned better posture, and the ability to move at lightning speed with coordination of head, waist and feet. If I got this right all the time, no boxer would ever hit me again – maybe! I thanked her for the time she had spent with me, and for her practical wisdom. I received a lovely, supportive smile in return, and a kiss on the cheek.

Charlie and I then took a lazy day to drive to Hereford, the headquarters of the SAS Regiment. I had a letter of introduction, which Charlie gave to the guard on the gate. He, in turn, used a mic to get a message to the right 'bod' to come and collect me. Soon, a sergeant drove up in a Land Rover, introduced himself as Tom, my team leader, and I said farewell to Charlie.

'See you in ten days,' he said, 'and good luck, man!'

Sergeant Tom got me billeted and kitted out, then introduced me to my squad of Tom plus five.

'The 'New Boy' won't need parade ground drills or shooting skills, but he will need hardening up. So, Day 1 will be running, Day 2 will be running with a pack, 10 kg or 22 lbs should be about right. That's one-seventh of your body weight, 'New Boy,' and then from Day 3, we'll take him up the hill, and keep him there for seven days. You'll have a radio – he won't – so contact me if there's any problem. I'll see you when you get back to do an assessment. Hooah!'

Tom turned to me and said, 'I'll be your logistics team leaders. Have you done any running recently?'

'Yes, some,' I said, not wishing to give away about the only advantage I had.

'Where?'

'Yorkshire.'

'Got some running shoes?'

'Yep.'

'Let's go!'

We were off, just the six of us. Tom stayed behind to act as liaison and back up if necessary. I started to work out what the current team leader would do with this chore. In his place, I'd try to run me into the ground, using fast runners and slow runners, hoping I'd try to keep up with the fast runners and wear myself out. After about two miles, that was precisely the plan they decided to use. I hadn't been working out my strategies in boxing only to neglect the rest of my life, so what strategy would I use to counter their tactics?'

Apparently, the training-exercise team leader would have to finish unless they had a really tricky plan here. So, I should follow wherever the team leader went. If he came in second last, then I would be last. No one had said it was a race, so last was fine.

They were very amused by my running boots, but that was okay. Taking the 'Mickey' out of the 'New Boy's' boots was also part of the hardening-up process. They were using the road, which was really easy, and after ten miles we all seemed quite comfortable. I was into my rhythm and doing it easy. Then we took off cross-country. I loved the springy grass on gentle slopes. This was a doddle after the Yorkshire fells.

We turned for home, and they started playing the game I had predicted. I stuck to my plan and saw some wry smiles from the troops. I realised that I must NOT be first home with a flashy sprint. That would blow my cover. So, I pottered along and came in after the training-exercise team leader.

'You did well,' he said, 'and I think we can start calling you Sam, since you're not a 'New Boy' after all. Get changed, and we'll see you in the Mess for dinner.

The billet was quite comfortable without any crap bits and pieces. I showered, changed and went to the Mess. I had one beer with my meal, and the questions started. To get it over and done with, I gave them only what I wanted them to know.

'OK, look, my name is Sam Smith, and I come from Whitechapel in London. I'm married with two girls aged six and four, and I'm a professional boxer. I have a long 'istory of boxin' on a poorly paid amateur basis, but 'ave now got some financial backin' and turned professional. I've never been put down, and very few of my fights 'ave gone more than five rounds. Within twelve months I 'ope to be the World Welterweight Boxing Champion.'

'What makes you so good? Have you got a killer hook?' asked one.

'No. I'm fast, punch 'ard and accurately, and 'ave a defence that's mostly movin' around very fast. My main asset is my thinkin'. I try to find my oppos' weaknesses and use those against each individual boxer. I've got pretty good at that after all the fights I've 'ad. A lot of it is counterpunchin', so timin' is most important.'

'Give us an example of this thinking,' said another.

'Well, take the run today, for example. I soon worked out that being an outsider, you would try to run me off my feet by usin' different paces by different people. You proved me right, but my counter to that was to tag on to one runner, stickin' with 'im and whatever 'e did. So, I negated your strategy by usin' different tactics. I chose the exercise team leader because 'e would be the fittest and would have to get back, come what may. You may 'ave been in a race, but I wasn't.'

'That's not bad,' said Tom. 'How are you on carrying weights?'

'I think you've got me there, but we'll see.'

They loaded me with a knapsack with the 22 lbs of weight in it, and we started out on a different run. Here, there were more hills, and I began to feel the weight quite soon. I thought, *My legs are good from swimmin' and skiin', plus the runnin' in Yorkshire, so they should be fine. But what's going to cause the fatigue? Answer: my back.*

I'd had scuba tanks on my back, but they didn't weigh much in seawater. So, how would I combat this problem? The ballet, and the balance lessons I'd had, came back to me. I straightened my back until the weight was centralised, and also used my legs and the rhythm of the pace to reduce the impact on my ankles, knees and lower back. From then on, I was running normally, just like going into a headwind.

At the Mess that night, they wanted to know how I'd run fifteen miles with a weighted backpack. I told them that I'd had some leg strengthening exercises and ballet lessons.

'Did you wear a pink tutu?' asked one wag.

'You do remember what I do for a livin'?' I said, looking him in the eye but with a smile on my face. 'I balanced the load to be vertically centred and used my legs to get into a soft rhythm that didn't stress any part of my body as I landed each time.'

'Now that's clever,' remarked Tom. 'You must have been super fit when you arrived because we've never seen anyone complete that course with the weights, and you're only little. So, well done. Now, tomorrow you'll go with the squad into deepest, darkest Wales, and be gone for seven days. You'll carry everything you need. If things get too tough, or you get injured, the team leader will have a radio, and I'll come and get you out of there.'

The following morning, we packed up a Land Rover, and drove over the border into Wales. Where we stopped, I didn't know. Where we went, I didn't know. I did know we slept out under the stars, the clouds and the rain. We ate the British equivalent of American K–rations from WW2, drank stream water, ran, walked and stalked, and much more.

At the end of the seven days, I was as hard and as fit as I had ever been but had started to yearn for Donna and the girls – and a boxing ring, strangely. The SAS boys had done the right thing by me. There was no abuse, possibly because of my boxin' skills, but I didn't think so, and I had developed a lasting connection with that squad. We left as best mates.

'If you want some extra money, and I come up to a world title fight, put your money on me. The odds should be good, and there's no way I'll lose after all this trainin'. See you, boys, and thanks for everythin'.'

Charlie picked me up and dropped me home. I needed sleep but stayed awake long enough to tell the family some of my exploits. Donna shunted the girls off to bed and told me she had really missed me, in more ways than one. Thankfully, I had a day off tomorrow, then a meeting with everyone on the team the day after. Life was going to be even busier from now on.

Chapter Fourteen

Charlie had been right when he told me that no matter how much razzamatazz there was, we still ended up with just two people in one boxing ring, and in there I was on familiar ground.

So, there we were. Me! At Wembley Stadium! Who'd have ever thought that? A boy from Whitechapel made good. Mind you, I'd done quite a bit of work for it, but you always had to do that – earn it, that is – not take it for granted.

Nice change rooms, and Charlie had looked after me, talked to me and had now left me alone. I liked that. It left me relaxed and calm, and I seemed to see things clearer when I got out there. I'd done my stretching exercises as suggested by Jean Smith. There should be a bit of noise tonight – cheers, shouting, whistles and all that stuff. First, I needed to win; everything else would come after that.

Time to go. Love you, Donna. Let's dance.

***

'Good evening, Ladies and Gentlemen, this is Bob Clark reporting to you from ringside at Wembley Stadium on behalf of the BBC. There's some time before tonight's fights begin, which I predict will prove an entertaining evening for you. Before I start reporting on the fights themselves, I'd like to give you a bit of background information on one of our fighters tonight.

'It's fair to say that little is known about Sam Smith, aka "Simple Sam," who is a welterweight, fighting here tonight. I've known Art Dutton, his current international manager, for many years. Art has managed three world champions and is highly knowledgeable about everything to do with boxers and boxing at the top level. I caught up with Art, here in London, for a few words, and this is what he said, and I quote:

"Sam Smith is a 26-year-old welterweight, and his nickname of 'Simple Sam' is about as wrong as anything can be in this sport. Sam has been fighting all-comers for more than two years and is very experienced. He's fast, has got a range of good punches and has never been put down. He has worked his way through a number of the London cards in his weight and beat the #3 welterweight in the UK, just after turning professional. He took a low blow from that boxer, got up at the seven count, and immediately dropped the former #3 with one of the fastest and crispest punches I have ever seen." Unquote.

'Art also told me that after that fight, Sam simply dropped out of sight for two months, and when he came back from wherever he'd been, Sam was a different man: hard, steely-eyed and confident, which was something he seemed to lack before. He had been competent, but not that confident.

'Art also said, "If I were in his weight, I'd frankly have second thoughts about going into the ring with him. Sam's greatest talent is his analysis of his opposition's technique, which finds the weaknesses that we know all boxers have, and then he exploits those weaknesses to win fights. With his newly found ultra-fitness, he could go all the way, so keep an eye on this one. He's also a fine young man with a loving family."

'So, Ladies and Gentlemen, we are about to start the programme here at Wembley Stadium tonight. I'll pass you over to Bill Fleming, my fellow commentator, for him to tell you about this evening's fights.'

'Thank you, Bob, and good evening Ladies and Gentlemen. That's quite a wrap for Sam Smith from Art Dutton, who knows more than most in this business. Sam is up against Chris Martin tonight. Martin is from East Dereham in Norfolk, a small market town, I gather. Martin is fit and a bit of an ambusher. He tends not to lead the fight because he is a counterpunching specialist. It will be interesting to see how Sam deals with him. Sam is coming into the ring now. As usual, he's covered up and being led by Charlie, his ring man and trainer, who is another specialist in his field. Sam seems to have collected quite a team around him, all thanks to a Mr Reuben Goldstein, who has also been in this business for a long time. Back to you, Bob.'

'Thanks, Bill. Sam disrobes and looks slowly around for his opposition. Martin is walking in with his entourage now, and, as he climbs into the ring, Sam is watching him like a hawk. I wonder what he sees. Martin seems to have longer muscles than Sam, so may have more speed but not the power or durability of Sam, I'd say. I can't see anything else, but Sam might.'

Bell!

'Martin has claimed the centre of the ring, and has a slightly crouched stance with his gloves held high. Sam comes within range, but Martin doesn't throw a punch, and I guess that will tell Sam a lot. He comes in again, bobbing and weaving, but still no punch from Martin. What's he waiting for, a written invitation? Sam comes in again and throws a jab, which kicks Martin's head back, but with no response. What I think we are seeing here, maybe, is a boxer who thinks he's a "one-punch wonder". I think Martin thinks he can finish this with one punch and is waiting for precisely the right set of circumstances. Sam circles to the right then to the left, throwing the occasional left jab, which always connects.'

Bell!

'For a first round, you could say that was almost a non-event. What do they say these days? All show, no go? Is that it? Anyway, Sam is taking this very slowly, testing and probing. He's trying to get a reaction from Martin. Let's see what Round Two brings.'

Bell!

'Sam is circling Martin who has claimed centre ring once more. Left jab followed by a right. There's no reaction from Martin. Another, and another. Sam is scoring at will. When will Martin unleash? Those punches have shifted Martin from the centre of the ring, which Sam now holds. That's clever, because Martin was in his comfort zone there, so Sam has shifted him out of it, claiming his territory. I'm going to have to concentrate quite hard on what's going on here because Sam has proved himself to be a very clever thinker, and this is like a story unfolding within a story. Every time Martin approaches, he gets Sam's jab. Martin explodes into action with a flurry of lefts and rights after one jab from Sam that was no different from any of the others. Where was Sam? He was out of range, and none of those punches landed. How did Sam do that? He was extremely fast in getting out of the way. But at least we got some action.'

Bell!

'How interesting was that? Sam has been baiting him, trying to get him to come out of his shell, and when Martin finally went into action, Sam was nowhere to be found. I still don't know how Sam moved back that fast, but nothing landed. Sam's got a slight grin on his face sitting in his corner. I think he's sussed him out. This is a twelve-round fight, but I would bet money it won't go the distance.'

Bell!

'Sam's out first and claims that centre-ring position, which I think is calculated to upset Martin. Jab, jab, right, back. Jab, jab, right, back. Jab, jab, right, left, right and back. Martin got conned into almost making an attack, was halfway into a counterpunch when he saw that Sam wasn't there. I would call him 'Sneaky Sam', not 'Simple Sam'. There's nothing simple about Sam Smith, in the boxing ring at least. Martin's way behind on points, and probably needs to get a move on here. It still makes me believe that he thinks he can put Sam down with one well-placed punch, and Sam must be thinking the same thing. What's Sam going to do now? Martin's low stance is higher now, with high gloves covering his face. I wonder if Sam's noticed that, and will think of going for Martin's body? Ha! I must have picked up Sam's wavelength because he followed his jab with a straight right just above Martin's shorts, which made Martin drop his guard, and Sam took full advantage by putting a left hook to the right side of Martin's head. I thought I saw a leg wobble there, just for a moment. Sam has allowed Martin back in centre ring where he is most comfortable.'

Bell!

'Bill?'

'Definitely Sam's round. Sam's body shot to Martin rattled him, and the left hook to the head took Martin totally by surprise. He's now wondering how Sam can counter-punch so effectively since Martin thinks that's *his* strength. Martin has a worried look on his face in his corner and is getting so many words thrown at him that he will be totally bamboozled when the next round starts.'

Bell!

'Sam's jabbing like he was before, sometimes following with a right, sometimes not. He's built up a lot of points, so Martin needs to do something soon. Sam's ducking and weaving in front of Martin, who throws a jab and misses. He throws another jab, and that misses too because Sam is just too fast. Martin throws a jab then follows with a wicked right that clips the side of Sam's head, and Sam goes wild. Lefts and rights rain down on Martin, who's trying to cover up. Sam is getting past his guard wherever Martin puts it. Sam puts in two quick body blows and follows with a beautiful crisp right to Martin's now-uncovered jaw, and its, "Goodnight, Chris Martin".

'Sam is in a neutral corner and seems quite relaxed. I only remember one punch hitting Sam all night. It makes you wonder what Martin was waiting for. Maybe he thought he had a big punch? However big it was, it's useless unless it's used. Yes, he's down for the count. The Ref raises Sam's right arm; Sam raises the left and winks at the crowd. They go crazy. The noise in here is huge, and it's a big place. Sam is bowing and clapping his gloves together to the four sections of the crowd, thanking them for supporting him, and they are clapping and cheering him as if he were Ali. Nicely done, Sam. I'm going to keep my eye on you. You really made me think, which I haven't had to do for ages, but please don't tell my employers that. Hey, Bill, what did you think of that?'

'You're right Bob, Sam is a thinking-man's boxer. You mentioned a story. I think Sam tells you the story of his thoughts through his actions, their reasons, and the strategy and tactics behind what he does, if that is, you are experienced enough to read that story. A bit of a challenge for your usual boxing commentator, but you did very well in spotting it, Bob. He's an interesting young man, and you're right, we'll keep a close eye on him. If he doesn't get hit much, he could be around for a while, and we haven't had a British contender at this weight for quite a while.

'I would agree with you. That Sam is a thinking-man's boxer we have established. That he is fast, and has a great punch is also true, but time will tell us how much he wants it.'

'The next fight...'

Chapter Fifteen

When I'd showered and dressed, the gang was there, and Art asked me about the fight. Where before I might have said, 'Easy! He didn't lay a glove on me, and his tactics were a bit obvious,' I now had to give them the whole story so they could see it through my eyes.

'When 'e came into the ring, I could see 'is muscles were trained for speed, and I wondered if 'e was going to be a brawlin' 'andful. Imagine my surprise when I couldn't get a punch out of 'im. What was I meant to do? Stand there with my 'ands by my side to give 'im a chance? I decided 'e 'ad to earn the right to 'it me, so I started in on 'im, slowly uppin' the ante. It took 'im to the second round to offer me anythin', and then it was a waste of time because, as you saw, I wasn't there.

'It became obvious what 'e was tryin' to do – get me sorted with one punch, and my guess? It would have been a right cross, probably angled downwards. I didn't let 'im get to that because I kept movin', and 'e showed me 'ow unsure 'e was of 'ittin' me. 'e definitely needs more floor-to-ceiling ball practice. Anyway, 'e got in a lucky knock to the side of my 'ead, and I thought, "blow this for a joke," and gave 'im both barrels. I couldn't learn anythin' else from 'im except how strong 'is "special" punch may 'ave been, and I wanted 'im to keep that to 'imself. So, who's next?'

'Love your attitude, Sam,' said Art. 'Love your hunger. Wembley is a big deal, and I have wet ink on a contract for the next one, but I'll confirm that soon, and you can get together with Reg to find out about your next oppo, and then with Charlie to find out how to counter his technique. The rest is up to you, Sam, but you did really well tonight.'

'Thanks, Art. I think that was my experience payin' off.'

'I agree, and you earned a nice amount of money from this one. What will you do with it?'

'Reuben said 'e would take care of it for us. I 'ad a long talk with Kit over money, and the consequences of not doin' the right thing. For the moment, I will just keep doin' what I'm doin', and livin' as we're livin' and keepin' the money in the bank. Later, I'll look at puttin' it into some enterprise to earn a little over the cheap rates the banks are givin' just now. But I'll be careful, for the sake of Donna, Anna and Ella.' Art nodded in agreement.

I continued. 'While we're all 'ere, guys,' I announced, 'I want to talk about this fight game we're in. A bloke, who has done a bit of boxin', drinks at the Waterloo and knows Reg, asked me if anyone 'ad asked me to throw a fight yet. I said 'No,' and 'e seemed surprised. Can you talk to me about this, everyone?'

Reg said, 'Sorry mate, it happens. I'd have thought you'd done enough now to be above all that crap.'

Reuben interrupted forcefully. 'Sam, listen to me very carefully. I'd never allow anything like that to happen to any of my fighters. See, it's all about reputation and respect. Once there is even just a hint of a taint of corruption on a boxer for throwing a fight, then he, his manager and all his staff get thrown under the same bus. They never get rid of the stench.

'So, Sam, I hereby give you my solemn word that I will never ask you to do anything but your best in the ring. You're a good man, a good boxer, a good husband and a good family man. But I have to say that you'd make a lousy actor, and if you ever tried something like that on your own, I would bury you in so many ways, you'd never box nor work again. I know some very hard men that would do almost anything for a grand, and your hands would be first. Understand me?'

'Reuben, I was goin' on the attack for no one to do that to me! I would never think of doin' a thing like that off my own bat. Why? Because, I told all of you when we started that I wanted respect for my boxin' skills, my behaviour, but mostly for my own self-respect. OK? I also know it would reflect on the team, and that's another reason I would never think about it. You've been really good to me, and that's not 'ow I would ever repay you. But I 'ad to know where we all stand.'

Reuben looked mollified but added, 'If anyone breathes even a whisper of a suggestion to any one of us about even the faintest possibility of fixing a fight, bring it straight to me, and it will be on the front page the next day, complete with pictures of him in a hospital bed. I take that sort of thing very personally.'

'Well, that sorts that out,' agreed Art. 'I guess it had to come up sooner or later, and I'm pleased we all feel the same.'

Chapter Sixteen

The next fight was to be in Birmingham. My oppo had fought and lost to the champion as the world welterweight contender, so he was up there, but not quite 'the goods'. Art talked to me about that fight, which he'd seen, and was able to give me some drum about his style. I was most interested in 'why' he had lost, and 'what' had made him good enough to be up there in the first place.

His name was Arthur Taylor. He was African American, had a fast mouth, flashy ways, and more gold around his neck than Fort Knox! He was quick and had a solid punch. The chink in his armour was a glass jaw, which was rare in black boxers although Patterson had one, too. He had been a smooth black panther in the ring until someone discovered that fact. It ended his career.

Most importantly, he was a southpaw, a left-handed boxer. He's going to lead with his right hand and right foot, totally opposite to the orthodox stance. So Sam is going to have to learn some new moves to counter this difficult situation.

Arthur Taylor was apparently over in England for a holiday, and to see some relations in London. He also wanted to live it up a little. He thought our fight was a bit beneath his dignity but had agreed to it because it would give him some funds for his holiday and widen his fan base. That was from Art, who always took a broad brush to things.

Reg told me he was fast and accurate with jabs and combination punching, but recognised his weak jaw as his Achilles heel, so he would be very protective of his head. *Fine, I thought, so I'll batter him downstairs until he has to drop his guard, then I'll take him.*

Then Reg talked to me about southpaw fighters, their tricks and their weaknesses, and strongly suggested I talk to Charlie about getting some sparring partners who were southpaws.

I practised the art of jabbing in the ring, while moving my head. This meant that I could hit without being hit. If it became a problem, I could always overextend his elbow to bring him into line. Charlie let me into a professional secret about boxers who watched eyes, which in an oppo could give away the timing of an attack and its direction. He said that if a fighter did watch your eyes to gather such info', then he could be deceived, and left me to ponder that one.

The two months before the fight flew by. Our family had been on holiday to Brighton and stayed at a hotel, which had seemed very posh but was nowhere near New York standards. They did cook us English breakfasts, which were far out. The girls went on the funfair rides, and we had long walks on the promenade and the pier. We even went to the Brighton Pavilion to see how the real Toffs used to live. I told Donna that I didn't want to do any of that, and she told me she was very pleased about that!'

However, she did want to see furniture for some reason, and we went to some big furniture showrooms just out of town, and to the beautiful little shops in the 'Lanes' of Brighton, with their antiques that were bloody expensive, but 'cherry', meaning old but in very good condition. I reckon there were some 'five-finger discounts', meaning stolen, among them. We had ice creams and fish and chips, but not jellied eels. Strange for a Londoner perhaps, but I really don't like 'em. Oysters? Now you're talking – with brown bread and lashin's of salty butter. They're a real treat.

Of course, I ran in the morning and evening to keep up my fitness, but I knew I was in for a big workout when I got back to Charlie. Still, I'd had a lovely twenty-seventh birthday party with just my family. We went for a meal in the restaurant at our hotel and were surprised by a cake with candles, and the staff singing the birthday song. I took a bow to the rest of the guests and got a round of applause. Maybe they did know who I was.

Returning from Brighton, I was asked by Reuben whether anyone had recognised me. I told him, 'Not really.'

'Good,' he said, 'because that may be about to change. When you beat Arthur Taylor, you'll become a household name. You may like to work out a disguise for your everyday life; otherwise, you may not be able to go out without getting mobbed. And I don't mean false wigs, beards or funny glasses with a built-in nose. Usually, a pair of large, dark glasses are enough, and a hat or cap of some sort. Talk to Donna and talk to Art; he's got some experience with his fighters, and Donna will know if you look like a flake.'

'Thanks, Reuben. That's not somethin' I'd ever considered would be a problem for Sam Smith of Whitechapel.'

'It will. Trust me, Sam.'

Chapter Seventeen

The change rooms in the Birmingham Arena smelt like boxing establishments the world over: chlorine and Lysol, sweat and smoke. However, the 'testosterone' in the sweat still turned on a particular group of girls, whose company, in turn, seemed very necessary for the blustery businessmen with these fun-loving dollies in the audience. A lot of noise also seemed necessary for this sport too. It added to the excitement and the over-arching tension that grows when large sums of money were on the knife-edge of potential exchange.

My job was really simple, relative to the complicated lives of some of those in the audience, with their bets, their booze and their bimbos. My job was to hammer rather than get hammered. I had the skill set, the fitness, the speed and the need to do this. If I did get beaten, then it was my fault, so I had to make sure that didn't happen – not only for Donna and the girls, but also for the team.

Charlie, as usual, had told me the pluses and minuses of the fight, and left me to myself. His advice seemed to go into my mind and be assimilated – a long word for me, but I knew what it meant. I was remembering Brighton and Epsom: good times with the family. And let's not forget New York. My! Didn't the girls' eyes sparkle, but they were very well behaved and held each other's hands. To lose one of them in that crowd would have damned near killed me, but it had turned out to be a great experience, fears aside.

I could have all that if I went on winning, with enough to give our girls everything they needed for a good start in life. Wouldn't my old mum have been proud if she were still with us!

Time to go; work to do. Love you, Donna. Dance time!

I walked with Charlie, covered up as usual against all the razzamatazz. That's for others, not for me. I climbed into the ring and saw Taylor, who had his back to me. It looked strong. His body had been oiled. Under the lights, the muscle-groups in his back looked as though a master craftsman had carved them from an exotic wood, then smoothed and gloss-varnished them. All this was meant to intimidate me, but I'd get his jaw involved, and then we'd see. Also, I'd have to punch straight otherwise my energy would be partly wasted as the punch was deflected off the oil. See? That was good gen, and I wouldn't have known that unless some geezer in the tents hadn't tried it on. He lost too, mainly for the reason that I'd sussed out that fact before the fight started.

***

'Good evening Ladies and Gentlemen. This is Bob Clark coming to you from Birmingham Arena on behalf of the BBC. We've got a massive crowd in here tonight to witness a number of boxing matches. It's virtually a full house of

15,000 people, who are all very excited. Our very own Sam Smith is fighting Arthur Taylor from the USA tonight. Sam has attracted an increasingly large fan club, which is making most of the noise in here tonight, I would guess.

'I would like to introduce my friend and fellow commentator, Bill Fleming. Bill, what are your thoughts on this fight; do we have a little time?'

'Hi Bob, and good evening everyone. I see this fight as a major challenge for Sam tonight, if only because Arthur Taylor is a southpaw. For those who don't know, the southpaw stance is the mirror image of the orthodox boxing stance. So, instead of having his left glove out in front, a southpaw will have his right glove out in front, and his feet will likewise be reversed from the orthodox. What this means in practice is that, for an orthodox fighter, he's fighting a mirror image of himself, and it's extremely confusing unless you have had some practice at it.

I do happen to know, because I had a word with Sam's trainer, Charlie Browne, that three southpaw fighters were procured as sparring partners for Sam. Let's see what tricks Arthur Taylor, as the southpaw, has up his sleeve, and how Sam deals with them.

This should be a fight where a large number of punches are thrown. Taylor is known for his combination punching, and Sam is no slouch in that area either. It's a twelve-round fight, but I can't see it going the distance. However, which way it goes is anyone's guess. If our wily Sam finds a way to take Taylor out, he will be a National Hero, if only because Taylor, on his arrival at Heathrow Airport this week, is quoted in the Press as saying, "Nothing of any value to the boxing world ever came out of the UK!"

'Taylor has been a world champion contender but lost to the current champion, so if Sam can set the record straight, he will be seen as a hero – our hero in fact. Back to you, Bob.'

'Thanks, Bill. Both fighters are in the ring. Taylor has his back to Sam, showing off his oiled muscles under the lights. I think Sam will be thinking, "I'm fighting your front, not your back, you narcissist!" And he'd be right, of course.'

Bell!

'Round One, Ladies and Gentlemen, and Taylor strode across the ring very quickly, jabbed and threw a right at Sam, who dodged both and clipped Taylor across the head as a message. I can almost see Sam smiling at that engagement, which has given him so much information.

'Again, Taylor comes in with a right jab and a round-house left, just the opposite that you'd get from an orthodox fighter. Again, Sam has slipped those punches and has punched Taylor on his right bicep. I saw Taylor's eyes open in pain. Taylor aims a wickedly fast left cross, his main weapon, to Sam's head, which he ducked, but gets a left hook to the body as a return message from Sam. Right-left-right combination from Taylor, dodged by Sam, who returns with a left-right-left of his own, which sees Taylor backpedalling. His back hits the rope and Sam gives him another combination to his mid-region on his return.

'Now Taylor has extended his leading right glove to touch Sam's glove. I know what's coming. I've seen this move before. Yes, Taylor moves forward and snakes three very fast and straight rights to Sam's face. The first caught Sam by surprise and bounced off his forehead, but the other two missed.'

Bell!

'Well, Bill, that was somewhat different from Sam's last fight with Chris Martin.'

'Sure was, Bob. Taylor is the aggressor but got punished by Sam every time he mounted an attack. I've seen Sam punish bullies a few times, and I think that's what he's doing now. Hurt them early on and take the upper hand. Sam is quick, but he's playing a slightly longer game than usual. He seems to be able to deal with the southpaw approach though. His round definitely.'

Bell!

'Thanks, Bill. Both fighters are circling. Who will take the initiative? Taylor jabs with his right, but Sam slips it. Taylor jabs again, and Sam jabs at the same time but moves his head. Taylor misses, Sam connects. I don't think I've ever seen a boxer who could do that. Maybe it was a one-off. No! I'm wrong. There goes another one. Taylor's right jab misses, but Sam's left jab kicks Taylor's head back. I think Taylor is getting frustrated because he didn't think for one moment that he wasn't going to dominate this fight and bring it to an early conclusion.

'Because of the difference in their stances, Taylor has just trapped Sam's leading left foot under his leading right foot. Sam struggles to get it free and in doing so stumbles backwards, trying to regain his balance, leaving himself without any defence. Taylor advances thinking he can finish this right now with a devastating roundhouse left cross, but Sam is not there. All the fancy footwork that Sam has used over the years is not just for show, it's for balance, and he has managed to duck out of there with his head doing a circle around Taylor's hoped-for finishing punch.

'Sam drives a right to the "breadbasket", and Taylor winces, backs off and drops his guard about an inch. Left jab from Sam, and up comes the guard, and I believe I know precisely what is about to happen. Taylor will be on the canvas this round. Let's see if I'm right. Another left jab from Sam that connects, and immediately another right to Taylor's solar plexus; there's the wince, there's the dropped guard, and there's that beautiful crisp right to Taylor's jaw, right on the "button", and he's down. Will he be counted out? ...eight, nine, ten! Yes, he's gone, and the crowd erupts in whistles, cheers, shouts and clapping – well, you can hear them, but I don't know if you can still hear me! Bill, your comments?'

'Thanks, Bob. Boy, you are getting really good at this. That was a prediction that nobody, except you at that particular moment, could see coming. What made you say that, or even think that?'

'I saw two consecutive punches to Taylor's solar plexus, which told me Sam was trying to get Taylor to drop his guard. There was only one reason for that – to hit him on the jaw. Now, if you recall, Taylor lost his fight against the champion by a punch to his jaw. All the pundits at the time said it wasn't hard enough to put him down, but down he went, and down he stayed, just like tonight. So, it must have been a plan of Sam's to get to that jaw. He did, and it worked.

'Also, his work with the southpaw sparring partners means that Sam was not uncomfortable with dealing with the different stance. He did, however, nearly get caught by one of the known southpaw tricks; that of standing on the leading foot of the opponent. To no avail, happily for Sam.

'At this moment, Sam is thanking the audience, mainly his fans, for their support by winking and clapping his gloves together and bowing slightly. That's clever, because the little bow says, "thank you for your support", the clapping gloves says his boxing was good and successful. His wink, however, is just cheeky, and is reflecting his "cockney sparrow" origins, since he was born and still lives in Whitechapel. Back to you Bob.'

'Thanks, Bill. Ladies and Gentlemen, you've just witnessed a master class in boxing again tonight from young Sam Smith. He's taken the world welterweight number two, an awkward southpaw, and made mincemeat of him in only the second round. This news will go around the boxing world like wildfire, and I think we'll see Sam as a contender to the title not that long from now. His record has been very impressive, dropping all his opponents in under five rounds. By conventional thinking, this should mean that he has a blockbuster right or a killer left hook, but as we know, that's not the case. He's just a good all-round boxer who beats opponents by out-thinking them. That's unique, isn't it, Bill?'

'Ali was good, but I don't think even his level of forethought or 'round' predictions were anywhere near Sam's, even though he made a feature of it by predicting the round in which he would beat his opponent. Anyway, a short fight, but a good one. Maybe Taylor will change his mind about the quality of boxing that comes out of the UK!'

'Nice one, Bill. And now, on to the next fight.'

Chapter Eighteen

'You need to go in front of the Press, Sam,' encouraged Art.

'I've never done anythin' like that, Art. You've got me confused now!'

'Yes, I'm sorry, Sam. We've neglected this aspect of your training, which we'll sort out later. In the meantime, can you count to three?'

'Art, I'm a boxer. I can count to ten.'

'OK, Sam, listen to me. One: "Thank you, Ladies and Gentlemen of the Press."

'Two: "I'm pleased to have won tonight. I'm sorry the fight was so short, but I have an allergy to getting hit. How about you?"

'Three: "Now, I'll be going home to my family for a bit of a rest before my next fight. I don't know who or where that will be, but we'll let you know. My thanks to you, and all my fans and supporters."

'You can do that, and don't answer any questions, just walk away. They won't think you're rude. You've just been in a boxing ring and they haven't, so you'll be fine.'

I walked outside to a crush of reporters and cameras, with my mouth as dry as a crunchy brown autumn leaf.

'Thank you, Ladies and Gentlemen of the Press,' I said, and there was instant silence. 'I'm pleased to 'ave won tonight. The fight was short because I 'ave this allergy to gettin' 'it. 'ow about you?'

There was much laughter at this, and I relaxed a bit. 'I'm goin' 'ome now to my lovely family, to 'ave a rest before my next fight. I don't know who that will be, or where, but you'll be the first to know. Thanks to all my fans and supporters. Good night.' I turned and fled back to the change rooms, where Art had a smile on his face.

'Sam, you did a hell of a lot better than I did on my first press appearance! Well done.'

Our 'Famous Five' met the following morning at Reuben's house for a chat about the immediate past, the present and definitely the future.

'Sam, tell us your opinion of the fight,' said Art, getting straight down to business.

I gave them a blow by blow of the fight as I saw it, including the parallel thinking that drove me to the successful knock out.

'If Art 'adn't first mentioned the glass jaw and Reg 'adn't re-enforced that, and if Charlie 'adn't worked with me on the counter jab, then I would probably still be in the ring, fightin', and wonderin' what I would be gettin' for breakfast. But it was a good result.'

'Now, Sam,' said Art, 'you got a fair amount of money out of that fight, so I'll talk to Reuben about that. We're all delighted with our money, and you have the lion's share, of course, doing 90% of the work.' I winked at him.

'Now we come to your next fight, and that's a puzzle. If we go for the title, then you're going to have to beat the champion. If you go down, that would be the end of you with not very much money. If you beat the champion, there would be a lot of money, and even more for a rematch. Then what you do, you open a bank, fight contenders, and pour lots of lovely money into your bank. First, your thoughts, Sam, then I'll come to the rest of you.'

I considered what Art had just said. 'Guys, I could take all day discussin' this, because I 'ave put a lot of thought into it already, but there are other considerations. I'm the best I've ever been, right now. I'm twenty-seven years old, my knowledge and experience are as good as they've ever been, and my reflexes are as fast as they will probably ever be. In two years, at around twenty-nine, I may be 'arder, more knowledgeable in the field of professional boxin' as a whole, 'ave nearly the speed I 'ave now, but with a much less time to continue boxin'.

'I could take the chance, and if I'm successful we'd live in clover. I could leave it for two years and then have a go at the title, but again, it's the same odds as now. Lose, and I'm finished. Win, and I have two fewer years of earnin'. I'm inclined to set a limit on the money I need to earn, but I'll talk to Reuben about that and work towards a point that I'm comfortable with.

'But this is not all about me, I know. All of you 'ave homes and families and commitments, so your opinions count too. Personally, I'd like to see enough to go round, so we are all set for life. As a preference only, you understand, I'd like to take that shot as soon as possible.'

'You really are a thinker, Sam,' said Art. Nice match summary too, by the way. Reuben?'

'I'm a money-bags, me. I'd just like to make a fortune because I have no idea of what I'd do if the boxing game fell through. So, I'll go along with the plan that makes the most money. Selfish, I know, but honest.'

'Charlie?'

'I've never trained a better boxer than Sam. We know his qualities, and thanks to his extended training, courtesy of Reuben, he's a much harder Boss-man now. He also has a much broader view of the world than he had before. I'd say that if the wait for a title match wasn't too long, then he's ready to give it his best shot. And the fact he feels ready too, means he is ready.'

'Reg, what about your thoughts?'

'My life has been spent thinking, living and breathing boxing, but I've never been so close to a boxer to see what it takes to get anywhere near the top. In the fifty or so years that I've studied boxers, I have never seen one who has what Sam has. I've seen them with all the talents there are, but Sam thinks them on to the canvas. If we show him the fights that the champion has had, and Charlie works with him, especially on some of the things that together we can spot as potential weaknesses, then I think he's got a great chance. Look, he's never been put down, he's dropped all his opposition in five, and he's out-thought each and every one. I'd say he's ready, preferably with some tough training for about a month before the fight,' said Reg.

'And last but not least, it's Art!' said Art, parodying a final bow. 'Since I'm the only person among us who has had any experience of being close to world champion boxers, well, apart from Charlie, I feel I have something to say on the subject. I'm sorry if this comes as a lecture, but for what it's worth, here's what I think.

'What makes a world champion? Well, there's speed. If someone is faster than you are, he will land more punches, and generally, "he, who lands the most punches, wins."

'It's no use using many punches if they don't land. Therefore, accuracy has to go along with speed.

'Also, you can punch a man all night with powder puffs, without doing him any damage, so power in those punches is equally essential.

'So, you have those three. That's really good. But if you have no defence, and your opponent has, then he gets to hit you every time, but you don't punch him every time. The result would be a foregone conclusion.

'So far, Sam is unproven when it comes to conditioning. We haven't seen him go twelve rounds yet, but he will, sooner or later. Standing up, with all his skills, facing an opponent with all his skills in the tenth, eleventh or twelfth round, is nowhere near the same challenge as in the first few rounds when you are both fresh. Being hard, and lasting many rounds needs a tremendous amount of work and self-discipline, and you will need more of that, Sam.

'Having mentioned discipline in that context, I also include it in your way of life, which will include a strict diet, the required amount of exercise, and strangely, enough sleep.

'"Guts" and "courage" are usually taken for granted in a boxer, but if you are really, really tired, and just about out on your feet in the eleventh round, and you still haven't defeated your opponent, knowing he has some steam left, then it takes a lot of courage to continue.

'Lastly, in my list of what it takes to be the best, is boxing intelligence, and we know Sam has that in spades.

'So, ticking the boxes that Sam has to his name, I'd say he is ready to go forward. However, there are some other considerations. What you don't know about Sam in the two months he was away, is that he learned how to scuba dive, ski, take dancing lessons including ballet. He spent ten days with the SAS out in the wilderness, and also went climbing and walking in the fells and dales of Yorkshire.

'Why the hell ballet lessons?' I hear you ask. 'Well, that was for balance. Dancing to fast rhythms gave him improved coordination with his feet, to make them fast and never tangled. Scuba was to learn to control his breathing, to become unafraid of being underwater. He was also able to see some things under the sea that are so stunning in their strangeness and their beauty as to bring tears to the eyes and wonder to the soul.

'Skiing was a natural progression to being in the snow in Canada, but also the rhythm of skiing, and how to control the skis, to breathe correctly, and especially to harden the legs and ankles. It also speeded up his reflexes when it came to foot movements and anticipation.

'He did all that in two months, which is why you saw a difference in him when he came back. He's seen Madison Square Garden, a beautiful indoor arena that holds 20,000 people, and he's explored New York with his family. I'm sure I don't need to tell you about the ten days with the SAS. Let's just say that he's a harder man now than he's ever been, No one in jail ever had it harder than the time those SAS boys gave Sam.

'So, after all that, Sam's ready for a shot at the World Championship Welterweight Title, in my humble opinion.'

There was a round of applause. That was some lecture, and I loved every second of it. I had been scouting around forever, looking for the priorities that I'd need to be a good boxer, but no one had ever been able to concentrate it like that. All my fights had led me in this direction, but it would have been so much easier if I'd have had this knowledge at the beginning, rather than at the end.

Or would it? Wasn't that the point? You couldn't become an expert at the top of anything without knowing what was happening on the bottom rung of the ladder, starting with the first steps leading to the hard grind to the top. Any other way would quickly show you as a fake, and if you were my oppo in the boxing ring, I would call you, 'Easy!'

I said, 'Can we have a space of three days, thinkin' about what I'll need in the way of trainin', then meet to discuss a programme of work up to fight time, and when that will be? We know the current champion is Trey Maxwell, another African American. Can I get some background 'istory, some film footage and a programme of work until the fight date, please?'

'Sure,' agreed Art, 'I've got most of the stuff on Maxwell at home, and I'll get you the date and venue as soon as I can. Charlie, please think about Sam's fitness and work out a progressive programme. Reuben, I'd like a private talk with you about finances, venue, betting odds and many other things. You and I will meet here tomorrow. Reg, we need your ear to the ground for any info you can glean on this cove, right?'

'Right you are, Art. I'll let you know what I come across. Go for it, Sam.'

Chapter Nineteen

Art told me that the fight was scheduled for Madison Square Garden in seven weeks. We'd fly out a week before that date to get in some work 'in situ'. I wondered where 'situ' was.

I had a long talk with Donna and the girls about what I was going to do – when and where – and what I hoped the outcome would be. I explained what I needed to do, and that I may be away some of the lead-up time. Also, that I would be going with my team, but this time, the family would have to stay at home.

I spoke to the girls, who needed to know from me, among so many other things, that most fathers/husbands worked every day at a bank, a shop or an office, travelling backward and forwards daily for the whole of their life, then they retired aged sixty, or sixty-five. I told them that this was not how I wanted to live my life, and that the Good Lord had given me some talents, which I'd worked hard to improve. I told them I loved them very dearly, and that if all my plans worked out, we would live more comfortably than we were at the moment, AND that I would have much more time to spend with them. That was the clincher, and I was so proud of them for not making a fuss about me going away.

Donna just said, 'Sam, you told me you would always do your best for us, and I know that's what you're doing. You never said "How", but I accept this is what you want to do, and what you're best at. I want you to know that you have my love and my backing, all the way. I hate to think of you coming home after a beating, but if you do, I'll tend you and heal you and love you just the same. There, I've said all I needed to say. So, go and do what you need to do, and get this done.'

'I love you,' was all I could think of to say. 'I'll speak to you nearly every day, but if I don't give you my full attention until the fight, it's because my mind will be in the ring, not for any other reason. And it'll be temporary, I promise.'

The fight against Trey Maxwell was scheduled for June the seventh, and we'd fly out on the first of June so I could get in some training at a gym in New York, not 'situ!' Charlie let me down lightly about that one, without taking the Mickey. This was the thirteenth of April, and I was fit, healthy and quick. What more did I need?

Charlie said 'hardening', so I went back to Yorkshire with him, to their beautiful walking tracks to everywhere, it seemed. Running, rather than walking these meandering trails, I saw fab cloudscapes, got surrounded by cloud, but mostly I just got rained on. First, I started with a tracksuit, but after three days I was in a T-shirt and shorts, with my ace running boots protecting my ankles, and my 'Charlie-designed' backpack.

After one week, I could run all day, covering an astonishing distance, come rain or shine. Charlie drove a rented Land Rover to where I was and took me back to the hotel for a shower, a massage, a meal and an early night.

Charlie kept a record of all distance covered in whatever time it took. He said that if the fight game didn't work out, then the Olympic Marathon might suit me, since I was close to their times, but was doing a heap more miles than a simple 26-mile marathon.

Then it was back to London and into the ring with many new sparring partners, plus some bag and ball work. A week of that brought us to the end of April, giving us just a month left until we flew out. Charlie said that over-training was even worse than under-training, and that I should take a few days off to let my body grow the muscles I had stimulated with all that running in Yorkshire, and let the lessons learned in the ring settle into my reflexes. Then I'd need to get back into the ring. My last week would be in the company of my SAS mates in Hereford. Strangely, although the squad had put me through so many hoops, I was lookin' forward to their company.

When I got to Hereford, we did some running that really surprised them, so they loaded me with heavy rucksacks, and we had to try it again. A different story, but I still earned their respect. We slept outside with no tents, just a sleeping bag, but it was May and the weather had started to warm up. Occasional showers at night would wake me, but, being so tired, I quickly went back to sleep. They gave me an excellent farewell with a pint of Guinness in the Mess and wished me the best for the world championship fight. They had their bets on already, they said.

I caught the train back to my family. They were surprised at how brown I was, and the fact that I was down to one hundred and forty-five pounds. I could undoubtedly fight at this weight, but it also gave me leeway to add a couple of pounds in New York, if that happened. Again, under Charlie's tender care, I took some time off to let my body assimilate the strengthening of the muscles and ligaments I had been working so hard to improve.

On the first of June, Reuben Goldstein picked me up from the house and took me to the Tube station where I met Kit again with a brief handshake. I told Reuben that I would see him in New York, and not to worry. He smiled a sad little smile, and I realised he had outlaid an awful lot of money on my training and education, and he was wondering whether I could produce 'the goods' that would get it back for him. Since his self-confessed religion was 'money,' I felt for him – then forgot it because it wasn't my problem.

Kit and I took the Tube to Heathrow, caught the flight with little fuss, and slept over the Atlantic, waking on our approach into Kennedy. The immigration man said, 'Aren't you the guy who's fighting Trey Maxwell for the welterweight title?'

'That's me,' I confirmed.

'Go break a leg,' he said with a great big smile. 'I've got my money on him.'

'Of course, you 'ave,' I said, with an even bigger smile. 'See you when I come back because you'll still be workin' 'ere.' He gave me a sign that I didn't recognise. We got to the hotel, checked in and then took a cab to the gym, a short distance away. Such noisy traffic! Why was everyone so angry? Not my problem.

Charlie was already there and welcomed me with open arms.

'How are you feeling, you contender, you?'

'Good, but strangely, not sharp.'

'That's honest, and it's because of the flight. This is why you came over a week early. Can you imagine going into the ring feeling like crap? We'll get all those bloody kinks out, then tomorrow I've got a few sparring partners sorted for you, courtesy of Art. We'll have you in tip-top form before you know it!'

That week went by so quickly. Suddenly it was 'fight day'. I awoke in a very comfortable bed, indoors, not in a sleeping bag out of doors, wondering what the day would bring. I'd done all the preparation, felt a million quid and was actually looking forward to the competition. Was he so great? Was he so fast and all-powerful? Well, I knew he was a human being just like me, so let's see who'd done the most work, shall we?

Ablutions, breakfast, a walk, which was sometimes easier in department stores because of the crush of people on the pavement – sorry, sidewalk! Then I ate lunch. I took some time to lie on the bed, and actually dozed off for an hour. By that time all the crew was there and we had a final briefing.

Reg started off by saying that Trey Maxwell was a competent boxer, with speed, accuracy and power. His defence was not quite as good as it could be, and his accuracy wasn't 100%. However, he was proficient and fairly fast, and had won his fights on those attributes.

I said, 'That means I'll 'it 'im more times than 'e 'its me, and if I can find the flaw in 'is defence, I may 'ave a chance at droppin' 'im to the canvas.'

'Also,' suggested Reg, 'he's good with a one-two combination, but I don't think he has ever come across your three- or four-punch combos. So, check that out too.'

'Thanks, Reg. Good advice. That gives me all I need. The rest I'll work out for myself.'

Art asked how I was feeling, and I told him a million quid, but that I wanted to get in the ring to find out about this man for myself.

We climbed into some rented vehicles. The whole gang was quiet and subdued. I started to bubble and fizz at the chance to get in the ring again, to find out what made a champion, and whether I had done enough work. They patted me on the back and left me in the change rooms with Charlie, who looked at me, smiling a huge smile.

'What's that for, Charlie?' I asked.

'I'm a little envious of you, Sammy boy, going into the ring with an unknown man and working out if he's as good as you. You've done all the work, and more, you're brighter than any other boxer I've ever known, and the fact that you're looking forward to the fight is all I need to know that you'll win tonight. Just show him who's the boss, because he thinks he is, and you know how to deal with that, right?'

'Oh yes! Get in first and 'urt 'im. Takes all bullies down, does that.'

'Go for it, Sam. I'll be in your corner, as always, so we'll talk, as always, and you'll take him. Have some time to yourself now.'

I let my mind settle and calm. Took away the music, the audience noise, the team, all the lead-up stuff. It was then I knew I was ready. I connected with Donna and the girls in my head, and saw again the images of our times together at Epsom, Brighton, and of course, here in New York.

Whoever would have thought that my hard-working, single mum, Mrs June Smith's little boy, Sam, would be sitting here across the other side of the world, waiting to climb into the ring to fight a world champion boxer? She would have been so proud. Love you, Mum. Then my mind went back to Donna and the girls once more. This was my work for them. I was going to work at doing what I knew best, and what I enjoyed doing. If I did this right, it would set them up for life. Now it was time to go to work and 'get this done'!

I robed, and Charlie escorted me to the ring amid a huge amount of noise. Climbing into the ring, I looked around for Maxwell, but he was not here yet. Off with my robe, and then I checked out his corner. His team were looking hard at me. *And what do you think you see? I thought. You see a new champion, that's what you see, and in only half an hour from now. Get used to it.*

Major music blared and Trey Maxwell entered – my oppo for tonight. Seemed funny, having only the one fight. I'd got used to five or more per night – fighters in the tents of unknown talents, strengths and weaknesses. This time there was just one fighter, and he was of known proportions. He disrobed, and I saw a good body, strong muscles at the neck, strong arms and good back muscles, so he'd got a punch. He looked at me for the first time, and for some reason I smiled at him. Now where did that come from?

He developed two little furrows above his nose. Gotcha! *You don't know what I'm doing, do you? I shouldn't have done that according to you. I should be frightened of you, Mr World Champion. Well, I'm not, and I'm about to show you why.*

The Ref got us in the centre of the ring, gave us the talk, and we touched gloves – his a little aggressively. *Gordon Bennett! If you wanted to show me your power, you should have thumped them. I think you're going to be a show pony, Trey Maxwell. Here we go. Let's dance!*

Chapter Twenty

'Good evening Ladies and Gentlemen. This is Bob Clarke reporting to you from Madison Square Garden on behalf of the BBC in London. I'm here with my fellow commentator, Bill Fleming. We'll be calling this World Welterweight Championship fight between the champion, Trey Maxwell, and our very own Sam Smith from Whitechapel in London, England, as they say over here. We feel very privileged to have been invited by the American authorities to be here to call this fight on behalf of all the people in the United Kingdom and around the English-speaking world, don't we Bill?'

'Indeed, we do Bob, and thank you for the introduction. Bob and I extend an extraordinary welcome to everyone listening in the UK, and elsewhere around the world. There's great hope, here tonight, that Sam Smith can bring home a World Welterweight Championship belt to the UK. Bob and I have followed this young man through many fights leading up to tonight's very special bout. We've both said that he had the talent to go all the way. We knew Sam was a good boxer, had all the skills but, above all, we recognised that Sam was a thinker. He seems to work out weaknesses in other boxers and then capitalise on those weaknesses. We have seen him do just that, time and time again. I must say, Bob, just before I hand back to you, that I've never seen Sam look so fit and hard. You won't be disappointed in this fight, Ladies and Gentlemen. Back to you, Bob.'

'Thanks, Bill. You are absolutely right. Sam looks spectacular. Ah! The games have begun. Did you see that Bill?'

'No, what did you see?'

'Sam smiled at Maxwell, and Maxwell looked momentarily concerned. That means he's lost some of the control he thought he had over Sam, who is so, so good at all this stuff.'

Bell!

'First round, or what I call "the sniffing out" round for Sam. They circle. Maxwell tried a jab. It missed, and how often have we seen that. Maxwell jabbed again, and again it hit the air. Maxwell closes, and there's another jab, and a right cross and Maxwell is left stunned as neither of his punches hit Sam, but Sam found Maxwell's chin with a very fast left hook. They circle. From nowhere, Sam landed a left-right-left combination and stepped back quickly to assess the damage. Maxwell came in with a left-right combination and was again clipped on the head for his trouble. About thirty seconds to go and Sam unleashed a left-right-left to the head, stepped back, then went in and did it again, but with the right going to his breadbasket, that sweet spot just below the navel. Maxwell looked confused, and I think that last right-hand punch took some of the wind out of his sails.'

Bell!

'Bill?

'Bob, definitely Sam's round. He is feeling out Maxwell and countered the somewhat 'wishy-washy' combinations that Maxwell tried with some quite robust combinations of his own. I don't think Maxwell has seen such speed and accuracy in a three-punch combination before.'

Bell!

'Second round and I predict some more feeling out by Sam. I expect him to try to get Maxwell in a corner sometime soon just to see what that produces. Then he'll try him on the ropes. Sam's allowed Maxwell the centre of the ring and is circling, dodging and weaving. Maxwell tried for a left and right but didn't connect. He tried again with the same result, and then Sam unleashed a four-punch combination, all of which hit Maxwell hard. Maxwell returned a left and right, with exactly the same result as before, and got a left hook to the head for his trouble. Then another three-punch combo from Sam, who retreated to watch the result.'

Bell!

'Well Bob, that's definitely another round to Sam. What is that quote, "Doing the same thing and expecting a different result being the definition of insanity?" That's what Maxwell is doing. He's using his ineffectual two-punch combo against Sam's big three- or four-punch combinations, thinking that will be enough. At this point, Sam's running rings around Maxwell.'

Bell!

'Round Three, and it's about time Maxwell upped the pace and took the initiative. He's nowhere near as composed as Sam; his punches are not as accurate as Sam's, and he's looking weaker than Sam, but these are the early stages. Left and right from Maxwell not finding Sam, who moved sideways, but he got in a nice right cross to Maxwell's head. Sam's given him centre ring again, so what's he looking for in this round? Sam sends a barrage of blows to the body that has Maxwell covering up and retreating. Where to? Into a corner, of course! What was I just saying? Sam's seeing if Maxwell's corner work is any good. Sam got a good uppercut from Maxwell but beat him around the head with seven or eight good punches, and withdrew quickly. The champion did not enjoy that experience and is blowing a bit. Sam looks as relaxed as though he just came out of a warm bath.'

Bell!

'Bill, your take on that round?'

'Thanks, Bob. Sam is still working him out, asking questions and seeing what he gets back. The uppercut from Maxwell was quite a good one, but there's been no noticeable effect on Sam. Those combinations from Sam are quite stunning in their speed, power and accuracy, and I have to say that I think they are having an effect on the champion.'

Bell!

Fourth round. I expect Sam to make his mark in this round. Maxwell has got the centre of the ring again, and threw a left and right, and the right clipped the top of Sam's head. The return from Sam was a left and a right cross. The left jerked Maxwell's head right back, and the right was timed to hit his head as it returned to an upright position. There was a tenth of a second gap before Maxwell was back in focus after that. I'm now sure Sam's punches are having an effect on Maxwell, who doesn't seem to be able to hit Sam. A flurry of punches from Sam put Maxwell on the ropes, and Sam crowds him, punching head and body alternatively. Maxwell threw a couple of punches, but they just took away his guard for Sam's very accurate punches to penetrate. Finally, Maxwell slipped out from the ropes, and regrouped at the other side of the ring. There's hesitancy in Maxwell now. He's not got the confidence that he had at the beginning of this fight. Sam stalks him across the ring and lands another three-punch combination. Maxwell is wondering what he has to do to hit Sam, and what all this manoeuvring around the ring is about. Well, now Sam knows much more about his opponent. He's done his research and knows how he is going to finish this.'

Bell!

'Bill?'

'Thanks, Bob. Maxwell is yet to win a round and is looking tired and not a little confused as this hard, little man keeps chasing him, the world champion, around the ring and hitting him, apparently, at will. They're hard shots too. Maxwell has tried a few things, but they have failed. So far, I've counted only two punches landing on Sam, one to the head, and an uppercut to Sam's chin in the corner. He has shown no effect from these and is not even breathing hard. There is a steely look in his eye, and he's determined to win this bout. I, too, think he's made up his mind how he will finish it, and I predict it will be this round. He told me once, "I get bored when I've found out all I want to know about another oppo." The look on his face tells me that that has happened, and he now wants to hear Maxwell hitting the canvas. Bob?'

Bell!

'Round five, and Sam is taking the initiative. Left jab, another, and another. Maxwell only found air with his return jab. He tried a roundhouse right hook. Sam saw it coming and squashed Maxwell's bicep muscle against the humerus bone of the upper arm. I've seen him do that before and it hurts. I've just had a prophetic moment. The end is coming any minute now. Watch Sam's eyes! Watch Sam's eyes! See how they dropped to Maxwell's solar plexus. Watch! Maxwell's guard came way down as Sam approached him. Sam then hit him right on the 'button'. It was so fast, so strong and so accurate that Maxwell is down. The Ref's counting – seven, eight, nine, OUT! Sam's won! Sam's won!

'He's now the welterweight champion of the world! Well done, Sam Smith of Whitechapel. I know from my sources in the industry that he has worked harder for this than any other boxer ever has. His knockouts in the past have come in or under the fifth round. He learned about his opposition, and, as he says, he then gets bored and wants it to end, which of course, is in his hands – literally. Over to you Bill.'

'Yes, thank you, Bob. There's mayhem and chaos going on here. Twenty thousand Maxwell fans are unable to believe that a Brit has dropped their hard man, Trey Maxwell, to the canvas.

'However, I feel there is grudging admiration for Sam's style – his strength, his speed, and the power with which his punches were delivered. I know that Charlie, his ring man, who's really good at preparing fighters, has done an exceptional job here.

'Art Dutton is his manager, and it was Art who arranged this fight, perhaps earlier than Sam deserved. He's also got a background man, who has given him some much-needed info about the fighting style of his opposition. His original manager and finance man, Reuben Goldstein, will be thrilled and relieved. He's been in the boxing world, in and around London for years, but tends not to poke his head up too high. Now, as I understand it he'll have all his considerable expenses paid back in one shot. He certainly saw the talent in young Sam early on. Back to you Bob.'

'Thanks, Bill. You really do know your background. Ladies and Gentlemen, I'm sure I speak for Bill too, when I say it's been an absolute privilege to witness this fight. It's a confirmation that the actual 'Art' of the Noble Sport of Boxing has not been lost. This fight was based on the game of chess. Sam wanted to know his opponent's strengths and weaknesses so went about finding those out logically and clinically. For Sam, the 'Butcher's Shop' interpretation of what boxing is all about – in the eyes of the general public at least – lies, not in the hammer, but in the scalpel. Sam is a surgeon, not a butcher. This was a beautiful display of boxing at its best.

'We will hopefully catch up with Sam in London for a chat about this fight, and his plans for the future. Congratulations to Sam Smith and his team. We also send our best wishes to his lovely wife Donna, and their two gorgeous girls, Anna and Ella. Sam is okay, has been victorious, and will be home soon. I'm starting to sound like "Family Favourites," Bill!

'It's goodnight from me, Bob Clarke, and my fellow commentator Bill Fleming, from Madison Square Garden in New York, where Sam Smith has just defeated Trey Maxwell, and is now the new welterweight champion of the world. We now return you to the BBC Studios in London. Goodnight.'

Chapter Twenty-one

'Thank you, Ladies and Gentlemen of the Press,' I said, 'I'm chuffed to have won this fight. It's proved to me that what I have been doin' for my fitness and my trainin' has been right, and I think all my previous experience supported what I did tonight. I'll 'ave tomorrow in your beautiful city of New York, then return to London and my family.'

'The champ hardly laid a glove on you, Sam. How did that work?'

'Just speed, which was part of my trainin'.'

'One of your commentators said that you "think" your opposition on to the canvas. Can you explain that?'

'Boxers know what they can do, right? Boxers don't know what other boxers can't do, right? But I do. If you want to know 'ow I do that, 'ave four or five 'undred fights, and then come and talk to me. Actually, by that time you will know what I know. OK?'

'What's your next fight, Sam?'

'I'll leave that up to the experts, Art Dutton and Reuben Goldstein, and when I know, you'll know. Thank you.'

The cameras and flashes went off, and I held up a fist and winked with a grin on my face. That's the one that would make the front page. Thanks, Art, for your patience and tuition.

Reuben and I got a cab back to the hotel. We sat in the back seat, and he had a smile on his face that I'd never seen before.

'Tell me about the fight, or tell me about the smile,' I told him.

'Sam, when I was a boy in school, I was bullied a lot. I was no good at sport, and I was no good at learning. Just before I left, the headmaster told me that I would never amount to anything, and I took that to heart, him being "The Headmaster", who should know about these things. I now see that it was a wicked thing to say to an impressionable young lad. Years of struggle for my family and me followed, but I took an instant shine to the boxing game and have been managing boxers ever since. It hasn't been much of an earner, to be honest, but I got by hoping that one day a fighter would come along who would be good enough to take himself, and me, to the very top. You are that boxer, Sam. My years taught me how to manage you, and yours taught you how to box, and both of us have won a considerable prize tonight, Sam.'

'I didn't know you 'ad a family, Reuben.'

'Sam, my wife and daughters died in a fire many years ago, which is one reason why I love your family so much, and will always care for you, and for them. My smile, Sam, was a justification of all those years of pain, guilt and struggle that you have helped me cancel out.

'So, thank you for your dedication to boxing, to training, and for having the will to win. There, now you know! And I'll tell you another thing, Sam. I'm going to front that headmaster. I know where he lives even though he's now retired, and I'm going to tell him, "Now I am a man, I have learned that there is no need to beat you up. However, you now know that you failed me when I needed just a little support from you, which would have cost you nothing. I have now succeeded in my business, but you, as a headmaster, failed in yours!"'

'And you 'ave won, Reuben, because you're a much bigger man than 'e ever was. So, put that smile back on your face, and let the welterweight champion of the world buy you a drink!'

We walked arm in arm through the hotel lobby into a private suite that Art had rented. What a reception! What a noise! What a wonderful group of friends. Someone put a drink in my hand. I turned to see it was Lou from The Garden.

'Well done, young Sam. I don't remember when I've enjoyed a fight more than that. Ya were terrific. Ya'll need some more fights, but concerning boxing, ya were everything ya said ya were, and I believe ya'll will attain 'Legend' status. Did you collect ya "energy packets?"'

'Didn't need to, Lou. Next time, put your money on me!'

'I did, Sam, and won a heap, so thanks. I'll keep my eye on ya. Let me know when ya'll be comin' to The Garden again, and I'll tighten those ropes just to ya likin'!' He let out one of his great big belly laughs.

I found a quiet corner and phoned my missus. She was over the moon and wanted to know when I was coming home. I told her tomorrow, and did she want anything?

'No,' she told me, 'just you home again, my Sam.'

'I'm on my way, my darlin'. See you very soon.'

My back got slapped more times than I'd been hit in my professional boxing career. Charlie's wise words came back to me yet again when he'd said, 'After all the razzamatazz is over, it always comes down to just two boxers in one ring.' Everyone was having a great time, so I snuck up to my room for a well-earned sleep.

After breakfast, I walked to the jeweller's shop where Donna had bought my ring. The same assistant was there, and I told her what I wanted. She remembered our family, as much for the kiss I had given Donna as for the sale of the ring. I told her I wanted a diamond and a blue sapphire in a gold setting, and she went off to search. She came back with a tray of 'bling'. One stood out immediately, and I pointed to it.

'Will that one fit, I wonder?'

'Oh yes,' she said, 'once I have seen a woman's hand, I never forget her ring size; it's a professional thing. This is a tray of rings that will fit your wife, so you are covered – generous husband! I assume she'll wear it on her right hand, the third finger?'

'I'd think so, but "Lady Protocol" isn't my strong suit,' I said with a wry smile. 'What about a necklace with a pendant and two similarly coloured stones each, for the girls? Maybe with the letters, "A" and "E," for Anna and Ella, or "Accident" and "Emergency," as Donna calls them!'

'Sir, I think that would be a splendid present for them. I'll show you a selection of letters and chains for you to choose from, and if you give us about an hour, I can have one of our craftsmen arrange the stones for you. We'll put them in beautiful presentation cases, and they will be cherished for life.'

'Thank you. You're a real smooth talker, Miss, but you've given me exactly what I want.' Where had that phrase come from? Then I remembered: it was an Australian who I'd met in the gym, here in New York. I'd heard him say that when a waitress had brought him his cup of coffee, and it had just rolled off my tongue. Ah! Travel, and the broadenin' of the mind.

I spent an hour over a cup of coffee with some newspapers. The photo of me was the one I had wanted, with my smile and my wink, and the report by Bill Fleming was pretty accurate. I phoned Reuben to let him know what I was doing, collected the jewellery and went back to the hotel to pack. Reuben had looked better, so I expect the team had partied until the wee small hours.

Thanks to Kit's training, I took over the role of travel facilitator, getting us to the airport and on to the plane. We both slept over the Atlantic and woke to grey skies and rain as we dropped into Heathrow. Customs and immigration went smoothly, and the tube, followed by a taxi ride got me home. Reuben waved me away to go to his lonely home.

I got 'girled' aplenty once I'd got through the front door! Smothered, spoilt and hugely hugged, and then it was 'gift time'. Donna was blown away by my gesture of getting her a 'look-alike' ring, which she loved. The girls clapped and sparkled at my presents, while I congratulated myself on choosing different necklaces that wouldn't be fought over.

It was great to be home, with some 'home-time' for Donna and me, for some loving and some planning, with yet more adventures in the offing.

This article is reproduced courtesy
of:
Boxing Weekly Magazine
By Bill Fleming ©
BBC Boxing Commentator
April 1965 edition

I aim this article directly at anyone who has any interest at all in the art and skill of boxing, and who, for whatever reason may have missed out on the live coverage of the match between Trey Maxwell, the world welterweight champion, and the contender, Sam Smith from Whitechapel in London.

I believe it's not hyperbole to say that another chapter of boxing history has just been written about the skill and dedication of boxers in general, compared to one boxer in particular, who fought at Madison Square Garden this evening.

A young British boxer called Sam Smith, who comes from Whitechapel, London, England – as they say in the United States – has given us a masterful demonstration of boxing skill tonight. Sam is a welterweight, who took on Trey Maxwell, the reigning champion, at The Garden.

Sam's background in 'the tents', as they are known in the UK, began nearly three years ago when he started fighting all-comers for a small fee. (The authorities ignore these 'unofficial' matches as long as they are well managed and there is no bad behaviour but you didn't hear that from me.)

Sam, managed by Mr Reuben Goldstein, spent two years gaining experience by fighting all-comers of approximately his weight, mostly five or more per Saturday night. His record, in this Saturday night 'boxing lottery' was exemplary in that he has never been put down, and has won his fights, almost exclusively, in five rounds or under, which is quite extraordinary!

At some point, his manager decided that Sam was ready to go professional and brought in a team to help with Sam's transition. His team includes Art Dutton, who had been very successful as a manager of three world champions. However, a few years back he suffered a heart problem and the boxing world wrote him off. Apparently, reports of his incapacity were 'greatly exaggerated', and Art appears to have done it again.

Also in Sam's team is Charlie Browne, who had been an unsuccessful contender for the heavyweight world championship. Bad luck dictated that Charlie slipped getting into the ring for his title fight, damaged his spine, and suffered a humiliating defeat. However, Charlie is known as one of the premier 'ring men' and trainers in this business.

Lastly, there is Reg, a local boxing expert, who lives in London, and is well known throughout the industry for his prodigious knowledge of fighters, their history, and their styles.

So, Sam turned professional and won his first few fights, at which time Art Dutton began to take an increasing interest in him. Sam's team put him through an extremely vigorous exercise programme, the details of which remain a secret, with training sessions that included viewing old films of old fights going way back.

The upshot of all this, Ladies and Gentlemen, is that Sam became a tough nut to crack, as fit as any boxer I have ever seen, and highly experienced even at such a young age.

Now comes the exciting part. Sam's quote to me in an interview that Bob Clark and I did with him, was:

'My fitness allows me to improve the timin', accuracy, speed and power of my punches. My real secret is in the chess game I play with my opponents. I think 'em on to the canvas by findin' out their weaknesses, exploitin' those weaknesses, and droppin' them. Then our team all go home for an early night.'

He also told us, 'It was a tough road to get to that fitness level. I owe a great debt to my team, especially Mr Reuben Goldstein who has stuck with me for such a long time. Thanks too, to my fans and supporters for helpin' me get through all the challenges, or should that be, challengers? Finally, thanks to my family for their love, patience and belief in me over such a long time.'

The fight against Trey Maxwell, the now 'former' world welterweight champion, was an eye-opener. When Maxwell came into the ring, Sam smiled at him. Please understand that that was the beginning of the chess match. Maxwell was confused by this, losing some of the control that he thought he had as the world champion. Score one to Sam, even before a punch had been thrown.

A young, intelligent and very experienced boxer is Sam Smith from Whitechapel, and both Bob Clark and I are really looking forward to seeing his next fight.

As a small postscript to this article, I'd like to quote my friend and fellow commentator, Bob Clark, who explained this fight in this way: 'A change in perspective from the "Butcher's Shop Theory of Boxing", i.e. basic brutal boxing, which the majority accept as The Rule of what takes place in a boxing ring, was made here today. Sam Smith, now the world welterweight champion, brought into the ring a pair of precision scalpels. Every other boxer brings two hammers, and that's because they have always brought two hammers, and think boxing is about competitive hammering. As the French say, "Vive la difference". Today, the more precise pair of scalpels prevailed!

Bill Fleming from Madison Square Garden.

Chapter Twenty-two

Three days after I returned home from America there was a meeting at Reuben's house in Hampstead. The 'gang' were all there. We needed to see where we were going from this point on.

'Well, Gentlemen,' began Reuben, 'We have to congratulate Sam all over again for his magnificent win over Trey Maxwell and thank him for cancelling out all the bills that had built up, as well as providing some very welcome funds for all of us.'

Laughter and clapping!

'Now, we have to plan out the future, where the main priority must be Sam's wellbeing. I think, Art, you would have the most advice here, given your background.'

'Thanks, Reuben. When I say, "I've seen 'em all," I mean it, and from every angle.

'I've seen boxers win a world title fight who are broke the day after. I give you examples of two actors who also did that – Peter O'Toole and Omar Sharif – both blew the whole of their income from six month's work on *Lawrence of Arabia* in one night at a casino!

'I've seen boxers win a world title fight, and then give up boxing because it was too hard, or they couldn't handle either the discipline or the knocks.

'I've seen boxers who haven't won a world title fight but have lived very happy, productive and rich lives from the sport. It's not just what you do with the money, it's how you plan what you want to get out of your life, and "plan" is the most important word here. Since Sam is the breadwinner, he should have first say and we'll try to fulfil his wishes. What do you think, Sam? Where do you want to go?'

'First, I'd like to give my thanks, again, to everyone for all your support and wise counsel. I've given this a lot of thought and discussed it with Donna. We think that we should look at three stages.

'One: I'm still young, and I 'aven't been 'it much, so I should actively box while I'm still in good shape, and win as many fights as I can, gettin' as much money for my retirement as I can. We agreed to the title fight with Trey Maxwell now, rather than in two years' time, so it gave me a longer time to fight and earn.

'Two: I'm aware that in two to five years from now I should be thinkin' about retirement, and plan for that. When that 'appens, it should be a planned decision, not because I've taken one beatin' too many.

'Three: I need to 'ave a plan for what I want to do in my retirement. Do I go to some educational establishment, 'oping to get a qualification of some sort? Do I go back to my old job in the construction game?

'My only real skill is in boxin'; it's what I love to do. Maybe there will be some value I can pass on to the young ones comin' into the sport. There are far too many disadvantaged boys and girls out there too, who really need to 'ave some sort of focus, and maybe boxin' could be one of those. Maybe I can give some mentorin' and skill-trainin' for 'em to keep 'em off the streets. Without my boxin', and some incredible luck, I too, could 'ave been in their shoes. What do you think?'

Art was the first one to speak. 'Well said, Sam. You've a good head on your shoulders. My suggestions are as follows: Reg will go on a consultancy basis and will be paid handsomely for whenever he is needed, having full access to Sam and the rest of us at any time. Charlie will be on a full-time salary, with bonuses for wins. Reuben will be Sam's full-time manager to oversee Sam and his family's arrangements where appropriate, of course, on a day-to-day basis. I believe that within that management, Sam should have progressive tuition in public speaking, so that when he finally comes to mentoring, he can stand up in front of anyone, anywhere, and talk naturally about his skills and beliefs. That leaves me to arrange international matches as Sam and Reuben think fit.

'At this point, I think we need one month for Sam to organise another house to live in, which he will buy as an investment, against which he can borrow if needed. This month will also include his buying a car, settling the girls into a new school and arranging for new bank accounts and so on. Reuben can certainly help with some of that.

'At the end of that month, we will meet and discuss a realistic next fight after all the "hoo-ha" has settled down. How does that suit everyone? Sam?'

'That's brilliant! I'll be needin' some 'elp with all that, and I'll call on Reuben's expertise for 'is 'elp. Concernin' the next fight, the sooner, the better; certainly, within three months of the Maxwell fight, or my fitness will start goin' backward, and I can't afford that.'

'Reg?'

'Guys, this is really very good of you. The fact that you pay me for my "consulting time" won't stop me from doing background work on potential oppos for Sam. So, yes, I'm delighted with that.'

'Charlie?'

'I will usually be actively employed for a maximum of two to four hours a day. Would anyone mind my mentoring and training other athletes in my off time?'

Everybody chimed in with, 'No! Not at all!'

So, we had a plan. Art said he would get something organised in about three months and would tell Reg as soon as he knew who the boxer was, and where the fight was going to be held. Charlie would tailor my training to the information that Reg supplied. Look out, boxin' world!

Chapter Twenty-three

You have no idea of the number of decisions we had to make in that month; then again, maybe you do. Choice of a house was a top one. Donna and I had to make a list of what we wanted, and then we searched. We found a mock-Tudor, semi-detached brick house with four bedrooms in a tree-lined avenue in Hampstead, which suited my wife to a tee! 'Happy wife, happy life!'

But this is a boxing story, so let's get back to the boxing.

We all met at the Waterloo pub, one month from the previous meeting. I got a massive welcome from Reg and his mates before we sat at a corner table with some privacy.

I gave them a rundown on our family situation, and then we turned to Art.

'How are you, Sam?'

'I need a month to get back to my best,' I said. 'What's the prospect for our next fight?'

'Trey Maxwell wants a return match, but not yet. His manager thinks six to nine months. Maybe he thinks your fitness level will come down by then, but he would be wrong – right, Charlie?'

'Not on my bloody watch,' grinned Charlie.

'Sam, in two months I can get you a fight with an Irishman named Danny Walsh, from Dublin. We can get either Wembley or Birmingham Arena. It's your choice. What do you think?'

I said, 'Wembley is closest for me. Reg, what do you know about him?'

'He's five feet eleven inches tall, with a reach of at least 74 inches. He looks like a gangly white spider, but he's fast and has a great jab, which he uses to keep people away from him. This makes me think he worries about his middle. What do you think, Sam?'

'Slippin' jabs to get inside, or even knockin' them sideways are both available to counter those. An oppo's 'eight is never a problem as long as I can reach 'is jaw, and I can muck up 'is jab in any number of ways – back and forward, sideways, knockin' away or slippin'. If he gets really annoyin' with it, I'll hyperextend his elbow. Once inside, I'll 'ave to use all my power to see 'ow 'ard 'is middle is. A 'eart shot to slow 'im, some lower shots to drop 'is guard, and then I'll drop 'im in the fifth. Art, why not just send him a letter to say that I've already got 'im covered, and save 'im 'is fare from Dublin!'

Art chuckled, 'Sam, as a champion, you have to learn that when money is offered, even when it is a certainty, you are duty-bound to take it with both hands, remember your manners and say, "thank you".' I just grinned.

'Having said that, if you were a girl, Sam, I'd marry you. Isn't that just the best analysis of an appropriate defence strategy you have ever heard, folks? I love this guy. And, you know the best thing? I know he can do it because I've seen him do just that! Reg, anything else you can get on Dublin Danny would be welcome. Any footage you can get on him would also be an advantage. Charlie, you know what to do?'

'Got it all covered, Art. Sam, this fight will "look" spectacular. There you are at five feet six, with a reported reach of maybe seventy inches on your best day, against this white giant-like all-powerful albino spider, who will have to punch downwards most of the time. Nobody is going to give you a chance on appearances, so the betting should be very much in our favour. The general public still has no idea of your thinking processes, or the skills you have to back them up, especially the ballet and dance movement training. I have to say that's paid off big time. Who would have thought that poncy dancing could help a world champion boxer? We may have to measure your actual reach one day, but that's for after the game has finished. Until then, Sam uses all his skills and knowledge, and makes everyone a lot of lovely money,' said Charlie.

Art said, 'OK guys, we will have a fight in about two months from now. Wembley is closer, and there should be a good crowd. They will be highly entertained by what Charlie says will be a visual treat. We'll meet back in one month to see where we are. We've done all this before, and while we will not get complacent, we do know what we've got to do. Everything all right with that, Reuben?'

'Yes, Art, but I didn't really think you could get all that organised in such a short time.'

'Stick with me, Reuben, and I'll teach you how to manage world champions!'

Chapter Twenty-four

One month out from the fight with the tall Irishman, and we met at our new place. Art invited Donna to stay for the meeting since she would be intimately involved in everything that would be happening from now on.

'Thank you, I've often wondered what you boys talked about,' she said graciously.

'Only boxing,' said Reuben, 'but Donna, it's a different sort of language, so please don't let it upset you. Now, where are we all? Sam, what are your fitness levels like these days?'

'I've been runnin', and while not up to my Yorkshire days, it's comin' easier every day. In ten days to a fortnight, I'll be there. The bags are easy, and the sparrin' is goin' well. I've 'ad a couple of tall sparrin' partners to test that part of the fight.

'I've nearly finished a fight plan, which will be my boxin' lesson to the world. I'll unveil it on fight day and 'ope I don't 'ave it backfire on me by losin' the fight!

'Seriously, if I'm goin' to be respected for my skills, I can leave a film record that can be shown many times. The first three rounds will all be defence, the fourth will be gettin' past 'is jab, and the fifth will be attackin' past the jab, and puttin' the boxer on the canvas. 'opefully, there will be lessons in there that will show what can be done with "scalpels," rather than "hammers". That's from Bill Fleming's piece about the fight at The Garden.'

'You're not getting a bit too fancy, I hope,' said Reuben with a worried look.

'No, I'm not, and trust me on this. If things at any time look like goin' south because my plan is not fittin' in with what's actually goin' on, it will mean I'm not controllin' the fight. Then, I'll leave the plan and just drop this oppo to the canvas.'

'Reg?'

'I can't add much to my first description. The Irishman has had less than twenty fights, won sixteen of them, seven by knockouts. His long, left jab is his big weapon, and he uses it because of his longer reach. If he follows up, it will be with a right cross, and we all know how Sam deals with those. Walsh likes to chase, not stand in the centre of the ring. He's a hunter by nature. I think he sees his oppos as his prey, which is fine until you look at his defence, which is patchy at best, and useless at worst. I also get the impression that his fitness and conditioning are not up to par, so by the fifth round he could be tiring. Anything else, Sam?'

'No, Reg, that's just perfect. That fits right in with my lesson. After I 'ave shown 'im what a good defence looks like, I'll show 'im an even better attack in the fifth and drop 'im. Does 'e ever uppercut with 'is right, Reg?'

'Not that I know; it's mostly right crosses he gets into. But since he's had only twenty or so fights, there's not much to go on.'

'Thanks, Reg, and we've all seen lucky punches from rank amateurs do damage to professionals who don't watch what's happenin'. That will not be me!'

'Charlie?'

'Yes, Reuben, he's coming along a treat. Sam lost about a tenth from his month off, but we've nearly caught up with that, and he's sharp. He'll be ready. After a few rounds, my tall sparring partners wished they were shorter!'

'Art, where are you?'

'Gang, we have a fight at Wembley in a month, on the sixth, with the 'White Spider' aka Danny Walsh from Dublin. The Wembley event machinery has gone into full promotional mode with adverts, leaflets, press releases and all the other innumerable ways of letting the public know that this fight is on. They have five other fights too, and we'll be last on the list at around 9 pm.

'We've negotiated the purse, which is quite rich, even though young Danny is quite new to the game. The Irish paid us heavily for the opportunity to fight a world champion, probably thinking that it could fire their boy to the top in one go. We've also been there; remember Trey Maxwell? Obviously, they know much more about promotion than they do about boxing. So, we'll take their money, remember to say, "thank you" and go on to the next one. Are you OK with all this, Donna?'

'Yes, I really am, and I'm so pleased that you are treating my Sam as a man, and not a commodity to be bartered and manipulated, which, I have to admit, I was afraid might happen. All my fears about what he's doing have been brought down. He obviously has a team of very competent people who value him highly. My message to Sam is always, "Go to work Sam, and get it done!" I'd like to be there this time, Reuben, if that's all right with everyone. I won't get in the way, I promise,' she said with a little smile.

'It would be a great pleasure to have you with us, my dear. I'll get you a seat and will sit with you for the company. I have to say that not all the fights are as clean and disciplined as the ones that Sam fights, but we'll be far enough back not to get splattered,' said Reuben, carefully looking at her for undue squeamishness.

Standing up with her fists on her hips, she stared at Reuben and said, very loudly, 'My name is MRS DONNA SMITH, and I am the mother of two babies! Does that tell you what you want to know?'

That got a big round of applause! Well done, my girl!

Chapter Twenty-five

The next meeting, which we held one week before the fight, settled everything down. I was ready, according to Charlie. Wembley was preparing for a big crowd, according to Art, and Reg had finalised all the information on Danny Walsh. Now it was up to me. It was fight night.

Reuben picked up Donna and me while the rest of the gang went in Charlie's new Ford Transit van. I still reckoned the change rooms were posh but not as posh as The Garden. I wished Lou was here, but he'd probably be able to get the broadcast in the US of A.

I had lashings of time before my fight, and I watched some of the other guys prepare. They all acknowledged me with a nod or a touch of the gloves but stayed within themselves. Charlie gave me his usual summary, then left.

I visualised this 'white spider' and wondered whether the 'spider' would bite me or be squashed by me. Why the doubt? I don't like spiders but don't fear them. So, what was it? Maybe it was their reach or the unpredictable direction of their movement. *For crying out loud, Sam, concentrate! Forget spiders! Think only of your plan to exhibit your boxing skills. If you start to deviate from the plan, this fight could end badly, and you wouldn't want that for your family, that's for sure. So, get to work. It was time to dance.*

There was huge noise from the crowd, plus a brass fanfare. I didn't need it. I wanted to see the oppo. Tall, yes. Big reach, yes. Lean muscles, so I would see how fast he actually was. I planned to frustrate him by not getting hit in the first and second rounds. We'd see. But if he was there to be hit, I'd hit him.

'Ladies and Gentlemen, this is Bob Clarke, back with you again. We come to the last fight of the evening, and the one I've been looking forward to the most.

'Sam Smith, our Welterweight World Champion, is taking on a relatively new and unknown boxer from Dublin, Danny Walsh. Walsh has a big height and reach advantage over Sam, so it will be fascinating, and probably very instructive, to see how Sam deals with these disadvantages. Bill, any comments from you?'

'Well, Bob, we've seen what Sam can do, and frankly, nothing would surprise me. Sam's got a good defence, and moves like lightning, so let's see what he has for us this evening. The fact that Walsh is very new to the game gives Sam a chance to show us his skills, but I'm equally sure he realises that a lucky punch by Walsh could change the fight.'

'Thanks, Bill, and that's the truth. Well, here we go,'
Bell!

'First round, and Walsh is stalking Sam, sending out long, long jabs. So far, Sam has not been present when they reached the end of their journey. Walsh incorporates a right cross in about one in three of his jabs. Sam is backpedalling, and so far, has not been hit. His head is never where the jab goes. Walsh tried a rush and threw three quick jabs in a row. Sam was not there. In fact, he was behind Walsh. As Walsh turned to find him, Sam gave him a perfect right to the jaw. Walsh staggered back with his eyes opened wide in surprise.'

Bell!

'Bill, tell me, what's Sam's plan for this boxer.'

'Bob, I think Sam is going to display his skills for us this evening, and if so, I really want a record of it. Round One was a lesson in, "Not getting hit by an opponent with a height and reach advantage, by backpedalling!" Next round, I think the lesson may be, "by going sideways". Let's see.'

Bell!

'Thanks, Bill. I just love the style and class of our man from Whitechapel. He's amazing in his cool and his control. And I can see you are spot on, Bill. He's using sideways motion to avoid Walsh's jab and right cross, or uppercut. He's just not there when the punches get where Walsh puts them. Walsh is still stalking Sam around the ring, but Sam's dancing feet take him out of range or out of direction, every time. Sam's bobbing and weaving make him difficult to hit, and I can see a degree of aggro coming into Walsh's shots. Frustration is building, and I believe this, too, is part of Sam's plan. The round is nearly over, so how will it finish? Walsh jabs twice, fast and furious, and again Sam skips round to Walsh's back, and gives him a very solid knock to the jaw as he turns.'

Bell!

'I have to say you were spot on, Bill. Round One was backward and forwards, and Round Two was sideways.'

'Yes, Bob, that's what I saw coming. So, what's next? Incorporate both in round three? If so, then maybe round four is, "how to beat an opponent's height and reach advantage by slipping punches and getting inside", and round five maybe, "how to put down an opponent with superior height and reach." I like this game, Bob, and begin to see what you saw in his technique so many fights ago. Back to you.'

Bell!

'Thanks, Bill. If you are right, our next drink is on me! Round Three, and Walsh is trying to get all over Sam, who is skipping away, leaving Walsh to run after him. Some of the audience have appreciated what Sam is doing and are starting to laugh; mainly at Walsh's inability to hit Sam, who is making him look like an amateur in the process. A huge swinging right slices through the air, right where Sam's head was, but he ducked at exactly the right time, bringing his own left into Walsh's rib cage. I heard the explosive escape of air from Walsh, who waits a moment before continuing his attack. In that moment, Sam punished Walsh's head, having got inside the jab. It was one of Sam's special three-punch combos, and we know how much they hurt. A jab from Walsh, and Sam pushes it away to the left with his right hand. Another jab from Walsh but Sam hits the right side of Walsh's head, which it looks like he can do all evening.'

Bell!

'Bob, I think I have broken the code. The third round was a combination of forwards and backward, and side to side. Now, if I'm correct, Round Four will be the lesson on, "how to get inside the guard of a boxer with superior height and reach". That will leave Round Five for the demise of Walsh.'

'Thank you, Bill, and yes, I think you've found the pattern in this one, too.'

Bell!

'Round Four, and Sam goes to the centre of the ring, waiting to see what happens. Walsh approaches cautiously and sends out a tentative jab, which Sam is instantly inside, and punishes Walsh with a four-punch combo to the body. Walsh is shaken, so I think his defence is not as good as it should be, probably because he thinks of himself as the aggressor, and his musculature has not been hardened in the same way that Sam's has.

'Another jab, dodged by Sam, and another, which Sam slips and dodges inside again, giving Walsh three more body punches before slipping away out of range. Walsh doesn't know what to do now. If he attacks, he gets a counterattack for which he has no answer. Another jab and a right from Walsh, and again Sam slips both punches, this time concentrating on Walsh's head with another three-punch combination that's so fast. Walsh's eyes show us that he's not altogether with it, and Sam hits his jaw with a very crisp right. There's a distinct wobble in Walsh's legs.'

Bell!

'Lucky timing for Walsh, that bell. Bill, what a perfect execution of the ability to get inside another boxer's defences?'

'Yes, Bob. Sam slipped those jabs so easily, but that's the mark of a master: "Making the difficult look easy". And Sam is a master. I've been in this business for more years that I will admit to, and I've watched films of old fights covering more years than I will admit to as well, but I've never seen such an accomplished and clinical boxer in all that time. You have to have all the skills, all the strengths, be perfectly fit and have no weak points. Tell me the boxers who could be described this way, Bob.'

'You've got me. Ali maybe. Johnson, Dempsey. Certainly, no more than a handful, but we have the great privilege of having a live one, right in front of us, right now.'

Bell!

'Round five, and usually Sam makes it the last round. If Sam follows his usual plan, he will drop Walsh's guard and put him on the canvas with a right cross or left hook to the 'button'.

Sam slips a jab and punishes Walsh's body – and again. He dances away to see what's going on. A wicked swinging right comes whistling through the air at Sam's head. Sam ducks and watches it goes way past the left side of Walsh's body leaving his head defenceless. Sam had ducked to the left to avoid that right cross, so is now in a prime position to execute the coup-de-gras, using his left hook to Walsh's 'button'. "Goodnight, Danny Walsh!" A brave fighter, but no cigar. Walsh is on the canvas, doesn't make any attempt to get up, and is counted out. Sam wins again. Bill, your comments please.'

'Bob, Ladies and Gentlemen, you may think you have seen boxing matches before, but you may never see such an exhibition of clinically-delivered boxing technique as we have just seen here tonight. That's why Sam Smith is the world champion. In his own words, Sam has said, "I think them on to the canvas". He has proved that again tonight, which we can show you because both Bill and I have predicted what will happen in each round, and we couldn't do that if there was no pattern.'

'Bill, thank you for your very welcome comments my friend. What a privilege this has been. We will have to have a chat with Sam in the BBC Studios, as we did after the world championship fight at The Garden. Let him settle down, and then we'll ask him to talk to us about this fight. On behalf of Bill Fleming and the BBC, this is Bob Clarke returning you to the BBC Studios in London. Goodnight, everyone.'

Chapter Twenty-six

'Good evening Ladies and Gentlemen. I'm Bob Clarke, here tonight in the BBC Studios in London, with my good friend and fellow BBC Boxing commentator, Bill Fleming. Last Saturday night, at Wembley Stadium, we were extremely privileged to watch a boxing match that we predicted would go down in boxing annals as a classic.

'By now, you will all know of Sam Smith, our World Welterweight Champion from Whitechapel, who went over to the United States where, in Madison Square Garden, he fought Trey Maxwell. That he was successful in that fight meant he became the world champion. However, we noticed some things in that fight that we'd love to talk to Sam about. We also watched Sam's latest match, and need to speak to Sam about that, too. Bill, your input, please?'

'Thanks for the introduction Bob, but I'll leave that until Sam joins us.'

'Very well. Ladies and Gentlemen, please give a wonderfully warm welcome to Sam Smith, the welterweight champion of the world.'

I walked into the very brightly lit little studio with only a small area to sit, among a considerable amount of black equipment that was virtually in the dark.

'How on earth am I going to deal with this?' I had wondered.

Reuben had said, 'Just talk to them, Sam. They want information that you've got. They ask the questions; you tell them the answers. And yes, Sam, it is just that simple.'

I shook hands with both of these guys and sat down. I knew, from what Art had said, that these two BBC commentators were two of my biggest fans. 'So be nice,' he'd said.

'Welcome Sam, we've both been looking forward to this interview with you. Bill, you first.'

'Thanks, Bob. Sam, we boxing aficionados have watched you in awe of your technique. You have a great defence and an equally great attack. Where did that all come from?'

'Thanks for 'avin' me on your show, guys. If we go back three plus years, I started in the tents, and we won't say too much about that except that I fought at least four and sometimes six fights every Saturday night. My oppos were unpredictable and varied in every respect. If I wasn't goin' to get too many beatin's, I 'ad to work out what they were goin' to do. I knew what I could do, but I 'ad to work out a speedy way of readin' their strengths and weaknesses. If I could predict those, then I could find a way to drop 'em in the shortest time, and not get 'it too often myself. Over time, my readin' got better and faster. I rarely get surprised now, and if I do, I do 'ave some surprises of my own.'

'What changed you from the tents to becoming professional?'

'I have to say, "external forces". I'd started to think that I would need more money to bring up my girls, and I wanted to earn enough to make a lovely home for my family. My wife was thinkin' about this too, but it was my manager, Reuben Goldstein, who first brought up the subject, and once I understood what was needed from me, it was all systems go.'

'What training did you do for the world championship fight?'

'Guys, I'm not prepared to go into that. What I can say is that Mr Goldstein put a great team together, and they worked out an educational trip for me, which involved fitness trainin' at the same time. I am so grateful to 'im for financin' that trip and 'avin' faith in me. I will be indebted to 'im for life.'

'How sure were you that you would win the Trey Maxwell fight?'

'As sure as anyone can be about anythin'. I 'ad told my wife I would win, and I would never let 'er down. Besides, with the trainin' I'd done, I was probably fitter than any other boxer on earth. Put that together with my experience and technique, and I wasn't about to find out what "'ittin' the canvas" felt like.'

'This latest fight against Danny Walsh, both Bob and I spotted a pattern. We were then able to predict what would happen in each round. How much of that was planned?'

'All of it. I felt confident enough to put my technique on show. How'd it look?'

'Frankly, Sam, it was a master class, and a great pleasure to watch. I would put that on a film and sell it, if I were you, because boxers the world over would give their eye-teeth to have the ability, speed and technique that you have. What's your next fight?'

'At this point, I'm not sure. Trey Maxwell will probably opt for another shot, but that's down the road. We'll be in touch with you as soon as we know.'

'Thank you, Sam, for spending time with us. We both think you are a legend in the making. Go well and look after that lovely family of yours!'

'Thanks, guys, I sure will.'

That seemed to go reasonably well, I thought. *Let's see what Donna and the girls thought about it. That's always the real test.*

When I got home, I called a family meeting.

'I wanted to touch base with everyone to see what you thought about what is goin' on.

'I think our family is as together and happy as we've ever been,' suggested Donna. I just love this house and this area in Hampstead, with the park close by with its trees and flowering bushes. I feel safer here than in Whitechapel, although we will still be Whitechapel people for as long as we live. I feel there is room to move and breathe here, and it's quieter and less stressful. What about you, Sam?'

'If my family is happy, then this is the best thing since sliced bread! I'm doing somethin' that I love and am good at, and my family is happy. That's the bee's knees – the ultimate – for any 'usband and father. So, am I safe to think that you're settled enough for me to stop pretendin' I'm any good at dealin' with mortgages, insurances, rates, taxes and that, and get on with my boxin' career? Good. I 'oped so. Reuben is competent in those areas, but 'e can't box for toffee! So, 'e'll look after the finances for us, and I'll take care of the income.'

That little family discussion settled my feathers down about all the extra stuff I was trying to do, and the need to get back into full-time training. There was a meeting coming up with Art, Charlie, Reuben and Reg. I think Art had something cooking.

Chapter Twenty-seven

I was right! Reuben had bought a black Homburg hat, which he showed off to us at the next meeting at home. Donna, knowing that we held meetings at home with up to twelve people, had decorated our big front room with chintzy sofas and armchairs, standard and table lamps. It looked a bit pre-WW2 but was comfortable and homely. With a bay window, it was a charming and welcoming low-stress environment, too.

'I've just won a couple of ponies on that 'at,' I said, clapping his somewhat showy entrance to our house, and pointing to his new hat.

'Off of who?' he asked.

'I'm not tellin' you that! What have you got for us, Art?' I said to change the subject.

'I think I've got a rematch with Trey Maxwell, here at Wembley,' said Art. The thing is, if he fights here, there's \$n in the kitty, but if we go over to the States there is \$2n, and I have to tell you that "n" is a vast number indeed. So, this is open to discussion. Sam, you first.'

'There is one other consideration, and that's security. If there's 'uge money on this fight, there may be some people over there that know some people over here, to put pressure on my family for me to lose. I'm very tough physically, as you all know, but mentally, I'd cave with a threat like that.'

'Where the hell did that come from?' shouted Reuben. 'I wouldn't allow that to happen. Where did that come from, Sam? You're a straight boy, I know, and we have *always*, always, done things by the book. There's never been a hint of this in the air. Do you have anything else to go on?'

'No, Reuben, I don't. It's just a background vibration that I've picked up, and I don't even know where it came from.'

'Anyone else know anything?' demanded Reuben. There were shrugs all around.

Art said, 'I've got many contacts on the other side of the pond, so I'll put out some feelers, very gently, by people who won't make waves, and I'll get back to you, Reuben. Just thinking that over, it could be part of a plan that the sweetened pot is to get Sam out of the way, though. That's maybe a bit paranoid, but hey, we need to think about it.'

'If anything like this did become a threat, I would contact some coppers I know, and do it very quietly, but officially,' said Reuben. 'We'd get the family out of the way, Brighton or somewhere, and put in some lookalikes to live here, but also with 24-hour surveillance from outside, back and front,' he continued. 'At least Sam could then stare down any threats. Everyone! Keep your ears to the ground to see if there's anything out there. Art, back to boxing, if you don't mind.'

'Right. Well this time, Trey Maxwell will be much fitter, will have improved his attack and defence, and will be more aggressive. Sam?'

''e can be as aggressive as 'e likes. If 'e brawls, I'll box 'im. 'is attack will be the same, but different. 'e may have a three-punch combo by now, and 'e will 'ave tightened up 'is defence, but 'e's just a boxer, and I 'ave the advantage: I've fought 'im before, so I know 'im and 'is ways. For all 'is increase in performance, 'e didn't stretch me in our previous fight, and I will 'ave a heap more to offer in this one. And, I know 'ow to beat 'im,' I confirmed with a smile.

'The Garden it is then,' said Art. 'I'll let you know the date, but I would think six to eight weeks. I'll talk to Lou and get that sorted. There'll be more money from this fight than we will know what to do with,' he said. 'It may be Sam's last fight.'

'What?' I said. 'Where did that come from? I want to keep fightin' for at least a couple of years. Why should it be me last fight?'

'Trey Maxwell may have improved enough to beat you?' said Art.

'There's no way 'e can beat me. I 'ave better reflex speed, better punching power and frequency, a much better and faster defence, and I'm much faster around the ring than anybody. It's true, he could get in a lucky punch, but with my fitness, I should be able to cope with that – and more. Charlie, tell 'im!' I pleaded.

'Well done, Art,' said Charlie, clapping his hands slowly. 'You threw a baited line into the water to see if there were any fish there. Does that answer your question? He's got all the skills and he's bloody well committed. Trey will be a very hungry badass, trying to get back what he regards as his, but he's got to take it, and I don't see Sam letting that happen, do you? Honestly?' said Charlie.

'He won't!' said Donna, joining in for the first time. 'Sam's told me he will win, so he will.'

And that seemed to finish off that particular piece of conversation.

'Can you get me a fight before then?'

'Sure,' said Reuben, 'I can always get you a fight, Sam. With you being world champ there's never a lack of takers. Where, and why do you want it?'

'I want to keep all my stuff together. There's been so much goin' on that sometimes I lose sight of my goals. I want to get back to basics, preferably with a keen, young fighter who 'as got a chance. I'll let 'im down lightly and talk to 'im afterward.'

'You'd do that?' asked Art.

'Yes, of course! We want to promote boxin', not annihilate promisin' young boxers. Apart from me, who do you know that 'as never lost a fight?'

'Point taken, Sam. I think your future is calling.'

I smiled because Art had remembered my talking about my wish for a mentoring and teaching life after boxing. 'I'll get something organised for three weeks' time. That OK with you?'

'That's fine with me. Charlie, we 'ave some work to do!'
The meeting broke up with a little buzz of excitement in my stomach about going back into the ring.

Chapter Twenty-eight

'Good evening Ladies and Gentlemen. This is Bob Clarke, here with Bill Fleming, reporting to you on behalf of the BBC on a series of boxing matches held here at Olympia stadium this evening.

'For those who don't know, London Olympia, situated in the Royal Borough of Kensington and Chelsea in West London, was built in 1885. It has had many upgrades, and some famous people have performed here, people as diverse as Jimi Hendrix, Dr Who, and the boxer Chris Eubank. It's mostly an exhibition centre but holds top-notch boxing matches from time to time.

'There are seven fights on the card tonight, but the one that has primarily brought us here tonight is Sam Smith versus Wally Shaw. Sam, who we all know and love, is a Londoner from Whitechapel. He won the World Welterweight Championship title from Trey Maxwell at Madison Square Garden. Shaw is an unknown boxer to me, but maybe my friend and co-commentator, Bill Fleming, has something to report on that. Bill?'

'Yes, thank you Bob, and the answer to your question is "no". I know nothing about this young man. I have the impression, however, that Sam is having the equivalent of a shakedown fight before meeting Trey Maxwell again in a few weeks' time, back at The Garden. That means he's giving an unknown boxer a chance to fight a world champion, which I'm coming to realise is the sort of future that Sam is looking for after his boxing days are over. Bob, I'm really hoping that Wally Shaw doesn't oust the champ. Back to you, Bob.'

'Thanks, Bill. You are as informative as ever. Your timing's pretty good too as Sam is just climbing into the ring. Shaw is yet to arrive so Sam will get a good look at him before the fight. Sam is looking very fit and very focused. Bill, where would they get Wally Shaw? How would they pick an unknown?'

'I think Mr Reuben Goldstein, Sam's manager, would have looked around for a suitable candidate. He would have to be able to really box, and be very hungry, I would think.'

'Shaw is climbing into the ring now. He's slight, by comparison to Sam, and he doesn't look like much, but I've been mistaken about appearances before.'

Bell!

'Both boxers approach and circle. Shaw throws a jab, Sam backs away. Shaw throws another but follows through quickly and lands a right to Sam's head. Sam thought the jab was all there was going to be, but Shaw outfoxed him. Sam jabs and Shaw backs. Sam jabs again and mimics Shaw's approach by moving forward quickly with a right, but Shaw is not there. He's dodged the right but lands a right of his own to Sam's head. Shaw is ahead on points against the champ at this particular moment. Can you believe that? Shaw throws a jab to Sam's head, and follows with a right to Sam's midsection, which lands.'

Bell!

'Bill, would you believe that Sam is behind on points after the first round?'

'I wouldn't have put money on it, that's for sure. Shaw looks very composed, attentive and focused, and has obvious ability. I'm now wondering how this fight will progress. What will Sam do? What will Shaw do? This is great stuff!'

Bell!

'Again, they circle, but Sam has decided to take centre ring this time, seeing what will change or modify Shaw's behaviour. Left from Shaw, missed, another left from Shaw, another left from Shaw and followed up with a right that hits Sam's left side. Sam releases a three-punch combo, but Shaw has danced away, and for the first time in my memory, Sam misses. Sam dances, coming forward with another combo, which takes Shaw by surprise. To his credit, Shaw returns with a three-punch combination of his own to Sam's body, and Sam retreats. Sam comes forward, I think to get Shaw either in a corner or on the ropes, but Shaw is ahead of him and slides out, giving Sam a right to the head before retreating. Sam tries again, but again Shaw avoids an obvious ploy by Sam.'

Bell!

'Another round to Shaw, Bill?'

'Yes, I would say so. Shaw is awake to Sam's plan, but he also has the skills to get around being crowded into a corner or onto the ropes. If Shaw can last twelve rounds, doing what he's doing, he will win this fight, however crazy that sounds.'

Bell!

'Round Three, and Sam looks much more determined, more aggressive. He throws a jab and an immediate right cross that catches Shaw on the chin. Shaw throws a jab of his own, but it misses. Sam comes in again and pummels Shaw's body but not before Shaw gives Sam a crisp right cross to his chin. Sam crowds Shaw again with a flurry of blows, but Shaw covers up to the degree that, although it looked good, allowed none of Sam's punches to hit their target. This is quite extraordinary. Sam is now backpedalling. Shaw drops his eyes to Sam's solar plexus. It was just a moment when he was at the right angle for me to spot it. Shaw approaches and throws a swift right, not to the solar plexus, but to Sam's chin. Amazingly, Sam fell for it and dropped his hands at the last instant to protect his body. He's in a clinch with Shaw. I think that blow hurt Sam.'

Bell!

'Bill, what are we seeing here?'

'Bob, we're seeing is a very talented young man, who was able to get, not a lucky punch, but a predetermined punch through Sam's defences, and I haven't seen that in a long, long time, if ever. This young boxer, Wally Shaw, may have looked "slight" and "lacking in confidence" when he came into the ring, but he's shown guts and considerable ability. In fact, I would put him ahead of Sam after three rounds, which in itself is extraordinary. Bob?'

'Yes, Bill. Shaw is faster than he looks and packs a kick into his punches, too. He doesn't seem to be tiring either, so one way or another, this is a nice little match-up if it wasn't for the fact that we have a world champion versus a rank amateur in the ring. I still back Sam because of the enormous depth of his experience and his obvious fitness level.'

Bell!

'Bill, I believe what you said, especially about experience, so I'll back Sam to the limit at this point, too. However, we have an intriguing and unfolding potential defeat right here in front of us, and it is a boxing jewel to behold.

'Sam has jabbed and followed with jab after jab, moving forward, crowding Shaw. Shaw attempts to move sideways and gets punched in that direction, so he moves the other way as a mirror image with the same result. Now Shaw is caught. He retreats and is on the ropes. Sam applies his combo, forwards not sideways, which pushes Shaw even further back on the ropes. Just as Sam is about to apply a barrage of punches, Shaw ducks sideways out of harm's way, cracking Sam on the chin as he goes. This is fascinating stuff. Sam follows Shaw across the ring and starts another barrage of punches to both upper and lower body. Shaw is having trouble shielding both areas, so some of Sam's blows are starting to tell on Shaw.'

Bell!

'Bill, I think Sam has started to get the upper hand.'

'Bob, I agree. That was definitely Sam's round, and the momentum has shifted. Sam is much more aggressive now. His punch per round ratio has increased dramatically. He is saying to Shaw, "OK my friend, you've shown me what you've got, and it's quite good, but now let me show you some of my skills!" That was the fourth round, so now we have Sam's "put you on the canvas" round. Let's see how this plays out. This is not just a good boxing match; it's an intellectually stimulating competition. It's like watching high-speed chess.'

'Thanks, Bill, but aren't you getting just a tad over-excited?' They both grinned.

Bell!

'Anyway, let's see how Sam will finish this, if he can. Sam is playing aggressor, chasing Shaw around the ring. Shaw reverses direction and catches Sam napping with a right to the head, changes direction and tries to do it again, but Sam is awake to that, slips inside and punishes Shaw's body. One of those punches was a right to the heart, and, yes! Shaw showed a distinct wobble in the legs.

'Next comes more punishment to Shaw's body and here we go. Shaw's guard drops, and there is that crisp, beautifully timed right from Sam to Shaw's chin. Shaw drops, raises his upper body and shakes his head. The Ref starts to count...6...7...and he's up! The Ref checks him, and he's cleared to continue. Now that's another first. There's about 20 seconds left in the round. Shaw circles, amazingly dancing on his toes. Sam moves in with a jab, Shaw slips it and gives Sam a stunning right to the jaw. His head spins away, sweat sprays into the crowd, sparkling in the lights as it goes. Shaw goes in for the kill with another right that has lots of 'toe' in it, but Sam has already ducked out of the path of that punch and delivers a huge right of his own to Shaw's jaw. This time, the Ref counted eight...nine...ten, out.'

'Well, Bob, that fight was the closest Sam has ever come to being defeated in his long history of boxing that we know about. That is a definite plus for young Wally Shaw. Young man, you have done a mighty job here tonight at Olympia, and may you go on to succeed to the title after Sam has hung up his gloves.

'Boxing is mostly about tenths, and sometimes hundredths of a second. You can have twelve rounds of routine boxing, and a match is won or lost in the last seconds because the challenger took a chance, or the champion decides that on the basis that "winner takes all", he puts in a punch from a direction no one expected. That last exchange of blows – Shaw to Sam's jaw, then Sam to Shaw's jaw – took maybe half a second, but it was the defining moment of the match.

'Here tonight, Sam was hit fair and square on the chin, and was just about gone. If he had not anticipated that next blow from Shaw, he would have been the one on the canvas being counted out. That would have been embarrassing, but Shaw would have deserved his victory. He punched Sam very hard on the "button". Sam was knocked sideways but must have either seen or sensed that Shaw was ready for the next one and dodged out of the way, and please note – in such a way as to be ready to deliver a punch himself! That last punch of Sam's not only saved the fight, but it also won him the fight. That is why Sam is so good, Ladies and Gentlemen. Back to you, Bob.'

'Thank you, Bill. That was a great fight, but we have to take our collective hats off to Wally Shaw. He put on an excellent show, winning the first three rounds against the reigning world champion.

'That, Ladies and Gentlemen, was the last fight from Olympia this evening. We hope you have enjoyed the evening's entertainment. From Bob Clarke and Bill Fleming, we wish you well, and return you to the BBC studios. Good night.'

The audience started to leave the arena, which was now almost silent. The two commentators sat in their chairs, silently re-running the fight in their mind's eye, while taking and giving scoring-points, points of interest, points of flair and style, attack and counterattack – not at all unlike a World Championship Chess Tournament.

'That, my friend, was a hell of a fight. If I got knocked over by a bus tonight, "God forbid", I would die a happy man knowing that I had witnessed one of the best fights in history. That had everything, including the genuine possibility that an unknown fighter very nearly took away the world championship from one of the best boxers we've seen in a long, long time. Inspirational! What more can I say?'

'Not a hell of a lot, Bill. I'm stuck for words too. We'll have to have a sit-down talk with Sam about that in the coming days and get to see it from his perspective.'

'Amen to that. Let's get a drink, then I'm going home.'

Chapter Twenty-nine

'What the hell happened to you out there?' asked Charlie. 'You looked flat, man, and I know you're not. So, what happened?'

'Charlie, believe it or not, I ran into an outstandin' boxer. That's *One*! I'm also guilty of fallin' into my own trap, that's *Two*! And *Three*? I've been too successful, which is why I fell into my own trap, as per number Two. This was a very timely wake-up call for me. Reuben handpicked that young man, Wally Shaw. 'e's been pickin' my oppos forever and 'as always challenged me. If 'e thought 'e saw a flaw in my technique, 'e would choose an oppo who could take advantage of that, so I always 'ad to be on the lookout for such things. Because I 'ave been so successful, I've developed a routine that even the BBC commentators picked up.

'Tonight, I was challenged by a young man with plenty of talent, plenty of hunger, and plenty of 'eart. 'e was not overawed by my status. 'e wanted to see what I 'ad, and what I could teach 'im about my technique. 'e knew my plan and 'e messed it up, just as I would 'ave done in reverse. 'e took chances, ruffled my feathers and generally played with me.

It took me until the third round to realise that I could be taken out of that fight, so I 'ad to get serious. I 'ave to tell you, Charlie, that if I 'adn't 'ad the sense to duck that last blow of 'is, 'e could well 'ave finished me.'

'I agree, Sam. He is a good boxer. Just maybe I have become a bit lazy and complacent in my thinking of your need to do something different, too. There's one good thing that can come out of this near-disastrous fight.'

'What's that, Charlie?'

'You can bet your bottom dollar that Trey Maxwell will watch this match over and over again, and will see your weaknesses, and that's good!'

''ow?'

'Because he'll think they are weaknesses, and they are not. They were caused by complacency, by a plan for a fifth-round knockout, and an exhibition-type performance. Nobody but you and I will ever know this, so that gives us a huge advantage. Maxwell will think he's got your weak spots covered, only to find that you have no weak spots, as proved by the fact that you will drop him in four,' he said, with a beaming smile.

'Charlie, you're a clever man! Now, 'ow do I explain this to Reuben, Donna and the Press?'

'Hey, chill out, man! You tell them he is a good boxer, and that Reuben chose well. That's fact plus a little flattery. To Donna, the Press and anyone else who takes that much interest: you wanted to see what Wally Shaw had to offer. You can afford to congratulate him greatly on his talent and wish him well. Then you say that you hope you don't come up against him in the ring in the future! This is tongue-in-cheek humour, Sam.'

'Brilliant. This ploy, then, is a win/win situation for everyone. Thanks, Charlie, there's more to you than meets the eye. You're a dark 'orse if ever there was one.' Charlie just gave me a big toothy grin, showing me gold.

In my head, I muttered, 'Think, Sam, think! Is that all that went wrong? No. I underestimated him, and that's unforgivable in a boxer – more so if he's a world champion. It's because of my status that I thought I was bulletproof, and he very nearly proved me wrong. I have always said, "Never, ever, underestimate the oppos!"'

So, it comes down to an attitude problem. Since I've realised it, faced it, understood it and accepted it, I can adjust it. How? Simple. I recognised that every boxer I fight wants not only to take my championship away but, much more importantly, the future for Donna and the girls! That should do it. New Mantra: "How dare you think I would let you 'arm my family?"

I turned my attention back to Charlie. 'Since we are being extremely and personally honest with each other, Charlie, I 'ave already changed that big mistake, which nearly cost me my first-ever defeat. That's done. Now my thinkin's clear on it. Tomorrow let's analyse what Maxwell will make of the fight, what 'e will come at me with, and 'ow I can anticipate and counter those plans of 'is. And since we're talking about this, I know virtually nothin' of your background. I don't want to know any special stuff that you may not want to be known, but, 'ow old are you, and are you married?'

'Sam, I don't know where you're going with this, but I'm forty-seven and unmarried. Why?'

'Fair question. I've done very well with you as my trainer and ring man, and we 'aven't 'ad a cross word. Mostly, we've been on the same page. It's far too early to make any real plans, but floating an idea on the outer limits of my imagination – what if we were partners in a gym, plus learnin' centre, plus mentorin' facility? Would that hold any interest for you? You know I'm straight, and I've found no tricky little silent areas in your personality, so maybe we could continue to work well together? And maybe Reuben could contribute some of his talent and money to the enterprise. Think about it, Charlie. You only have about five years!'

'Yeah! OK, Sam. My turn to say, "Thanks, man".'

Chapter Thirty

'Welcome, Sam, and thank you for coming to spend some of your valuable time with us in the BBC studios, again.'

'Thanks, Bob. Bill. Always a pleasure to talk to guys in the know.'

'Sam, first question, and the hardest – what happened in your fight with Wally Shaw?'

'Yeah, I thought you'd get on to that fairly quickly. I knew nothin' of Wally Shaw before the fight and, given my extensive experience in the tents, 'e should 'ave been easy to beat. However, not only was 'e an outstandin' boxer, with great speed and technique, 'e also 'ad no fear, and, to my irritation, no respect for my status. This, of course, I found out during the fight. We 'adn't scoped him out because 'e was an amateur. As with the tents, I decided to find out what 'e 'ad, going gently with 'im to start with. I found out by the third round that 'e 'ad far more than I expected, and that if I didn't get my act together, I could lose the fight. So, I upped the ante. 'e managed to catch me a beauty and, 'ad I not anticipated 'is next punch, it could have been curtains for me. I did, and it wasn't!'

'You found him a talented fighter?'

'Most certainly, and frankly, I don't fancy ever being in the ring with 'im again! Wally, if you're watchin', please accept that as my ultimate compliment, and I'd like to get together with you for a talk soon. Please ring me.

'Oh! I'm sorry guys,' I said, with a sheepish smile, 'I didn't mean to use your programme as a communication channel to my oppos.'

'That's absolutely fine, Sam. Where do you go from here?' asked Bob.

'Trey Maxwell wants a return bout in a few weeks, so I'm workin' 'ard towards that. 'e thinks 'e can beat me if we fight in The Garden, which 'e thinks of as 'is patch. It means that the money is much better if I fight 'im there, so that's what I'll do. I don't mind where we fight. I'll still beat 'im.'

'Sam, I've heard you have made some lifestyle changes since you won the Belt.'

'Sure 'ave, Bill. We've found a new house, which pleases Donna, and the girls 'ave found new schools where they are 'appy.

'Will you be fully fit by the time of the fight?'

'Hell, yes! You can bet your boots on that. My staple programmes are runnin', ball work and sparrin' with some very serious boxers. At one point, I was runnin' up to seventy miles a day, and that's in the country not on a track, and feelin' really good after it. I'd probably need a little lead time to get right back to that, but there are other aspects to 'avin' an 'ard body for boxin'.'

'Such as?'

'Every boxer's footwork can be improved, and you 'ave seen 'ow fast I can move around the ring. It's a big part of my defence. Breath control too is important, as is balance. All of those I 'ave improved. 'avin' 'ardened and improved my body in many areas by workin' outside the gym, most of the others can be sharpened in the gym. Speed and accuracy of punches, and then the power behind each delivery can be practised in the gym. But the final exercise to put all this into practice is with a sparrin' partner. That's when it should all come together, and if you put in enough time, the whole attack-defence thing works like a well-oiled machine.

'Then, there is the mind! Since my boxin' is 90% mental, can you both give me 20,000 words on, "The Mental Aspects of Boxin'?"'

'Actually, Sam, that's a bit of a challenge,' said Bill, 'I'll think about it.'

'Sam, we're out of time. As always, it's been an absolute pleasure to talk to you, and thank you again for giving us your time and your insights. Go well at The Garden, Sam. Needless to say, we'll both be there.'

Chapter Thirty-one

The phone rang.

'Sam, it's Reg. Listen, there's a whisper, just a whisper, of something not quite right. I've told Reuben. He told me he'd be in touch with you. The word is that "the other side" are quietly confident that Trey Maxwell will beat you on his turf, but they want to make absolutely sure before the big money is placed. You there, Sam?'

'Yes, Reg. Any idea of the direction of the threat?' I asked, thinking of my family.

'Not yet, but I'm keeping very close to it.'

'Good man, Reg. I'll hear from Reuben, and we'll see. Thanks again, Reg.'

I put the phone down, and it rang again immediately. It was Reuben.

'Sam, we need to meet. Out in the open. You have a park near you. I'll see you there in half an hour. Can you make that?'

'Yes,' I said, and he rang off. I got there in my running gear and saw him sitting on a bench seat under a tree.

'I've 'eard from Reg,' I said.

'So, have I, and I've been worried sick since he picked up that vibration. There's just three weeks before the match, and two weeks before we take off for New York. The most important thing – and maybe the only thing I have to tell you – is that your family will be safe. I positively guarantee that, Sam. You must totally believe me about that and go about your business as usual.

'I mentioned a plan before, when we were talking hypothetically. A little nearer the time we'll put that into play. Your family will be taken somewhere else. I said Brighton at the time, but it won't be there, and you'll not know where, but I repeat, no harm will come to them, I promise. They are as close to me as my own family was, so they'll be cared for. I'd give my own life for them if it would help.'

'I seem to spend my life sayin', "Thank you" to you, but I owe you another one; so, "Thank you for carin' for my family, Reuben." Can I talk to Donna about this?'

'I think it's better if we all go out to dinner tonight, my treat, and we'll all talk about this, then and there. I'll meet you at the Indian Restaurant on the High Street at six-thirty. I've got to go.'

'See you then.'

If Trey Maxwell had anything to do with this, or even knew about it, I'll kill him in the ring, or at least maim him for life. What do they say: 'Beware the anger of a patient man?' That's me, a very patient man, but my family is everything to me.

I could feel the anger building within me, but I knew there was no direction for it. So, it was 'Discipline time'. *Drop it down, hide it away until you can bring it out and unleash it on a suitable target, Sam.* If I found out Maxwell was involved, I'd know exactly where to direct it. He was going down anyway; it was just a question of how that would play out. *Quiet, Sam. Quieten it down for now. Bury it. It's useless now, so save it. Tuck it away in a dark corner for later.*

We met Reuben over Biryani, Chicken Tikka Marsala, Naan bread and Pav Bhaji. It was delicious. Being early in the evening, the restaurant was quiet, so we had privacy, although why we needed it this far away from home, I wasn't sure.

Once the girls fell asleep with their heads in Donna's lap, Reuben turned his attention to me and Donna, and began in a low voice. 'Donna, I have something to talk to you about. There has been a rumour, a whisper really, that someone, or more probably some group of people, is most interested in Sam losing his next fight in the States. Now, American society plays by different rules to those we have in Britain, so we are thinking of taking a few precautions to keep you safe. I have already brought the police into this, even at this early stage, and I'm getting outstanding cooperation, not only because Sam has a very high profile in this country, but that his family may also be involved.

'This is most important to all of us. I guarantee you will come to no harm. Everyone wants to protect you, but the police also want to capture the guilty parties. They are liaising with the FBI, an organisation that doesn't work outside the USA, but they can exchange information with our crime people. Understood?'

Donna gasped and clutched my hand, but nodded mutely, casting fearful glances at the girls as they slept.

'So, what's going to happen is that sometime soon, you will leave your house and be taken to a nice holiday place; and no one, except the police and me, will know where you are. There will be three people stationed in your house, one will look very much like you, Donna, but she will be a trained police officer. She will use clothes similar to your clothes, which, in turn, of course, will mean shopping for more clothing for all of you. There will also be around-the-clock observations from outside your house, both front and back. You will stay in hiding until this problem has been resolved. OK?'

Donna looked shaken, but managed to ask, 'How long will that take?'

'As long as it takes to make sure the coast is clear. We'll clear it with the girls' school, so they won't be missed. The school will know that you are on holiday, but no one will know where you've gone. As far as they're concerned, you've had the offer of a touring holiday abroad and have taken advantage of that, meaning you'll have no fixed address. You won't, of course, be going abroad.'

'Donna,' I announced, 'if I thought there would ever be any problem of this sort that was directly caused by my boxin' career, I would be deliverin' coal or be bricklayin' right now, instead of puttin' you in any sort of 'arm's way. I 'ave Reuben's word you'll be safe, and the police are involved at this early stage.' My wife clutched my hand tighter in response.

'When the time comes, don't take anything with you except the clothes you stand up in,' interrupted Reuben, 'and I do mean anything at all! That includes toys, clothes, keepsakes or jewellery. Just the clothes you are wearing. It'll probably be in the dead of night, and you may not know where you are when you get there. That's all right. Just enjoy some time in the country. When you get back, your friends will want to know everything, yes? Just tell them there was a rumour of a security problem to do with the fight, and you were taken away for your own protection. You don't know, and won't know any more than that. Is that all right with everyone?'

Donna said she would keep the girls calm by making it out to be a holiday adventure courtesy of Sam's career, but thought the move should be soon because young girls find it very hard to keep secrets.

'Great point, Donna. We'll bring up the schedule to tonight, which will get around that problem. Sam, your family has gone on an overseas touring trip, so they have no fixed address. You'll miss them, but you have the fight to concentrate on. Everyone understand all that?'

We nodded.

After getting home, we decided on an early night. Donna and I had some intimate conversation because we were well and truly married, hating to be apart, even for a short time.

Sometime during the night, my phone rang.

'Now. Backdoor. Quiet, and no lights,' said a voice.

'Right.'

I alerted Donna, who got dressed while I went through to the girls' bedrooms to get them organised to dress in dark clothes, in the dark, in silence: all the while telling the girls that this was part of the adventure. We made the back door in about three minutes, carrying nothing. I kissed each of them as they climbed into a dark car, which drove off without lights.

My heart felt bleak, knowing I wouldn't see them, or be able to cuddle them until I returned home from the US.

Later that night, my phone rang again.

'Backdoor, no lights.'

For one terrifying moment, I thought my family had been hijacked and that these were the real police. My heart was in my throat. When I opened the door, three people in dark clothes, one woman and two men, walked in silently. These were my family's replacements who would be living with me until I took off to the States. They sent me back to bed, using the sofa and armchairs without turning any lights on.

In the morning, the woman, Christine, was already up with the coffee and toast sorted. She looked a bit like Donna, while the two men said they would stay out of sight upstairs.

I talked them through the house: cupboards, clothes, routines, car and my security measures. The habits were the most important. Christine wanted to go out as infrequently as possible, which made good sense. I would come and go as usual. She would shop, get petrol and so on, as little as possible, while wearing Donna's clothes. The headmistress of the girls' school was in a limited loop to cover potential leaks.

Chapter Thirty-two

We had a meeting at Reuben's house.

'Sorry to bring you bad news,' Reg told me.

'I'm just very glad you did, Reg. It was an early warnin'. But I do miss 'em already.'

'Everyone's fine,' interrupted Reuben, calmly. 'They've settled in very well, and we have the best of the best looking out for them.' I was relieved. Now I could focus my energies on the up-coming fight.

'Sam and Charlie will travel to New York on Sunday, ready to start at the gym on Monday. The fight's on Saturday, so that's just right, I think. Sam?'

'I'm glad my taper is at an end so I can work extra 'ard this week, because no one messes with my family, and if Maxwell is involved, 'e's in for a lot of pain. Either way, 'e'll hit the canvas in five – maybe before.

'Guys, after my last fight with Wally Shaw, Charlie pointed out that I 'ad been a bit complacent. I remedied that by accepting it to be true and decidin' not to let it happen again. To make sure, I've added a mantra to my pre-fight preparation, which is: "ow dare you think I would let you 'arm my family?" Little did I know 'ow pertinent that would become, or 'ow soon. But it's solved my problem of complacency. I will put Maxwell down, and I will 'urt 'im. All I need is a little sharpening in a gym for a couple of days. Art?'

'"All systems are Go", from my end,' said Art, stealing a line from space engineers at NASA when launching rockets.

'The Garden is in full promotion mode. Lou's on side, and we're ready. Just add two boxers.'

'Reg?'

'The word is that there's a heap of big money being put on Maxwell, and that he's a bit stressed about the outcome. In my opinion, based on what I've heard on the grapevine, he's working on his fitness a tad too hard, and will continue until the day before the fight. What effect would that have, Charlie?'

'His condition could actually go backward. His fitness, hardness and reflex speed could suffer, and his focus could be all over the place. That's why I make Sam work so hard up to about ten days before a fight, then chill out and taper down until he's raring to get back into the ring. Then I get him sharpened in situ, and believe me, by that time he's ready to rock and roll! The big money has probably sealed Maxwell's doom. They shouldn't have told him about that. That's just bad management, right Mr G?'

'Absolutely. It starts to look easier and easier, but no complacency Sam, right?'

I nodded to appease him.

Reuben was not happy at having to stay at home, when 'his boy' was fighting at The Garden, but he had promised to look after my family.

After the meeting, when we were alone, I said to him, 'Reuben, I don't know what's going to 'appen to my family, and that makes me very confused. I imagine that they'll be taken to a remote farmhouse somewhere a long way away, maybe Yorkshire, and there'll be a couple of armed police officers livin' with 'em for protection. If the actual situation turns pear-shaped, do remember that I 'ave Tom, plus his squad of five SAS soldiers, very much on my side, and I'm sure they would do a lot to protect my family.'

'That,' said Reuben, 'is one excellent idea, Sam. That's one very effective resource that never crossed my mind. Just in case, I'll have a word with their Liaison Officer, through whom I sorted out your training programme. God forbid, my boy, it would ever come to that, but that's definitely a backup asset I'm happy to have on our side.'

***

Charlie and I flew into New York on Sunday, and by pure chance, the same immigration officer I'd seen last time was on duty.

'Hey!' he said.

''ey yourself! Tell me, are you goin' to make the same mistake as last time?' We were both grinning away with the underlying innuendos.

'Well now, that depends.'

'Depends on what?' I asked.

'Depends on what you tell me this time, that's what.'

'Well,' I said, 'if you are an American who 'as never been out of the country and feel that everything America produces 'as to be the best, then you'd have to follow your instincts. 'owever, if you were one smart immigration officer, who 'as travelled, seen and experienced some good things outside America, then your broad mind might just favour the smarter option, which in turn, may mean that you may not 'ave to work here that much longer. Your choice.'

'Nicely, nicely,' he said.

'Stubby Kaye, Guys and Dolls,' I said.

'Now I know you're smart! Love to buy you a drink.'

'Save it for your lady-love.'

'And that tells me that you are one wise and brilliant man. Good luck!'

'Thanks. If you come to England, ever, look me up.' He gave me a mock salute and a warm grin.

We settled into the hotel, and on Monday morning I started on some sparring partners and workouts under Charlie's eagle eyes. On Tuesday I went to The Garden and saw Lou again. He and Reuben had been mutually, but deceptively, rude to each other, but he greeted me like a long-lost brother.

'How's my all-time favourite boxer, then? How the hell are ya, Sam?'

'Just great, Lou. Lou, this is my ring man and trainer, Charlie Browne.'

'Hello, Charlie,' he said, and shook his hand. 'Sam, although he doesn't get the publicity some prima donna boxers that I know receive, everyone in this business knows of Charlie Browne, and acknowledges his worth. Shame about ya fight, Charlie. I was there and saw what happened. Still, you've found an important niche, yeah?'

'Yes, Lou, and thanks, man.'

'You got the ring tuned, Lou?' I asked him.

'Ya'd better come an' check it out. We haven't raised it to the floor yet, but it's ready unless ya tell me otherwise. How's Rube been treating y'all?'

'Really well, thanks.'

I had checked with Reuben about whether Lou was in the loop about the threat to my family. He told me yes, since he was a trusted friend, who not only knew everybody but had his enormous ears to the ground too.

'Have you 'eard anything, Lou?'

'Well now, let's just say, between ourselves, that certain clever people, who always wear the colour blue, have an angle on this that's pretty promising. I'm also told that there are some clever people in your country who always wear the colour blue, too. It seems that our blue-wearers talk to your blue-wearers quite often, an' that they're all on the same wavelength. Our boxing officialdom is extremely keen to keep clean – not only the actual sport – but the image of the sport. I can also tell ya there is a considerable weight of focus in the background, which is being kept very, very quiet. This is because they are hunting "wabbits". I don't think the "wabbits" have heard them yet, an' they won't until after the fight. How's that coming along, Sam?'

That was my cue, and it was no weight to lift.

'I would say that your good sense last time will pay even better dividends this time, so just keep doin' what you do. Let's see those ropes.'

The ring, being in the basement, was in the dark, but I jumped up and tested the rope tensions. It was the top one I was interested in.

'About two and a half to three inches too far at the centre, or about an extra two turns on the turnbuckles, which will probably suit both boxers. It's not just in my favour. If we were big heavyweights, the current tension would have to be beefed up even more, but we lighter weights like to 'ave a slightly stiffer top rope than is there now. That OK with you, Lou?'

'Absolutely, an' I'll get it checked with the match referee before the bout. Sam, I'll see ya after the fight. It's great to see y'all again, Charlie. I'm very pleased that things are going well for ya. Ya certainly have a winner in Sam.'

'Amen to that, Lou.'

Chapter Thirty-three

I have always been grateful to Charlie for the way he sorts out my pre-fight time, and he was also on hand to help me through the weigh-in. This is the official scrutiny of our body weights to make sure we comply with the appropriate Boxing Association's category weight rules.

Charlie and I were well out-numbered by the crush of Maxwell's sycophants. I ignored Maxwell, got on the scales, hit my 147 lbs, got off, and was leaving because I had nothing to say to anyone here. Maxwell made an effort to get up close in front of me, so I gave him a false smile and waved at him, even though he was only six inches from my face.

'How's your family?' he asked. 'You think they're safe? They're not. We have them, so just be a good little family man and lose this fight, or…' Then he smiled and raised his eyebrows.

It hit me like a 'rabbit' punch. My head spun, I couldn't breathe, and my blood pressure dropped like a stone. I was in shock. Charlie's big hand came around my arm, and he half-propped and half-guided me out.

'Don't make nothing of that, Sam. Walk, man, just walk. Now!'

We made it outside, and I saw a bench. My legs gave way, and I sat heavily.

'What the 'ell?' I said. 'Charlie, 'e knows, and 'e's in on it! 'e's blackmailing me through my family. Can you believe a boxer would stoop so low, just to win a fight? The bastard! 'e will rue this day.'

I was close to tears at the thought of my family in danger, and furious that I couldn't do anything about it.

'Oh! God, Charlie, I 'ope they'll be all right.' I sank down with my head between my knees.

'Sam, listen to me hard, right now! Reuben said he would take care of your family, so you have to trust him to do that. You know he's got great backup resources. Concentrate all your energies on the fight tomorrow. Think, man, think! There is nothing you can do for them from here, except win this fight. You have a job to do, and you have to trust other people to do their jobs too.'

'I know you're right. Let's just sit 'ere for a while so I can get my breath back. Maxwell is going to regret that. Imagine, terrifying my little girls just so 'e can win a fight. Who'd do that? That's absurd, Charlie, and 'e's goin' to pay for that in the ring! Let's run back to the 'otel, and then I want to make a phone call. The run'll 'elp get rid of all this adrenaline. Thanks for gettin' me out of there. I was in danger of fallin' down.'

'I know, man. I saw a white man become a whole lot whiter – like a ghost, man, and I worked out that's what was happening. The shock dropped your blood pressure, that's all. Now run, Sam, run!'

Chapter Thirty-four

My pre-fight routine had become precisely that: routine. I had my stretching exercises, á la the lovely Jean Smith, the ballet instructor but no relation, and I had my mantra to stop any complacency. Then, once the gloves and the boots had been settled and were comfortable, the overall physical check was done by Charlie, the sit-down précis, then the last minute check of my eyes, which told everything there was to know about a boxer's state of mind to a good ring man, then I was alone.

My first thought was always of my family. I offered a prayer for their safety. It was evident that whatever was going on behind the scenes was being kept a secret from me, for which I was grateful. I remembered their leaving our home like thieves in the night, which was none of their doing, and none of mine. Somewhere out there were some greedy, faceless bastards who wanted to change my behaviour, and they were using and abusing my family to do it. *Thank you, Reg, for catching on to it so early. I'm missing them so much. Yes, Donna, 'I will go to work, and I'll really get this done!'*

Just then a man in gym clothes walked over to me and said very casually, 'You've been warned. Lose this fight if you want to see your family again, otherwise they're dead meat!'

It wasn't a hard punch from me. But he was on the floor in an instant and not moving. I went outside and motioned to the police officer assigned to me. He came at a run. I pointed and told him what the man had said.

'I'll take care of this, Sam. I'll get it sorted for you, and report it in.'

I sat down, put my head between my knees, pushing the mood I needed to the forefront of my mind.

We've got a great team who work so well together. I'd get it done for you too, guys! Just then my mind, all on its own, skipped to Yorkshire and my running around that beautiful countryside, and to my mates in Hereford in the SAS, who would normally be tuned in tonight. Maybe they wouldn't be tonight after my earlier phone call to them.

Now it was time to go. I had work to do. I was going to hurt that arrogant bastard who thought he could terrorise my wife and my little girls. The cheek of him! I was fizzing! I was first in the ring and watched Maxwell as he approached. He looked toned but had stress lines and sweat on his forehead already. I thought he may start with a burst of speed and a flurry of blows designed to put me on the back foot to intimidate me. It didn't matter because I knew he was going down. He was getting a pasting because of his blackmail attempt through the kidnapping of my little family. It was time to open the box that was hidden in that dark, deep corner of my mind.

Chapter Thirty-five

Town and city dwellers, for the most part, find the country weird and threatening. At night, that same country becomes really spooky, alien and distinctly sinister; hiding unnamed horrors in every shadow. There were no street-lights, no shop-front lighting, and no vehicle lights to create the albedo effect that ensured cities were never dark. 'Townies' got lost within minutes in the country, even in daylight, because of the lack of street signs and known landmarks like pubs or bookshops.

In this part of the English countryside, in the County of Shropshire that we're concerned with, which just happened to be next door to Herefordshire, the home of the SAS, the night air was still and cold. The sky was cloudless with a three-quarter moon bleaching all colour from the land-scape. Leaves, tree-trunks, branches and gates were black unless a glossy surface shone a tiny mote of reflected silvery-white light. The ground and other flat surfaces reflected the silvery moonlight that poets and romantics had worshipped for millennia.

A keen observer might have just noticed a patch of grey colour moving slowly across a field of silvery-grey grass towards a farmhouse. This patch was, in reality, a squad of six of the most highly trained SAS soldiers - some of the best in the world. They were at the same time stealthy, silent, yet somehow menacing.

At one point, the grey patch of six soldiers bunched together, split into two groups of three, and both changed directions. After several seconds, the front three slow-moving figures carefully approaching the farmhouse. The other three separated and surrounded the farmhouse, but at a distance, with angles of four, eight and twelve on a clock face. They appeared menacing in that they were each apparently carrying a very big and bulky stick or cudgel. These were, in fact, very accurate rifles complete with silencer and a night vision device known as an AN/PAS 2, which allowed quite reasonable vision at night, especially on a moonlit night like this.

At some point, all six figures stood still; their camouflage ensuring their virtual disappearance into the landscape. The three nearest the farmhouse then moved stealthily towards it, one to the front door and two to the back door. The remaining three started slowly circling inwards, giving off the chilling menace of predators closing in on their prey.

The two near the back door began to search the outer buildings for potential ambushers. When they opened the door of the second building, they saw four bodies lying on the floor, drenched in their own blood.

Increased tension developed within the group of six when the report of the bodies of four young police officers had been discovered and communicated to the rest of the team. There were also the remains of the police radios that looked as though they had been smashed underfoot. Fists were clenched, jaw-muscles bulged and teeth gritted as 'murderers' was added to the list of crimes attached to the six American criminals that an infrared device had identified, together with their positions, within the farmhouse. That anger fuelled speed, efficiency and emotion-free action.

The scene was set.

Chapter Thirty-six

'Good evening Ladies and Gentlemen. This is Bob Clarke from the BBC outside broadcast unit, coming to you live from Madison Square Garden, where our very own Sam Smith, the welterweight champion of the world, is having a long-awaited rematch with Trey Maxwell, the former champion. Good evening too, to Bill Fleming, my co-commentator. Do you have anything to report for us, Bill?'

'Good evening Ladies and Gentlemen. Yes, Bob, as you say, it's a long-awaited fight for us. Sam is looking good; what's the phrase, "Trim, taut, and terrific?" He's relaxed but standing completely still in his corner. He looks more like a nail – tough and indestructible. Trey Maxwell has, apparently, been training extremely hard for this fight, right up until yesterday, and I can't help thinking that a tapering-off time before a major event is beneficial. So, has that harmed his timing or his condition? We are about to find out. Back to you Bob.'

'Thanks, Bill. We're under starters orders, and I'm so looking forward to this fight.'

Bell!

'First round, and Maxwell comes out very quickly and throws a three-punch combo at Sam, which misses, and gets he one from Sam in return, which doesn't. I'd say from that exchange that Maxwell's timing is off by just a smidgen.

'Sam now attacks with two solid punches to the head, and a wicked third to the solar plexus, and yes I saw a reaction from Maxwell. Sam dances back, then circles until Maxwell starts to get the rhythm, then circles back leaving two great rights to Maxwell's body. Maxwell rushes forward throwing blows, four, five, six – all of which Sam dodges, but he gets inside Maxwell's defence, donating a fierce four-punch combo to Maxwell's body.

I'm now looking at the places that Sam is hitting. He usually dodges about and doesn't get hit in the first few rounds, dispensing fast, accurate punches later in the fight. He's changed his modus operandi tonight, and I wonder why? Again, Sam has gone for the body – a hard blow to the ribs, and another to the left kidney. I think Sam is aiming to make a mess of Maxwell. I wonder what has caused that?

'Maxwell comes in with a jab. Sam slips so Maxwell's left wrist is against Sam's neck for a moment as Sam punches his elbow in the wrong direction for that elbow to pivot. It's called 'hyperextension,' and if you'll forgive the expression, it hurts like hell! Sam's swift left to the bicep of Maxwell's left arm immediately follows that punch. Ouch! That's got to hurt too.'

Chapter Thirty-seven

The voice of one of the SAS soldiers near the front door of the farmhouse sang out, 'Milk and papers. Come and get 'em!' The door burst open, and an American emerged quickly, holding a handgun pointing into the dark. He immediately collapsed from a blow to the neck, and his gun was removed. He was dragged by his coat-collar, away from the door.

The back door was thrown open at precisely the same moment, and two more SAS soldiers in camouflage and balaclavas rushed in at two other American men with guns, who were just about to exit and circle round to the front. Two wrists were broken, two guns were removed. Two little shrieks of pain from two overwhelmed Americans were uttered, before both necks received sword-blows from the side, by two separate, tight, extended hands of those very practised soldiers. Two unarmed, unconscious bodies sank to the ground where they remained immobile. *Balletic,* thought both soldiers, smiling behind their balaclavas.

They were at the bottom of a short, but broad flight of stairs leading up to a newly installed loft or mezzanine, which looked quite large and carpeted. There was a slight movement at the top of the stairs, appearing to be more Americans with guns. There was a pause and silence.

The loft window in the roof had a fire-escape ladder leading down to the garden outside, which the 'Milkman' had climbed very quietly. From this window came three quick metallic taps from a hard object like a knife blade, and the two soldiers in balaclavas tore up the stairs to see two more Americans with handguns: both were looking up to identify the noise. Big mistake! Two American wrists were broken, two American handguns were removed, and two short shrieks pierced the night before those two Americans, now unconscious, were discarded like refuse over the balcony to the floor below. Their trajectories meant that they landed with a skimming action, resulting inevitably in deep carpet burns to their faces. Two balaclava-covered SAS heads nodded at each other.

The back door slammed shut, and one standing figure put his finger to his ear and spoke softly.

'One out, to you.' No reply was made or expected.

Three more figures were spotted by one of the SAS soldiers, cowering in the near darkness at the back of a large bed against the far wall under the low ceiling. Their legs were pulled up for protection, and their faces showed a high degree of fear. The soldier took off his balaclava revealing a military buzz cut and a beaming smile.

'Hello, Donna, Anna, Ella. My name is Tom. I know Sam, and we have come to get you safely out of here. Are you all right?'

Donna tremulously nodded that they were. Tom held up his hand for silence.

'Stay there for just a moment until I get the all clear.' He waited.

Across the field, the last American gangster was running, or more accurately, stumbling, away from the farmhouse. The only sound in the still air was the gasping of the stumbler's breath from his unfit body, but he had his gun. Nothing in the landscape appeared to change until suddenly, a light appeared right in front of the stumbling figure. It was a set of bright, white teeth, belonging to another of the SAS soldiers, which shone in the parody of a smile in the moonlight with, apparently, no visible means of support – such was the effectiveness of his face and costume camouflage. The gangster's wrist was broken, his gun was removed and, after his prolonged shriek of pain, he was guided back to the farmhouse by the SAS soldier, who put a finger to his ear and said, 'Got him'. There had been no shots, no disturbance, and, apart from the conversation with Sam's family, and some inconsequential screams, no noise.

Tom, the team leader, removed a radio from his pocket and said, 'Come and get them. Six stars and stripes, plus four in blue, plus three live innocents.' He turned to the rest of his squad and said, 'Cuff these Yankees! Believe it or not, Gentlemen, these six murderers have managed to summon up the courage to frighten a mother and her two little girls. And please note just how brave they are; they even needed handguns to do that!'

The SAS crack team, led by Sergeant Tom, secured plastic ties to the six American gangsters, whose broken wrists went unheeded amid cries of pain, pleas of innocence and prayers for mercy. Deafness too, seemed common in that area of Shropshire on that particular night for these particular American murderers, kidnappers and blackmailers. Perhaps their alien Yankee accents were too unfamiliar? It seemed more likely that their hopes, which were falling on deaf ears, had much more to do with the four dead police officers that had been found in an outhouse on a sweep search? Perhaps too, it was a case of everyone being far more concerned about the health and welfare of Sam's family rather than their six former jailers?

All in all, things were not looking good for these American criminals.

Chapter Thirty-eight

Bell!

'A bit going on in Round One, Bill?'

'Yes, Bob. I've not seen Sam like this before. There's something behind this. Sam always wants to win fights, of course. He is, after all, the consummate boxer. This evening, however, there's something else on his mind and he's out to hurt Maxwell. I take your point about where Sam is aiming his punches. I think Maxwell is soon going to be in a world of pain. Back to you Bob.'

Bell!

'Thank you, Bill. Sam is the first out for this, the second round of this fight. He immediately smashes a right through Maxwell's defence, right on the nose, and yes, I think it's broken, but there's no blood from it – yet! Maxwell throws a left jab, followed by a right cross, his stock-in-trade. Sam performs the mirror image of his attack on Maxwell's left arm, by using a short left to Maxwell's right elbow, then a right to Maxwell's right bicep. I'd say that has about halved Maxwell's attacking power, leaving Sam more chance to mess up his body. This is a vindictive Sam; one I haven't seen before. 'Vengeful' may be a better word, but Sam is starting to go for the body in earnest, and Maxwell is backing off, trying to protect himself. A wicked right upper-cut to the jaw by Sam, followed by a very fast left-right-left to the head leaves Maxwell staggering. A huge punch from Sam to Maxwell's midriff as he was leaning forward literally lifted Maxwell off the canvas. It's now obvious he can't get his breath. Sam attacks his right kidney with a short but wicked left, then a right to the jaw. Maxwell is in big trouble here.'

Chapter Thirty-nine

Several vehicles, including two ambulances, arrived quietly at the farmhouse a little time later. The first out was a uniformed police inspector. Sergeant Tom, the SAS team leader, met him.

'Good evening, sir,' he said, and saluted.

'Good evening, Tom,' said the inspector, returning the salute. 'Been having fun?'

'Yes, and no, sir. Yes, taking down these Yankee bastards – sorry sir, these American ne'er-do-wells, was a great pleasure for us. It was all done by the book, on time, and with not a shot fired from either side. They were expecting us, however, so we would really like to understand where the leak originated, if only to stop that happening again.'

'Of course, we'll get to the bottom of that one as soon as we can, and I'll be in touch, Tom. What else?'

'At a guess, you sent a bodyguard of three armed police officers to cover Donna and the girls, I suspect. When you didn't receive the hourly phone call, you sent someone to investigate. Is that right?'

'How would you know that?'

'Some bad news, I'm afraid. Come with me.'

The inspector followed the SAS sergeant to the out-house, where the four bodies were.

'Shot in the head, execution-style, if you were an American criminal, that is,' said Tom.

The inspector grimaced. 'Losing four young police officers is appalling. I'm relieved Sam and Reuben were able to call on you chaps. I'll see to it that those Yanks never see the light of day again. To kill four young officers and terrorise children just to win a boxing match is absolutely unforgiveable, no matter how much money is involved.'

'I agree wholeheartedly, sir. You'll have a detailed report from me on your desk as soon as I can get it to you. May I suggest you have a meeting with all involved at Sam's place, soon after he gets back from New York? None of our team needs to be there, of course, but you can give Sam and his team a watered-down version if you need to. Just let Sam know we played our part, please. We have a good relationship with that very talented young man. How did he go, by the way?'

'He is slaughtering Maxwell, almost literally, as we speak. Apparently, Maxwell was in on it and taunted Sam about his family at the weigh-in. Sam is battering Maxwell! Now, excuse me, sergeant, I have to see to my poor dead officers, and get those Yanks charged and housed. Busy night.'

'Thanks, inspector. We'll be off before anyone wants to talk to us. We were never here, of course.'

'Of course.' The SAS squad naturally fell in behind their sergeant as they faded into the countryside in silence, leaving no evidence they had ever been there.

Chapter Forty

Bell!

'Bill, I'm left flabbergasted by the ferocity of that round.'

'Yes, Bob, the exact word I was going to use. Sam's in a zone tonight, and after just two rounds, Maxwell is basically gone. Sam seems impregnable, and is deliberately hurting Maxwell, who is going to be an absolute mess when this is all over. Can he last another round with Sam in this mood? We'll see.'

Bell!

'Thanks, Bill, you ask a big question. That Maxwell is hurt is shown by the slow and tentative way he gets out of his corner. They've put some plaster over his nose, so I think it is broken. Sam's first punch is a straight right to the ribs followed by a left to the chin. Sam dances back just as Maxwell was thinking of counterattacking, but he dances in again and cracks Maxwell hard in the ribs again. I have a feeling that was a big enough punch to crack at least one rib, and I see Maxwell is starting to favour that side. Sam throws a left to the ribs on the other side, and a right to the head. The headshot was the kindest because it could have saved Maxwell from more pain to his body.

'This is a massacre by Sam. I've never seen him like this before. Something has got him really riled at Maxwell. There's another shot to the ribs, then both eyes come in for some attention from a quick two-punch combo. A three-punch combo lands to Maxwell's body. Sam dances back then delivers another, and another. Now Maxwell is on the ropes, and that means only one thing. A big uppercut from Sam means that Maxwell's head goes way back, but as he comes forward, Sam gives his best yet; he jumps in the air and, as he comes down, Sam delivers an incredibly fast right hook, crashing right on the "button". Maxwell is down. Yes, Maxwell is down. The Ref is counting, six... seven... eight... nine...OUT!

'Sam has beaten the ex-champion in an awesome display of power punching. That's as powerful as I have ever witnessed from any welterweight in my lifetime. Over to you Bill.'

'Bob, Ladies and Gentlemen, that fight has shown Sam's undeniable right to the title of World Welterweight Champion. His speed, power and accuracy have shown him to be among the greatest welterweights we have ever seen in the ring. In recent times there have been heroes, but I believe history will dictate that Sam will be in the Hall of Fame, right up there with the elites. That was an awesome display of power. Just totting up the potential damage: Maxwell has a broken nose, cracked ribs, probably on both sides, two eyes that are now both closed, but will end up doing passable raccoon impressions, I would think! Add two hyperextended elbows, both biceps in need of considerable repair, and possibly a ruptured spleen. Sam's final blow, the right to the chin, almost certainly broke Maxwell's jaw. There may, indeed, be kidney damage too. However, the most critical thing that Maxwell takes away from this fight is his broken spirit. He was demolished, and made to pay for something, it seems, which is unknown to everyone else at this time. Selfishly, I would have liked that fight to last the full twelve rounds.

'As for Sam, there's not a mark on him. He's not even breathing hard. In fact, he has more breath right now than I have. Maxwell, on the other hand, is still on the canvas. I think he's really hurt. Back to you Bob.'

'Thanks, Bill. That was a really nice description. All the razzamatazz that Americans love so much is in full swing. I'm looking forward to talking to Sam in the studio when we are all back in London. Wow, what a fight! Bill, you mentioned before the match that Sam looked like a "nail", standing in his corner. Frankly, I don't think you could have hurt Sam with a hammer tonight!

'Sam is being escorted out of The Garden by his ring man and trainer, Charlie Browne, who is a very talented man in his own right. Bob?'

'That's all from us on behalf of the BBC, until we have the privilege to bring you our next report. From Madison Square Garden, this is Bob Clarke and Bill Fleming returning you to the BBC Studios in London.'

Chapter Forty-one

Charlie fussed over me while I showered and changed. Just before we left the change rooms, he asked, 'Mind telling me what the hell that was all about? Last time, I saw you win the fight against Trey Maxwell. This time you have hurt him very badly. Why?'

'Charlie, remember what Maxwell said to me at the weigh-in, about not seeing my family again? Well, neither of us know the outcome of that yet, so there's no further info at the moment, but you will understand later. I'm absolutely terrified that my family 'ave been 'armed, but I won't know until we get 'ome. I knew from what Maxwell said that 'e was part of that, and in a way I was protecting my family.'

'Is there anything I can help you with now, Sam?'

'No Charlie, but thanks. Just stick close until we get back to London. It will all be sorted then.'

We got a cab back to the hotel, where Lou was waiting with a drink in his hand for me.

'Wow, Sam! What the hell did he say to ya?' asked Lou, manoeuvring me into a corner, hiding me with his big frame.

'Lou, 'e asked me at the weigh-in, "ow's your family?' And 'e told me they were not safe, and that I 'ad to throw the fight to get them back safely. 'e was smiling as 'e said it. Then I knew 'e was in on it. Nobody messes with my family, Lou. No one!'

'Yeah, Sam, I do understand. Listen, I'm a big man, and I used to be fast, but I would not have wanted to be in that ring with ya'll tonight. Maxwell is hurt real bad, but I guess he had it comin'. I mean, kidnappin' and blackmail? What the hell is this sport comin' to? Anyway, give my best to Reuben. And Sam, I owe ya. I cleaned up! Tell Reuben I'll be in London in about a month, an' we'll have a great dinner at the Dorchester – an' it's my treat. Tell him that. He'll probably go an' buy a pair of runnin' shoes to make sure he gets there first!' Again, there was that great, loud belly laugh that Lou was so well known for.

So many people – so many slaps on my back. I escaped and went to bed. Just before I turned in, I phoned Reuben's number. He answered almost immediately.

'Hello?'

'Reuben, it's Sam.'

'Oh! God bless you, Sam! You need to know about Donna and the girls. They are tucked up in bed right now. Their own beds! At home! I'll tell you the full story when you get home tomorrow, but they are fine, Sam, and so looking forward to seeing you again.'

'What 'appened?'

'Let's just say that your mates from Hereford saved the day. The Yankee connection sent over a bunch of nasties to "look after" Donna and the girls. They murdered the four Brit coppers guarding them. But your lads, led by Tom, took down the Yanks, who are spilling their guts about their gambling scheme as we speak. You gave Maxwell a severe beating, Sam. Why? You're not usually like that.'

'At the weigh-in, 'e asked about my family, Reuben, and 'e told me they weren't safe. 'e 'ad a knowing smile on 'is face. 'e told me to lose the fight if I wanted to see them again. So, 'e knew! That's why. I just wish 'e'd 'ave lasted for the twelve rounds and I could 'ave continued to demolish 'im! Tonight, they could 'ave given me six world champions, and I would've seen them all off. No one could 'ave beaten me tonight, and you can believe that.'

'I believe you. Get some sleep, Sam. I'll meet you and Charlie at Heathrow tomorrow, and I'll tell you everything at a full meeting the next day, at your place. I don't think Donna wants to leave her home at the moment. The girls are all fine, shaken, but unharmed, so you can relax now and sleep tight.'

Chapter Forty-two

I slept like a baby for twelve hours but woke with a crushing concern for Donna and the girls on my mind. I had breakfast with Charlie, got a cab to the airport and slept again on the plane. Woke to rain and wind. Welcome home, Sam.

There was a mob of fans with placards at Heathrow, and I spent about twenty minutes talking to them. I thanked them all, and then we met up with Reuben. We set off east, and then down the Edgeware Road for home.

My front gate was suddenly beside me. I leaped out of the car and raced indoors. I got thoroughly 'girled.' It has to be one of the greatest pleasures for any husband and father in the universe. It was a spectacular group hug with everyone wanting to touch everyone else, and never let go.

Charlie embraced me before going home to his pad.

'The Best!' was all he would say, slapping me on the back. I would guess it was a combination of the best time, the best fight, the best result, and possibly, the best boxer. He was a lovely man – surprisingly gentle for all his boxing background: slightly rough around the edges, but a lovely man, all the same.

Finally, we were left alone, with lots more hugs. To spend the maximum amount of time together, we got Indian takeaway. We spent the evening being close to each other. I kept asking the girls for memories of the three farms they visited, bringing the images back to see who had the better memory recall. Ella won that non-competition. It also diminished some of their fear surrounding the American bad guys, and the knowledge – but luckily not the experience – surrounding the deaths of the four British police officers. That, of course, was my sub-plot. I might have known that Donna, with her special little smile, would be way ahead of me. She totally understood and approved of what I was doing in trying to take the emphasis off the violence.

Finally, they went to bed after I told them I would definitely be there for breakfast with them tomorrow. They were still rattled and clingy, and I expected to be joined in our bed by one or both during the night. Hopefully, all that fear would leave them with the re-establishment of home, routine and safety.

Donna wanted to know about the fight. I told her I wasn't very proud of my role. I was just so angry that my family was at risk. I told her too that Trey Maxwell knew about the plot to blackmail me by kidnapping them, so I concentrated on him. Not that I wouldn't have liked the chance to focus my punching power on all the others too. Finally, we went to bed, in our safe home, with the echoes of violence receding to less substantial images and impact.

The following morning, the girls didn't go back to school, although they had their pre-prepared stories. I had a talk with them after breakfast that all the silly stuff they had been through was all over now, that we were all safe in our home, but it would take a little while for that to settle down.

We decided that the girls should have a few days at home with us. Hopefully it would be enough to help heal the potential for nightmares and other side-effects of the emotional trauma they'd been through. I could see the relief in their smiles, and Donna suggested they play in their bedroom for a while, which was the safest place in the world for them.

The gang all came around about eleven to debrief all the circumstances surrounding the fight. I was surprised and delighted to see Tom, the SAS sergeant team leader, and also a senior police officer, both of whom were accompanying Reuben. With Donna sitting in on the discussion, we started at the periphery.

'Reg, what's the news in your ear?' I asked.

'You really made a mess of Trey Maxwell, Sam. He's in hospital, and likely to remain there for weeks. May I ask you why you did that to him? Was it essential because, after all, it was only a fight? You only had to win, not to maim.'

'Right, Reg, everyone, please listen. At the weigh-in, Maxwell confronted me. I smiled and waved to 'im as I did in the first fight, which, if you remember, threw 'im off 'is game. 'e smiled back and asked me 'ow my family was. He said that I thought they'd be safe, but that "we have them, so just be a good little family man and lose the fight, or...!" That's 'ow, and when, I knew 'e was personally involved. 'e knew what was going on and 'ad condoned it. Kidnapping my little girls! I ask you.

'Somehow, my mind 'ad focused on punishing 'im. In truth, I'm not proud of that, but nobody messes with my girls. I did what I would have done to win the fight anyway, only 'arder, mainly because I could not believe that a world-ranked boxer would kidnap my children to get me to throw a fight. Also, a Yank in gym-gear came to me just before I was called to the ring, and said, "Lose the fight if you want to see your family again!" I think I must have punched 'im because 'e went down, and a Yank copper dealt with that.'

'Yes, Sam,' said Reg, 'I can see that now. I don't have a family, but if I did, I would like to think that I would defend them as fiercely and successfully as you did. Let me know when you need info on your next fighter, and I'll be there with bells on, mate.'

'Thanks, Reg. Tom, I'm delighted to see you again, and a 'uge thank you for rescuing my family from that bunch of American bad guys. Tell us about it, please, with all the details.'

'Sam, I'll give you everything I can, but do understand that there will be a heavily edited version for everyone else, which will not include our services.'

Tom told us about being called in for that job; how it was such a pleasure to take down these bad guys for Sam, and to rescue Donna and the girls. No details about the SAS modus operandi, just the successful takedown, no blood spilled, no shots fired, and minimal injuries.

He told us about the third choice of that Shrewsbury farm as a venue for Donna and the girls to be near to Hereford and the SAS HQ in order to get a minimal response time, should that become necessary. All the vehicles had been geared up before being called, so they were on the scene very quickly. The local police, who had failed to get a pre-arranged signal, had alerted them. Also, he told us about the discovery of the four bodies but left the details to the inspector.

'I wasn't going to attend this meeting, but the inspector thought I should, if only to congratulate Sam personally on his stunning win, and to thank him for topping up our Mess fund!' There was a big round of applause, which lifted the mood a lot.

It was the inspector's turn.

'Two days before your fight, six very nasty characters with American accents and loaded handguns turned up on the scene. They killed the three police officers guarding your family and smashed their radios. They kept your family indoors, with threats of pain, and even death, for any infringement of the rules they set down. One of those guys was, according to the girls, very creepy and interested in them particularly. Bless them, they have identified him, and we shall be paying him some exceptional attention, shall we say? When our police guard didn't check in on the hour, we sent someone to check. Again, there was no hourly communication. That's when Reuben called in the SAS boys, as suggested by Sam, before the fight.

'I don't have to tell you how sad we are at losing four young and promising police officers. Their funerals will be announced shortly, and we'll let you know the time and place, as I expect you would like to be there.'

'Yes, we'll all be there,' said Reuben.

'Reuben,' interrupted Sam. 'I would like to 'ave a meetin' with you and the police inspector after this, to sort out a way for me to say 'ow sorry I am that these families 'ave lost loved ones. If they 'ad children, I would be very 'appy to pay for their private education for as long as they need. If they didn't 'ave children, I'd like to discuss with the inspector 'ow

I can 'elp in a practical way, like paying off their mortgage. I don't just want to say 'ow sorry I am that this whole episode became so bloody. We don't 'ave a gun culture in these fair Isles, and we find it shockin' when we come face to face with a society that does. But I need 'elp with that, is what I'm sayin', to do this right. I'd like to visit the families with Donna to tell them 'ow sorry we are. Do you have time after this meetin', Inspector?'

'Yes, Sam, I do, and I thank you for your concern. It was a bad business, but we will all do our best in these circumstances.'

'Some good news is that the FBI is rounding up all those bad guys on their side of the pond, who were involved in what has turned out to be a huge criminal betting syndicate. We haven't single-handedly cleared the FBI's books, but we've taken their caseload down by a large percentage. The courts, however, are going to be fully employed for the foreseeable future. So, if you ever go back to the States, Sam, there would be some extraordinary privileges available to you. Of course, I wouldn't be silly enough to go anywhere near Las Vegas, if I were you.'

'Thank you, inspector. I get the impression that I won't be invited to the US of A at any time soon, 'avin' been rather effective, shall we say, against one of their best.'

'Only one thing remains unexplained to me,' I said to the inspector. 'How did the Americans find my family, after their move to three different locations?'

'Yes, we had that puzzle too. By logic, it had to be Mr Goldstein.'

'WHAT?' he roared, jumping out of his seat. 'How bloody dare you say that?' He approached the inspector menacingly, who held up his hands for calm.

'Steady on, sir. I didn't mean that you, personally, gave the game away, but your phone did. Mr Goldstein is, of course, in no way responsible for any of that.

'The Americans came to Britain illegally by flying into a private airfield. They were part of an organisation based in Las Vegas that had contacts over here, one of whom was particularly good at spy craft. They illegally entered Mr Goldstein's home and placed a bug in his phone and were thus able to identify all the conversations between all the parties, so they knew where, when, who, and how many they had to deal with. They knew about the police personnel, and the SAS boys. That, in my book, makes the SAS takedown even more impressive since they were expected.'

'On my life, I'm so sorry, Sam, Donna. I wouldn't have allowed that to happen if I could have done anything about it, but I didn't know, honestly!' He was almost in tears.

'Reuben promised that my family would be safe, and so it came to pass. When I get free of "stuff" again, I'll send a nice present to the SAS boys, with a great big "Thank You!"' I said.

'Charlie? What are your thoughts?' I asked, trying to get Reuben away from the limelight. He felt bad enough. I had also noticed that Tom had moved to intercept Reuben if that had become necessary.

'There has been rather a lot going on, in case anyone missed it! My job, as I saw it, was to keep Sam on the straight and narrow towards the fight, and not let him get distracted by other "stuff". I needn't have worried. He dealt with what he had to, then switched that off, concentrating only on the fight. It wasn't so much a fight as a demolition. Sam has never punched so hard or so accurately. Maxwell had no chance at all. He never has had the skills to challenge Sam, nor defend himself from such an onslaught, so he went down hard. That was the best fight, and overall this has been the best time I've ever had in the fight game. I'm so proud to have been associated with you, Sam, and very grateful to everyone else.'

'Thank you, Charlie. We're a good team, you and I, and we work well together. There's never been a cross word between us, and I've learned a lot from you. We 'ave some plans, yes?'

'They would be great to explore.'

'What plans?' asked Reuben brusquely, still angry, feeling responsible, and not a little left out.

'We'll talk later,' I told him. 'But don't worry, they will include you.'

'Art, what have you got to say?'

'Well, kid, I gotta tell you, that was the biggest beating I've ever seen anyone get in a boxing ring. From what you say, it was well deserved. But boy! He is in a world of pain right now, and he won't look so good even when he does get out from under his medical care. I'm pleased for his sake that the fight didn't go twelve rounds. He'd have been dead by five. Sam, Reuben, where does that leave me?'

'We'll need you to find fighters and venues into Sam's future,' said Reuben. 'You had mentioned earlier to Sam, at the stage of development he was then, that he would have a rough time with the top ten fighters in his weight category. We need those fighters to try their luck with Sam. Probably, it would be wise to leave it a while for current affairs to settle down a bit, yes? This team is good, we work well together, and we should stay together. All the pressure is off, but we need to regroup. I'm going to get myself a secretary to handle all the stuff that comes in for Sam.'

'Donna could 'andle that role,' I said quickly, 'if that's all right by you.'

'I would be more than happy with that arrangement, Sam. She's clever, quick and knows a bit about office machinery, and she can type. I was thinking about starting a fan club for you, but she would be the best person to keep that under control. What do you say, Donna?'

'It would be wonderful to be part of this team. Sam hasn't had the exposure he needs or deserves, so I might subcontract a marketing team. They can do press releases and news items. We will contribute magazine articles, giving Sam a much bigger profile, and an even bigger income from his boxing.

'We'll organise some endorsements too. There's lots of money to be made there, which requires extremely little work, apart from looking good and taking direction at a photo shoot. Gentlemen, I give you the real-life examples of the Beatles and the Rolling Stones, and Stirling Moss and Jim Clark in the Grands Prix championship. They make a fortune by endorsing expensive items like watches and car brands. If anybody has any ideas at all, please pass them through me, and I'll explore them.'

'See?' said Reuben, 'she's lost me, already.'

'Well,' I said. 'I feel like 'avin' a month off to settle our family down. I think a little trip abroad would be nice, with some sunshine and a beach with warm water. The west coast of Barbados calls. When I was in Jamaica, I 'eard about a 'otel right on the beach there called the Sandy Lane 'otel. It came 'ighly recommended, so we'll try that for a while. I'd take Reuben, but 'e doesn't look like a "beach" sort of person in 'is 'omburg 'at and pinstripe trousers. 'e would stand out like a total sore thumb and give 'olidaying Brits an even worse image than they 'ave already!

'After that, I'll get into training for my next fight in about three months. Art, we'll choose an American, but 'e will have to travel to us, and the purse will have to be 'uge. Charlie and I have a gym to design and build, with Reuben's help – and financial contribution, of course!'

There was much laughter from this band of brothers plus one sister. I took Donna's shoulders, looked into her eyes, and saw some caution but mainly hope, so I didn't need to ask her about the future.

This article is reproduced courtesy of:
Boxing Weekly Magazine
By Bill Fleming ©
BBC Boxing Commentator
June 1966

Last year, I wrote an article about the fight between Trey Maxwell, then the world welterweight champion, and Sam Smith from Whitechapel in London. Sam dominated that match to take the world championship away from Trey Maxwell at Madison Square Garden. I said in that piece that we had witnessed a 'masterful demonstration of boxing skill'.

Well, in truth, this return match about a year later, which was also held at Madison Square Garden, was arguably the most dominant, the most aggressive, and the most one-sided boxing match in history at world championship level. I'll give you some credentials for my being able to make a statement like that.

I'm in my late fifties and have been following boxing matches, individual boxers and venues since I was five, to the exclusion of almost everything else - just ask my wife! Only one man I know is more knowledgeable and dedicated than I am, and he's another Londoner, called Reg - and no, I don't remember his last name.

My employment by the BBC for many years to attend the main boxing matches throughout the world has been a real privilege. Together with my friend and co-commentator Bob Clarke, whose voice quality and knowledge of radio protocol make him the lead commentator, we share a common love and understanding of the boxing game.

Having said all that, I have to tell you that we witnessed the most ruthless demolition of a former world champion, at any weight in recent history, when Sam Smith had a rematch with Trey Maxwell last week. Sam has always been super fit, but for his first match with

Trey Maxwell, he was also super-hard too. His training programme was kept secret, but he was arguably in absolute top condition for that fight. However, his actual condition for the rematch was slightly down on that, but it was more than compensated by his dedication, his need to dominate and his total focus on winning.

During that fight, I referred to Sam as being 'vengeful', which was an astute and true description, although unbeknown to me at the time.

Anyone who had any interest in this fight will by now have either seen it originally, or caught up with the innumerable replays of what happened and will agree with me that 'savage' was the appropriate word I thought of at the time to describe it. I asked myself, 'Why would Sam try to assassinate Trey Maxwell? It was a boxing match, after all.'

Sam Smith is a family man. He is a gentle, friendly, and loving man away from the ring. So, what could have provoked this attack?

Well, Ladies and Gentlemen, I have now been told why all that unfolded as it did, and I can tell you this much.

Since his first fight with Trey Maxwell, Sam has not been beaten. He was, in fact, virtually unbeatable. Consequently, he was at very short odds to beat Maxwell in their rematch. This means that the odds on Maxwell winning the match were long. A group of American criminals - not to beat about the bush - thought they could make a vast amount of money by influencing the outcome of that fight. How could they do that?

It is known that Sam is as straight as a die, and you can't bribe him. So, you find out his weak points and you attack those, a strategy every good boxer knows.

A cartel of American criminals went for Sam's family and kidnapped them, even though they had been taken to a place of safety. At the weigh-in on the day before the fight, Maxwell confronted Sam, and, while smiling, asked him how his family was? He also told Sam his family was not safe and would not be safe until Sam lost the fight. That was how Sam knew that Maxwell was in on the kidnapping and blackmailing scheme. It was a totally stupid thing for Maxwell to do, giving away his complicity unnecessarily.

One of the conspirators confronted Sam in the change room immediately before the fight, telling him that if Sam wanted to see his family again, he should lose the fight. Sam flattened him too! And THAT, Ladies and Gentlemen, is the reason that Sam did what he did to Maxwell. In his mind, I think he believed he was protecting his wife, Donna, and their two little girls from Maxwell-the-Monster, who had threatened to kill them just to win the fight. Looked at objectively, this was a totally insane way to make a lot of other people rich by illegal means. It was over-planned, over the top, and over here.

Sam could have thrown the fight. He could have made it easy for Maxwell to win, but he had friends and resources backing him in England that he trusted to protect his family. That's why Sam 'went for the jugular' so to speak, and why you will almost certainly never witness such a beating of a boxer in a boxing ring at that level, ever again. My comments of 'vengeful' and 'like a nail, straight and unbendable' were totally justified when that background came to light.

There are quotations in the literature of such events: 'Revenge is a confession of pain;' 'Revenge is a dish best eaten cold;' and, 'Revenge is not a noble sentiment, but it is a human one.'

To finish this on a happy note, I can report that Sam's wife, Donna, and his girls, Anna and Ella, are safe and well. They are all reunited and unharmed. Art Dutton is going to be arranging fights for Sam into the foreseeable future. Reg will continue his lifelong study of the pugilistic arts, mostly at the Waterloo pub, not far from Sam in London.

Meanwhile Sam, Charlie Browne and Mr Reuben Goldstein are planning to build a boxing centre and gym – a teaching and mentoring facility for boys and girls who are, in some way, disadvantaged. I suspect that Sam may also take some top boxing talent under his wing to promote British boxing to the world.

There is, in all this, a circular train of thought, making a complete joke of Arthur Taylor's comments at Heathrow Airport, when he said, 'Nothing of any value to the boxing world ever came out of the UK!' (I'd like to see that rematch!)

Bob Clarke and I will follow Sam Smith's career with great interest, and bring you descriptions of his future fights, courtesy of the BBC outside broadcast unit.

Bill Fleming from Madison Square Garden.

Chapter Forty-three

Lou's great booming laugh bounced off the beautiful wood panelling around this very high-class, private dining room at the Dorchester Hotel in Mayfair. In English, Mayfair is spelled, 'M-o-n-e-y', and this hotel was the ultimate machine for extracting the most money from the people who have the most! It's proved very successful in doing that over a long period of time.

We were all gathered for dinner here, courtesy of Lou of 'The Garden' fame. Reuben was giving the first of many toasts that evening to me and my family, to Art, Charlie, and Reg as team members; to Lou, Bob Clarke and Bill Fleming as Home and Overseas Communications, and to Tom, the SAS team leader, and the police inspector, as security. We were a little group of thirteen people who had, as a team, helped to win and defend a World Championship Boxing Title. Most had also survived some extremely nasty criminal behaviour.

'Here's to Sam, first and foremost, for his work ethic, his talent and his patience, without which we would not be rich and not be here,' said Reuben. 'Here's to his loving family, who have always makes us all so very welcome. To the team backing Sam; to the two 'B's' for taking such an interest in Sam, and to Tom and his team plus the police inspector, who allowed us to survive a seriously bad situation. And finally, to Lou's generosity, allowing us to gather together in such beautiful and expensive circumstances. Here's to each and every one of us!'

Lou stood. 'My friends, when I met 'little' Sam, 'little' compared to me that is, I thought there wasn't much to him. Then he opened his mouth, and pure 'boxing' language came out of it. He knew – in the way that only old souls in the boxing fraternity know – not just the terminology, but the feelings of the fight, the sense of cunning, of attack and defence. He knew the internal reality – not the press-release reality. He was also totally aware of the sweat, dedication, an' the discipline needed for prolonged hard work. He has the sense of individuality that allows him to stand alone, having done the work an' learned the lessons; takin' with him that confidence wherever he went. That he is a loving husband and father I have no doubt. However, to do all *that* successfully, *an'* to be able to stand alone among a very select peer-group, means that Sam is doubly blessed. You are a wonderful man Sam Smith, and I envy ya, more than I can say.

'This little party is to say a big "thank ya'll" to everyone involved in making me a tremendous amount of money, extracted with great glee from some very unscrupulous men, in a hitherto reasonably scrupulous game. So, all those bad men are financing this evening, and frankly, I delight in that. Enjoy, Ladies and Gentlemen. And Sam, just keep doing what ya'll are doing, and I am always here at any time to he'p ya, in any way I can, OK? Cheers everyone!'

It seemed like my turn was due. I hadn't prepared anything but felt very strongly about this group of people, so I decided to 'wing' it.

'I realise, and I 'ope you do too, that I could not 'ave achieved what I 'ave, without each and every one of you. Donna, you are my rock, and, with Anna and Ella, you totally fulfil the softer side of my life. I guess if I were a 24/7 thug, I wouldn't need that, but you define the real me and I love you all.

'When I'm not thinkin' of you, there's Reuben, another rock to lean on. His knowledge of the ways of the world balances my naivety – and all 'e needs is money! That's not strictly true, as you will also know, and our family is there for you too. Art, Charlie, Reg, I think Reuben chose very wisely, and I 'ope our little team will stay together and prosper in more ways than just money.

'Bob and Bill, your insightful reporting 'as not done me, or my image, any 'arm at all, as my growin' fan base will tell you, so my thanks to you both. It's great to be able to share some time with you, out of the public eye. Also, Tom, you and your squad saved my family when I was unable to be there for them. Tom, please say, "Hello, and thank you" to the squad when you get back. My very grateful thanks go to you and the police for what you have done for me and my family. Enjoy this evenin'.

'Lou, many thanks for this evenin', and for bringin' "our gang" all together for the first time. That the bad guys are payin' makes it so much sweeter but thank you anyway. I 'ave a feelin' that we'll be in close contact over a project that Charlie and I are just startin' to think about. Ladies and

Gentlemen, please raise your glasses to boxin', and our success!'

Donna left early with the girls, who everyone treated very gently, and the 'boys' were left to themselves.

'What's this project ya'll have in mind?' asked Lou.

'That's Americans for you! About as subtle as 'ouse bricks! Well, Lou, since you brought it up, my life after boxin' 'as to be considered, and Donna and I 'ave 'ad to do the considerin'.

'Usin' my world championship as a platform, I should be able to attract and mentor a stable of British boxers who are the cream of the crop. If my sponsorship brings results to one or more becomin' world champions too, that would be a good thing for boxin' in general, and British boxin' in particular. It may 'elp to pay for trainin' some disadvantaged girls and boys, too. To 'elp with this, I thought "we" could build a facility that included an extensive gym, which would be open to the general public, 'ave several boxin' rings, and a lecture theatre with a projector for lessons and talks. We could design some dedicated space for mentorin', discussion groups and so on. Some of the facilities and space can be rented out when not bein' used. Charlie wants to mentor, as do I, and we both have knowledge and experience to offer.

'I 'ave no details about where or what size or even 'ow much. I do know that if we run out of cash, I can have another fight. We'll bank the proceeds, I'll 'eal, and we'll get on with the project. I'd like to do this on a share basis. Those who want in will be given shares to the amount they invest. Then profits, should there be any, will be given out in that ratio, and please! Would someone stop me before I start to sound like an accountant.

'Sorry, but I didn't realise that my "backroom," or "subconscious" to you, 'ad been so active in this area. If you 'ave any thoughts about this, perhaps you would jot some ideas down on the back of an envelope, and let me, or preferably Donna, 'ave them at your convenience?

'In answer to your offer, Lou, maybe there's something like that already in America that Charlie and I could come over and 'ave a look at? Anyway, that's the hint of a plan, which may or may not become a reality.'

Everyone started talking at once, and the whole party began to deteriorate into a free for all. Wild ideas were thrown around. 'Adapt, adopt or discard,' I once heard, and this seemed appropriate to our ever more alcohol-fuelled creations.

Tom, Charlie, the police inspector and I left the rest to carry on as we tried to rescue our sanity and our livers and took taxis home. Just before Tom and I parted ways, I asked him what he was goin' to do, post–SAS.

'Sam, you must be a mind reader because it's something I've been concerned about for a while now. I have about six weeks left in the Service, and then I'm on the street. Why?'

'When you get out, will you come and see me, please. I think there's a way to use your services for our security, 'ave you teach some stuff you know, and learn more about bankin' and personal security, and proper ways to protect all our paperwork and our personnel, for example. I'm tryin' to think long-term, and our organisation is goin' to need those services, which, if you can learn, you can also teach. That approach will give you short, medium and long-term employment in something you obviously enjoy. Think about it and get back to me. It could save you from thrashin' around in tropical jungles – unless, of course, you want to thrash around in tropical jungles?'

'Thanks, Sam. That appeals more than you would believe, because I have a young lady in the background. I would like to see her more often and, as you so rightly say, thrashing around in tropical jungles is not conducive to true love. I'll be in touch, and thanks again.'

'I'd like some idea of your skills, your thoughts, and your wishes. I like 'appy people around me, so let's see if this can work. You might like to write me a small summary, nothin' formal, and we'll talk.'

Lou, Art, Reuben, Reg and the two 'B's' made the most of a unique opportunity to discuss boxing for a whole night. They moved to a private bar, and saw the night out with stories, reminiscences, lies, jokes and even more stories. Reuben and Reg were absolutely in their element. Lou and Art contributed the most, while the B's gave their British perspective, easily holding their own.

That was a night to remember, for everyone.

Chapter Forty-four

Over the next three weeks a huge number of phone calls were exchanged, many thanking Lou for his generosity. There were others about our plans, which I gave over to Donna to start a file of ideas, which may or may not be useful in the long run. At one point, Charlie, Reuben, Donna and I had a meeting at our house so we could throw these suggestions around and come up with what looked like a viable business plan.

We certainly had enough money to do a whole feasibility study to make sure the concept was sound, what it would cost, how it would be paid for, and how we could charge to get some money back. It was a fascinating exercise. We tried to predict what it would look like in five years and ten years, and what the money flow would look like. Then we came back to the original motivations for the idea of continuing to do what we enjoyed. If we didn't make an absolute fortune that would be okay too, because we would be working in an environment we could control, that is, be the bosses, and be busy doing something we thoroughly enjoyed. Not many people in the world get to control those choices.

Lou phoned to say that there was a place in New York where a woman had started the sort of thing that he thought we had in mind. He gave us the address, said he had contacted the owner who, of course, was a friend of his, and had made an appointment for the fifth of the month for us to look over this facility and meet the owner.

I cleared with Donna that Reuben, Charlie and I would be spending two nights away to have a look at possibly our future, and yes, I'd bring lots of photos home.

We flew out on the fourth. This was to be my treat to say a big 'thank you' to Charlie, and in part make up for the huge investment that Reuben had made in me. While the hotel was lovely, it was nothing compared to the Dorchester, but we were comfortable. I took all four out to dinner to a place that was Lou's recommendation. It was another great night of stories.

In the morning, we went to 'Gym Plus,' as I thought of it. Lou introduced us to the owner, Anne, a lovely redhead with knowing eyes. She must have experienced quite a lot in that environment. She was a younger version of Rhonda Fleming, quite beautiful, but very much in control.

'So, this is the "Boy Wonder",' she said. I put a small smile on my face and extended my hand. She shook it hard, looking into my eyes as she did.

I smiled even wider and said, 'Good morning, Anne. Thank you for your time. I 'ear you 'ave a gym that caters for both men and women, and we're thinkin' of doin' somethin' similar in London. We'd be very grateful for some 'elp.'

'Well, as a boxer, you made a real mess of our world welterweight. I wouldn't have believed it if I hadn't been there. To have won would have been enough; you didn't need to slaughter him, even if you could. Why the hell did you do that?'

'Anne, I 'ave to tell you that I'm not proud of my performance that night, but 'e was on the inside of plans by a bunch of bad–boy Americans from Vegas to kidnap my family. They did this to blackmail me into losin' the fight. I took my rage out on the man because 'e told me 'e was part of it, without realising how deeply it ran. It'll certainly never 'appen again. But I will win again,' I assured her.

'Well, well, well,' she said. 'You do run deep. OK, Sam, what can I help you with?'

'How long can you spare me?' I asked.

'As long as you like, "World Champ!" Seriously, whatever you want from me concerning time and information, it's yours.'

'Anne, I 'ave in mind to build a place where I can mentor the cream of the boxing crop in Britain, as well as take care of some disadvantaged children. I want space for lectures, displays and so on. There'll be spaces for mentoring, which could just be some comfortable chairs and a coffee machine, with a degree of privacy. There'd be a 'uge, clean and airy gym for both men and women in a safe environment. Basically, this is what I'd like to do after I 'ang up the gloves.

'Charlie 'ere, is my trainer and ring man, so, together with my boxin' experience, we 'ave a strong foundation for all this. This is our retirement project idea, so the fact that you are a step ahead of us could mean savin' us a lot of time and mistakes, and a 'eap of money. Maybe, some shortcuts, too. We're at the very early plannin' stage, and anything you can 'elp us with would make us very 'appy.'

'You Brits have such lovely ways of saying things. OK, here's how this will go. I'll show you what we've got and what we're doing with it. Then we'll talk about where it came from, how it was financed, the basic business plan, and how that worked. Also, how we could have done much better, and where we're hoping to go. I'll tell you what the market is, over here anyway, and how our costing works. Then, I'll take you into the realm of hope about where we'll be in five years and ten years' time, at which point you can all take me out to dinner!'

'Wow! That would be fab, Anne. We'll be all ears, especially Mr Goldstein 'ere, who "does" money! Charlie can visualise many things, internal plans among them, so let's go.'

Lou said, 'Anne, excuse me. I've seen your place, but I'll meet ya'll for dinner. This will be Sam's treat in gratitude for all that hard-earned information you're going to give him.'

'Yeah, Lou, see you tonight.' When he had gone, Anne said, 'He's one lovely man. If he was twenty years younger and half his weight, I might just encourage him. Now, to business. Sam, have you ever started a business before?'

'No, but Mr Goldstein 'ere has.'

'What's your ratio of win to lose? And what is your name? I can't keep calling you Mr Goldstein, it sounds altogether too Teutonic; and a name like Goldstein makes me feel almost guilty.'

'It's Reuben, but not R-e-u-b-e or R-u-b-e.'

'OK Reuben, what's your ratio?'

'I've got three businesses that have made it past the five-year mark, and two that didn't. The two came first, and the three later.'

'That makes sense, and good work. Walk with me, and I'll talk as we go.'

We looked over Anne's business, and I saw things I liked, and things I didn't, or thought I could improve upon. I took photos of everything, havin' first got Anne's permission. They were for Donna and the project, for which we hadn't yet got a name. 'Sam's Slammer' was probably funny the first time, but I sensed it wouldn't be good commercially. That could wait.

The day whirled away with endless coffee, talk, suggestions, flow-charts, licences, taxes, profit and loss accounts, key-indicators and more. Anne really knew her stuff, and I hoped that Reuben was keeping all this information in a safe file in his head.

Finally, when my head was about to burst, Anne left for her apartment upstairs to change for our dinner together. We went in a cab and met Lou at a not very nice-looking place.

'It may not look much,' said Lou, 'but you'll get full value from the food and the wine.'

I needed a glass of good red wine after all the coffee and talk, and asked the waiter for his recommendation. He suggested a French Burgundy, which by chance seemed to suit everyone's taste. I started talking about Donna and the girls, and the large number of photos I'd taken today for them and the team to look at, and to act as discussion points.

Since the Americans do steaks really well, and as this was by way of a treat for Anne and Lou, that was what most of us decided upon, with baked potatoes and lashings of salty butter, and a touch of salad to keep me healthy. The wine? It had a Wow Factor. I'm not usually a dessert eater, but chocolate profiteroles, covered in praline and filled with clotted cream was probably a once-in-a-lifetime indulgence. Anne had that self-satisfied look one gets after a good meal in good company. She said, 'Thank you, Sam. That was definitely worth the time and information I gave you today.'

'Anne, if we ever do get our project up and runnin', I'd love for you and Lou to come over to the openin'. I also 'ad a thought today that since we'd be the first to do this, you 'ere, and me in the UK, we may, much, much further down the track, possibly think of a franchise connection. It would basically cost us nothin' financially but could reap rewards for both of us, for the cost of a little trust and cooperation. You've shown your trust and cooperation today; now we'll 'ave to demonstrate our trust so that you can 'ave faith in us too. But that's a long, long way ahead. Any thoughts?'

'Sam, there are some things I know about life. One is that you do not get a happy wife, a happy husband with two equally happy kids if there is not a great degree of trust, to the point that honesty is something that is taken for granted. So, apart from some sort of meltdown beyond your control, you already have my trust. And please, give Donna my best. I look forward to meeting this lucky lady!'

We caught the flight back the following day, with ideas swirling around about the scale, the cost, the location, the money, and so on and so forth. I was seriously wondering whether I had bitten off more than I could chew. It was also about time I started to think about my next fight, too. We'd need some lead time, and then some serious discussions about the location and the cost of the new gym with Charlie and Reuben. This would give me an idea about how many fights I would need to have in order to finance this project that was in severe danger of getting way out of hand. Even though the money from fights at my level was astronomical, so were the taxes, and the cost of land and building in London. The cost of the land could be recouped in a sale, but, if the structure was too specialised, it might affect that price should we ever have to sell it. This whole project was a way of putting an asset into our pocket rather than just giving a large chunk of money to the government as a tax for them to play with, or squander.

Chapter Forty-five

It was obvious that my fights had brought in a life-changing amount of money, but if we were going to follow our long-term dream, we'd need much more. So, I had to go back to work at what I knew best, as long as I didn't get my block knocked off!

The other thing that suddenly came to mind was that my head was all over the place from being involved in the thousand and one details needed for all these changes. So, I needed to knuckle down with no distractions to do some serious ring work.

The front doorbell sounded. I opened it to find a sort of familiar face that I couldn't immediately identify.

"ello,' I said.

"ello, Mr Smith,' he said, smiling, and leaving the pause to extend. He knew I didn't know his name, and he let me dangle.

'Gotcha!' I said. 'Wally Shaw. I didn't recognise you without your gloves on. Come in. Coffee for you? I'm about to 'ave a cup, and do call me Sam.'

'OK, and thanks to both.'

We settled on the couch.

'What are you doin' with yourself, Wally?'

'A bit of this and that with some training in a gym near me.'

'You did very well against me. I'm proud of you. Where do you live, Wally?'

'Balham.'

'What do you want to do with your life, Wally?'

'I'd like – no, I need to be a boxer like you, and kick arse at the very top!'

'How do you propose to do that?'

'At this particular moment, I 'ave a very positive attitude about things, and 'ave a feeling that my dream will 'appen. From the outside it looks very slim, I would agree, but I live in 'ope. And, you did ask me to contact you. I thought havin' an invitation over a BBC TV programme from a world champion boxer was really cool. I got some major "street-cred" for that.'

'You should 'ave got your "street-cred" for your boxin' performance. That was outstandin'.'

'Thanks, Sam.'

''ave you got anything on at this moment, Wally?'

'No.'

I picked up the phone and dialled Reuben.

'Reuben, Sam here. I 'ave Wally Shaw with me, and it would be a great idea if you could come 'ere for a chat with 'im. What do you think?'

'I think that would be a good idea. Do we know where he will fit in? Yes or no.'

'No.'

'Good, so no promises, and we have time. I'll be right over.'

Reuben arrived about ten minutes later and was welcomed with an introduction to Wally Shaw.

'Hello, Wally, you made an excellent fist of your fight with Sam. First, some questions, if that's all right with you.'

'Yeah, sure,' said Wally, bracing himself a bit.

'How old are you, what do you weigh and where do you live?'

'Twenty, around 145, and Balham.'

'What do you want to get out of boxing?'

'I told Sam: to kick the daylights out of whoever is at the top of my weight division.'

'And afterwards, Wally? After you become a world welterweight champion, what then? That's after Sam has hung up his gloves of course. What do you want to do then?'

'Well, boxin' is all I really know. School and I didn't see eye to eye. I can read, write and do arithmetic, but readin' a boxer's ability and 'ow 'e will go about fightin' you, is excitin' and easy for me. I so nearly 'ad Sam! Maybe an extra two- or three- 'undredths of a second and I would 'ave got that last punch in, and it would 'ave been all over. I 'ave no idea how you got me first, but that taught me a lot. Sorry, I got a bit off track there. So, I want to stay in boxin'. Doin' what, I'm not sure.'

'What trainin' have you 'ad, Wally?'

'None of what you could call "formal training", but I've watched fights, 'ad some fights in the gym, and I seem to know instinctively what the other boxer is goin' to do. I 'ave no idea where it comes from, but right now you are thinkin' of throwin' out a quick left to see how my reflexes are. Correct?'

'How the 'ell did you do that, Wally?'

'Watched and knew, somehow.'

'Write down your address and phone number, and we'll be in touch. Don't get your hopes up yet. Our plans are long term. Do you have a job that brings you in enough money to live?'

'Yes, Mr Goldstein. And a thousand thanks for giving me a chance to fight Sam. If I go nowhere else in my life, I will cherish that experience.'

'Wally, you did very well and showed a lot of heart, and that really counts in the boxing fraternity. I'm sure we'll be in touch with you, but it may not be for some time, so be patient.'

'Thanks, Mr Goldstein, Sam. I look forward to our next meetin'.'

When he had gone, I asked Reuben what he thought.

'He's a promising young man, not only as a boxer, but there are some good personality traits and some manners in there. What twenty-year-old these days uses a word like "Cherish"? No, there's some good stuff in there. I'll think about him. At twenty years old, he's way ahead of where you were, Sam. Sorry, facts are facts!'

'I know, and I could get quite attached to 'im in a brotherly sort of way. His intuition that I was goin' to throw a left was spot on, and 'e knew it almost before I did. What about some tent work? 'e could be quite charmin', but 'e will have to be taken out of 'is current crowd. They're keeping 'im down.

'What do we know about 'im? 'e responded to my invitation. At twenty, 'e very nearly put down a seasoned world champion. 'e's personable, well-mannered and 'as bags of potential. We do know that 50p plus "potential" will buy you a cup of coffee, but 'e very nearly beat me, so there's some good stuff there. That just leaves: what do we want 'im for, and how do we train 'im?'

'I'll think about it and get back to you. Then, we'll have a meeting of the whole gang with Wally, to see what they think. Incidentally, where are you at?'

'A good question, and it's one that I was thinking about when Wally rang the doorbell. I've been so involved in all the changes that my 'ead is bein' used as an egg whisk. I need to get my fitness up and get into the ring again. Most importantly, I need to leave all the 'detail-itis' behind and start focusin' again. I'd be slaughtered by very average boxers in my present state.'

'I doubt that, but I take your point. I'll get a local lad for a match soon, say a month, so you'd better get your skates on. I'll ask Art to see if a contender is available to come here for a championship fight say, in two months' time. How would that suit?'

'That's about right. I'll get on to Charlie, and get Donna to take over all the decision-making except the big bits. Think about young Wally. 'e could be useful as a sparring partner, yes?'

'Absolutely, but think about some long-term plan for him, then we'll talk sparring.'

A most productive meeting was that. Donna was at her new desk when I found her, talking to an attractive, statuesque redhead. She introduced her as Margaret, who ran a slick and professional marketing group.

'Nice to meet you, Margaret,' I said.

'So, you are the product we have to sell and promote. Donna, this is going to be the easiest money I've ever earned. He's yours, right?'

'Oh! Yes, he is really mine, and don't you even cast a look in his direction, or you and I are going to have words, Margaret, in a ring, with no rules, girl!'

'Donna, please trust me when I say I have my own preferences, and he's not one of them. He looks yummy, but he's safe!'

'Steady on, girls! I'm a boxer, so I 'ave no 'ope of keepin' up with you. I love your accent, Margaret – Roedean School, perhaps? It's very Maggie Smith. And what do you want from me, Margaret?'

'Well spotted, Sam. I am impressed. Our family has a stately home with a couple of thousand acres near the New Forest. My preference for business in general, and marketing in particular rather broke the mould from our stockbroking background.

'Donna, I'll get a proposal to you in about a week, and then we'll have a meeting, at which I will have a plan about the best exposure for Sam, some product endorsements for your appraisal, and a photo shoot. Sam, think of the photo shoot as a butcher's shop. You will be a "rump steak", and the photographers will feel about you the same way as a butcher would think about that steak. You'll be dressed in different clothes, and told to look here, look there, do this, smile, don't smile, hold your hands just so, and so on and so forth. Smile for me, Sam.'

I smiled, turned my head, looked over my shoulder, smiled again, and then looked fierce with a sideways turn of my head. Margaret grinned.

'You'll be fine, Sam. Where did you learn to do that?'

'I 'ad a mate who lived in Barnet, who 'ad started to fool around with cameras an' things at school. 'e thought 'e'd make it as a society photographer, an' I did some work with 'im. It's just playin' silly games, but if that's what you want, I'll try to make it easy for you, and I'll be patient.'

'We'll do hair and make-up and, as a boxer, if you can put up with that for two hours, you'll be a dream, making my job that much easier. How do you want to be seen, Sam?'

'That, Margaret, is a good question. The reason I do this is for Donna and the girls to 'ave a better lifestyle. At the same time, I want respect for my boxin' skills in the whole sportin' community; like Ali, and like our 'enry, the great Mr Cooper.'

'Sam, I want your image to be what you want it to be; otherwise, the whole thing becomes false, and it will show. What about background – what do your fans think of you?'

'I'm Sam Smith from Whitechapel, who was lucky enough and talented enough to take advantage of an opportunity given to me by Mr Reuben Goldstein, my manager and promoter. We 'ave a great team with some long-term plans after boxin'. They include effectively helpin' disadvantaged kids, and also trainin' some talented boxers at the very top of their weight.

'My family is the closest thing I 'ave to 'eaven, and I would protect them with my life. Our plannin' includes whatever the girls want to do, way down the track: university, travel, literature, science or languages. I'm 'oping to 'ave enough time and money to make that possible. Does any of that make sense, Margaret?'

'Absolutely perfect, Sam. I can work with your hard side and your soft side, and create some mystery out of that, because very few people in the world can run those side by side. I'll see you in about a week with some ideas that you will need to adapt, adopt or discard. You won't upset me, whatever you say, because they will be suggestions, not rules set in concrete. I will say that you are one of the sanest and luckiest men at the top of their game that I've ever had the privilege to meet. I can, and will, do some great things for you that will have both depth and veracity.'

'Veracity?'

'Look it up!' said Margaret smiling. 'I will see you in about a week, Sam. Donna, I'll ring you for an appointment.'

When she had gone, I looked at Donna to see what she thought, and I realised that she'd been silent during that 'interview'.

'She's nice, but safe, right?' I ventured.

'Yes, I agree with you, and I think she's honest in herself, and she's going to give me a whole new Sam Smith from Whitechapel to play with!' I stuck my tongue out at her, and she squealed and ran away.

Chapter Forty-six

Charlie worked me hard in the ring, on the bags and with the various balls, and then got me back to running. By the third day, I thought I was getting old and starting to lose it. By the fourth day, it was starting to become more natural, and I was looking forward to the ring again.

After a fortnight, I was running well, my wind was good, and my punching was starting to feel sweet again. The timing was not quite right yet, but I thought that would come closer with a little more ring time.

'What do you think, Charlie?'

'Coming along, but you're not right.'

'What do you see that's different? What's not right? I know my timin' is not quite up there, but it's gettin' there, and I'm only twenty-seven, for cryin' out loud!'

'Don't shout at me, Sam. I'm just saying that something's not right. Have you got any changes in your body?'

'Sorry, Charlie. I've got absolutely no reason to shout at you. I do seem to be a bit slower than normal. I'm gettin' tired just a little bit before I should, and my guts sometimes cramp, but I've put that down to not 'aving trained for some time, and the fact that you're puttin' me through one of your commando exercises.'

'Maybe, but we'll keep an eye on it, and keep up the pace. You've got a fight in two weeks. We don't want another fright like Wally. I'll see you tomorrow at your place when we have a full meeting.'

'Thanks, Charlie.'

At our next meeting, there was Art, Charlie, Reg, Reuben, Donna, Margaret, Wally Shaw and me. I did all the introductions.

'You've now met Margaret, our new marketing consultant. Margaret, we all need to be in on this proposal from the start, so we'll all waste less time if you go first before we get to things you don't need to know about, saving your precious time.'

'Thank you, Sam, Donna, Gentlemen. I have taken a broad-brush approach to get feedback from you. Sam, I mentioned your hard and your soft side, and if you think about the marketing brand of Pirelli Tyres and the calendar they just launched, or any number of car ads, aeroplane travel ads or household appliance ads, you are getting close to what I have in mind. Those are for "things" or "services" and are being produced in glorious Technicolour in magazines. However, I have in mind some heavily contrasted black and white posters, with Sam offering a number of top-of-the-line products, which will promote him while he is being paid a huge amount of money just to be in the picture. I initially propose to introduce Sam to the world, or those few who don't know him, with some equally startling boxing stances. This may sound passé to you, but I have two photographers who can do miracles.

'For example, smooth hair in one photo, but ruffled hair in the other, which is otherwise identical. An identical pose with gloves, boots, and shorts in one, with the other in an immaculate suit by "Brand X", cologne by "Brand Y" and a timepiece by "Brand Z". The only difference is that the watch is hanging on a shelf in the boxing one and displayed with a lot of linen in the suited one. Lean on a car of some sort, and you have four endorsements on one advert. The homily would be something like, "Sam from Whitechapel. You can make it, too." I'm thinking of getting you known as Sam, rather than Sam Smith, to make you closer to being a friend to everyone. Everything, and I do mean everything, sells with sex, so these will be total eye-candy for the ladies. And yes, we will have products for the ladies to be endorsed by you too. But mainly, you will be an obviously successful, alpha-male role model for the wannabes.

'So, if you are agreeable to my approach, give me Sam for two hours, with three weeks to work up the posters, and we'll have a showing, at which time you can tell me if I've got it right. Trust me when I tell you it will not be a waste of time, and there will be more money in it than you can believe.

'Margaret, that's fantastic,' I said. 'I could follow that through to the extent that I think I know how the pictures will look. Black and white, yes? A tad gothic, maybe?'

'Donna, did you know you had an artist in the family? Yes, Sam, that's exactly how I see it too. I have a couple of very gifted photographers who can do a fantastic job on that, but it may run over the two hours. Could you handle that, Sam?

'If I must!' I said, in a Noel Coward-style feigned apathy, with the back of my hand to my forehead. I got a round of applause for hamming it up.

Margaret pressed on. 'I have yet to get the products I want, and the permission to do multiproduct promotions, but we're working on that. First, I will do just "SAM!" There will be three pictures of just you, in boxing gear, in three different poses. They will be black on white, with a boxing pose, and some sweat in the air from someone just off frame. These will be the introductory ones and need two months exposure, not three, and not one. In two months, all those people who have to ask, "Who's Sam?" will have been told.

When the next ones come out, people will all say, "Hey, that's Sam!" I'm hoping that eventually, it will be, "Hey, that's our Sam!" I do not want it to be London-centric because that would lower your fan-based coverage. I want Scousers, Brummies, Geordies, even the Welsh and Scots to be equally enamoured with you.

'We'll get coverage in cities with big posters, plus TV, plus magazines and newspapers, with some talk shows later on. When the multiproduct poster/adverts come out, they will carry the words, "That's our Sam". This will take two to three months to get organised with all parties at the table. In case you are wondering why Aston Martin would be in the same advert as Rolex, Brut Cologne and Johnny Walker Black Label Whisky, it's because they will all get the same coverage, but at less cost than if the ad was directed to one product alone. Any comments, Sam?'

'I love all that. If the watch is sittin' on a shelf next to the cologne, the effect is: "when my watch goes on, so does my cologne," in the same way that night follows day.

'Also, I gathered my original fan base by not only winnin' fights and fightin' fair, but with my wink. You may want to think about incorporatin' that in at least some of the work. The "sweat" from the oppo, out of frame, is inspired.

'One other thing maybe you can do for me is to give me some 'elp with doin' interviews and speeches. I still 'ave a 'orror of bein' in front of a crowd of questionin' faces!'

'Sam, you are a lot cleverer than I believed. Yes, of course, I have seen the "wink" pictures, and we can certainly incorporate that in some of the posters, if not all. We have on our consulting staff a little lady called Patricia Ryan, who tutors and mentors on public speaking. What she doesn't know about that topic isn't worth knowing. We can start on that when it suits you.'

'Thanks, Margaret. Anyone, any questions? No? Thank you, Margaret, we won't take up more of your valuable time, but keep in touch with Donna.'

'Thank you for your time, everyone,' farewelled Margaret.

'All this is predicated on your not losing a fight, yes?' asked Art. 'How is he, Charlie?'

'I'm not sure. Something isn't right with Sam. He's fitter than 99.9 recurring of the rest of the world, and his stamina is fine, but his timing is a little off. It will come back with more ring work, so I can't put my finger on it. I've said that we'd keep an eye on it, and we will.'

'Sam, how do you feel?' asked Reuben. These questions from the team always have to be the whole truth, so I said,

'Pretty good but not 100 percent. We'll keep an eye on it, as Charlie says, but I'm sure there's nothing to worry about. The occasional stomach cramp, a little fever occasionally, not as 'ungry as I usually am, and my stamina seems a little down. Otherwise fine. Donna, 'ave you noticed anything different?'

'Sam's appetite is down is all I can say, and that could be put down to some factors that have nothing to do with boxing.'

'True,' said Charlie. 'It's not major, and we'll have this next fight, but I think I will get him medically checked before the contender fight. Any details on that, Art.'

'Yeah, I've got a boy who's very hungry, but young. His name is George Ellis; he's twenty-two, from Alabama, and about your height and weight. He wants to be the youngest world champion in history. He thinks he's running now, but he hasn't learned to walk yet. His backers have put a huge amount of money up front, I must add, but not quite á la Trey Maxwell. So, be fit for that one, Sam, and there could be enough to finish your project.'

'He'll be fit,' said Charlie, with considerable emphasis.

'Reg, anything about George Ellis?'

'Not yet, mate. They seem to be getting younger by the match, crawling into the ring with their nappies still on. I'll see what's out there and get back to you. I have to say that I like the idea of all those posters, especially with the wink. Get that right, and they'll be beating down your doors, Sam.'

'Reuben, you've been very quiet. What are your thoughts about all this?'

'I think Charlie should get you checked out as soon as possible. If there is something wrong, I want it sorted soonest, because there may be a lag time for healing whatever it is. All my fighters have to go into their fights in peak condition. So, let's keep to that rule.

'I think where Margaret is going with those posters is brilliant. From a business point of view, all her expenses will be tax-deductible. Your popularity will be used to promote products with no loss to you except a few hours here and there. There will be big payoffs from the product manufacturers. That's one thing. The other is that Sam's popularity will increase – always assuming things go well – which in turn means that his audiences will be bigger, and purses will get bigger from greater exposure, and of the products too. Sam, as long as you keep winning, we'll all be in gravy.'

'Yes, Reuben, but I've got the runs on the board, just to mix my metaphors. My experience, my fitness under Charlie, my management from the team, includin' Reg to give me background information, should all ensure that it will continue, especially with the "Project" as a goal to aim for. Any progress on that?'

'I'm still looking at locations, either old buildings that can be renovated, or old buildings that can be knocked down and re-built. Leave it with me.'

'Art?'

'This one, George Ellis, thinks he's good, and he is fast and fairly aggressive. I don't know how many fights he's had. He was presented to me with a cash offer that I really couldn't refuse. Where do you want to fight him, Sam?'

'Let's go to Birmingham Arena. I must try not to 'ave too many fights in London. Spreadin' the fan base is the better business ploy, as Margaret said. Reuben, who 'ave you got for me to fight in a fortnight?'

'He's a local lad from Balham, second generation here from Trinidad and Tobago. He's George Kitchener, same weight but taller, and he is really looking forward to getting in the ring with the world champion to teach him something about boxing!'

'Really? That should be fun. Charlie let's get a good doctor to sort me out. I 'ave been skirtin' around this, but I should really take it more seriously because we all depend on my fitness.'

'Harley Street, here we come,' said Charlie.

Chapter Forty-seven

I was ushered into a very classy office, having been sitting in a similar-looking waiting room. The doctor, smartly tailored, shook my hand and gestured to a very comfortable chair.

'You're THE Sam Smith, are you not?'

'That I am. Do you follow boxin'?'

'Indeed, I do, and I love your work. You made a real mess of that American. I'm just glad I'm not his surgeon. One wonders where to start to repair that sort of damage. Now, you have a medical problem for me?'

'My trainer, Charlie Browne, says somethin' is off with me. I've been trainin' 'ard for a fortnight after some time off, and it's all going well, but somethin's not quite right.'

'Whatever it is, I think you have caught it early. Describe what you, and those around you, have reported.'

'Donna, my wife, says my appetite is down. I get the occasional abdominal cramp, which I put down to the 'ard trainin' regime. Occasionally, I feel slightly sick, and yesterday there was some blood from my back passage. Doctor, 'ave I got bowel cancer?'

'My dear Sam, I do not think so. Tell me, have you been overseas in the last year or so?'

'Yes, as part of an extensive trainin' regime, a few months back, I went to Jamaica, Canada and the US.'

'How long did you spend in Jamaica, and where were you?'

'I arrived in Kingston, but travelled to Montego Bay the next day, where I spent a week scuba divin'.'

'Lucky you! Did you ever walk about without shoes on, or more probably, thongs?'

'Well yes, sometimes I did after my feet got toughened to the 'ot sand. Why?'

'Because I'm pretty sure you have picked up a hookworm infection. The larvae can wait in the sand, go in through your foot, work their way around your body, eventually lodging in your intestine. It has been long enough for you to be leaking blood and seeing it in your faeces.'

'Can it be cured?'

'Oh yes, very easily. I'll give you a prescription for Vermox, which is the trade name for Mebendazole, although you can buy the medicine over the counter in any pharmacy. We have some very good anthelmintics, or 'worm-killers' to you, these days. Take one tablet per day for three days. I would suggest after breakfast. They are even orange flavoured and chewable to make life more pleasant for you.

'I'll need my nurse to take a blood sample from you to see whether it has caused you to be, in any degree, anaemic. If it has, you'll need to eat more red meat for a fortnight or so, but there should be no ill effects from any of this after about a week. My nurse will arrange that test now, and she'll be able to tell the extent of the anaemia at once. If you wanted to use both "belt and braces", so to speak, you could also buy some special iron and vitamin C tablets from the pharmacy at the same time. All understood?'

'Sure thing and thank you for settin' my mind at ease. My imagination 'ad started to work on some pretty gory details. Thank you again, doctor.'

'My pleasure. And do keep up the good work. By all means, come and see me any time you have a problem, even if you only *think* you have a problem!' he said with a smile and a handshake.

Ten minutes later my problem had been sorted, together with the background anxiety that had started to rise. My 'feathers' had all come down.

The nurse had returned from her testing and reported that my haemoglobin was in the one hundred and thirties, when it should have been in the one hundred and sixty to one hundred and seventy ranges. I thanked her, went to the pharmacy, and spoke to the pharmacist about this. He was very kind, and talked to me about the Mebendazole 100 mg tablets, and adding some special iron complex and vitamin C tablets to promote the growth of more and healthier red blood cells. He said that my low haemoglobin would be sorted quite quickly because it wasn't too deficient; the cause was being treated, and the iron and vitamin C tablets, plus some red meat, would do the rest.

'Good luck with all that, Sam, and keep on winning!' encouraged the pharmacist. I thanked him and went home to start on all this stuff. I settled Donna and Charlie down with a full explanation, and we decided to ease the training for a couple of days, eat plenty of rare steaks and keep taking the tablets.

There would be two days gentle training, and then accelerating up to three days before the fight, then taper. *Do not take this oppo, or any other oppo for granted, Sam. Remember Wally Shaw.*

This gave me time to catch up with what Donna was doing, and our conversations were excellent, bringing us even closer together. Those talks allowed us to see where we were in the present and appreciate that we were both on the same path to the future.

'How do you feel about all this?' I asked her.

'Very excited. I still find time for the household stuff like cooking, cleaning and doing this work, and I'm not in any way neglecting the girls. The last thing we need is to have the girls not included in all this, and yet more importantly, have them feeling left out.'

'I agree. I've only looked at this from my point of view – a typical selfish male, I know – but please, Donna, let me know when you want some 'elp and I'll get a 'ousekeeper in, to cover whatever you need 'er for. Actually, come to think of it, Wally could do some of that stuff for you, couldn't 'e?'

'He could, but would he? Would his ego as a boxer get in the way of menial tasks like washing and ironing and shopping?'

'Maybe, but think what a catch 'e would be down the track if 'e could competently run a household? 'e'd be around us, and all our boxin' talk, as well as some work in the gym. It would keep 'im close. I'll ask.'

Donna and I also discussed the project, money, prospects, fitness and the girls. They had their relaxed smiles back on their faces, good positive attitudes, and were doing well at school, even though it was early days yet. Their fears of the past mental trauma seemed to be waning as their focus was centred on new stuff at the new school with new friends.

I caught up on sleep, and at the end of three days at home, I was very keen to get back in the ring.

Margaret rang about a photo shoot, but I told her that should happen after the next fight, as I was deep into training.

Three days before the fight we had a meeting. Art and Margaret were absent.

'Reg, what do you have for me?'

'Sam, his name is George Kitchener from Balham, and I mentioned him to you before. His parents came over from Trinidad and Tobago in the late forties. He's got a bit of a height and reach advantage, but he's quite young. Wants to give you a boxing lesson. Otherwise, he's just another boxer with dreams in his head and stars in his eyes. Resilience, I doubt, but quite fast for all that. Hasn't been a professional long, and thinks he's taking the easy way to big money. That's about it, except to give the normal warning to you about amateurs.'

'Thanks, Reg. Reuben?'

'He's young and hungry, and like most youngsters, he cares about his image. I don't think he has anything hidden away to compare with Wally Shaw, for example. I would remind you to remember the wink at the end. It could help Margaret.'

'Charlie, am I ready for this?'

'Yes. You are not in the peak of fitness like you were for Trey Maxwell's first bout, but you're close enough to that. Your haemoglobin has come up to just over one hundred and sixty, so that's good. By your next fight in a month, I'd like to see it over one hundred and seventy. So, we're good to go.'

'Just before we go our separate ways, this seems to 'ave been a long break, and so much 'as 'appened since my last fight. My 'ead's a bit "all over the place", and my body 'as been hit with this worm infection. This fight will be good, but it's one I need to get both my 'ead and my body back to the efficiency I used to know. Thanks, everyone for your 'elp with that. See you on Saturday, and I'll remember the wink!'

Chapter Forty-eight

'Good evening Ladies and Gentlemen. This is Bob Clarke coming to you from Balham in South London, with my co-commentator and friend, Bill Fleming. We will bring you many fights this evening on behalf of the BBC outside broadcast unit. Bill, we have one fight, in particular, that should bring a large audience to this establishment; talk to us about that.'

'Thank you, Bob. Well, Ladies and Gentlemen, our very own Sam Smith, the welterweight champion of the world, is fighting a local man this evening. His name is George Kitchener who was born in this Borough. His parents originally came from Port of Spain, the capital of Trinidad and Tobago in the Caribbean. He's a local hero because he recently turned professional. He has a height and reach advantage over Sam. We're told that he is fast with his fists. So, Bob, let's get this show on the road.'

'Your timing is improving with old age, Bill! Kitchener is coming to the ring now, already firing shots at an imaginary opponent. He climbs into the ring, continuing to bounce and shadow box. Frankly, his energy is making me feel old and tired. A huge cheer goes up as Sam enters the arena, walking covered up, and led by his ring man, Charlie. He climbs into the ring, sheds his robe and immediately looks at his opponent, who smiles and sends a roundhouse right in his direction from his corner. Sam returns the smile but remains still. The Ref gets them together, gives them the talk. They touch gloves and retire to their corners.

Bell!

'Sam takes two steps forward and stands still. Kitchener almost runs across the ring and sends an incredibly fast right at Sam's head, which suddenly is not there, but a left from Sam as Kitchener's right swings away leaves an open area for Sam to hit. That left hit Kitchener on the cheek. If he understood what's going on, Kitchener would realise that Sam has just given him a lesson about speed and accuracy, and that the left could have been on the "button". It would have been "goodnight, Mr. Kitchener". Jab, jab, jab from Kitchener, none of which touch Sam. A jab and right cross from Kitchener misses, another left from Sam finds Kitchener's body. Left jabs coming thick and fast from Kitchener, and Sam looks as though he's doing the Quickstep or the Samba, but none of Kitchener's punches hit the target. He insists on coming forward only to have Sam move sideways, or out of range. I can see young Kitchener getting frustrated. He's saying in his head, "Stand still, why don't you, so I can hit you?"

Bell!

'Bill?'

'Thanks, Bob. That was a lesson from a "not very old" pro to a young boxer on how to deal with an attack without getting hit. Sam's speed of feet and head are always impressive, as we know, and his apparent dancing got him out of any trouble. A good lesson for young Kitchener. Reminds me of the "Old Bull" joke, Bob.'

'Yes, I read you. Very old!'

Bell!

'Sam walks to the centre of the ring, and I smell another lesson coming up.

'Kitchener circles around Sam, throwing an occasional probing jab. He darts in with another jab only to find Sam inside his body space, putting a three-punch combo to his head until Kitchener's guard comes up, then he gets another three to the body. Kitchener's guard comes down, and he gets three more to the head. Sam retreats and takes centre ring once more. Kitchener jabs and follows with a low right hoping to catch Sam unaware. Sam spins sideways to avoid the blow, pivoting on the ball of his foot, building momentum for a hard right to the "button", which has been exposed. Kitchener staggers back on to the rope, seems to make a supreme effort, and puts everything he's got into a huge right to Sam's jaw. But Sam isn't there; he swayed back but came forward again after that right had gone past and plants a beautifully crisp left to Kitchener's chin, and now it's, "Goodnight, Mr. Kitchener".

'Sam goes to a neutral corner, waiting until the Ref has counted Kitchener out, then he raises Sam's gloved left hand. Sam raises the other fist to his cheek and gives the crowd his famous wink. When the Ref releases his hand, Sam goes to each side of the ring, and gestures to the crowd, bringing them to him, and rewarding them with his wink. Sam punches his gloves together, makes a little bow to thank the audience for coming, and then winks again.

The crowd is trying to take the roof off this building. Sam turns, waves and leaves the ring. Bill, your thoughts?'

'Well, Bob, that was another boxing lesson for those who appreciate such things. Sam's footwork got a real workout, and I've never seen him do that better or faster. His lesson was "don't try to hit what is in front of you, hit where it ends up". Kitchener had heaps of energy and optimism, but he's got a considerable amount of work to do, just to be in the ring with Sam. However, I sincerely hope he continues his boxing. Back to you, Bob.'

I sat in the dressing room and re-ran the fight in my head. My conclusion was that my fitness was good, my coordination and timing were good, and with some hardening during the coming month, I would be ready for some real competition.

'How was that,' asked Charlie.

'How did it look?'

'It looked like a seasoned pro in the ring with an amateur. You gave him a lesson or three, then showed him how it was, not how he wanted it.'

'That's what it felt like too. I'll need some runnin' during the next month, and, with some ring work, I should be ready for the next one. Charlie, I'm startin' to lose count, not only of numbers but also of names and identities. Is that wrong, or bad? Am I losin' it?'

'None of the above, Sam. Your opponents are optimistic and opportunistic boxers who are trying to take what you've earned away from you. So, once they fail, they don't matter in your life. Go on to the next one and use it to build something worthwhile, which is exactly what we are doing, yes? Incidentally, Reuben spends much of his time keeping records of who fights who, when, where, with a description of the fights, so you can always refer to that.'

'Good, Charlie, and thank you for your counsellin', yet again.'

Reuben took us home, pleased with my performance. Something said I should have a quiet talk with him soon. He seemed to be receding into the background, and I wondered why.

When I got home, Donna gave me the once-over to see if there was any damage to me, as she always did.

'All good,' I said with a smile and a gentle, enveloping, warm hug.

'Of course, but I want you to stop before any real damage is done.'

'Me too, and that should tell you all you need to know. Are the girls asleep?'

'No, they're in their rooms and would appreciate a visit.'

I bounded up the stairs and knocked on Anna's door.

'Come in,' she called. I went in, and she jumped off her bed and came to me with a big kiss and a hug. 'You all right, Daddy?'

'Yes, darling, as good as gold.'

Just then Ella came bounding in for her share of Dad's hugs and kisses.

'You all right, Daddy?' she also said.

'Yes, darlings, as good as gold.'

'What happened?'

I gave them a funny account of the fight, that made them both laugh.

Things were starting to crowd me again. Reuben needed to be brought back into the fold. Donna would need some domestic help soon, so I needed to be talking to them both.

I also needed to get together with Art, Charlie and Reg to get a reading on - what was his name again? George Ellis, that's right. If there was anything different about his style, I might need to get in some practice with Rollo to sort it out well before the fight. I'd use the project to get back into Reuben's mind and share his thinking.

There were just too many balls in the air, even for a good magician. Could I manage?

Chapter Forty-nine

Epping Forest was one of those places Charlie used to drive me that had running tracks I could use, but which was also close to home. The Downs and the New Forest too were used for my long-distance runs. Charlie drove me because he could keep an eye on my progress, and also because my family had finally cracked up at the smell of sweat, body and foot odour in our car. Charlie said he didn't mind since he didn't have anyone to complain to him about the smell in his.

We would drive and talk about many things from the project and the fight to some technique or other that he thought I could improve on. I told him that I was taking public speaking lessons from Patricia Ryan, an expert on such things, as well as my diction, allowing me to relate to more people. Londoners talking to Londoners was fine but smoothing out some of my more local dialect would help me with everyone else.

At some point I realised it was all about work, so I started to ask him his taste in music and such, only to find that Charlie was a bit of a closet classicist. He had learned to love

Shakespeare, but stuck mostly to American authors: Fitzgerald, Twain, Steinbeck, and Kerouac, with his favourite being Joseph Heller's *Catch 22*.

Then I discovered that my ex-heavyweight champion contender was a romantic. His top composers were Tchaikovsky, Rachmaninoff, Grieg and Mozart. His favourite painters were Gainsborough, Turner and Edward Seago from the Norwich School, all of whom painted startling landscapes showing the beauty and moods of the British countryside. Who would have guessed? I wondered why he was alone with no wife, but that was a bit private and the English are rather reluctant to dive into other people's preferences. He took care of me like a father, so there might have been some background there, but I left him to talk to me, if and when he felt like it. My job was to run and run and run until it felt normal to run, rather than to stand or walk or lie down. Time to suss out my next oppo.

Gathered at our next meeting were Art, Reg, Charlie, Reuben, Donna and me.

'Reg, you first.'

'Thanks, Sam. George Ellis is a twenty-two-year old from Alabama, of African descent, weighs 145 lbs, has had forty fights, won thirty-three with seventeen by KO, and lost seven. He relies on speed, is pretty accurate and can go the distance. The interesting bit is that of his seven losses, six were from combos to the head, not the chin, but the head. This says to me that his weakness lies in shaking his brain about in its box, so to speak, either backward and forwards or side to side, rather than one punch to his "button". That's a new one to me. The odd man out was an uppercut that put him down, which tends to point to the same thing. Agreed?'

'Yes, Reg. I can see where you're comin' from. So, 'e 'as speed, accuracy and can go the distance, so no tiredness comes into play unless I induce it. 'owever, if I can get a few three and four-punch combos to 'is 'ead, 'e should go down, right?'

'That's the best I can do for you. Ellis never fought Trey Maxwell, but he was working his way up the list, so you are a prize the Yanks will pay dearly to fight, although that's not my department,' said Reg, suddenly realising he had got himself into an area outside his expertise.

'Art, what do you have for us?'

'Reg got that down pat. He is quite experienced, more so than you are, professionally speaking. He's also correct in saying the Yanks are paying heavily for the privilege, so open another bank account, Sam. You'll fill it up again after this one. It's all arranged for Birmingham Arena in three weeks, which is interesting if you have a certain turn of mind, because he comes from Birmingham, Alabama! Any thoughts, Sam?'

'It seems quite straightforward, but I'm wary. Forty professional fights make Ellis very experienced, and if I were George Ellis, I'd 'ave a plan for beating me, with a few surprises in store. So, this one I will take slowly to suss out 'ow 'e intends to do that. 'e's no slouch, but I'm fit, fast and ready. Charlie, you'd agree with that, I hope.'

'Yeah, man, two more weeks hard work with a week to taper, and you'll be spot on.'

'Reuben, what do you have for us, right across the board that is?'

'Taking a broad brush, I can see things progressing very nicely for both the team and the project. I have picked out two sites to develop for our project, which I won't explore with you until after the fight. Donna mentioned the possibility of getting some domestic help as her administrative duties are taking up more and more of her time.'

'That's actually rather good timin',' I said, 'because I 'ave been thinkin' of a role for Wally Shaw. 'e's told me 'e can cook, and with a little direction from Donna, 'e could manage some other routine chores around the 'ouse. 'e doesn't live far away, so weird hours probably won't be a problem, and imagine 'ow eligible 'e would be on the marriage market as a successful boxer who's 'ouse-trained!' Laughs all around.

''e will also be around boxers and boxin', and we can incorporate 'im in the sparring routine. 'e can work in the gym too, so could be employed full-time, 'oldin' down several useful roles. How would that suit you, Donna?'

'I think he will do very nicely. I was, in truth, getting a little frazzled. Any help would be appreciated.'

I said, 'Donna, you should 'ave said somethin' earlier. I'll ask Wally to come and see you. You can sort out what you want 'im to do, 'ow long it will take, and what time 'e will 'ave to work in the gym. For a young boxer to 'ave to do domestic duties will test 'is determination, which in turn will lead to the strength of 'is dream. Does that suit?'

Donna nodded a yes.

'Reuben, I didn't think you 'ad finished.'

'Only to say, that I seem to be less involved than I used to be. Not that that is a bad thing, but I'm not making the sort of decisions I used to.'

'Please listen to me,' I said. 'You've been the best and most consistent member of our team, but I 'ave to say I've felt your lack of involvement. I thought it was a good thing, in that it allowed you to manage other boxers, and/or 'ave some time off when you felt like it.

'As far as I'm concerned, we'll need all the 'elp you can give us to design, build and people our new project. One thing I can predict is that you are goin' to need skills that you don't 'ave at the moment. So, why not take any courses you might need, make appointments with builders, plumbers, electricians, structural engineers and architects, and pick their brains, use their time, and we'll pay for it. I really do want you to be a big part of this team that, I 'ave to say, YOU built! Think of this as a break in your workload, and if you feel like goin' on holiday, say a river trip down the Rhine, tastin' a range of beautiful wines, then go and do that because, as God made little apples, you are soon goin' to be as busy as a bee in a colander. 'appy now?'

'You bet. Sorry, Sam. I've always been in the thick of it, and just felt a little left out somehow.'

'There's absolutely no need, you daft old man. You've always done right by me and my family. It's just that the money and the workload 'ave got to the point where some dividin' of responsibility 'as been necessary if we're goin' to follow the plan of my boxin' for the next two or three years. You 'ave a buildin' to build, and facilities to design for maximum efficiency.

'Just now, I 'ave this fight to concentrate on, so go and do what you want, while you 'ave the freedom. After the fight, we'll get together about which site, and the best design and facilities. I've just 'ad another thought; maybe we could incorporate some hotel type rooms, not bed and breakfast, just sleepin' accommodation on the top floor, but we'll get to that later. Does anyone else have somethin' to say? Yes, Donna.'

'Sam, I got a phone call from Margaret for the photo shoot, asking about timing.'

'I think that after the fight I will be more focused on what I need to do. Tell Margaret that, please, and if you like, choose a date. Our fight's on the fifteenth, so pick anywhere between the twentieth and thirtieth at 'er convenience. I would like you there too, so I don't make a total prat of m'self. OK, thanks, everyone. Forgive me bein' elsewhere for the next three weeks, but I've got a fight to win.'

I had two weeks of hard work with Charlie before the taper began, and I needed every bit of focus.

Chapter Fifty

'Good evening, Ladies and Gentlemen, this is Bob Clarke and Bill Fleming coming to you live from the Birmingham Arena on behalf of the BBC. We have a packed programme of boxing matches for you tonight, none more important than our very own Sam Smith, the Welterweight World Champion from Whitechapel, who is fighting George Ellis from Birmingham, but in Alabama in the southern United States. Bill, have you any comments on this fight?'

'Thanks, Bob, and good evening, Ladies and Gentlemen. Sam is in the process of going through, if I might use that word, some contenders whose job it is to take away his title, while it's his job not to allow that to happen. After a recent birthday, Sam is now twenty-seven and has had an enormous number of fights. He has fought the previous world champion on two occasions – once to beat him for the title, the other to "beat on him" if I may say that in the American parlance.

'George Ellis is only twenty-two but has had forty professional fights, so we'll see how this goes. I guess that Sam will take this very slowly to see what the other fighter brings to the table. The boxers are starting to come into the arena, so it's back to you Bob.'

'Thank you, Bill. Concise, succinct and to the point, as always. George Ellis is climbing into the ring now. He looks very fit and assured. Ellis is not looking around for his opponent, Sam, who has just entered the arena with Charlie Browne, his ring man. Sam is covered up and now climbs into the ring, removes his robe and looks over at Ellis and his corner staff. He stands completely still, which is almost a shock, because every person of the approximately sixteen thousand people in this huge auditorium is moving. He's just smiled at Ellis, and I do believe it has had a detrimental effect on Ellis, who can't quite believe what he has just seen.'

Bell!

'Sam claims the centre of the ring, standing in his stance, waiting for Ellis to make the first move. Ellis has a low stance but keeps his gloves high. This protects his head and keeps his middle away from being hit, without his ability to counterpunch effectively being impaired. Ellis throws a jab, which Sam dodges, and another and another. Ellis is moving slowly around Sam who is still in the centre of the ring. Another jab from Ellis followed by a right cross, which Sam has walked inside and delivered a short, but very sharp uppercut. He dances back just as a swift, right-hand scythes through the air in a hook to where Sam's head was a moment before. Ellis is fast, reasonably accurate, but has not given much away regarding tactics as yet. He tries another jab and cross, but Sam has moved back, waiting to see what else comes his way.

'Ellis makes a rush towards Sam, flailing a three-punch combination, but as regularly as clockwork, Sam dodges sideways, and lands a cracking blow to the side of Ellis's head. There was a momentary hesitation while Ellis got his wits back, but that hurt him.'

Bell!

'Fairly standard first round for Sam, don't you think Bill?'

'Yes, Sam's getting his measure. Ellis thought he was doing quite well until Sam showed him who was the boss with that cross to the head. Sam looks sharp and very focused. This should be good. Back to you Bob.'

Bell!

'Thanks, Bill. Sam has not claimed the centre ring this time, and it's part of Sam's interrogation technique, if I may put it that way, to find out just what strengths and weakness his opponent has. Sam circles Ellis, not throwing a punch. Ellis can't stand the "silence", so throws a jab and a cross. Sam is inside him in a flash, pummelling his middle, then steps back just in time to miss another roundhouse right hook, which, when it had gone past Ellis's left, Sam gives Ellis's now unprotected right side a very solid left of his own. Ellis's eyes are much warier now, so Sam gives him a jab and right cross, mirroring Ellis's own attack technique, and it's evident that Ellis can dish it out but doesn't know what to do with it in return.

'I sense that Sam is getting bored with Ellis. He doesn't seem to have anything other than a jab, right cross and a roundhouse right. I think Sam will get him on the ropes or into a corner soon. Ropes it is, with a couple of three-punch combos pushing Ellis back. Ellis leans back on the rope, but ducks to his right before Sam can set him up. That's good from Ellis.'

Bell!

'Bill?'

'Yes, Bob. Sam is reverting to his usual "feeling out" process when he realised that there wasn't much depth to this fighter's armamentarium. He has tried being "in" centre ring in Round One, and "out" of centre ring in Round Two. In Round Three, he will see what getting Ellis involved with the ropes and the corner will bring. If Ellis negotiates those well, Sam will have to dream up another way of taking him down.'

Bell!

'Thanks Bill, and sure enough, Sam has blustered Ellis with three combinations to get him in a corner. Ellis has covered up, but Sam is concentrating on his middle. Ellis is now leaving his head unprotected. Sam has just delivered a five-punch combination to Ellis's head, so quickly that I wasn't sure I counted correctly, and Ellis is down! Sam has gone to a neutral corner, leans nonchalantly on the ropes, not breathing hard. Ellis is counted out, in only the third round.'

'Bill, your comments?'

'Bob, I have to say that I've never seen a five-punch combination before, and there was a lot of body-swing in it, so they were not by any means powder-puff punches, as proven by the body on the canvas. Ellis is only twenty-two years old, but he needs a lot more practice to be at this level. He's had seventeen KO's in his career, and I would think they all came from that roundhouse right hook with which he kept trying to nail Sam. Another contender bites the dust. We might get Sam into the BBC studios for a chat, Bob, what do you think?'

Yes, Bob, great idea, especially since I think he is a legend who will eventually be in the Boxing Hall of Fame.

Chapter Fifty-one

''ow was that, Charlie?'

'Yeah, that was OK. You were fit enough to be able to dodge those big rights, and Ellis had no idea about corner work. Getting his head unprotected was critical, and you did that well. Tell me about your five-punch combo? Where did that come from?'

'Seriously, I 'ave no idea. I just wanted to finish it because 'e was very shallow in his range of punches and appeared to 'ave no strategy to beat me. Just as an exercise, Charlie, as an ex-boxer, 'ow would you beat me?'

'Now that's an interesting question. Let me get back to you on that.'

'OK. Now, I 'ave to get into some private activity, like bein' photographed, becomin' an architect, builder, site manager, interior designer, staff manager and "media tart" on the BBC before my next fight. My fitness is good, the money is pilin' up, an' we should soon be able to retire from that and look for some new challenges, Charlie.'

'That's a shame because I like what we're doing. You are really very good, and I'd like this to keep going forever.

You've been hit very infrequently; your reflex speed is still good. Now is the time to get these serious contenders out of the way while your bank is still open for business!'

A couple of days later, I got a visit from my old friend Tom, the SAS team leader. Tom was a user-friendly version of Michael Cain in his role as 'Alfie'. He had a warm smile that showed nothing but friendship – unless you looked deep inside it, and then you could discern the watchfulness, the awareness and the potential for violence. That he was capable of considerable violence, I didn't doubt, but somehow, I felt safe with him because such violence would only be relative to the threat and its direction. His was not a violence released to be enjoyed. His presence had a calming effect with no pressure.

'Hi Tom, good to see you, mate. Come in! Come in! What 'ave you been up to?'

'Finally, the regiment has had enough of my services to the point that they have pensioned me off. Truthfully, I've hit the age limit for active service in the SAS. So, I'm on Civvy Street, and you did mention that you'd like to see me when I got out, so here I am.'

'Firstly, it's terrific to see you again. Did I really do all right, or were you partly coverin' for me?'

'No, we weren't, and we wouldn't. I have never seen anyone, especially in your weight range, deal with a fifteen-mile run with a 10 kg knapsack first time. That was quite extraordinary. Could you do it now?'

'Probably. I've just 'ad a fight, and you need extreme fitness for twelve rounds against a very active oppo who won't leave you alone.

'Now, regardin' employment with us. There will be some areas of security that you'll not be able to talk to me about from your previous employment, and that I totally understand. I think that not long from now there is goin' to be a need for security in our whole organisation, which is growin' nicely, although I 'aven't yet told you my plans.'

Tom butted in, 'That you are going to build a boxing and mentoring centre with Charlie and Reuben. Reg and Art won't be needed when you give away the gloves, but you will need advertising, and Margaret is excellent. Donna is doing well with the admin side of things, and the girls are thriving at school. How did I do?'

'My God, Tom, where the 'ell did you get all that from?'

'Easy! Providing you know where to look and who to talk to. All that took one week, and just to put your mind at rest, I didn't talk to any of "your" people.'

'All right, 'ere we go. There is nothing secret about the business we are 'oping to start. In fact, the wider the message is spread, the better. But our safety, as you well know, can be compromised. So, I see a place for you in our organisation as a security expert – that's bankin' in general, money in particular, and its physical movement, policy, plannin' and personal security. Your presence reflects my thought that "Prevention is better than Cure". I think I may 'ave to go over to the States again to box, and it would be very re-assurin' to 'ave you with me. Charlie is good in the ring, but against real-life bad guys you'd be my choice every time. I'll 'ave to talk to you at length about our structure and plannin' to fill you in on everythin' that's goin' on, but at a later date. Just keep an open mind.'

'I'm in,' he said.

'What? Just like that?'

'Yes. No "ifs," no "buts". You are solvent so you can pay me. There's nothing that you are likely to ask of me to do that I can't do, or get someone else to do, and you are all good people to be around, with a heap of integrity, which is very rare. So, yes, I'm in.'

We shook hands, and it was settled.

'Thanks, Sam, see you. And you may like to see what I have been doing,' he said, giving me some sheets of printed paper. 'My CV.'

Margaret rang to make our appointment and had asked me to bring my boxing gear, a suit and tie, shirt and shoes. When does a boxer get to wear a suit?

I walked down the hill from our house to a local Jewish tailor, who had had a business there for three generations, according to the locals. Walking into his business, I saw a dowdy shop with poor lighting, no displays, a scratched glass counter and an old-fashioned cash register. He swept out from a back room that had a heavy curtain across the doorway. He greeted me warmly, although I had never met him before. He was a smaller version of Lou, with expansive gestures, an expansive girth and a warm expansive smile. His tie looked pre-war, but which war was debatable; the sleeves of his cream shirt were half-rolled up, and he wore a sleeveless, burgundy wool cardigan that had also seen much better days. I spotted a tattooed number inside his left wrist, which completely changed my perception of this scene.

'On my life, it's Sam Smith from Whitechapel! How are you, my boy?' he enthused, holding out his hand, then grasping it in both of his.

'Just grand, thank you. I need a suit for a photo shoot next Thursday week.'

'That will be no problem at all. Tell me about the photo shoot. Will it be in colour? What are you promoting? How good will the photography be?'

'All good questions,' I said. I explained to this tailor what was going on by echoing Margaret's words.

'Ah! Good. I have it. You will need a grey suit. As the whole thing is aimed at a dark image then a black suit would recede into the background. A grey suit would look warm, personable, and make you stand out as an individual: a real "mensch", yah? I will make a beautiful grey suit for you that will be ready on the Wednesday before, and I'll marry that with a beautiful white shirt, striped tie, and black shoes. You could go to the palace in that suit, yah?'

'That will be just fine. How do you know me?'

'Is Reuben Goldstein not your manager? Are you not on TV for all your fights? Do you not know Lou at the The Garden? You are very well known to us, and to everyone, Sam Smith. I will personally make a beautiful suit for you. Three minutes for some measurements, and you can go back to beating Americans on to the canvas. This, I enjoy watching. Who are you fighting next?' he asked, as he seemed to throw a tape measure around without counting or recording anything.

'Right now, I 'ave no idea. I just hope I won't need to return to the States, although it would be good to see Lou again. How do you know 'im?'

'By marriage, of course. Lou is family. A long way away, I admit, but he is family. Tell him I made your suit and said "Hi!"'

'No wonder Lou gave Reuben such a hard time when they met in New York. I'll tell 'im I've met you, and that you made me one of your finest suits. I'll see you next Wednesday, and thank you, Mr Moser.'

'Call me Mose. Everyone does. Oh, and a fitting on Monday, yah?'

Apparently, the majority of the Jewish population in the UK was in my fan club. Somehow, I'd like to recognise that network; not dramatically, but subtly.

Monday, 11 am came around very quickly, and we had a very full lounge room.

I introduced Tom and briefly described his role in rescuing my girls. We organised Reuben to get my next fight for three months' time. Donna told us that she had employed Wally Shaw, who was doing well at his domestic chores.

Reuben had selected two potential sites for us to evaluate, arranged to pick us up tomorrow at 10 am. We discussed finances, the design, long-term plans and all that boring stuff that people other than boxers are concerned with!

Margaret wanted me for the photo shoot, and we made a rough date for that.

I just had to get rid of all this detail and get back in the ring. I started to feel like a bloody accountant, for crying out loud!

Chapter Fifty-two

There were three months until my next fight, so I needed to get as much done outside the ring in the first month as I could.

The first potential gym site that Reuben drove us to was a decrepit old warehouse that looked as if it had been built before the First World War. The bricks had been painted different colours on many occasions. There were no windows, no doors, and no roof although most of the trusses were still there.

'This is a dump,' said Charlie.

'Yes, it is,' agreed Reuben, 'but you have to use your imagination. This old wreck will have to be demolished, of course, but then look at the space you will have, and I'm thinking of parking. Ignoring the building, this is an extensive site. Now, in your mind, build a really modern four-story structure with big windows, spaces that are light and airy, with a large, paved car park with fir trees that don't drop leaves.

'The best bit is that there is a Tube station within fifty yards and a public car park about the same distance in the other direction, which would be virtually empty after working hours. So, if parking is not a problem, the building can be more significant. This is the drab part of this area, but when the new building is here it will raise the level of sophistication of the area, which in turn will increase the value of the land. I estimate that it will at least double in value, in real terms, within five years.

'The area is just better than half an acre, which is enormous for any real estate in Greater London, and the asking price is only a hundred and seventy-five thousand pounds. Take the cost of knocking down the old one, putting up the new one, give or take, paving the car park, and you'll have a final cost of four hundred thousand pounds, which, at the going price around here is definitely worth it.

'I've found it's always important to walk around the area to get the feel of the place. It's well worth the price, trust me on that. So, go and have a look around for yourselves. Meet you back here in fifteen minutes.'

Donna and I walked off hand in hand to the street. I looked back at the admittedly big space and, in my imagination, put a modern building on it, and it changed the atmosphere of the whole area.

After drinking a local coffee, we drove to the next site, also north of London, but a bit further out. Here, there was what used to be called, a 'Bombsite' – an empty piece of ground that, once upon a time had had a building on it. With parkland surrounds, it lightened the spirit because of the country 'feel'. I could visualise our building here and it seemed to fit in nicely. I wasn't building a really nice house, but commercial premises, and that's very different.

'Tell us about this, please,' I asked Reuben.

'As you see it's virtually in the country, which is both good and bad. There are fewer patrons locally, which is bad for business. However, the price is lower, per, and it's bigger and cheaper than the last one. Plus, you wouldn't have to take down an existing building. It's about three-quarters of an acre at about the same price as the last one, so that's with half as much area again. No demolition costs, but a bit more for the new building, so about the same price, but a much better outlook.

'The old adage for business to follow is: "Location, location, location!" We do have a Tube station close by, and it's a much nicer neighbourhood. All of which gives you a decision to make. I'll give you three days to mull that over.

'Sorry, I have a photo shoot on Thursday, so let's make it Wednesday,' I said.

We travelled home in silence, each alone with our thoughts.

On Monday I visited Martin Moser (Old Mose) for a fitting, and my 'so-called suit' looked like a rag! I wondered if he really knew what he was doing. Afterwards, I sat in the local library, and wrote down my thoughts in my shorthand "Plus and Minus" system – a technique I'd learned long ago.

It seemed very confusing at first, but after an hour it all came down to lifestyle. Money was apparently no object, which helped with the decision, and, since this was going to be a showpiece for possible future franchises, the depressive area with the old warehouse dropped out of the running for me.

Additionally, if we were able to hold international boxing matches at the gym, it shouldn't be in a sleazy area. That was part of the change we wanted to make in the minds of the general public as far as the philosophy of our gym was concerned, changing the image of boxing to be cleaner, fresher and more open.

The road approach to the second site was easy and relatively straightforward. There was a Tube–train connection not far away, and then I realised that aboveground car-parking space was a waste of money. Put the whole building on top of the car park, and you would have a heap of space left for future building expansion. A couple of lifts, and we'd leave the security arrangements with Tom.

At the Wednesday meeting it was decided that the second site was unanimously the favourite, mainly for its fresh, open-air quality.

Now, if you don't mind, I have a suit to pick up from my tailor, who is related to Lou, would you believe?'

'What? Who's that,' said Reuben.

'Martin Moser.'

'Old Mose? He makes the worst suits of any tailor I know,' he laughed. 'No! Seriously, he does a beautiful job, but related to Lou? How amazing.'

The suit came with some accessories. There was a pair of unfussy, soft leather black shoes that were high-sided and probably called, 'Half-boots'. There were a couple of shirts, white and pale blue, and a selection of ties. The suit fitted like a glove. I thanked Mose and told him I would be in touch with Lou shortly.

Thursday was the photo shoot with Margaret and her two photographers. Donna was with me to make sure I didn't make a complete idiot of myself. In these fashion-conscious times with all the new styles, I sat beside Donna as she had watched the catwalks on our TV, so I had some idea of what Margaret would need from me. I was a good boy! Doing what I was told, and in two hours we were done.

'Thank you, Sam, Donna,' said Margaret. 'That went much more smoothly than I had anticipated.'

'I have some big names on board as sponsors, but there is a lot more work to be done before I present you with the finished product. I will phone you when we are ready. Could you come here to my studio?'

Friday found me at the gym and in the ring. Comfort through familiarity at last, although few would understand that. Here, I knew what I was doing. After a useful session with Rollo, I showered, changed, and sat down with Charlie.

'OK Charlie, so how would you beat me in the ring?'

'I've been giving that a lot of thought. After the beating you gave Trey Maxwell, I thought you may be invincible, but no one has attained that status. So, I would crowd you, and cover any chance of your escaping by slipping sideways. I'd keep hammering at you, body and head, putting all my energies into one huge assault. How would you defend that?'

'I'd be taking blows anyway, so taking them to escape seems like a no-brainer. I'd slip sideways, and counter-punch hard, turn the tables, and beat you senseless.'

'Yes, you're right about the odds. "You're damned if you do, and you're damned if you don't", so you might as well take an escaping punch to get free and go to default. That's good, Sam.'

A week later, Reuben and Charlie joined us to discuss the design of what we would need in the new facility. We thought it should be called, "Sam's Healthy Gym". It would contain both male and female facilities, and have a well-lit, underground car park that extended under the whole area, so we didn't have to worry about that at a later stage. Above it would be dedicated space to many disciplines, and some space that could be rented and paid for by individual private practitioners. They would pay us rent for their area, which would cover our mortgage repayments, administration and management fees, as well as a reasonable maintenance fee – proportional to the area rented. But it would be theirs to work as hard or as little as they wanted to. They could include yoga, massage, osteopathy and physiotherapy practices, as well as peripheral health-oriented shops selling health-oriented goods. It could be worked out on a 'per square foot' of floor space basis. Our office space would be located well away from everything else – and so on and so forth.

Margaret called to say the posters were ready, which I have to say gave me a tickly little feeling in my stomach. *Vanity, Sam Smith? Maybe, but keep it to yourself.*

Margaret welcomed us and ushered us into a darkened studio. There were spotlights on five easels, which were covered in black cloths.

'We have done five. Three will be the boxing introduction, and two are with the finished products. Tell me your first impressions, and we'll get your longer-term impressions later. Just say the first thing that comes to mind.'

'One!' she called. A willowy young man removed the first cover. There was a beautifully timed chorus of, 'WOW!'

'Well, that's gratifying,' said Margaret. A very realistic picture of me in a boxing stance in shades of black and dark grey on a stark white background, from which my image appeared to be coming out of the poster at me. My face looked serious, and frankly, I would think twice before getting into the ring with that man. My hair was ruffled, and my body looked as though it was about to unleash a match-winning punch. The picture didn't move, but it looked as though it was about to. In truth, it was a work of art. It just said **'SAM'** at the bottom, all in capitals. The whole poster was about a metre and a half by a metre; quite big.

'That's a work of art, Margaret, with enormous impact! Next, please.'

The black cloth came off the next and the next, and there were two more boxing stances that looked as though they were in motion. In the last one, I was throwing a right jab with my body extended, towards the left-hand side of the poster. The glove stopped about six inches before the left edge of the poster, and a spray of 'sweat' was apparent in that area, giving the illusion of my having just punched someone. It, again, was a work of art with huge impact, with **'SAM'** written on the bottom.

'Now,' said Margaret, with a lovely, warm smile, 'here's my "piece de resistance".'

The last two were classic masterpieces. I appeared relaxed and sophisticated in my beautiful suit, leaning against an Aston Martin, a Rolex on my wrist below the cuff. The picture had apparently been taken in an immaculate garage, and there was a shelf behind me with a bottle of Brut Cologne in a pump spray with the lid off, close to my left shoulder. From the right-hand side of the poster, there was a silver tray holding a bottle of Johnny Walker Black Label Scotch Whisky, and a short, chunky cut glass tumbler about a third full. A white-gloved hand, with a white linen cuff and a short length of white, uniform sleeve with three gold rings, supported the tray. The effect was of unhurried sophistication. The caption was, **'SAM from Whitechapel. You can make it too!'**

I'm pleased they didn't make me wear a bowler hat, although it did feel very 'Whitehall'.

'Margaret, these are brilliant. The income from them should be considerable, and I've just realised that as my name is still out there, we can change formats and products.'

'Who's a clever boy then? Yes, we could, but I've got to make sure our approaches on this are the best they can be. If I can negotiate with your tailor to allow Hardy Amies to claim the endorsement of your suit, please note, not "claim to have made it", then we add another product. Your tailor could undoubtedly retire on that endorsement. Give me his name, address and phone number, and I'll go and see him. He'll never make another suit that brings in so much money. Is that all satisfactory to everyone?'

Reuben was bedazzled by the artwork, the business insight behind the concept, and its execution.

'How much money will it bring in?' he asked.

'I can't give you a figure yet, but have you ever dreamed of drowning in money? About that much,' said Margaret with a broad smile.

'I'm off to buy some scuba equipment,' he said, with the second biggest smile of his I'd ever seen.

'Can I get copies to show Art and Lou when they come from America?'

'Absolutely not! They will come here, or they will miss out and have to wait for the launch. There are copyrights, patents, loads of registrations and licences involved, apart from the legal contracts and the element of surprise in the marketing strategy. Bring them here anytime, Sam, but these posters do not leave here until I'm ready.'

'Right, ma'am,' I said.

As we drove home, I told everyone that it felt as though I was holdin' the responsibility for all this stuff in my head, and my boxin' was goin' to suffer if I didn't get rid of it.

Donna got me straightened out by telling me to get back to where I did the most good – in the ring – and that she would take care of the rest.

We met again when the American connection of Lou and Art finally joined us. I got a bear hug from Lou and told him about my suit and Martin Moser.

'Old Mose?' he said, 'Yeh, he's family, but I haven't seen the old boy in a t'ousand years. I'd love to pay him a visit.'

'We'll do that, but I want both of you, Tom and Charlie to look at the advertisin' programme we are settin' up. Donna has seen the posters, Wally and Reg don't need to, and we'll go this afternoon.

'Now, Art, I need your wise counsel. I want to have two more fights only. There are many reasons for that, but Donna is the main one. We have plenty of money, both for our future and the project, so how do I go out in a blaze of glory – undefeated?'

'It might seem too simple, but you have to win your last two fights. That's the absolute baseline, and don't take it for granted. Remember your mantra? Follow it and get your fitness way up there again. We'll get a Yank over here, then pick someone in America that we can hype is going to ruin your record. If I can find a boxing friend of Trey Maxwell's, then I could turn that into a perfect grudge/revenge match. Everyone in the States hates that you beat their champion, but secretly admire your guts and technique. So, if I can put a heap of emotion into that fight, we can clean up. Prepare to be hated – at a superficial level. Be like a politician; they don't take anything personally. If pollies have a problem with people hating them, they say, "That's your problem". Think Teflon, Sam!'

'That's brilliant, Art. Reuben will take you to see the ads, and you'll meet Margaret, who is inspired. If you leave the last fight until about seven or eight months from now, she may 'ave some ideas for the States, which could also raise the stakes. It could increase the actual audience and, most importantly the TV audience, by a factor of ten, and that should be worth a lot,' I said.

'Sam, you really are getting quite good at this, aren't you?' said Art. 'I'll go with Lou, Reuben and Tom, and we'll talk again. If I'm right, I should be able to launch the challenge as; "The United Kingdom against The United States of America." Countries, not boxers! Wow, Sam, this could be really big. See you this afternoon.'

It was beautiful to see those old men so enthusiastic about such a project. Reuben had someone in mind for the UK, and we'd hold that bout in Manchester Arena, which could hold around 21,000 shouting, screaming fans. That would be after the original posters had been released. It should be fun and held in about a month.

The last fight would be in the States at The Garden again, and, with all the advertising to be done and the partisan feelings whipped up, we would hold that in about eight months from now.

Art's salutary advice about winning both bouts naturally came first. So, I went back to Charlie, the ring, the running, the balls and sparring, while still spending as much time with Donna and the girls as possible.

'Accident' and 'Emergency' were doing so well at school. They were still bubbly, and twinkled in their smiles, which told me everything I wanted, and needed, to know.

Donna and I talked almost nonstop about our environments: the plans, the adverts, the project and the bouts. Wally, bless him, took over much of Donna's domestic workload, but I realised that I needed to get him more involved in the boxing side of things. Charlie said that Wally was coming along nicely in the ring, and that's quite an accolade from him.

Somehow, I had to disentangle myself from this extensive set of trivial details to focus on my fitness. Making that more difficult was Art and Lou's enthusiasm for using the posters to try to drum up support across the Atlantic, knowing full well that, done well, they would be a red rag to a bull! More 'smoke and mirrors'.

The first three posters were launched, and Bob and Bill from the BBC wanted me on their TV Show again. Reuben, Donna and I went to Shepherds Bush where we met with them. After make-up, I was introduced to an audience that was nowhere in sight.

'Good evening, Sam Smith of Whitechapel, and World Welterweight Boxing Champion. How are you?'

'Just "Sam", and I'm well, thank you, Bob,' I said.

'Of course, Sam. Those magical posters we see of you around the country really are beautiful artworks.'

'And I would absolutely agree with you. Those posters are the result of the great talent of a young lady called Margaret. She's a genius, inspired.'

'What are they for?'

'If I say, to get my face known even more than it 'as been, I hope you'll be able to read between the lines and avoid dentin' any BBC protocol.'

'So well put, Sam.'

'If you think those are good, just wait until you see the sequel; they are so far out!'

'What do they look like?'

'No advanced descriptions,' I said, waggling my finger to their smiles. 'You'll have to wait until Margaret releases them.'

'I can't wait.'

'I hoped you'd say that.'

'Sam, who and where is your next fight?'

'It will be at the Manchester Arena, but as yet I don't know who.'

'Then, how do you know how to beat them if you don't know who they are.'

'I believe in myself, and my ability. I'm young, so my reflexes are still in good shape, and I believe I can beat any boxer at about my weight. My fitness is about 97%, but will be perfect by then, thanks to Charlie Browne, my trainer.'

'How long do you plan on continuing to defend your title?'

'I'm pleased you brought that up, Bill. There will be two more fights: one 'ere in Manchester, the other in the States, which will be my last.'

'Seriously? That's a crying shame, Sam. You have been an absolute delight to watch in the ring, but we'll be there for both fights, all being well. Thank you for coming to see us, and good luck, Sam.'

'Thanks, guys. Until we meet again.'

Chapter Fifty-three

An excellent workout for about a fortnight brought me up to speed, accuracy and strength. Early on, I talked with Charlie, Tom, Reg, Wally and Reuben about my UK oppo.

'I've found you a young, hungry and quite talented boxer from Scotland,' announced Reuben. 'I've seen him on a couple of occasions, and I think you'll have a good match.'

'And whose side are you on, exactly?' I joked. 'Reg, what do you say?'

'Yes, I've seen him fight, and he's a bit of a wild man to be honest. Lots of activity with some wild swings, all of which have to be dodged or conquered. Sam, you've never been the full twelve rounds, but he's a boxer who could do that. He seems tireless, has tremendous energy, but not a lot of discipline. He just keeps coming at you, so if you can slow him down, it would help your victory.'

'Thanks, Reg. I can see I'll 'ave to be on my game not to get caught by one of those wild punches. What does 'e favour: jab, hook, cross or uppercut?'

'All of the above. He's a whirlwind.'

'Charlie, what are your thoughts?'

'I'd recommend that you do what you always do and keep out of trouble for the first couple of rounds to see what he has, what his preferences are, then, having understood his pattern, work out a way to drop him. You'll probably have to do some major back peddling, but that's your best defence until you can break his code,' advised Charlie.

'That sounds good to me. Talk to Rollo, Charlie, to see if he can mimic his style, and we'll see what 'appens. Any news from Art about an American oppo?'

'Not yet,' said Reuben, 'but he's got an advertising group in New York to liaise with Margaret for material and strategy, and there's still nearly three months to go. Get this one over in Manchester, and then we can spend some more time getting you to the fittest of your career for the American fight.'

I turned to Tom and said, 'Tom, I wanted you to be 'ere for this so you can fit in with our thinkin' and preparation and suss out any unnecessary risks in our groundwork for the American trip. You may feel the need to 'ire some support staff, so please keep us up to date with your thinkin' too.'

'Sam, you've got a lot on your plate at the moment. I'll come with you to Manchester so I can see how all this works. Then I'll fly over to see Lou. We'll talk, and I'll see what The Garden supplies in the way of security. At that point, I'll be able to evaluate whether I'll need more help, where it should be, and why. The geography of the place is important too, and that must be seen first-hand. Does all that suit you? I have any number of top lads who would give their "eye-teeth" to be a part of that.'

'That sounds fine, Tom. Just keep the details away from me until after this fight. Talk to Reuben about it. I go into my taper next week, and that means almost a meditative state, so I'll see you after the fight.'

Charlie sorted out Rollo, my main sparring partner, to attempt to mimic the actions of my next oppo in Manchester, and we tried a few things. Some, like a jab and cross, didn't work because it took too much time to execute, and then left me too vulnerable during the regroup – assuming my oppo was that fast. Other ploys, like a three- or four-punch combo with alternating punches to head and body, did seem to work, primarily because they were too hard to defend. It also could be that as a 'hard man', he was prepared to take a punch to give a punch. My plan to deal with that was: a) to trade one of his for three or four of mine, and b) that my punches would hurt him more than his hurt me. It took two days to get that sorted. I felt ready.

We had the taper in hand with just some running and ball work, and I felt a million quid. I had Charlie take me to the two potential building sites again, to re-evaluate our original thinking. The first site and its neighbourhood looked even sleazier than it had done initially, while site number two was even more appealing. I wandered around it for an hour, dreaming dreams and building lovely buildings with squeaky-clean facilities that all worked like clockwork. Disadvantaged children, who could work when they wanted, for however long they wanted, and of course, they would be paid. I would put a beautiful garden over the underground car park that wasn't initially built on, which we could remove if, and when, we needed to expand.

Strangely, I felt fully restored after this time alone; from what, I had no idea. Decisions made in my 'backroom' subconscious maybe, or a settling of spirit. It was the same feeling I had experienced after my Yorkshire runs. Maybe we city people miss out on something spiritual in the country with its fresh air, trees and birds, green grass and big skies. This was opposed to looking at the sides of commercial buildings all the time, as city dwellers do. When we got a chance, our family would have to explore this countryside more fully.

Chapter Fifty-four

'Good evening once more, Ladies and Gentlemen. I'm Bob Clarke, here with Bill Fleming, and we are coming to you live from the Manchester Arena on behalf of the BBC's outside broadcast unit.

'We have a busy evening here with eight fights on the programme. I have to say that we are privileged to be watching Sam Smith in action again tonight. He's fighting a Scotsman by the name of Joe Barr. I'll pass you over to Bill Fleming, my friend and co-commentator in this business, for his thoughts. Bill?'

'Yes, good evening, Bob, Ladies, and Gentlemen. First, the bad news is that this is Sam's penultimate fight. We talked to him in an interview in the BBC Studios in London a few weeks ago, and he said he would fight twice more only. Should he not be beaten, he will be one of the very few undefeated world boxing champions. In the welterweight division, I can think of only four.

'Second, the good news is that we have Sam here tonight, against a Scotsman of unknown potential. Joe Barr has been called a "Wildman", the "Glasgow Grappler", and the "King of the Picts". Until I've seen him in operation, I can't tell you which is the more accurate, but I think that Sam may have his hands full with this boxer. As usual, it will be a pleasure to find out what Sam's tactics will be, and whether his vast experience will stand him in good stead. We'll look forward to having a chat with Sam in the studios once more after this fight. Back to you Bob.'

'Thanks, Bill. Sam is approaching the ring as we speak, covered up and being led by his ring man, Charlie Browne. He climbs into the ring, sheds his robe and looks around. I'd say Sam looks relaxed but sharp. I don't know how I can judge what is apparently a paradox but he's obviously in good shape. Sam is watching the approach of this Scotsman, Joe Barr, who is bouncing around with nervous energy. Barr looks slightly taller than Sam, and may have a slightly longer reach, but, as we have seen before, Sam can easily negate those advantages. Barr has a good, strong-looking body, so perhaps he's got a good punch. They walk to the Ref, touch gloves and part.'

Bell!

'Barr runs across the ring and launches himself in the air, descending on Sam, aiming to take his head off with one blow, but he's down on the canvas! What happened, Bill, did you see?'

'Yes, Bob, as he was coming down with his right primed with enough energy to take down the "Twin Towers". Sam dodged, and hit him with a very fast and crisp left on the side of his jaw and has retired to a neutral corner.'

'Thanks Bill, I must be slowing up! That whole piece of action took no longer than half a second. That was absolutely extraordinary, yet beautiful, in a balletic sense. The count is seven, and Barr is on his feet. They touch gloves, and the fight continues. If he had stayed down, it would have to have been the fastest knockout in history – about a second and a half from the bell.

'However, it's a much warier Barr who is circling Sam in the centre ring. Barr jabs, jabs, and jabs again, approaching a step with each punch. Sam just backs up, keeping clear. Barr tries a jab and right cross, which also misses Sam. Sam is continually assessing Barr's condition, which seems to be all right now. Barr tries a three-punch combo to Sam's body, which misses, and Barr gets one in return that hits alternatively high and low. I haven't seen that one before, so it's new to Sam's armamentarium. While he's thinking about that, Sam gives him three more quick punches to the head.'

Bell!

'What do you make of that, Bill?'

'I want a film of that piece of action so I can play it over and over, a frame at a time, well into my old age! Sam must have the reflexes of a cat to have been able to deal with that. Barr must be really tough to take that very sharp left from Sam and still get up from a seven count. It certainly dented his confidence. Next round? I think Sam will try a corner or the rope. Back to you, Bob.'

Bell!

'Thanks, Bill. Look at that! Barr has turned southpaw and has started leading with his right.

Sam moves sideways at each jab or hook and kicks Barr's head sideways with left crosses in return. I can see Barr getting annoyed; he's getting frustrated at not being able to hit Sam. If Sam can bait him, he may lose his cool altogether, and his coordination will go out of the window. My impression is that Barr has a short fuse. Sam's is staying back out of reach. Barr seems to be running to catch up, and the audience is starting to laugh. Barr's lost it. Sam's back hits the ropes, but he ducks away to his left just as a huge right from Barr fills the space Sam's head had just inhabited. Barr almost topples over the rope forwards, turns to look for Sam, who gives him a cracking right fist, right on the "button". Barr wobbles with his guard now high, and Sam gives him another right to the heart. More wobbles in Barr's legs. The Ref steps in to make sure Barr is all right to continue. He is, and tries to take Sam by surprise with a fast right. Imagine his surprise when it hits the air, and he gets a crashing left from Sam to his right side.'

Bell!

'Interesting change of stance from Barr, Bill?'

'Yes, Bob. I guess he thought he could outfox Sam with that, but all his surprises have turned to trash, thanks to Sam's reflex speed and experience. Sam's working on instinct, I believe, because you couldn't possibly think that fast. He tried another "swifty" on Sam after the Ref had checked him, but it's hard to beat Sam at this game. Definitely, two rounds for Sam; not that I think this will go much further. Look out for the ropes. Sam wants to get him back for the rope thing that went wrong for Barr.'

Bell!

'Bless me! Barr has run across the ring to deliver another huge right to Sam's head! Barr's on the floor again, but this time he was propelled across the ring, sliding across the canvas into his corner by a huge punch from Sam to his solar plexus or near to it. He's still down, and Sam is standing in a neutral corner, breathing a bit heavily. The Ref has counted him out, and it's all over. The Ref raises Sam's arm, and Sam is blowing kisses to the crowd and winking! After those beautiful posters we've seen recently, he's using the wink to his commercial advantage, and, as they say in Australia, "Good on yer, mate!"

'Yes Bob, that was an amateur trick Barr tried to pull on the world champion. He would have been an absolute hero if it had come off. However, when dealing with someone of Sam's calibre, the chances of that happening are, to say the least, slim. That was a very different boxing match to Sam's usual pre-programmed ones. However, he showed us his class once more, has entertained Bob and me, sadly all too briefly, and we have one more fight to savour before Sam retires.

'I gather he's building a gym, unlike any that we have seen before, somewhere in North London. He will cater for the ladies too, I understand, and it will be open and airy and spotless, unlike some of the old sweatshops we have seen in our time, eh Bob?'

'I hope we get an invitation to the opening, Bill. I'm looking forward to seeing what this extremely and, may I say, unexpectedly talented young man has dreamed up. Those of you who know about such things, will know that I use those words advisedly, since "new" ideas originate first in someone's imagination. Whether dreamers have the resources to follow through is another matter altogether, but our Sam has, or will have.

'Now, our next fight is...'

Chapter Fifty-five

The gang was crowded around for my debriefing.

'Art, did you see the fight?' I asked.

'Yes, Sam, I caught it at the airport. It was – different! Please tell us about it.'

'His initial lunge from 'eight nearly did for me. It's only thanks to Charlie's fitness regime that my reflexes were fast enough to deal with that. 'e could 'ave dropped me easily, and 'ow would that 'ave looked? Amateur, unprepared and incompetent, that's what! The Scots would 'ave voted for a new annual 'oliday in 'is honour!

'But 'e didn't. I saw it comin', and my survival instinct just took over. 'is punch 'ad to miss me as a first priority. Second, it provided an opportunity, so I took it. It could 'ave taken 'im out, but it wasn't to be. 'e's one tough Scotsman. 'is rope attempt that I evaded was all down to trainin' specifically with Rollo. Reg, a thousand thanks again, mate, for your very accurate report, which could 'ave saved the match.

'When 'e tried his original trick at the beginnin' of the third round, my head said, "Enough of this". And I clobbered him. I don't know what damage I did to 'im, but I gave it all I 'ad because I didn't want any more of 'is nonsense. Then, I 'ad to concentrate on the post-match frolics with my thankin' the crowd and winkin', which should tie into our advertisin' campaign quite well. Charlie?'

'I could not believe that first punch, but I saw yours, and it should have put him down. What was his fatal flaw, Sam?'

''is lack of discipline! If 'e had started the first two rounds slowly and brought that aerial punch in at the beginnin' of the third or fourth round, he might well 'ave succeeded. He could 'ave been a formidable foe, but for that.'

'Spot on, Sam. Otherwise, your fitness, speed, power, and accuracy were just fine,' said Charlie. 'You will have to harden up some more for this next fight. Any idea about who that may be, Art?'

'Ladies and Gentlemen, here we should have a drum roll, because you are just going to love this! I've got a rematch with Trey Maxwell for you! Apparently, he's healed, and has been working on his fitness and hardness for a long time, just to have another go at you. The "powers-that-be" obviously thought that the beating you gave him was enough punishment for his involvement in those crimes, or that there was insufficient proof of his complicity. They've only got your word of what he was alleged to have said to you, and they must have thought you would be biased, and ignored it. Anyway, he's had some recent fights but he needs revenge on you so badly he can taste it. Do you have any reservations or comments about that, Sam?'

Yes, I bloody well 'ave! 'ow can that bastard get away with kidnappin', blackmail and murder? Eh? Frightening my little girls. I made 'im pay last time, and I'll bloody well do it again, see if I don't.

'Art, there 'as been somethin' in the back of my mind every day since I last fought 'im. It's somethin' to do with the energy I got from the injustices to my family. I would like to fight 'im free of that, but I don't know if I can after what I just said. 'e's a good fighter, but I can beat 'im. What's the purse, Art?'

'It's more than you would ever believe, Sam. I'll whisper it to Reuben.'

He did, and I watched Reuben's face. First, he blanched, then he seemed to almost collapse, then he just said in a whisper, 'My God, that's not possible!'

Art laughed out loud. 'I just love doing that,' he said. 'According to the American pundits, they still do not have a better welterweight boxer, and Maxwell has put up nearly half the money himself, which, I guess, is why he's working so hard. Charlie?'

'Yes, Art, this changes things just a little bit. The fight is in about nine weeks' time, so we'll taper Sam, from now for ten to fourteen days, then slowly build up over the following six weeks, maybe with Tom as company under my direction, with a taper for the last week, before getting in some ring time at the gym in New York. That should do it. Any thoughts, anyone?'

'I'll be happy to accompany, Sam,' said Tom. 'The chances of them being silly enough to think they could influence the outcome a second time would be astronomical; but how silly would we be not to consider it?'

'A good point, Tom. That's a plan,' consented Reuben. 'Item two. We've agreed to the second site for the new gym. We've had a look at the facilities we think we'll need, and the number and status of the staff. We have selected a local bunch of young but very keen architects. They have a couple of building firms that they use and liaise with, and they all concentrate on quality finishes. Sam, none of this will come to fruition until your last fight is over, so don't spare any thought to it; it's well in hand. I give you this information so you can get rid of any cogitation until then.'

'Cogitation?'

'Worry, then, concern, OK?'

'OK. Reg, I know Maxwell better than you do but I need your ear to find out what 'e is doin' by way of trainin'. Me? I'd re-think my strategy to beat me. I don't think 'e will do the same thing, hopin' for a different result. I also don't think 'e'll come screamin' across the ring at "moment one" to try to take my 'ead off, like Barr. So, anythin' will be useful, Reg.'

'Will do, Sam.'

'Item three,' said Reuben, taking control again. 'The ad campaign for the UK has gone brilliantly, Margaret. People are smiling and stopping other people on the street and asking, "Have you seen Sam?" I can feel that flowing out from London, and just at the moment there's a tremendous awareness. What's next, Margaret?'

'Yes, thank you, Mr Goldstein. It does seem to have gone well. The money to pay for that in the absence of product endorsement has come from a fund we have set up in your name, with resources supplied by your group, through Donna and yourself.

'The timing of the next stage has been set by Sam winning his last fight against, may I say, a memorable opponent! Everyone has been talking about it, with replays on TV news, current affairs, and sports commentary, so we strike now. The new posters, magazine adverts, news, current affairs and sporting channels will all want to talk about these too, and the posters will be going out tomorrow, after this meeting, having got your approval – I hope. Some of you haven't yet seen them, so I've brought the new ones with me.'

Margaret quickly assembled two portable stands and posed the pictures on them. There was a synchronous intake of breath from everyone in the room.

'That's magnificent!' said Art.

'I've seen them before, but they are even better than I remember!' said Charlie.

'If you were a girl, Sam, I'd marry you,' said Reg. 'They are just brilliant, Margaret. I definitely want one of those to put up in perpetuity in the Waterloo. I'll even pay for the framing.'

'Well, I'll take that as unanimous approval, then, shall I?' said Margaret. 'Now, I want you all to think about the American connection and similar posters to be used in the US before Sam's last fight. For the sake of the money, we will use the ones with the product endorsements, but we'll change the wording. There are a few weeks to go before these need to be finished, so please let me have your thoughts, say, in a week. It should take no more than twenty minutes of creative visualisation to come up with your best.

'What we want to do is to create a pro-British camp in the face of overwhelming odds. The object is to get people talking, and nothing does that more effectively than opposing emotions. I need wording to accomplish this, without, I hasten to say, starting another American War of Independence! Let Donna have your suggestions by the end of the week and we'll talk again.'

'Thanks very much, Margaret, and we all compliment you on the brilliant quality of your work,' said Reuben. 'Reg, Charlie, Tom and Sam, your work until the next fight is planned. Art, get all the details nailed down with Lou at The Garden, and talk to him about the advertising campaign. He may have some lateral thinking, being on the spot, and we'll run some suggestions past him anyway. Margaret, Donna will keep liaising with you. I gather from your body language that you are getting along well, yes?'

'Yes,' said Donna, 'we seem to be on the same wavelength in promoting Sam and his image and products.'

'Tom, I'd like you to go to New York to see Lou,' suggested Reuben. 'Phone him to make sure it's convenient, and take a copy of all the posters, "For his eyes only". Capisce?'

'Si, Senor Goldstein, Capisco,' said Tom with a challenging smile and a sing-song voice.

'I'll be working in the background on the project. Any questions? No? Well, that's it for now.'

That got me up to date. I found I was already pushing things into the back of my mind, bringing forward my needs for being entirely fit for the fight. I needed some massage for the kinks from the previous battle, which Charlie would sort out. I needed to sit down to plan the fitness programme with him and set some goals for checking each level on a weekly basis as we went along. I also needed some words for the pre-fight hype in America. I could think of that while getting a massage.

I told Charlie I'd be unavailable on Saturday and Sunday, as would our family. We desperately needed some private time, especially with the girls. I checked with Donna as to what she would like to do, and she, very sensibly, suggested that we have a 'weekend of slob'. Takeaways, talk, some TV, if we could agree on a programme that we all wanted to watch, and playing some of the latest music on record. We could play card games, have more talk, and sleep when we wanted, with maybe a beer or two for me. I call it healing, and I think that's probably true as there had been too little down time for a long while in all our lives. I hoped we'd be bored by the end of the weekend.

Before that, I met Tom and I talked to him about Lou – who he was, what he did, what he was like, and the fact that he seemed very pro-Sam. I told him that Anne should be included in the showing too, but I would talk to Reuben and Margaret about that.

He said he thought the posters were artwork, and very powerful. He asked me about money.

'Aren't you bein' paid enough?' I asked, in some dismay.

'Yes, Sam, of course. I've squared all that away with Reuben, but I was wondering about the project, and if you had enough for that. It sounds awfully expensive.'

'It will be, but yeah, we have more than enough. You wouldn't believe some of the purses at the sharp end of World Championship Boxing. I was almost too embarrassed to take that amount of money until I got a lecture, with finger pointin' and fist shakin', from Reuben! 'e told me that if people were willin' to give me an obscene amount of money, it would be impolite not to take it, and, because of the amount they obviously think I'm worth it. Also, I should not be prickly or ungracious about it in any way. 'e said it was good manners to say, "thank you", even if I did smile as I said it.

Tom, please give Lou my best, and see what ideas 'e 'as about the fight and the advertisin' and pass 'em on to Donna, who really enjoys bein' in the middle of this bunfight. I'm takin' the weekend off to be with my family, finally. It feels like we've almost become strangers, and I can't let that 'appen. Before you go, are you 'appy in your role in our team?'

'Yes, I am, but the role will have to be expanded over time as the gym starts to work.'

'Keep your ear to the ground then.'

'Gotcha. See you when I get back, Sam.'

Chapter Fifty-six

On Saturday morning we all woke late – for us. I got the coffee and juice. Donna organised cereal, toast and marmalade, and we sat around in our pyjamas and dressing gowns. By around ten o'clock, the girls wanted to watch some TV. Their choices included Blue Peter, Magic Roundabout, Play School and Rupert Bear. They were quite engrossed so we left them to it.

'My lovely Donna, at last we have time to talk. There's you lookin' after the girls and the home, plus all the administration with Reuben. And there's me, with my fitness and boxin' matches, the project and the ad campaign. It's all been a bit 'ectic for both of us. Are you 'appy with what you're doin' and where we're goin'?'

Donna nodded. 'We're young enough to burn the candle at both ends when we need to, and I know you're building something for our future. I love being a constructive part of that. It's got my brain working again. Housework is not at all a mentally stimulating pursuit, and Wally has now taken a lot of that really mindless stuff off my hands.

'Sam, I haven't had a chance to thank you yet, but your giving up fighting, for me, is a very great gift. I have felt an alarming level of stress and anxiety whenever you've fought, even though I know you're very talented. I've always felt that there's a faster and harder puncher out there, and I have nightmares about you ending up like poor Trey Maxwell.'

'Poor Trey Maxwell? 'e kidnapped you, and our girls! Why would you 'ave any compassion for 'im?'

'I think he got caught up in something that got out of control.'

'What? You mean, like breakin' the laws in the United States and the UK, kidnappin' and terrifyin' a mother and 'er little girls, and then murderin' policemen just sort of slipped 'is mind? 'ow the 'ell did 'e escape jail time, and be allowed to fight again? Anyway, I will take great pleasure in acquirin' a 'uge amount of 'is own money by beatin' 'im in the ring, yet again. 'e's puttin' up about 'alf the money 'imself for this fight. 'avin' beaten 'im twice, once severely, I will now take all his money away. When this fight is over, I 'ave a feeling that Art is goin' to be puttin' the boot in, to bring Maxwell to justice. I cannot believe 'e skated that, but I'll do my part, and you'd better believe it!'

'I agree, Sam. I'll just say this, "Go to work and get it done". Then I'll have you home with us all the time, and I'll be as happy as any wife and mother can be.'

'It shall be done, my love.'

Tom visited New York and talked to Art, Lou and Anne. They discussed a campaign of "Yanks vs. Limeys", and were invited to send brief descriptions to Donna of inflammatory language to set tongues wagging.

He had looked over 'Gym Plus,' then accompanied Lou to The Garden where he sorted out exactly what he wanted in the way of security, melding The Garden's own security, with a couple of New York's finest at the external door, and assessing the need for one more SAS member as extra cover.

We gathered the team together, one month before the fight.

'Charlie, how's Sam coming along? We have what feels like an incredibly short time before the biggest bout of Sam's career,' said Reuben.

'I think you may be getting nervous for no reason, but I will tell you that's Sam's fine; better than right on pace, and is working hard, with Tom for company. They have spent some nights in open spaces, with the rest of the day spent running and climbing. I've also had him in the ring with a variety of sparring partners, and he's doing just fine. Two weeks will have him ready, and close to his fitness level before the first Maxwell fight. He'll lose a bit in the travel, but we'll bring that back in the practice ring in New York. OK?'

'Thank you, Charlie. I didn't mean to query your competence, but an awful lot is riding on this fight.'

'No there isn't,' I said, 'unless there's somethin' I 'aven't been told? You 'aven't put a huge wedge on me to win, 'ave you? To the point that you're now startin' to sweat on it?

'Well, yes actually, I have. You won't lose, will you Sam?'

'I could slap you for bein' so silly, Reuben. Seriously, I'm not goin' to talk to you until this fight is over, so you'll have to sweat it out all on your own, right until the last punch. Of all the wise counsel you've given me over the years, and then you go and do somethin' as stupid as this? That takes the biscuit.'

Reuben looked at me, mouth open, displeased.

'But it'll be the last chance I have to make a real lot of money out of you Sam, after all I've done for you,' he whimpered. The others looked at Reuben in disbelief.

'Tom, tell me about New York and Madison Square Garden before I say somethin' that I might really regret,' I said, shooting Reuben my own look of disbelief.

'OK, Sam. Anne's place is fine, but I've got some ideas for doing more things, and better. Art, Lou, and Anne all got a hell of a kick out of the posters. Donna, expect some comments from those three.

'Lou was very cooperative, and we have the security as nailed down as it can be. I'll need one more guard, which I'll organise. The Garden has its own security. The police will give us a couple of sentries at the external door where Sam will arrive. I'm happy with what we have. In case anything untoward happens, there will be two very fit ex-SAS boys and a world boxing champion, so anything less than a Sherman Tank will be child's play. I'll talk to Donna and Mr G about travel arrangements, but we are good to go.'

'Thanks, Tom. Margaret, what do you have for us?'

'The poster campaign has outdone all predictions. The principals have asked – *Hey! Seriously, listen to this!* "The *Principals* have asked us to extend their contract for these posters, and subsequent ones, for *FIVE YEARS!*" You may not have been in touch with this market before, but this is unheard of, absolutely unprecedented! New buyers have been quoting their motivation for sales, and Sam's popularity is the defining feature. If we can keep this campaign fresh and current, it will bring in somewhere between fifty and a hundred thousand pounds per year! Is this good news, or what? And we have Sam and his cheeky wink to thank for all of it. I know he will do his best to win his final fight, for many reasons, but none of you will exactly starve if it all goes pear-shaped.

'I have finished the USA poster campaign. There are three winners, two are Sam's own, and one is from Donna. Sam gave us:

- 1783   Colonies 1   Redcoats   0
- 1967   USA   0   SAM   1

Then there's;

- TREY MEANS THREE – REMEMBER? SAM

And Donna's contribution was;

- 1773   Limeys 0   Tea–dumpers   1
- 1967   SAM   1   Carpetbaggers 0

'There should be enough ammunition in those to start a real emotional discussion, all of it centred around the fight, which should have an enormous audience on radio and TV.

I thanked Margaret and continued. 'Now,' I told them, 'I have two more weeks of hard work, a week to taper, and then it's off to New York for my last fight. I'll win, which will take away Maxwell's personal fame and fortune. Have we got security in hand at this end, Tom?'

'We have. I've a couple of ex-SAS soldiers to help, and you really wouldn't want to cross them, trust me! They'll be at home with Donna and the girls, and these two have special permission from the Home Office to be armed. There will be observers front and back too, so it's covered. Donna, you and the girls know what to do in the event of?'

'Yes, Tom, we've had a long talk with your soldiers, with some practice, and I'm happy we're in such good hands. Incidentally, our girls have mostly settled after their last traumatic experience, but this has stirred it up again. But they'll be alright. I'll keep them close to me, and ask Tom, their kind rescuer, to come and have a word with them. He's their hero!'

'That's great! Thanks again, Tom. Well, that's it then. I think we are all prepared, except for a certain silly person who is goin' to be sweating cobs until the last punch of this match! Thank you all for comin'.'

Chapter Fifty-seven

I had kissed the girls goodbye, leaving them in the capable hands of John and Paul, the two SAS soldiers. Tom had also introduced me to Denis, a man-mountain with an engaging, warm smile and an awareness that seemed to be permanently turned on. He was Tom's wingman, and we all caught a taxi to Heathrow. Having taken care of the luggage and immigration details, we went to the bar for a beer.

Denis told me a little of his background – places, rather than operational details. He'd seen a lot of action with the SAS in some far-flung corners of the world. Anywhere, in fact, that the safety of the United Kingdom was in jeopardy, either terrorist training camps, insurgents, or just some little politico who had got too big for his boots and/or was mixing with the wrong crowd.

'What do you do for relaxation?' I asked, thinking about him tearing telephone directories in half, or bear wrestling.

'Sax, man,' he smiled, 'you know, Coltrane, Hawkins, Jimmy Dorsey, Charlie Parker, even Dankworth. Get into a jam session and I can lose six hours easy, you know?'

I laughed. 'No, actually Denis, I don't. Music 'as never been a big thing with me. There 'ave been times when I've 'eard some beautiful music but 'ave never taken the chance to follow up. Or there's been somethin' else that took my attention. Would you play for me sometime?'

'I'd be pleased to, after this is all over. Are you feeling safe and comfortable, Sam? Believe me when I say I know how you feel. I've been into combat so often that, as long as my fitness and preparedness is fine in my mind, then it comes down to just killing time. That's when I play my best music. It's in the context of "I may never play again".'

What a fascinating man. I knew I couldn't employ everyone I came across, but Denis had such huge talent – if he was telling the truth. We'd see.

I woke on the descent into JFK airport. Unfortunately, my mate, the customs officer, didn't seem to be on duty. Maybe he'd had a massive win on my last fight and retired. It seemed unlikely.

I was confronted with a crowd of people with placards, saying "Go home Limey!" and "We're taking back what's ours!" and "I've got a cheap body-bag to get you home!" Things like that.

I smiled, waved and winked. Some people started taking photos, which I thought was better than throwing stuff like eggs, vegetables or rocks! I noticed that Denis had automatically moved in front of me for protection, which was a good sign. Tom hustled me into the cab. We stayed at a midrange hotel not wanting to fight crowds everywhere we went. Tom said he had arranged delivery of a VW Microbus with dark tinted windows for our transport from now on.

Charlie had been very quiet throughout the whole journey. I noticed him staring at me occasionally. I knew that look. It was his evaluation look. He always kept very close tabs on me close to fight time.

We had dinner in a private room, and an early night.

In the morning, we all travelled to the gym for some sparring that Art had set up. I needed to get the kinks out from the flight, and the one beer. Slow start, but after an hour, it was all back – speed, accuracy, and power in my punches, plus 'making like Fred Astaire!'

Denis said, 'Sam, you're good. You're such a little man; I didn't think you had much "oomph!" But you could take a boxer's head off with some of those uppercuts and hooks. I look forward to seeing some of the fight, but my attention will be mostly around you.'

'Thanks, Denis, but, just like you, I've been doin' what I do for a long time, too. I 'aven't been put down, and my oppos tend to go down in five. That will be my plan 'ere, but this is my third fight with this same boxer, and let's just say, we 'ave 'istory.'

The gym-time was strenuous, but I felt sharp, in control, with plenty in the tank in case this fight went more than five rounds. Charlie fussed over me, but that was just him being nervous – *his* pre-fight nerves.

The weigh-in came, and Tom and Denis flanked me on the approach. A man in a suit approached me, holding a brown manila envelope out to me.

'Security tags from Lou,' he said. Tom took them and nodded his thanks after peering into the envelope to confirm the contents. The suit said, 'Lou said to say, "Good Luck". He smiled and faded into the crowd.

I made the weight and was trying to leave through the crush of antagonistic people when Trey Maxwell appeared in front of me.

I was relaxed because of my bodyguards, so I gave him my best 'hard-man' look, which I know is effective. He didn't return it, but said, 'Whatever happens in our fight, I am going to end up a very rich man at your expense. Now, let's see who's done the most work, and who's the better boxer, shall we?'

'The first will not happen, unless you've fixed this one too, Maxwell, but we will definitely find out who's the best,' I replied, and walked out.

'That was interesting,' said Charlie.

"e's still goin' down, Charlie, and I'm goin' to get all his money. Maybe then 'e'll understand some other stuff. Discipline for example. 'e thinks gettin' up early to pound the track means 'e's disciplined; but that's not even 'alf of it, which you also know, Charlie.'

'Anyway, back to the ring for just an hour's practice, then I'm ready.'

'What did you feel when he came to you?' asked Charlie.

'I just wanted to smash 'is face in.'

Neither Tom nor Denis had any reaction, other than increased awareness. Maxwell had my message, so I went and did some ring work, showered, changed, had dinner and retired for an early night, after phoning Donna at 7 pm, of course. I slept the sleep of a baby.

In the morning, feeling totally refreshed, I breakfasted and walked the streets with Tom, wearing dark glasses and a dark blue beanie hat as a disguise, but soon the air quality was bad enough to drive us indoors again. Charlie joined us for a morning coffee in the hotel.

'How much have you got in the tank?' he asked.

'Feels like plenty. Why do you ask? Do you think this'll go twelve rounds, and if so, why?'

'It looked to me, from his body shape, that Maxwell has done a heap of training. He's much harder. He always was quick, and if he's developed a good three- or four-punch combo, it will even the score a bit.'

'So, what's your advice about this?'

'Conserve your energy. You may need it,' said Charlie.

'I can do that, of course, but why the sudden reassessment?'

'There were a large number of tiny indicators that have taken time for me to mull over since I saw him yesterday. Look, I don't want you to over-think this, so let's just throw it around a bit, nothing serious.'

'I'll buy into any discussion if there's somethin' new to think about,' I said warily.

'Do you remember when Maxwell arrived at the ring at the last fight? His forehead showed signs of stress, and he was sweating. That pointed to his anxiety and tension. We said at the time that his training had been too hard, with no taper. That put his timing off, his reflexes were slower, and his general lack of planning doomed his result. And no, I don't think anyone could have beaten you that night.

'This time, "the shoe is on the other foot". He has everything to lose. You have only your title and your unbeaten record, neither of which will hurt your survival. You are, in your head, a complacent, fat man right now, Sam, and in spite of all your training and all my advice, you are vulnerable – if he is as determined as I believe he is. It's your "end of term" last fight. You're already winding down in your head, becoming distracted by project details and advertising campaigns. You're not entirely focused. Am I right?'

'Charlie, I've just thought of a dozen arguments against what you've said; but yes, you're right. There's about 90% focus on the fight. What can I do about that?'

'What do you think you can do?'

'I'll 'ave an afternoon sleep, then re-focus and re-dedicate this fight to a controlled and very convincing win. Then, I'll be 100% on track, and that bastard is not goin' to take from me my title, my success, the comfort of my family or our future prospects! Stuff 'im! I will never forgive 'im for terrorisin' my family, or for bein' involved in all that. 'e will not get the better of me in this fight!'

'Now that's much better,' grinned Charlie, 'you say that as if you really mean it. And you should. He should be in prison! Do you see where I was coming from? More importantly, where you were coming from? It's important.

'Point your focus from this moment like an arrowhead, and each minute will get you more focused until the fight starts, and then your training, motivation and considerable experience will take over. You actually need this fight, for Donna and the girls. Nothing else stacks up against that, man.'

Chapter Fifty-eight

I thought about my mindset for beating this child-frightener, this greedy, lawless bastard who thinks he can avoid the consequences of his actions. Using that as a basis for my motivation was very powerful.

Now I needed a strategy. Charlie had said, 'conserve energy', so he thought this match would go more than five rounds. I had to be ready to do all twelve. He had asked how much I had in the tank. If I spent a lot of time and energy on dodging Maxwell's punches, it would frustrate any boxer who couldn't hit his oppo. Something in my head went, 'Tick!'

I knew that positive emotion supported effort. Now I suddenly realised that negative emotion leached energy from that effort. Yes!

Charlie knocked and came in.

'All sct?'

'More than ever.'

Tom and Denis were in the foyer and fell in beside me as though this was a parade ground. When the van pulled up at the business entrance to The Garden, there were two very large cops in uniform, looking alert. They checked our security tags and waved us through.

I took my time getting dressed. Denis had gone off to check on the ring with Lou. Three men came in through the door – two had handguns, and the one in the middle had a sour expression. They looked like bad actors out of a very bad Asian movie.

'Lose the fight,' the middle one said to me, as the other two pointed their handguns at me. I was about three feet to the side of Tom. In a flash, he had the two handguns forcefully to pointing to the floor before being wrenched free. Tom then jerked the handgrips upwards, hitting two noses, which flattened and bled. Their owners fell to the floor leaving me with the centre spokesman. One long step and I reached his nose with a right jab that dropped him too.

Just then, Denis arrived, saw the situation and immediately went to fetch one of the cops from the front entrance. Rather than come himself and abandon his post, he phoned The Garden Security, who sent people to collect and restrain these 'Three Stooges'.

'Nicely done, you two,' said Charlie, 'and we now know that Trey Maxwell is full of crap. You ready, Sam? Time to go.'

I had my hood off for once so I could savour my last visit to a professional ring. The razzamatazz was in full swing, and there were about 20,000 booing fanatics. It seemed my posters had had the required effect. I saw Reuben near the corner and winked at him. He smiled back in a relaxed manner, which I thought was unusual, bearing in mind his massive stake in this fight. I climbed into the ring, noticing that I was first, checked the top rope tension, and watched for Maxwell to arrive. Charlie was beside the ring; Tom and Denis were down on one knee beside my corner, on the floor at right angles.

'Bless you, Donna. I'll get this done, and we'll have no more interference in our lives.'

Chapter Fifty-nine

'Good evening Ladies and Gentlemen, this is Bob Clarke reporting to you from Madison Square Garden in New York, on behalf of the BBC in London. My friend and co-commentator, Bill Fleming, is here beside me as usual. We have an exciting boxing match to bring you, but with sad overtones. Is this not so, Bill?'

'Yes, Bob, indeed it is, and good evening everyone. Sadly, this is to be Sam Smith's last fight in his, so far, unbeaten career. In my opinion, Sam has given the world of boxing many masterclasses as he has dished out his interpretation of the ethics, talents and skills of this sport. His technique is almost flawless, and his speed, power and accuracy in punching probably outrank even Sugar Ray Leonard. His defence certainly does.

'However, it is his reading of opponents and their abilities that set him apart from all other boxers. I think he gets close to fighting in a Zen Buddhist state of mind. He has worked so hard at his fitness that he can forget it. He has worked so hard at his technique, both in attack and defence, that he can forget that too. All that has become virtually automatic.

'So, what's left? In reality, there's just the thinking, the understanding and the appreciation within the moment. This would include motivation, attitude and state of mind except that these too, have already been set in place before the fight. That just leaves his total focus on what's happening in every instant.

'Just to add to what I think are his extraordinary skills, I believe he can change time. Not actual clock time, obviously, but time perception for himself. Imagine, if he could slow time down just a little bit, then he could choose where to accurately place his punches, and work out a couple of, let's say "chess moves", ahead. That would make him invincible to we mere mortals. The fact that he remains unbeaten tends to support my theory.

'I sincerely hope, however, that my little talk doesn't lead to his losing this match, thus making a complete mockery of me, and my opinions! Back to you, Bob.'

'Thank you, Bill. That was inspired! We'll undoubtedly get Sam to talk about this the next time we meet back in London.

'Sam is approaching the ring with his hood down, which in itself is unique, especially since he has 20,000 spectators booing him at the top of their voices. What will Sam do? He climbs into the ring, takes off his robe and waves with his hand in the air. He smiles widely, and winks at the huge crowd here. There's a momentary hesitancy with a drop in volume, then a cheer is taken up, and the whole audience seems to have turned around one hundred and eighty degrees! They have started cheering him! How absolutely extraordinary! How in the world did he just do that?

'Trey Maxwell is making his entrance, climbing into the ring with a little smile on his face, which he turns on Sam. Sam smiles back very broadly, points his glove at Maxwell, and appears to drop the hammer, as per handgun. The smile has disappeared from Maxwell's face – his eyes have opened in shock. I wonder what that is all about? We'll ask Sam when we see him.

The Ref has called the fighters to the centre of the ring, given them his talk while both fighters stare at each other.'

Bell!

'Round One, and Sam has claimed centre ring with Maxwell dancing around him. Sam seems calm, focused and totally aware. Maxwell jabs and steps forward with his right cross. It's fast, but Sam is not there, and gives Maxwell a right to the head as he moves left. Maxwell again with a left jab but pulling back after it, which means it goes nowhere. I think he thought Sam would come forward himself, but he didn't, so Maxwell has started second guessing himself. Sam will make a lot of that and will keep him guessing.

My guess would be that this will be a round of jabs and misses from Maxwell, with Sam moving left, right, backward or forwards. That will continue Maxwell's confusion. A three-punch combo to Sam's head misses but Sam gives Maxwell a four-punch combo to the body, and there was a lot of speed and power in those punches. Maxwell retreats then comes forward with a right and left. They clinch, which is unusual for Sam, and Sam hits him four times in the breadbasket on the voluntary break. Maxwell's head is unguarded, and Sam hits it with a tidy right.'

Bell!

'Bill, what did you think of the opening round?'

'Sam started very conservatively. He got two good punches to Maxwell's head, and a lot of good work to Maxwell's body. If this is going to go on for twelve rounds, which it could in spite of past history, then the last man standing could be the man who conserves his energy. I wonder how much healing Maxwell has done since Sam gave him such a beating in their last fight?'

Bell!

'Round two, with Maxwell out first, firing three jabs at Sam, which again, all miss. Another two, and Sam moves inside, giving Maxwell a huge uppercut. It kicks his head back, but he ducks away to his left to avoid the usual Sam combo follow-up treatment. Sam waits again, and Maxwell brings a roundhouse right to Sam's head, which, thankfully wasn't there. The counterpunch by Sam was to Maxwell's chest. That has two possibilities. One was to see if there were any unhealed areas from their previous fight; and two, to get near the heart for its slowing effect to the legs.

Maxwell comes fast at Sam with a flurry of punches, and they clinch again. The Ref parts them, and Maxwell tries to punch during that official parting process. That's against the rules, and the Ref has stopped the fight, signalling to the judges to dock Maxwell a point. I can see Maxwell's eyes, and he is ... very upset! Sam's technique now is not to be hit and has gone on a dancing programme that sees Maxwell almost running after him to connect. Sam abruptly stops, but Maxwell's momentum carries him forward into a huge right to the chin from Sam. Maxwell stands stock still as if paralysed, and Sam says something to him.'

Bell!

'Bill, what did you make of that?'

'Bob, Sam is leading the dance, making the running and calling the shots. His dance was impressive, as was that big right hand to Maxwell's head. I could see Sam saying something to Maxwell, and the nearest I could get, with my very average lip-reading skills, was, "That's for my girls." Understandably, Sam has not forgiven Maxwell for having been involved with the criminal activity before Sam's last fight with him. I also think that Sam is getting Maxwell frustrated, and I'll tell you why after the next round Bob.'

Bell!

'Round Three and Maxwell seems sluggish at getting out of his seat. Query? A ploy, or for real? Sam takes his time and puts three high jabs on to Maxwell's forehead. Maxwell hunches forward, with his guard high. Sam does it again, and follows up with an uppercut, which catches Maxwell beautifully under the chin. Maxwell runs at Sam, punching wildly – three, four, five, six punches at Sam's head. One caught him enough to allow a second barrage to land, and Sam looks in trouble. He dances away but is chased by Maxwell, who obviously wants to repeat something that has finally worked against his nemesis. Sam reverses his direction and punches Maxwell's chin with a very fast and hard right. Maxwell wobbles, and Sam again says something to him, before backing off to see the results of his handiwork. Maxwell actually staggers.'

Bell!

'The bell timing came as a bit of luck for Maxwell. Bill?'

'Yes, indeed. Sam got hit by a couple of good blows during Maxwell's hissy fit! That right to Maxwell's jaw, I thought, was enough to drop him. He must have really hardened up. Again, Sam said something after that right to the chin. My guess would be, "and that's for Donna!" I think Sam has reclaimed some of the aggressive mindset that he brought to his previous fight with Maxwell, so I would say that Maxwell has got another loss coming up. I noticed a pattern in the last round relative to energy conservation. I believe Sam has been given some advice about Maxwell's improved fitness and hardness, and the thought has been discussed that this fight could go to twelve rounds. That means the last man standing will be the one with the most energy left. I'll continue this later, Bob.'

'Thank you, Bill.'

Bell!

'Round four, and it's Sam's turn to get out of his corner slowly. Now, why is that? Is Sam "taking the Mickey" for Maxwell's slow start last round, or is he fooling Maxwell into thinking he hurt him in the previous round. With Sam, you can never tell.

'Maxwell moves forward aggressively with a combo to Sam's midriff. It misses again as Sam back peddles, but he got in a nice left hook to Maxwell's head, followed by a quick left- right-left to his head again. Maxwell comes to him like a spider, with many punches from many directions flying everywhere, like a propeller that's become detached from a Spitfire. One punch lands solidly, and it's from Sam – a straight right that bored through all those thrashing gloves, directly to Maxwell's "button". Maxwell clinches, hanging on to Sam's neck. Sam bows unexpectedly, and Maxwell falls off his neck and drops to the canvas. The Ref starts the count with Sam in a neutral corner. Maxwell scrambles to his feet at eight, Ref checks him, and signals, "Box on". Sam is in there to finish Maxwell but gets a very fast roundhouse right to the side of the head, and in turn, goes down on the canvas. Maxwell goes to a neutral corner, and yells something to Sam, who gets up on seven, shakes his head, speaks to the Ref, and is ready to continue. There are thirty seconds left in the round, and Sam comes in swinging, landing punch after solid punch to Maxwell's body and head. It looks like a blur from here, and Maxwell's got no answer to it. He staggers and goes down once more.

Bell!

'The Ref counts, but Maxwell is up at nine and manages, somehow, to get back to his corner. Bill?'

'Maxwell seems to have that bell sorted out for just when he needs it most. That's the first time I've seen Sam go down. I think that's the first time that Sam has been down, ever. A real roundhouse that he must have missed, but he really made up for it once he retained the vertical! I have no idea about what Maxwell yelled at Sam. It may have been something of the order of, "You can give it, but you can't take it!" In the light of his last fight, I would think Maxwell is stretching the truth, somewhat. To any Americans listening to our broadcast; yes, that's what we call a "British understatement!" However, it's a great round of boxing, albeit with both boxers on the canvas. The fifth round is coming up, and I wonder whether Sam can retain his extraordinary record. Back to you, Bob.'

Bell!

'Thank you, Bill. Sam looks his fresh-faced self once more, while Maxwell looks as though he's hurting. Sam slams a hard left uppercut to Maxwell's midriff and follows with a right to the chin. Maxwell looks as though he doesn't know whether to double over forwards or fall back. Sam helps him make up his mind by sending a big right to the heart and a left jab to the ribs. Maxwell winces, and his eyes widen. I think Sam has broken another rib, and Maxwell looks all done in. I've just noticed that Maxwell has dropped his guard. Is that unintentional or on purpose? Sam hits him very hard in the stomach; right where his guard was!

He thought Sam was going for his chin, falling for the ploy of Wally Shaw's successful punch. Sam didn't fall for it and has done yet more damage to Maxwell. Now Sam's eyes have dropped to Maxwell's solar plexus. A jab from Sam, counter jab from Maxwell, which Sam slips inside, and throws a mighty right to Maxwell's jaw. It's "Goodnight, Mr. Maxwell" for the third and last time. The Ref counts him out! He holds up Sam's left arm, Sam raises his right fist to his chin, and winks.

'The crowd is going crazy! I'm just hearing them again since this match started. You can hear they are shouting, "Sam-my, Sam-my, Sam-my!" I have no idea what it was that turned them around, but I wish I knew how to turn around a massive audience like that, and then put it in a bottle! Bill?'

'Bob, that's a most extraordinary thing. There has been a huge amount of anti-British sentiment since those posters of Sam started to appear. Sam's team seem to have done an amazing job of marketing this fight by promoting our British Sam Smith against the American Trey Maxwell, which, in itself was very clever. Then, the anti-American and pro-British posters arrived, and set tongues wagging all over North America – pitting country against country. That was really clever. It didn't matter which side thought they had won the argument, because all the talk was promotion for this fight. I'd love to know what the TV audience count was.

'However, the fight itself lived up to its advanced billing, even though it didn't go the whole twelve rounds. From their fitness levels, it was pretty obvious that Sam was the fitter of the two and could have outlasted Maxwell. Earlier, I was speaking about "energy conservation" in this fight, and I think Sam, or Charlie, or one of his team members had the idea that the best way to drain energy from someone is to use emotion. There's no more efficient way to do that than to use guilt. I think Sam was saying to Maxwell, after a particularly big punch, "That one's for my girls," which would have had Maxwell revisiting the past, feeling both guilt and distraction that that whole plan fell apart. That's a perfect example of Sam's chess-player thinking. We may never experience the likes of which again.

'I also gather, from talk on the grapevine, that Maxwell put up a big percentage of the money for this fight himself. Sam won "big" in the first fight by taking the title away from Maxwell. He won hugely and got his family back safely after the second fight. This time he has crushed Trey Maxwell for the third and final time and has taken away all his money! That, Bob Clarke, is known as a Win/Win/Win situation, from which our Sam has emerged victorious, unbeaten, and very, very rich!'

'Thank you, Bill. As usual, you have delivered a concise, succinct but very rich narrative to end this era. We promise the listeners a long interview with Sam within a few days – all things being equal. This was not one of Sam's master classes, but it was an exercise in dominance, and apart from the Maxwell right that hit Sam, it was flawless.

'So, with Sam retaining his World Welterweight Championship against Trey Maxwell, it's farewell from Bob Clarke and Bill Fleming from Madison Square Garden in New York. We return you to the BBC Studios in London. Good night.'

Chapter Sixty

Charlie peered into my eyes to see if there was any damage from that one roundhouse right hook from Maxwell.

'Any soreness? What's your date of birth? Where do you live? What was your mother's maiden name?' asked Charlie.

'Yes, Charlie, got all those. There's nothin' amiss. No 'eadache, no vision problems, no neck pain. I'm fine.'

Tom and Denis were lingering around, trying to be un-obtrusive. They were about as successful as a couple of giraffes at the Chelsea Flower Show! I took my time showering and changing, and we went to the van, which Tom drove. He said he was the most qualified should any bad guys try to level the score, but we had an uneventful journey to another hotel where Reuben had booked a private room.

Every time, at the wash-up after a fight, the first person I saw was Lou, who had a smile and a drink of about the same proportions for me.

'Ring tension OK?'

'Yes, and thanks for all your 'elp and 'ospitality over time,' I said, and the tears began to flow! Where the hell had that come from? Why? Why now, just as it was all over? Lou spotted what was happening and quickly shoved me into an adjacent room, closing the door.

'Hey, hey, hey,' he said, 'it's OK, man. It's all over now, Sam! It's just the tension coming off from all that stuff just now. Ya'll are among friends and supporters, but ya don't need to hold all that in either, so let it out now. It won't be the last time but believe me when I tell ya that it's perfectly natural for the mind to react like this when all that pressure comes off.'

'You sure?'

'Yes, Sam, I've seen it before. Hell, I've experienced it before, myself. It's just ya head saying, "Thank God! It's all over." That's all.

'Now, ya got lots of people to thank, so take ya time, and when ya ready, just re-join us, eh? Nothing has happened for ya to be ashamed of. No one else saw ya, and I'm well known for keeping secrets. So, get ya'self together at y'own pace. This is a time for celebration, not introspection. When ya'll ready, come and make the other people feel good by acknowledging their help. All right?'

'Yeah, Lou, and thanks.'

'There ya go, starting already!' he smiled. 'Take ya time.'

Maybe Lou was right. It seemed as though a few days off were needed for me to level out all this stuff. I re-joined the group.

Denis had brought his tenor sax with him and was playing quietly in a corner. It was enough to soothe and yet heighten awareness at the same time, as good jazz at Ronnie Scott's Club, for example, will show.

The gang descended on me, and I played host, regaling them with some insights into the fight. My very last fight.

All too soon it was time for bed. Charlie came with me. To answer his persistent questions, I told him I would let him know the instant there was a symptom of any sort. You know: head becoming detached from neck, blood dripping from my eyes, or eyeballs actually falling out of their sockets on to the pillow – that sort of thing! He got the message, but to retain control, said harshly, 'Be sure you do, man!'

'Yes, sir.'

He smiled wryly.

I fell back on the bed and thought of a few things I'd heard this evening, even before some booze got into their heads.

Art had said, 'Sam, you are the best boxer I have ever seen. I had three world champs, but they were not even in your class. I'm so glad I could help. If you ever need anything at all, you call me, and I'll come running.'

Reg said, 'Sam, I've gone from being a sad old drunk living in a pub, to having celebrity status, riding on your coat tails. Thank you, Sam, for changing my life.'

'I couldn't 'ave done it without you, Reg, and that's the truth.'

Lou said, 'Ya'll right now? That just shows the soft Sam. Ya'll have been living the hard Sam for too long, and ya just needed to balance up, that's all. When ya get back to ya family, it'll be fine. It's been a great pleasure to know ya, Sam, and I count ya as a good friend, as well as the best boxer I have ever seen. Ya let me know if there's anything ya ever need, and I'll come running. When I'm in London, I'll call ya, on the understanding that if ya ever get Stateside, ya'll do the same. Deal?'

'Sure, Lou, deal. I count you as a real friend, and I'm proud of it. Go well, and many thanks for your wise counsel.'

Reuben said, 'Whoever would have thought that young Sam Smith from Whitechapel, working in the tents on a Saturday night could, or would, ever have achieved all this? Sam, you are the son I never had, and it will be an absolute privilege to work with you into the future. Anything I have is yours, and I am now a very wealthy man. I am also a successful man with a family and a project, new ideas, and lots of challenges into the future. Hang up your gloves with pride, Sam. You beat them all, my son.' There was a loving hug that benefitted both of us, individually and together.

'I think it's fair to say that together, we beat them all, Reuben,' I said.

Charlie said, 'Sam, you're the best, man, the very best. Over time I'll tell you why I say this. Now is the time for rejoicing and telling people that they are much valued.'

'Charlie, you've cared for me in great detail. For this, and much, much more I thank you. Hey, we've got lots of stuff to do together! We'll get crackin' after I've 'ad a few days with my family. You're a true friend.'

They were the main people, and I really felt the love. Looking at those conversations later I realised that it wasn't the words that mattered, it was the sentiment. I had brought them, and myself, money and fame. But that didn't matter as much as the togetherness, the unity of our team that had transformed all our lives.

I slept – waking in the morning with a wet pillow. No dreaming, no mid-night fractured sleep, no depression, so I must have used the night for starting to normalise my life.

There was so much more to do, which I could share with Donna.

Breakfast, airport, flight, Heathrow, where there was a massive crowd with placards full of compliments. I went over and thanked them all, telling them to watch out for my gym, and, if they made themselves known to me after it was open, I would give them each a signed gift and a group photo that Charlie had just taken. More cheering as I left.

Donna! She met me on the doorstep, and we hugged like there was no tomorrow.

'It's so good to be home, my love. I did it, and now perhaps we can 'ave a proper life with proper 'ours and a proper family doin' proper things.'

'Yes, please,' she said, her eyes dancing brightly.

'Did I tell you that Bob and Bill from the BBC are writin' a book about me and the world championship fights? They are goin' to call it *Counterpunch*.'

'No, Sam. Listen, Margaret wants to see you about future photo shoots. Mr Goldstein wants you to meet the architects, builders and engineers to look over some preliminary plans. Charlie wants to discuss his mentoring programmes, and also wants to know what he should be doing now. Tom has some security queries for you and wants to know about employing Denis. The bank needs you to sign some cheques, and have discussions with you about your plans, the mortgage, finance, and your future. The solicitor needs some discussions with you about the project and the insurances you will need, and there's a lawyer who has some documents to...!'

'Tomorrow, my darling Donna,' I whispered, holding her tightly. 'Tomorrow.'

This article is reproduced courtesy
of:
Boxing Weekly Magazine
By Bill Fleming ©
BBC Boxing Commentator
April 1967

You will have read my previous reports on matches between Sam Smith, the current world welterweight champion, and Trey Maxwell, the former champion, or you could find or request copies, courtesy of Boxing Weekly Magazine.

Sadly, this report will be my last to contain any information about Sam Smith in the ring, because he has decided to hang up his gloves. Why has he done that when he is still so young and has, potentially, so many fights left in him?

Well, in truth, it's a brutal way to make a living, which is why the pay packets in the upper echelons of this sport are so enormous. I think he realises that he's been extremely fortunate so far; having fought the number of fights he has and to finish virtually unscathed.

His family probably played a big part in his decision: wanting a husband and a father who still had all his marbles, all his energy, and all his abilities intact. After all, being a father is one of the hardest roles any man can play, and a father needs all his wits about him to cope with two beautiful children such as Anna and Ella.

Then there's being a husband, and how many roles does he need to fulfil for a wife to lead a happy life. She needs his respect, his communication, and his security to make her feel safe and comfortable in their relationship. A wife, who has those three and is cherished, is capable of miracles within a family, or so I have read.

Also, I have heard on the grapevine that Sam, together with his wife Donna and their business group, is planning to build a new 'Super Gym', which will cater for many diverse groups. Mentoring the cream of British boxers, training and employing disadvantaged children, and catering for women who want to increase their fitness - all in a clean, open and airy environment with loads of equipment and qualified staff to ensure safety, is the pattern of Sam's future.

These are among the goals of this project. We're not yet sure of the location of this developing masterpiece, but it needed a bucket-load of money, which has been part of the motivation for Sam's work. Apparently, he has achieved a level of finance that will allow him to fulfil this dream, and I can't wait to see the finished product.

Back to the boxing, and Sam travelled to New York last Monday with Charlie

Browne, his trainer and ring man, Reuben Goldstein, his manager, and two of the toughest looking characters I've seen in a long while. Apparently, they both had impeccable records with the SAS, and with that, I will say no more. Sam put in some ring work on arrival and pronounced himself 'fit and ready' on Thursday.

At the weigh-in, Trey Maxwell told Sam that he, Maxwell, was going to be rich after this fight, and they would see who the best boxer was.

The following day, when dressing and preparing for the fight in the change rooms at The Garden, three 'toughs', two of whom were armed with handguns, confronted Sam to get him to throw the fight. One of the SAS men disarmed and disabled the two armed gangsters within about a second and a half, and Sam knocked out the third. As he said afterwards, 'It was just a bit of a warm-up!' He referred to the three as "Lou, Curly, and Moe". Enough said.

In the ring, Trey Maxwell was all smiles until Sam pointed a glove at him and let the hammer drop, so to speak, with his thumb. That wiped the smile from Maxwell's face. Sam was saying that although Maxwell thought he had the fight in the bag, Sam had seen through that and was gunning for him - hence the falling hammer.

Sam must have got wind of the enormous amount of work that Maxwell was doing in preparation for this fight. I asked myself, before the match, that if I were fighting Maxwell, how I would defeat him?

Since both men were in prime condition, they could forget that aspect. Sam has all the moves, all the punches, all the footwork, and the reflexes of a cat. Both boxers had more than adequate motivation. Sam has a health facility to design and build, an unbeaten boxing record to protect, and a family to care for, whereas Maxwell desperately wanted his title back, and had put up most of his money on winning this fight. Well, what does that leave to think about during the fight, I hear you ask?

Well, there's planning, scheming and taking advantage of every opportunity. There's also conservation of energy because I think Sam, or one of his team, believed that this fight could go the full twelve rounds, and that the last man standing would be the one with the most petrol left in the tank. That had to be part of his plan. So, how did the fight turn out?

It was not a typical Sam-planned execution, if I may put it that way. Effective? Yes, very effective, and I think he was in energy conservation mode until he realised that the fight would not go the full twelve rounds. It was at that point Sam gave Maxwell both barrels for the third and final time.

After his first victory, Sam won the title. The second, he retained the title, earned a lot of money, and some revenge on Maxwell for the criminal activity aimed at his family to influence the odds on that fight. This, the third victory, has meant that Sam has retained the title, and confiscated the enormous sum of money that Maxwell, himself, put up to get this fight. 'Revenge is a dish best eaten cold,' it is said.

After a massive advertising campaign that supported first, Sam as a boxer, and then Sam as the UK representative, he was welcomed at Madison Square Garden by an onslaught of close to 20,000 'booing' fight fans as he entered the ring. His reply was to smile, wave and wink. In seconds, the audience was cheering him. How did that happen? We may never know.

To be cheered from the ring when he had won was an absolute credit to Sam personally, his boxing skills, and his overall ethical reputation. When his full story is finally told, he will be lauded as one of the greatest. If he can find out what it takes to turn huge audiences around within seconds - and then put that in a bottle - he will make another fortune!

Go well, Sam Smith, the "Wink" from Whitechapel. May you, your family, and your group be happy, healthy and safe, and prosper into the future. We, in the boxing world, salute you, your skills, your integrity, and your ethics. In the greater world of boxing, these stand out like beacons in the night.

Bill Fleming from Madison Square Garden

Afterword

A few weeks after I had finished writing this book, I decided to have a look at some boxers in action on YouTube. After some heavyweight bouts, I looked at lighter boxers, and I was transfixed by the skills of one boxer, whose name was Vasil Lemochenko, from the Ukraine. It took me ten seconds or less to see Sam Smith in operation, as I had written him. Fast fists, fast feet, unorthodox angles of approach and a huge work rate.

Lemochenko weighs in at around 130lbs whereas I had Sam Smith as 145+lbs. This allowed Sam to hit harder, but would, perhaps, have had a slower work rate.

I am at a loss to understand the parallels, so I'll just send my congratulations to Vasil Lemochenko for attaining all his skills. Sam knew how hard that was.

Chris Shaw

Acknowledgements

A special thank you to Armando Lepore, a former Southpaw and South Australian lightweight title fighter, for his valuable advice on this unorthodox boxing stance.

A big thank you to fiction and nonfiction author Stephen Chong for his encouragement early on as I wrote this manuscript.

Thank you to my editor, Dr Juliette Lachemeier at The Erudite Pen, for all her hard work in refining the story. Also a thank you to Christian Hildenbrand for his great cover design.

As always, thank you to my ever-lovin' wife Rebecca for her forbearance, patience and encouragement.

Last but not least, thank you to my readers, for coming along on Sam's journey with me.

Glossary

A lot of linen – at least an inch of shirt-cuff showing below the suit jacket, or uniform, sleeve cuff.

A 'Pony' – British slang for GBP25 (about $A50).

Bloke – a man, slang.

Bob's your uncle – 'you're all set,' or 'it's done.'

Both barrels – most shotguns in UK used to have two barrels and two triggers. While usually used separately, they can be used together to provide a greater impact.

Breadbasket – sweet spot below the navel and above the genital area.

Button – a spot on the jaw that is about one inch, (2.5cm), back from the point of the chin, on either side.

Camden – short for Camden Town; an area of London close to Regents Park and the London Zoo.

Cor - slang for 'God,' as in 'Cor blimey' meaning; 'God blind me,' (if what I have told you is not the truth.)

Extracting the Michael – 'Taking the Mickey,' or 'making fun of.'

Geezer – a man, a bloke, sometimes refers to a man of old age and/or eccentricity.

Gen – 'get the gen,' get the information/knowledge

Haymaker – a swinging punch, named after the motion of a reaper, or cutter of hay or grass.

Oppo – opposition, in this case 'an opponent boxer.'

Posh – upper class, well dressed, beautiful English accent, and flaunting it. See 'Dandy.'

Prat – an incompetent person, an idiot.

Pub – a Public House, a building licensed to sell alcohol to the general public.

Ready – slang for 'ready cash,' as in money available at once, rather than in the bank.

SAS – Special Air Services, a Special Forces unit based in Hereford, UK. Roughly equivalent to the Green Berets and Navy Seals in the US, and the Spetsnatz forces in Russia.

Selfridges – huge department store in Oxford Street, London. It has four floors and covers most of a city block.

Sweating cobs – sweating with large beads of perspiration; sweating profusely. 'Cob,' something large and round; cobble stones, cob as a stout horse breed, or a round loaf of bread.

The goods – the level of quality expected.

Threads – clothes.

Wapping – an area of London, north of the River Thames.

Wedge – a thick wad or bundle of notes; a lot of money.

ABOUT THE AUTHOR

Chris Shaw was born in 1939 in Felixstowe, Suffolk, UK. He lived there with his mother during the war years, with occasional periods of respite from the bombs and doodlebugs on his grandparents' farm in Longham village in central Norfolk. He is a prize-winning writer, and his stories have also been featured in *The Weekend Australian*.

Chris was educated at Framlingham College, qualified as a pharmacist and spent three years in London, then seven years in the Caribbean, travelling as a medical representative through the British-based islands.

With his family, he emigrated to Cairns, Far North Queensland, Australia, in 1973, working as a retail pharmacist until he retired in 2009. He owned two pharmacies.

In 1991, he married his beloved Rebecca at Trinity Beach, and they have never had a cross word.